On a time-bleached braided rug, spread in front of the fireplace, Cymel sat winding a hank of old, worn yarn into a ball. As she worked, the sound of her father's pen scratched through the snapping of the fire and the purring of the cats—and the words he wrote wrote themselves across her mind....

We must do better this time.
We must devise a way of protecting our records,
and not just protecting but retrieving them once the
Time of Chaos has passed....

The word *Chaos* expanded hugely and hovered in front of Cymel, the letters twisting and throbbing as if they were screaming at her.

She gasped, pushed out with her hands—and felt the word press against her fingertips. She caught hold of it and crumpled it up, though the letters were slick and greasy and made her gag. As if the word had unlatched a door, the fireplace, then the whole wall vanished. The kittens hissed and backed away, tails up and spines arched.

A man was looking at Cymel. He was young and fierce, and his mouth was stretched in a smile with no softness or humor in it. *Come here*, he said. She heard the words in her head, not with her ears, and with them came choking fear.

DRUM
WARNING

J O   C L A Y T O N

A TOM DOHERTY ASSOCIATES BOOK
NEW YORK

This is a work of fiction. All the characters and events portrayed in this book are either products of the author's imagination or are used fictitiously.

DRUM WARNING

Cover art by Greg Call

A Tor Book
Published by Tom Doherty Associates, Inc.
175 Fifth Avenue
New York, NY 10010

Tor Books on the World Wide Web:
http://www.tor.com

Tor® is a registered trademark of Tom Doherty Associates, Inc.

ISBN: 0-812-55122-2
Library of Congress Card Catalog Number: 95-53144

First edition: July 1996
First mass market edition: June 1997

Printed in the United States of America

0 9 8 7 6 5 4 3 2 1

For Kit Kerr and my sister Penny, without
whose help and support this book could
not have been written.

The Continent of
NORDOMON

GLANDAIR

Jinger Lakes

Banyakor

Kingakun University

Lake Mizukor

Idainamin

NIKAWAID

Higamin

CHUSINKAYAN

Nishamin

SEMMERTA
ISLANDS

Mionach

DOMAIN
EOLAIS

Pálamar River

the
Comcon

DOMAIN
PLANDA

DOMAIN
MIONMIOL

Fasalla

Teyas Brota

The Continent of
SAFFROA

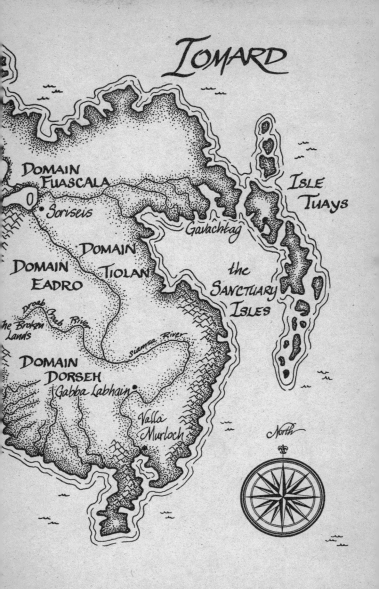

Drum Warning

1

Cymel

By the secret calendar of the Watchers, events dating from the 24th day of Ailmis, the second month in the 734th Glandairic year since the last Settling.

Cymel reached into the cage trap she'd brought from the barn, caught a mouse by the tail and flipped it over to Ymfach. The dusky black tullin snatched it in her right talon, hopped and kicked out, sending the mouse tumbling and squealing into a high loop; as it fell back, she captured it with a jab of her hooked beak and killed it by breaking its neck with a quick, hard jerk. Then she settled to the serious business of ripping the mouse apart and eating it.

Oorta was greedier and more direct. She caught her mouse without any flourishes, began tearing bits loose and gulping them down without bothering to kill it first. Cymel shivered and moved to the third perch. She didn't like Oorta much.

Heddig was the quiet one and the only one who liked her feathers stroked. Cymel ran a gentle finger over the smooth curve of her head and down her back, then she opened the pouch she'd hooked to the cage and took out the rabbit's leg she'd saved from last night's supper. For the past week Heddig had been having trouble with her stomach so she was being fed tenderer fare. Cymel held it up to let the bird see what she had, then pushed the leg onto the perch.

"How you feeling today, li'l love? I still think Pa should send to Osgotown and get the healwitch for you, but he says you're just getting old and no healwitch can cure that."

Heddig blinked dull eyes at Cymel, lifted her foot, set it down again, finally grasped the leg, poked at it with her beak, then tore a strip loose and gulped it down.

"That's the lady, that's the lovey. Eat it up. Yes."

Satisfied, Cymel crossed to the lattice door, unlatched it and went through into the colo side.

Dawn was still red in the east and the colos were white and gray mounds of feathers, their heads drawn down into their ruffs until they looked like a row of dusters laid on a shelf. They were day fliers, while the tullins belonged to the night.

"Lazy birds," she chanted in a soft whisper as she emptied the husks from their wooden food cups and filled them with cracked corn from the bin in the corner. "Colo colo sleep the day away, colo colo sleep the night away. Colo colo sleep from hatch to heaven, never ever quick or clever. . . ."

Tyfin, the youngest of them, uncovered an eye when he heard the rattle of the grain and greeted her with a sleepy *caroo-coo*, then he settled back to his doze.

When she was finished, she pulled at the lattice door to make sure the latch hook was properly set. Two years ago when she was only five, soon after her father trusted her with this chore, she'd left the door unlatched and it had come open; the tullins got into the colos' side and killed them all. Her father made her bury the little heaps of bones and feathers, though she was crying so hard she could barely dig.

Outside the birdhouse, Cyswe was stalking a flock of brown-birds. They flew away before he got close enough to pounce so he came back and jumped his sister Noswe, growling and chewing on one of her ears. The two cats wrestled through last year's dead leaves then broke apart and trotted decorously after Cymel as she headed for the barn.

Her father was milking Buhwin, leaning into the cow's soft brown side, the lines of white hissing rhythmically into the bucket. Bucochy's milk was already in the can; she stood with her tail switching as she chewed at the hay in the manger.

"Birds are done, Pa. Heddig liked the rabbit. She ate almost all of the leg."

"Good." He turned his head and smiled at her. "Get your mug, Mela. Buhwin's letting down easy and sweet this morning. Spring grass is good for her."

Cymel took her wooden cup from the nail and brought it to him, then stood drinking the warm rich milk, leaning against her father, feeling his shoulder move as he finished milking Buhwin, breathing in the earthy acrid smell of the cows, listening to the *siss siss* of the milk, the sound of Bucochy chewing and shifting her feet on the flagstone floor. She loved these early morning times when her father was contented and all there with her, not somewhere else in his mind.

She drank slowly, making the milk last as long as she could, but the moment ended, as it always did, and she went back to her morning chores, helping her father in the creamery, setting out one bowl of milk for the little gods and one for the cats, washing up the cans and bucket after he set the ward spells and filled the settling trays so the cream could rise and be skimmed off.

While he was busy in the barn, rinsing off the flags of the milking place and forking hay from the mow so he could feed the horses, she scattered corn for the chickens, collected the eggs, took them to the pantry, opened the gate of the corral and chased the cows out into the cloverfield.

* * *

After Cymel dropped the gate bar into its hooks, she rubbed the itchy place between her shoulderblades against the gatepost, then stood leaning on the post, looking past the barn at the house. She pinched up her mouth. It was turning into a beautiful morning, crisp and clear, not a cloud in the sky, perfect for climbing about the mountain.

She didn't want to go inside. She didn't want to do her house chores, all that dull dusting and making beds and washing dishes. And the kitchen floor was supposed to be mopped and the stove top scrubbed and blacked. And there were the lessons. The history of Nyddys. She was only up to the fourth Tyrn and there were twenty more to go and each one was more tedious than the last and most of them not nice people. She wrinkled her nose with disgust as she remembered the third Tyrn and what he did. The Order of the Year and what all the holidays meant. Reckoning problems. Times tables. And that poem she was supposed to learn and recite "with feeling," her father said, "not gabbling it out as if you don't know and don't care what the words mean."

He didn't scold her when she messed up in her lessons, but he'd call her Cymel when he spoke to her, not Mela, and he'd look so disappointed it was like a knife in her middle. She'd rather he took a switch to her like last year when she got lost in the cave and fell over a drop and nearly broke her neck. When he fetched her out, he was so mad he couldn't talk and her behind was sore for a week.

A loud squawk cut into her thoughts. A hen was doing a wild dance, hopping up and down, losing feathers, her red eyes madder than mad. A little god shaped like a mantis bug was perched on her back, clutching her tail feathers and using his spurred hind feet to jab at her.

Cymel pushed away from the gatepost and started toward the fuss. And stopped, staring.

The sky curdled, knots of blue in blue, streaks and whorls of blue on blue. The breeze that sprang up was full of whispers, sounds that seemed like words she could almost understand.

A breath later, all that was gone.

So was the little god.

The hen still had her feathers ruffled and was treading the ground as if she were trying to tromp her tormenter into the gravel. The rest of the flock was ignoring her and pecking up the last of the cracked corn Cymel had thrown down for them.

Cymel shivered, rubbed at her eyes. "Stupid pest. Stupid mean horrible *thing*!"

She walked slowly over to the barn, stuck her head in the door. "Pa, can I go up the mountain?"

He heaved the forkload of hay into the horses' manger, turned and leaned on the fork. "Mela, your lessons."

"I know, Pa. But I haven't got the poem right. It helps sometimes when I can walk around and say it out loud. Can I go, huh?" She thought a minute, added, "I'll turn the horses out and clean the stalls if you want, after I get my house chores done."

His face softened and his eyes twinkled at her behind those round spectacles that could hide what he was thinking when he wanted them to. "You be back before sun hits noon." He pushed at the fringe of hair falling across the glasses. "And if you see any of those boys fooling around up there, you come and tell me right away, you hear me?"

"Yes, Pa."

She fetched the paper with the poem on it, got an apple from the barrel in the root cellar and headed for the oak grove behind the house, meaning to climb up along the stream that ran through it. Noswe followed her a short distance, then went off about her own business. Cyswe walked beside her with the air of one there by coincidence, though his ears twitched from time to time when she began to say lines from the poem.

> *Sodden the soil*   *Streams in full run*
> *Blood blacks the water*   *War's woe is the bane*
> *Nor charms of the harp*   *Nor surcease of wine*
> *Dulls the hurt of the heart*   *At the death of a son*
> *Spear*

She stepped on a straggling lace as her sandal came untied, tripped herself and crashed onto her hands and knees. The little god who'd pulled the knot loose perched on a rock hooting at her, bent over with giggles that escaped its mouth like bubbles from a fish—until Cyswe swiped at it with his claws out. With a shrill *eep*, it vanished, appeared behind Cyswe, gave his tail a sharp tug, then vanished again as the cat swapped ends, snarling.

"Cys, you come over here." Cymel wiped her hands along her sides, retrieved the poem, retied the laces and got to her feet. "Cys, Cys, Cyswe." She snapped her fingers, the signal she made when she put his food out; he came slinking toward her, stopped just beyond reach. She put her hand down and let him rub his jaw against her fingers, then scooped him up and walked along, holding him against her until his body went taut and his hind feet kicked at her.

She let him jump down, wiped the muddy poem paper against her shirt and shoved it in a pocket.

The new leaves on the trees had a strong oaky smell, the smell of springtime, dark and damp but with a bright edge to it. Though there'd been no rain for several days, the dirt was wet and soft, oozing up to get between her toes and between her soles and her sandals. She stopped a moment and teetered back and forth, enjoying the slippery, slidery feel.

There was a giggle and a tug at one of her braids, but when she turned the little god was gone. It had snatched off the tie and the braid was starting to come undone. She pulled off the other tie, ran her hands through her long black hair, combing it loose from the plaits her father had braided it into.

Cyswe growled and went slinking off into the shadows, stalking something, maybe the little god. She thought about calling him back, shook her head, put the tie in her pocket and moved on. When one of the cats was on a hunt, she could call till her teeth fell out and all she'd get was out of breath.

That was the fifth little god she'd seen since Year Begin. She counted them on her fingers. There was the little round red one who looked like a coppernut with legs; it was the one that would turn the milk sour if you didn't leave some out for it. Even the avoid-spells Pa put on the pans to keep the flies away didn't work on the coppernut pest. There was the skinny one that looked like an overgrown bug who perched on her pony's head and maddened him into running round and round until her father wove a charm into the pony's mane—now it was fooling with the chickens, the nuisance. There was the one with huge eyes and batwings who made the chimneys all smoke; it tied knots in her father's spells and nothing he could do would keep it out of the house, until one day it must have got bored and just went away. There was the one that kept pulling all the turnips out of the ground so that most of them died—though she didn't know if she should count that one since she'd never managed to get a look at it and it could have been one of the others. Now there was this one who was like a mouse, with big round ears and a pointy snout and whiskers that twitched.

She pushed straggles of hair out of her eyes, and pulled the crumpled paper from her pocket. Little gods were worse pests than Orog Dyrysson and his gang of stupids from the other farms. She stopped walking and listened. All she could hear was the sound of the stream, the rustle of the leaves and some birds. That meant Orog and them weren't around. They thought they were mighty hunters, but they were always yelling at each other, and even when they weren't, they were noisier than a herd of stampeding cows. "Hunh!"

The stream that ran through the oak grove was full of rocks and white foam, but higher up the mountain there were gentler stretches where the sun turned the water to rippled glass and you could see the speckles on every pebble on the streambed.

As Cymel worked her way upward, she repeated the lines of the poem over and over, five verse-sets at a time, declaiming to the trees and a startled squirrel or two. By the time she reached the special pool she was hunting for, she had it mostly memorized, intonations and all.

"Done and done." She shook the paper and laughed, then tucked it away to leave her hands free.

The year before she was born, the one they called Dyf Tanew's Sorrow because it was so wet and cold, there was a terrible storm on the mountain and a lot of trees went down, one of them beside the durbaba pool. By now all the bark was worn off it and the wood was soft with rot. She crawled along the trunk, then stretched out on it, resting her chin on her fist and waiting for the durbabas to feel safe enough to creep from the reeds where they'd darted when they heard her coming.

Durbabas were not much bigger than her hands, tiny naked water people with funny frog faces, three-fingered hands and duck feet, wide and webbed. They looked as if they were made out of glass; Cymel could see their hearts beating and everything they swallowed and babies curled inside the little women who were pregnant. The men had fins like bright-colored ribbons on their wrists and ankles and they were always dancing, making circles in the water, the ribbons waving. The women ignored them and went around finding bugs and worms and roots to feed the children, who had tadpole tails instead of legs though their top halves were just like their mothers' and fathers'. The durbaba babies played their own games, tag or hide-and-seek or swim races or follow-the-leader. Watching them was almost like having family besides just her father.

She eased the apple out of her pocket and took a bite.

The air turned black around her and she was looking out of the blackness not at the durbaba pool but at a vast grassy plain. Two people were riding along a dirt road on smallish, sturdy horses, the hooves of their mounts kicking up clouds of pale dust. They were riding away from her and all she could see were their backs veiled and unveiled by the swirling dust, but something about them made her think they were women. They wore armor made from bronze-studded leather and had bow staves clamped to straps slanting across their backs and long swords on other straps. Both had glossy black hair and both had gathered it into single, loosely braided ropes that fell to their waists.

In the distance there was a herd of beasts about the same size as Buhwin and Bucochy, with long straight hair and curved white horns. Sitting slouched on what looked like large goats, two riders tended the herd—girls, Cymel thought.

The sun was near the horizon, close to setting, big and red as if it had a fever.

The scene blinked and was gone and she was back looking at the durbaba pool.

When the vision started, she'd dropped the apple into the pool. Now four of the little women were trying to roll it toward a pile of rocks thick with waterweed. They leaned their shoulders into it, shoved it along the bottom of the pool, only to have the stream's current tug it away from them and bounce it in the wrong direction. Most days she would have enjoyed seeing how their struggles came out, but right now she didn't feel like watching any more and she didn't feel like being up here on the mountain alone. She crawled back along the tree trunk, swung onto the ground and started for the house, trying to figure out what she should do about these visions; this wasn't the first, only the longest and the clearest.

She didn't want to worry her father. He seemed troubled about lots of things these days. He didn't like having to do farmwork, the neighbor boys were always poking around and he didn't like that either, and he wouldn't ever go visit the neighbor farms except when he had to take Buhwin and Bucochy to be bred or in Foolsreign and on Gifter's Eve and the Tyrn's Birthday. Or go down to Osgotown unless he needed something he couldn't make and no peddler had come by. And he almost never took her with him, though she begged to go. Sometimes he seemed so lonely that it made her heart hurt and she grew angry at her mother for going off and getting killed.

Even when she missed her mother desperately and cried into her pillow, she never spoke her name because she didn't want to make her father grieve again and add that sorrow to his other troubles.

When she got to the house, her father was gone to the tower at the back of the house for his Watching work, but he'd laid her lessons out for her and she settled to the familiar struggle with a sigh of relief.

Ellar Yliarson sat at his writing table in the small back parlor where he spent most nights. The light from the lamp shining on his hands, his face mostly in shadow, he was writing in a bound book, his Daybook, copying entries from scraps of paper piled up beside it. Now and then as he moved his head, the lamplight glinted from his spectacles or from the wire of their frames.

Across the room, on a time-bleached braided rug spread in front of the fireplace, Cymel sat winding a hank of old, worn yarn into a ball. Noswe and Cyswe stropped their sides against her knees, the light from the fire turning their eyes to melted gold as they watched her fingers move. When she was satisfied with the size of the ball, she looped the end and knotted it to itself, did that several times more so the yarn wouldn't come unraveled when the cats got their claws in it. As she worked, the sound of her father's pen scratched through the snapping of the fire and the purring of the cats—and the words he wrote wrote themselves across her mind. . . .

*The signs are coming more thickly these days—if what we know
is accurate, the Settling has to be near—734 years since the last
one—a long time—so many details get worn away by that much
time and so much was destroyed—the sun has a ring about it
every day now—only visible if you have the Sight, not like the ice
rings we get some winters—many stars have twinned themselves
and there are others that were not there before—new constella-
tions—there is one that rises with the full moon these days and
looks like a tasseled drum—one of those thin tapering tambourins
the Scribes of Iomard use for their solstice rites. . . .*

Though she understood little of it, she liked having the angular black letters scroll across her mind's eye; it was a comforting
and familiar part of her evenings, as if her father were holding
her on his lap and telling her stories.

And it only happened when he wrote. Round the end of Foolsreign there was usually someone visiting from Cyfareth University, come to trade stories and copy entries from her father's
Daybook. When the visitor was writing, she heard nothing but
the scratching of his pen, never saw the words that he wrote.
Knowing that made these evening sharings even better.

She jiggled the yarn ball past Cyswe's nose and swung it in a
wide circle as he pounced at it.

*During daylight the sky is more and more filled with the shift-
ing textures created by the currents of Pneuma flowing from
Iomard into Glandair and from Glandair to Iomard—one could
wish that during the last Settling the destruction of records had
been less complete so that we could measure the increase and
know from that more precisely when this next Settling will
come—we Watchers only know fragments that we fit together by
guess and will, never sure whether what we have created is a representation of reality or only a construct of our own minds. . . .*

Cyswe got his claws in the yarn ball, jerked it away from Cymel
and rolled onto his back, growling and attacking it with his hind

feet. Noswe dropped to her stomach and began slithering toward him, the end of her tail twitching. Cymel giggled and scooped her up, held the cat on her lap, rubbing along the limber spine and scratching behind the ears.

We must do better this time, we must devise a way of protecting our records, and not just protecting but retrieving them once the Time of Chaos has passed. . . .

The word *chaos* expanded hugely and hovered in front of Cymel, the letters twisting and throbbing as if they were screaming at her.

She gasped, pushed out with her hands—and felt the word press against her fingertips. She caught hold of it and crumpled it up, though the letters were slick and greasy and made her gag. She threw the mess into the fire, which popped and crackled while streaks of green and blue danced in the flames, then rubbed her hands on the rug, trying to get rid of the sick feeling.

As if the burning word had unlatched a door, the fireplace, then the whole wall, vanished.

Cyswe and Noswe hissed and backed away, tails up and spines arched.

A man was looking at Cymel. He was young and fierce and his mouth was stretched in a smile with no softness or humor in it. He leaned nearer, his body taut. *Come here,* he said. She heard the words in her head, not with her ears, and with them came a choking fear.

"Pa!"

"What is it, Mela?"

"He's looking at me. I can't move. . . ."

"Craïteh!"

She heard the noise of the chair pushed back and footsteps pounding on the rug; at the same time she felt the floor start to melt under her and something pull at her. Then her father was between her and the man, chanting something she couldn't understand, something that made her head hurt, his hands moving through the patterns meant to reinforce the words:

His strength flowed over her and calmed her.

The floor was solid. The pull was gone.

Cyswe and Noswe came to nestle against her, purring so hard her own body vibrated with them, and the remnants of the terror that had taken hold of her began draining away. Her father picked her up and carried her over to the window seat. Mewing plaintively, Noswe and Cyswe jumped onto the cushions and curled up by his knees.

After he'd held her on his lap until the last of her trembling was gone, he said, "Mela, I need you to tell me what you saw. Will you do that? It's important."

She nodded, her head moving against the old leather vest he always wore when he wrote. It smelled of ink and smoke and leather cream and it made her feel safe.

"This man who was looking at you, could you see where he was?"

She closed her eyes and worked at remembering. She was almost sure the place she'd seen was somewhere on Iomard, but she didn't want to say that.

"It was a cave," she said. "Like the one you spanked me for going into last summer, only lots bigger. I couldn't see the roof at all and the walls were a long way off. There was a big pool of water, it looked black like ink. And lots of candles burning."

"The candles—what color were they? Could you tell if they were wax or stone?"

"Um . . . red. Yes. That's it. Blood-colored, when the blood is new and bright. Stone candles?" She concentrated, but all she could remember was redness. "I don't know."

"The man—what did he look like?"

"Um . . . he felt young and he was mad at everything, I think.

You know, like Ryn Dyrys's bull gets sometimes. And his eyes were funny, one was green and the other brown. He wasn't wearing any clothes and he had lots of scars all over him and painted stuff. His hair was black and real long; it was all crinkly like he wore it in braids most of the time. And he had little tiny eyebrows, like half of them were shaved off. And his skin was a funny color, sort of like our teakettle gets when it hasn't been cleaned in a while. That's all I can remember."

"That's very good, Mela. Did he say anything to you?"

"Uh-huh. He said 'Come here.' That's when I got scared and yelled for you, Pa. I think he's a bad man."

"I think maybe you're right."

His voice was meditative in a way that made her feel shivery again. Before she could stop herself, she said, "Pa, will he Walk here like Mama did?"

When she realized what she'd done, she went stiff, but her father didn't seem to notice.

"I don't know," he said. "I think if he could, he'd have come across already. Don't worry, honey, I'll reset the housewards so they'll warn us if someone tries to Walk in. I won't let anyone hurt you. You know that, don't you?"

"Yes, Pa."

He stood, still holding her, then put her down on the window seat and wrapped the old blanket around her. "So. You curl up here while I write a note for one of the tullins to carry to the University, then you can walk to the birdhouse with me when I send it off."

She watched him take the thin sheet of strawpaper from the little box in one of the drawers of his writing table, then pick through the pen points in the tray until he found the crowquill point. He ground and mixed his blackest ink and began writing in tiny crabbed characters. For once she didn't want to see what he was writing, but the black words came anyway.

This night a Siofray Mage looked from Iomard into my house and
spoke to my daughter—a male and a powerful one—broke
through my usual wards as if they were cobwebs—I call to your
memories notes 7,986–990 from the year 9 concerning the role
that the male Siofray Mage Harbrai played at the last Settling
and the Fragments in Case 296 from the Settling before that, con-
cerning the male Siofray Mage Gart—further, the one my daugh-
ter saw was in the Great Cave on the Sanctuary Isles. I say to
you all this is the Final Sign. My child has described the man and
the cave so clearly that there is no room for doubt. I am fright-
ened and angry that it is my daughter who attracted his notice,
perhaps because of her mixed heritage and the Iomardi gifts her
mother may have passed to her, but I cannot deny what has hap-
pened. For all of us there is no more questioning possible. I say
to you all, the Settling begins. Ask the drums, and when they have
spoken, seek for the Hero.

Her father set the lantern on the ground outside the door to
the birdhouse so it wouldn't hurt the tullins' night-eyes; as he
eased the door open and went inside, he made the chirruping
sound that calmed the birds.

He came out with a tullin perched on the heavy leather of his
flight glove, the tiny letter tube tied just above its rose-pink
talons.

Cymel stayed very quiet so she wouldn't distract the bird, but
she smiled when she saw who it was. Ymfach.

Her father lifted his wrist, whistled the high, sharp fly-call. Ymfach powered herself up off the glove and darted away, silent and
swift, vanishing into the night with a few strokes of her black
wings.

Cymel latched the birdhouse door as her father stripped off
the glove, folded it over his belt and lifted the lantern, then she
took his free hand and walked beside him back to the house. In
a few days Little Noll would come here from Cyfareth, bringing

Ymfach back. He'd have a present for her. He always did, but he was the biggest present himself. He'd spend the whole rest of the day playing with her and she could show him the cave and the durbaba pool and all the other things she'd found, things that the mountain hid from everyone except those who knew it well.

There was another reason to be happy—she'd mentioned her mama and it hadn't made her father grieve. Maybe soon she could even talk about her, find out what she'd been like.

"Corysiam." Her father's voice was cold and unwelcoming.

Startled, Cymel stared at the woman standing on the path in front of the door.

Corysiam was a plump woman, taller than her father, with a round face that looked as if it were used to smiling, but was serious and unhappy right now. She had light brown hair that was short and stood out around her head in a thicket of tiny curls. And she wore odd-looking clothes, a white blouse that was cut full with sleeves gathered at the wrist and black trousers that were big enough around the ankles to look like a skirt. She wore a wide black leather belt laced tight to show off her small waist. When she spoke she had a deep voice that Cymel found familiar, as if she'd heard it in a dream sometime.

"Ellar, will you listen to me for once?"

"Talk."

"I know you still blame me for calling Doeta home and letting her get killed, but you knew her temper, you know how she'd have gone after us both if I hadn't told her our father was down with lungrot and probably didn't have much longer with us."

Our father, Cymel thought. *This is my aunt? My mother's sister?*

"You didn't have to let her go out alone and that late at night when you knew there were outcast bands attacking anything they found along that road."

"If you'd bothered to talk with me, you'd know that we tried to send someone with her, but she wouldn't wait for anything. You want to blame someone, blame Cousin Reädu, coming in with gossip about this witchman healer that lived in a stretch of Wildland a day's ride up the Riverscribe Road. Once Doeta heard Reädu's babble, she was determined to fetch him for Father, didn't matter what any of us thought, didn't matter what the healer thought. When she got an idea in her head, she wouldn't wait for anyone. Remember the uproar when she decided to marry you?"

Her father's hand tightened about Cymel's until the pain brought tears to her eyes. She didn't make a sound, though, just stared at the woman standing there in the moonlight, shadows from the needle tree by the door moving back and forth across her face.

"Why are you here?" her father said, the edge still on his voice.

"Am I supposed to shout my business to every ear the dark has?"

He was silent again for several breaths then he loosed Cymel's hand and turned to look down at her. "This is your aunt Corysiam, Cymel. Take her into the front parlor and get the fire going while I change the wards as I promised you." He touched her shoulder, gave her a slight push toward the woman.

Corysiam took the glass of cider that Cymel brought her. "Thank you, Cymel. I prefer fruit juices to tea. Tea keeps me awake too much. When I want something warm in winter, I just put the juice in a pot and heat it. And you can let the cats in, if you want. I like cats."

Cymel opened the door, then slid a hassock across the floor so she could sit beside her aunt; Cyswe jumped into her lap and Noswe sniffed at the visitor, then came and laid herself across Cymel's foot. "I can remember Mama a little," Cymel said. "She didn't look much like you."

"We had the same father but different mothers, that's all.

Families are . . . well . . . different on Iomard." Corysiam hesitated a moment, drank some of the cider, then sat holding the glass with both hands, the bottom resting on her thigh. "I've watched you grow, Cymel. I didn't want to disturb your father, but you're my sister's baby and I wanted to be sure you were all right."

Cymel bit her lip. The thought that this strange woman had been spying on her all these years made her feel itchy.

"Ah, well." Corysiam shook her head. "Sorry, Cymel. That was meant to make you feel loved and protected, but I see it doesn't. Prophet's Nails, I open mouth and insert foot all too often. So. What can we talk about till your father gets finished?"

Cymel scratched at Cyswe's purr spot, the one behind his left ear, and considered the question. She had a thousand things she wanted to know, so many she didn't know where to start. Asking about her mother behind her father's back made her feel queasy, but there was other stuff. . . .

"On Iomard," she said, speaking slowly, frowning, "do you have women who ride round dressed in leather with bows and swords on their backs?"

"Yes. They're called Scribes. A few years back, I was one of those riders. Where'd you see them? Have you been looking at us?"

"Well, kinda. And not on purpose, really. It just started happening this year."

"Huh. That's interesting. You're seven, aren't you? Young for that, did you know? My Sight didn't come to me before I started my courses. And I know your father was twenty when he first looked at us."

"I'm almost eight. It's only a couple months more before my birthday. You said you were watching. You didn't know that?"

"The years run a bit differently on Iomard, Cymel. Gives me a cramp in my head trying to figure out how the two times fit together." She wrinkled her nose, twisted her mouth in a grimace that made Cymel want to giggle. "And it never seems all that important, so I mostly don't bother. Do you ever see the sky go strange?"

"Um. A couple of times, but that's just little gods playing tricks on me, isn't it?"

"What do you see?"

"The blue goes all lumpy. Like cottage cheese does when it's making."

"No, that's definitely nothing to do with your little gods. We don't have them on Iomard and there's a boy over there called Breith who is seeing the same thing, that curdled sky, I mean. And his father saw it too. Ah. What's your father say about that?"

"I haven't told him."

"I see. Because he'd ask questions and find out about your looking into Iomard and that'd remind him of your mother and you didn't want to do that?"

"How'd you know?"

"I just thought of what I would do if I were you, and that's what popped in my head. You mind if I tell him?"

"I don't know. . . ." Cymel let the last word trail off into silence and sat listening to the rumble of the cat's purr. After a minute she shifted on the hassock, said, "Do you think I'll be able to Walk between worlds like Mama did?"

"No way of knowing yet. Dyar like your father don't Walk, so maybe you won't—but our family has lots of Walkers and even some Bridges, so maybe you will. Can't tell until you do it. The first thing is the looking, you have to see where you want to go. Then . . . well, one day the thing you see gets so real, you take a step and there you are. We do need to talk to your father about this, Cymel. He won't know that it's time to start your training otherwise."

"Agh! More lessons."

Ellar came in as Corysiam burst into laughter. "What?"

"Cymel was just contemplating her future." She set the cider glass on the arm of the chair and leaned forward as he walked over to stand by the fireplace, warming himself at the sullen little fire that Cymel had coaxed from the wood in the grate. "If you'll sit down, Ellar, so I don't get a crick in my neck trying to talk to you."

He shrugged and dropped on the settle beside the hearth, his back against the bricks. "You're inside and there's no one listening. So talk."

"It's a simple enough request. You're a member of Cyfareth University—"

He interrupted her. "A poet with no readers and an inherited sinecure. I haven't even been in a lecture hall for more than five years."

"Which we both know has nothing to do with what you really do. No. Doeta didn't say anything. Have you forgot who and what I am? I'm asking for help, Ellar. I'm asking you as a Watcher of Cyfareth to tell me what you know about the Time of Chaos. When is it going to begin? Do you know how bad it's going to be?"

Ellar's mouth went tight as it always did when he was angry at something he didn't want to talk about; when he did speak, he sounded as scratchy and sour as Beio Dyryswyf in a scold. "I have a duty to keep silent about the business of the Society."

Cymel bent low over Cyswe. She hated seeing her father act like this and she was getting angry at Corysiam for making him do it.

"You're just being stubborn, Ellar. This isn't about Watchers' secrets. Why do you collect this knowledge if it isn't to use it when it can help people?"

Ellar pulled a kerchief from his sleeve, took his glasses off and sat polishing them, his brows drawn together in a frown. "And why don't you Siofray do your own collecting?"

"If I could see the secret histories of the Domains, I wouldn't be bothering you." Corysiam slapped at her thigh. "The books the Scribes provide to our schools are worthless when it comes to the Settlings—or rather, the Corruptions, to use our Iomardi term. They're a mix of exemplary tales and theology with all the intellectual rigor of whipped cream."

Attracted by the jerking ends of the kerchief, Noswe left Cymel's foot and bounded across to Ellar, jumped for the end and snagged it with her claws. He let her have the square of cloth, slipped his glasses back on and for the first time looked fully at Cymel. "Mela, it's long past time for you to be in bed."

"Ahhh, Pa."

Cymel leaned against the door. She could hear the murmur of voices inside and if she slid her ear near to the keyhole she could probably hear what they were saying.

She didn't dare. One thing her father being a Watcher meant was that he knew where she was whenever he wanted to know, and hanging about the door when she was told to go to bed would bring a good hard swat on the behind and a scold and that disappointed look that she hated worst of all.

She walked down the hall, patting yawns and trying to convince herself that she wasn't sleepy. It had been a long and troubling day and she had enough to think about to keep her brooding for weeks.

2

Breith

By the calendar of the Domains of Iomard, events from the 17th day of Thairin, the first month of summer and the fourth month of the Iomardi year 6531, the 718th year since the last Corruption.

Breith swiped at the sweat trickling into his eyes as he crouched, his body tense, waiting for Gloy to call the signal. He couldn't see the target because Tel, Moggie and Trosc were ahead of him, blocking his view of the street. They didn't trust him not to fall over his own feet, not after what happened before, so he was last to go. On this run the Slapgame targets were ship captains, though they had quick hands and quicker tempers and if he or any of the others got caught it would mean a beating. But like Gloy said, no use going after easy game. What's the fun in that?

"One's coming coming coming. Go!"

Warbling the Slapgame hoot, Tel burst out of the alley and ran full out along the plankway, Moggie and Trosc following close behind, adding their yells to his. Breith sprang after them, caught his toe on a loose board and nearly fell on his face. Arms wheeling, staggering, he fought for balance, found it and ran after the others, his long legs cutting the distance between them. He raised his voice in the hoot, but it felt stupid because he wasn't really with the other three, not like it was when they were all whooping together, running together like a beast with eight legs. Gloy was watching, though, and he had to do it.

"Gotcha," Tel squeaked and slapped at the Ascalar ship captain, then skipped away as Moggie yelled "Gotcha" and tapped him, then Trosc. Breith was still a few steps away and got a terrifying look at the man's face as fury turned it purple, but he kept on, yelling like the others, swinging his hand for the slap.

"Perpwun brats." The Captain's hand shot out, caught Breith by the arm.

The deep magic that had protected Breith since he was a baby turned his skin so hot and slippery he pulled free. He left the Captain gaping at his mucky, burning hand and went running off, half blind in his panic until he trod on Moggie's heel and his friend's yelp brought him back to himself.

"There's one," Trosc yelled and took off, running head down, weaving through the people moving along Wharf Street, whooping, "Slap slap slap."

Breith and the others followed, running full out like him, caught up in the noise and the run and the game. They slapped the Captain and ran on, hunting for the next target. All the length of Wharf Street they played the game, shouting the numbers that measured their triumph, leaving cursing and furious ship captains behind, sending ladesmen scrambling to one side so their loads wouldn't get dumped in the street, shying away from others who tried to catch and hold them, leaping into alleys to escape the Watch but always coming back to the street; the game was the whole length of the riverfront and they only won if they got through clean and clear.

"Breith!" The icy voice cut through the noise of the whoops like a diamond-cutting glass.

Oh scane! Mam. Breith stumbled to a stop, straightened up. He scraped his hand across his face, smoothed his hair down and trudged toward the tall woman standing in the door to a chandler's shop. His shoulders were rounded, his hands were shoved in the pockets of his shirt, his eyes were fixed on the gray wood of the plankway. Hladdin miserable luck, she never said she was coming down here, two minutes and I'd a been past and she wouldn't a seen me. Prophet's Nails, I'm gonna get it, she's gonna yell at me all night.

He could hear the others getting farther and farther away, going on without him; he hated that, it was going to make his life miserable for weeks, especially Gloy, who'd keep picking at him and picking at him because his Mam yanked him out of the game before he could finish.

"Stand up straight, Breith. Look me in the face."

Still grumbling inside, he lifted his head, trying to keep his face blank like the Dips players he and Trosc used to watch playing cards over in Reilig Park.

"Breith, I'm not going to ask why you're here and not in school or what you think you're doing acting like some Houseless scurd. Not now. But you had best have an explanation ready when I get home." She lifted the timekeeper she wore on a chain about her neck. "It's third hour and twenty marks. I expect you to be walking through the gates at the House another twenty marks from now. Tell Gateward Neech to note the time you get in. Believe me, you'll be a sorry soul for every mark past twenty. Well?"

"I hear, Cay Faobran," he muttered.

With an impatient sigh and a shake of her head, his Mam went back into the shop.

Hands still shoved in his pockets, Breith went slipslopping home, simmering with resentment because Mam Fori had humiliated him in front of his friends, but not daring to take any detours. He'd rather she beat him like Moggie's Mam did. Instead she'd make him feel lower'n a worm and she'd tell Mum Yasa on him. Mum wouldn't say anything but she didn't need to. Her disappointment was the worst thing of all. And Da would tell him he was an idiot and Gloy was using them all to make himself look big and Tel had no brains and Trosc was a sneak, and he knew all that but he didn't want to think about it because these were his friends and it'd be a mess worse than the time Gath sicked all over his best boots and went and hid in the stables because he knew he did wrong and came crawling on his belly to lick Breith's feet, his tail sweeping fans in the dirt.

Scane! I'm not gonna crawl, I'm gonna stand up. Whatever they do. Oh Prophet, why did Mam have to be down to the wharfs today!

He felt the itch he got when the sky went bad and glanced up. Sure enough, the blue was all knots and swirls. He kicked at a crumpled wad of paper someone had dropped on the plankwalk; if that curdle didn't clear off, it meant he'd have dumb dreams all night and wake up feeling like someone had kicked him in the gut. "Gut gut gut gut," he said, and the scowl he got from a Scribe stumping briskly along the plankwalk brought a grin to his face. He hadn't actually noticed her, but she was a big, fat woman and figured like everyone else always did even when he wasn't that he was mouthing off at her. He shrugged off her grumpiness. He didn't know her, so he didn't care what she thought.

He stumped on round the bend in the street. It was quieter here where a lot of the big trading Houses were. Not just quiet, dead, he thought. Dead and dull. Dull and dead. Urfa House was on the bluffs above the river, high enough to escape all but the worst floods. Like all the others, it was a blocky structure built in four sections behind high walls: the servants' quarters and the stables, the main house with the public rooms and the private family quarters. There were three towers inside the walls, two shorter ones from which they could overlook the back and sides of the compound and a tower five stories high beside the gate; the Urfa House standard flew from a stubby pole on top of that tower, the house sigil—a green flag with a black falcon inside a black ring—embroidered on it.

The outer gates were open, pushed back against the wall. Actually he'd never seen them closed, though Munter, who used to be his tutor before he went to school, said they were shut when the old Urfa died and Mam Fori took over from her. And in the Trade Wars. Though there hadn't been one of those since before Munter was a kid. The wrought-iron gates were closed and locked. He shook them to make sure, then felt better. Whenever Mam and Da Malart were both gone, the locked gates told visitors to keep out. So Da was gone somewhere too, maybe to talk to his friends down at Scribe House, maybe just to read through those old dusty books he liked so much. Whew! There was one scold put off.

Breith tugged at the bell pull and scowled some more as Neech hobbled down the gatehouse stairs and came round with the big black key to let him in. He hated what he had to say, it was humiliating, but he didn't dare let it slide. He was in bad enough trouble as it was.

He slipped in as soon as the gate had creaked open enough. Over his shoulder, fast as he could get the words out, he said, "Ce Neech, Cay Faobran said write down the mark when I got here." Then he took off running for the main house.

Breith measured for a last time the heel knee he'd just finished carving then fitted it where it was supposed to go. With just a bit of pressure it slid neatly into place. He took the lid off his gluepot, painted glue on both ends and fitted the piece into the skeleton of the model boat he was putting together, a miniature copy of one of the Ascal oceangoers he saw every day when he walked to the Brothers' school.

He set the skeleton into its cradle so the glue could dry without disturbance, took up one of the branches he'd collected and dried carefully during the winter. Using the shaping knife with the thin, curved blade, he began removing the bits of bark that still clung to it. The branch was straight enough and about the right size for the mainmast and didn't seem to have any knots, cracks or other flaws that would waste his work, but he wouldn't know that for sure until he'd got it shaped and ready for rigging.

Gath was trotting about the patio, nosing into the bushes, barking at squirrelmonks who went running up the lineda trees where they sat on the lower branches, squealing and throwing the hard nubbly lineda fruits at the dog.

Whistling softly, the irritations of the day forgot for the moment, Breith scraped gently at the branch, turning it in his fingers to keep the roundness, shaving off strips so thin they were almost transparent.

Pain stabbed through his head; he gasped and the knife slipped, cutting his finger. Wild Pneuma. Harsh as acid on the skin. He dropped the knife and the branch, got to his feet, stood licking at the cut, eyes squinted against pain that went as suddenly as it had come.

Halfway across the lawn in the middle of the patio, a piece of air went hard and glittery; a moment later a woman stepped out through that hard patch into the patio. Gath left the squirrelmonks and came racing across the grass to stand in front of Breith, not yet growling, but taut in the body and serious.

She was facing away from him, looking toward the public rooms of the main house, but he knew her as soon as he saw her—Scribe Corysiam, one of his teachers from school. He had her for a class in the early history of the Riverine Confluence.

Huh! So she was a Walker. Nobody at school knew that. She must have just come over from Glandair. Coo, what a thing. He'd never met a Walker before. He couldn't wait to get to school tomorrow and tell Gloy and Moggie and the others; this would make up big for getting pulled out of the game.

She turned and saw him. "Breith. I need to talk to Cay Faobran."

Gath growled. His tail switched back and forth, hitting against

Breith's thighs. "I don't think Mam's back yet," Breith said. "Want me to find out if Mum Yasa will see you?"

"If you would. And Seyl Malart."

"I think Da's out too. Mum will know. Um, I'd better put this stuff away. I leave it out, Gath's bound to bust it and I don't want to waste all my work."

Cay Yasayl sat before her loom, running her fingers across the weave, checking the tension and the pattern she was creating, her sealed eyelids giving a tranquility to her face that was as real as it was hard won. She turned her head and smiled at Breith. "Oh yes. Corysiam. We spoke with her yesterday, Fori and I and your father. She's back more quickly than I expected. Bring her here, Bré, then go call Malart. He should be back by now."

"Mum . . ."

"I know. You've been doing something thoughtless again. I expect you'll keep being an idiot at times for the next fifty years. Out, out, Breith. Don't keep our visitor waiting."

Malart touched hands with Corysiam, then turned to Breith. "You'd better go deal with your lessons, Bré. Since you saw fit to absent yourself from your afternoon classes."

"No. Breith needs to stay."

His mouth dropping open, Breith stared at Mum Yasa as his father and the Scribe were doing. When she got that note in her voice, she scared him. It always meant trouble for someone and it looked like that was him this time. His throat went dry and his stomach knotted. A minute ago he was figuring out how he could finesse a way to stay, slide into a corner behind the yarn rack or something like that. Now, all he wanted was to get out of here.

Malart frowned. "Why, Yasa? Seems to me . . ."

"I don't know why, Mal. I have a sense that it is important for him to hear what Corysiam has to say." Yasayl of House Urfa had the rarest of all magic gifts, the ability to read and comprehend the tangled threads of might-be, a gift that came and went with-out warning, but couldn't be ignored.

"I don't like that, Yasa. I don't want Bré pulled into this business."

"No one will be untouched. This Settling or Corruption or whatever it is that you spoke of when we met before, Corysiam, it's going to be bad, isn't it?"

Breith came reluctantly away from the door and sat on the floor beside his father, his knees pulled up, his arms draped over them, his bowl-cut hair falling into his eyes. The whole thing sounded boring and too much like one of those long arguments about the business that Mum, Mam and Da sometimes had and brought to the supper room to chew over with the meal. He wished he was back in the nursery with his two-year-old sister. Bauli didn't have to fool with any of this stuff.

Scribe Corysiam sighed. "I'm pleased House Urfa thought to ask about the signs and disturbances. I'm forbidden to teach any of this, you know. Upsets the Domains, they call it the Apostasy and the Corruption, names like that. And our Priom is a fussy old besom who doesn't want anything that even looks like trouble. She's got the practice of not knowing what's happening around her down to an art." She wrinkled up her face, ran her hands through hair like brown springs. "All right, I'll get to the meat of it.

"The things you've been seeing, Malart, you and Breith, the curdled sky and the ghosts, they come from the Flow of the Pneuma between Glandair and Iomard. During the next five or so years, that Flow is going to get stronger and stronger till it isn't just the Walkers and the Bridges who'll move from world to world, but anyone caught in the current will risk being sucked away and find herself walking under a sun she's never seen before."

Scande! Breith thought. You mean I could Walk too? He rubbed at his nose and started listening harder.

"When that time comes, you'll have to be careful, Cay Yasayl, you and the Seyl Malart. With your gifts, you'll attract the Flow to you and you could land on Glandair with no way back."

No way back? Breith thought about being lost in a strange place where he didn't know anyone and couldn't talk to them if he did. This was starting to sound like one of those Ascal pirate stories where you got sold to slavers and spent the rest of your days in chains.

"Ellar Yliarson . . . him, the Dyar my sister married, he's the one I got most of this from . . . he's going to start a search in the records at Cyfareth University for ways of avoiding that tumble, not for me, but because my niece Cymel has very strong Sight, though she's only a baby yet, not quite eight years old. Already she's seen bits of Iomard."

Eight? Prophet's Nails, maybe I can look too, I never tried. Hm. Breith unfocused his eyes and stopped listening, though words and phrases twitched at him as he tried to think how one would look at a whole other world.

"Astonishing child . . . first Walker . . . Dyar . . . half Siofray, but only half . . . danger . . . protect her . . . my sister's sake he'll share . . . Malart . . . for you especially. And for Breith."

Breith lifted his head, met the Scribe's eyes, the calm measuring gaze that always seemed to scrape the back of his soul. He looked away.

"Yes, Breith. Pay attention or you could end up with the life sucked out of you like a fly in a spider's web. There's a Mage in the Sanctuary Isles. Or at least he was. Prophet knows where he is now, not me. A runaway daroc with the Sight and the fire in his belly to use it. Listen to me. You don't have to look at me, just listen. If you feel anything pulling at you, tell your father or me, whoever's closest, and if we're not around, you head home fast to Cay Yasayl."

Breith would have got up and stalked out if he dared. He wasn't a baby to run home to Mum every time he busted his skin.

"Prophet's Nails, here I go again, foot in mouth. Not because she's your Mum, but because she's Yasayl with more magic in her than anyone else in Valla Murloch. You *want* to be a daroc's slave?"

Refusing to look at her, he scratched at the floor beside his feet. After a minute of uncomfortable silence, he muttered, "No."

"Well, use the sense the Prophet gave you." She turned her attention back to Mum Yasa, took a roll of papers from her belt pouch. "Notes," she said. "I'll make a copy of them and send them over soon. From what Ellar said, the Domains are going to use this time to purify the Siofray. Which means most of the Riverine cities will be looking trouble in the face for a lot of years. And we're not really organized for it. If you'd spread the word quietly around the Merchant Houses, maybe the Riverines can get ready and hold on."

"Purify? What does he mean by that?"

Scribe Corysiam unrolled her notes, looked up, a crooked grin taking years off her round face. "Ellar figured the dates so you can count on them being right; me, the difference between the two kinds of year makes my head hurt. Sometime round the year 5000, which was the last but one Settling or Corruption or whatever, a Traiolyn and a High Cantair of the Prophet led a crusade against the Riverine cities. There was no Confluence yet and . . . well, you know all that . . . anyway, they burned down the cities, took everyone they could catch who wasn't pure Siofray and sold them to Ascal slavers and made the rest darocs and divided them up among the Domains. Last Settling, there were two Traiolyns feuding and a daroc Mage who was more than a little crazy going after the Domains, and the Confluence was getting started so we Riverines didn't have as much to cope with. Ellar thinks it could be worse this time than it was back in 5000, he didn't explain why. Um . . . I'm going to talk to some of the younger Scribes and hope word doesn't get back to the Priom. We can . . ."

Breith tuned out again. His father mostly taught him how to

hide his gifts, and at the school the Flow Management classes were only for girls, the Scribes wouldn't even consider him for teaching, though he knew he had more gift than most of the girls. And over on Glandair there was an eight-year-old girl who knew more than him already. And how did a daroc boy without more than a couple of years' schooling get to be a Mage?

The voices rumbled in his ears but he didn't hear any of it. He was dreaming of Shaping and Walking and being free with no one to tell him what to do or make him feel like a cabog with arms and legs jointed the wrong way and a permanent *duh!* on his tongue.

As Breith stretched out on the roof of the tower, the last rays of the sun came through louvers set in the crenels and painted bloody lines on the flat stones. He'd got used to his magic protecting him and to the sessions his father put him through whenever Malart had the time and remembered to do it, but he'd never really thought about studying it until he turned thirteen last year and was old enough to start in the Brothers' school. Though he'd pretended to himself that he didn't care, watching the girls go off and do stuff he wasn't allowed to try had really got under his skin. He could *feel* them doing it, but he didn't know what it was they were doing. He was always getting scolded for not paying attention in class, but how could he when all that other weirdness was happening all around him—the Pneuma they called it or the Flow, but it was just magic all the time, being pinched and folded and twisted.

He lay on his back and watched the sky churn, the lumps and strings purple now that the sun was going down. How? he thought. How do you look across the membrane and see that other world? An eight-year-old baby can do it, why can't I. How?

He closed his eyes but all he saw was the usual reddish darkness of the inside of his eyelids.

How?

Breith squeezed his eyes tighter shut and screamed, GLANDAIR , inside his head, but that only made his brain hurt and his magic just sat in a lump and ignored him. When he stopped trying to shove it the way he wanted, he could feel it uncurl and go reeling around inside him. Lots of times when he thought about it, it got agitated like that and went chasing its tail like Gath in a hissy fit. Da said to think of it as a river. It flows where it wants and most times all you can do is go with it, but sometimes there are eddies and if you can catch one of them you can turn the current your way.

He'd never really tried that before. When Da gave him exercises to do so he could learn to mask the magic, they were so boring he'd rushed through them so he could say he'd done them, but it was like memorizing Sayings for the Cantair who taught the Religion class. If you went, duh I dunno in that class, you had to spend extra time after school until you could play the Sayings back word by word. Ol' Meiger didn't want you thinking, he wanted you docile and pious, and it was easier to play his game and forget everything you learned soon's you walked out the door.

Breith rolled over onto his stomach and lay with his head on his arm as he dredged through memory, trying to call back those exercises. He could always ask his father to go over them again, but he didn't want to do that. Da was going to want to know why and Breith was sure he wouldn't like the answers he got. Besides, this was his business. Everyone else should keep their noses out.

He struggled with sorting out the Flow while the magic inside him grew more and more agitated and hotter and hotter; the sloshing and the heat made him so sick he was close to throwing up his supper. He rolled onto his side, pulled his knees up and just lay there for a while, eyes closed, not thinking, just breathing.

When he opened his eyes, it was full night, the sky a purple-black filled with swirls and sprays of stars. The moon was halfway up already, a fat crescent whose light smothered that of the scatter of those stars in its path. He pushed up, ran his hands through his hair. It was time to get back to his rooms; Mum or Mam, one of them was bound to come check up on him, and after the scold he'd got before supper, he wasn't up to dealing with more trouble.

He lifted the trap and lowered himself onto the ladder, thinking about the river. If he could watch it and see how the current went, maybe he could translate that to the Flow. He swung off the ladder onto the spiral stairs that wrapped round the hollow center of the tower.

Not a good idea to go out tonight and he wasn't going to do anything like going soppy over a river where Gloy and the others would see. Anyway, tomorrow the moon would be bigger and brighter.

As Breith left the tower, Gath was nosing about in the bushes beside the path that led to the stables where he was supposed to be bedded down. He yipped and came running, reared up and licked Breith's face. "Yech! Gath, your breath stinks major. You been eating old dead squirrelmonks again? Down. Now! That's a good dog. Shhhh. If you're real quiet, you can come in and sleep in my room. Shhhh. Yeah. Good dog."

He strolled along the path, the resentments and frustrations of the day faded to ghosts. All he felt was tired. So tired his muscles hurt worse than toothaches and his bones had gone rubbery. The House was so quiet, the thud of his feet on the gravel and the scratch scrutch of Gath's claws sounded louder than the dinner gong. The servants and stablemen were sleeping, his Mam and Mum and his Da were probably arguing over the business again or talking about him and what they were going to do about him. He burned with a brief anger, but that was snuffed almost before it began.

He followed the path through the arch to the patio, walked across the grass and pulled open the door to the rooms Mam Fori had given him the day he left the nursery. School wasn't going to be any fun tomorrow. Brother Bullan would snatch him bald for missing games class and Brother Meiger would have him doing penance till it came out his ears. He sighed and began pulling off his clothes. Might as well get some sleep while he could.

3

Lyanz

By the secret calendar of the Watchers, events dating from the 3rd day of the Winter month Degamis, the tenth and last month in the 735th Glandairic year since the last Settling.

[1]

Lyanz Kurrin wriggled in the hard chair and rubbed his thumbs on the battered surface of the worktable as he watched his tutor run down the list of problems and inspect with careful attention the answers written on the paper. He was fairly sure he'd got most of them right but the logic felt shaky in two. And Muali had a hawk's eye and a tongue sharper than a razor when he spotted lazy thinking. And Father backed the tutor every time, wouldn't listen when Lyanz tried to explain.

The door opened.

Lyanz didn't look round. He didn't have to. There was only one person who'd break into his schooltime. Marath Alaesh protect me, he thought. Let Sah Muali accept the reasoning. Oh please. Please.

Muali made two small checks, then set the paper aside.

Lyanz worked at hiding his surprise. What was he doing?

With a nod to Saretal Kurrin, the tutor took a box from a

drawer on his side of the worktable. He set it in front of him, opened it and began placing objects on the table.

There were three small slips of paper with writing on them and splashy seals that had an official look, though Lyanz had never seen those designs before. There were six coins laid out in a row, four gold, two silver. There were two gold bracelets set with gems, a dagger with a jeweled hilt and several unset semiprecious gems.

"Sah Saretal, will you inspect these, please? All of them have been spell-enhanced; some are wholly false, some are real. Look at them closely but without your touchstone, then return them where you found them."

Oh, Lyanz thought, that game again. At least it's not something hard.

Muali waited until the last stone was returned to the desk, then he leaned back in his chair and crossed his arms. "Lyanz, we've done this before so I don't need to explain."

Lyanz nodded, then began the sort. He didn't even have to touch the items to know which was which. He could see right through the glamour spell-cast onto them. It was so obvious he didn't understand why anybody was fooled by such silly tricks.

Last month Ol' Muali had taken him to the bazaar to buy Sunreturn gifts. At a traveling cutler's kiosk he used a gold zar from his allowance to buy a folding knife with horn insets that he thought his father might like. The cutler tried to hand him dross as the change, but Lyanz protested and Muali put the touchstone to them. When they turned dull and leaden, the man apologized profusely and produced proper coin, but the look he gave Lyanz when they walked away was not a kindly one.

"Done." Lyanz pushed his chair back from the table and stood with his arms folded across his chest. He kept his face still because he knew his father would be annoyed at any trace of smugness, but he was excited, sure of himself and waiting for praise.

"Try them, Sah Saretal."

"I assume you're certain of the outcome or you would not have called me here. The point of this exercise?"

Lyanz felt his triumph congeal. Every time he did something special, this is what he got. Cold voice, cold eyes hiding whatever he was feeling—if he felt anything. His father had never got over losing Kyodal. Lyanz knew he was second choice, a way back in the dust second choice, and nothing he did would ever make him equal to his older brother.

Even Muali was disconcerted. "Sah, I thought it would be a useful turn for a merchant to be able to tell true from dross at a glance."

"A trick, nothing more. Relying on facile tricks like that, a man forgets to use the intelligence Marath Alaesh gave him." Saretal Kurrin got to his feet. "Teach mathematics and logic, Tutor. That's what I hired you for. Leave tinsel glitter to street vermin."

[2]

"Get you gone, boy."

Kha Baja had been his mother's nurse, then his brother Kyodal's and finally his until he was out of baby dresses. When he left the nursery, she demanded and got the job of warden of the Women's Quarters. Two years ago, when he reached his twelfth birthday and was formally named Heir, Baja made it clear he wasn't to run in and out as he had before. She shocked him because she seemed to enjoy saying that and because she looked at him as if she—well, *hated* was too strong, but *disliked* wasn't right either—as if she would be glad if a Dyv popped up from the Underworld and swallowed him whole and not just him but every other man.

After that first time, she didn't let it show, but he never forgot what he'd seen and being around her made him nervous.

"I'm supposed to play a game of shatra with Ahmery. Ask Mum."

"Ahmery is indisposed. Go back to your rooms. You'll find a note there saying she can't see you for the next week."

"Oh."

Lyanz looked at the books he was supposed to read. Though he usually liked reading and even math, today he was just too restless to settle.

The day was windless and warm for the time of the year, the air crisp and dry. Much too nice a day to waste inside, especially when all he'd be doing was going over and over the thing with his father.

He left the family court and wandered about the compound, watched the Smith awhile as he made spikes for repairs on the front gates, then went to the stables. A mare was being bred. When they chased him away from there because somehow he was making her nervous and she was kicking at the stallion, he went round a corner of the barn and watched some silkwool goats being sheared. But that was boring, too, because they wouldn't let him help.

He had no real friends. There were lots of cousins more or less his own age living in the compound, but since he was named Heir, they were afraid of him and treated him just as they did his father. They were no fun at all. They always let him win even if they were better players. Sometimes he heard them laughing, running in tag games, playing Finjin Finjin Catch the Ball, but as soon as he showed his face, everything stopped and they waited for him to tell them what to do.

When he was still in the Women's Quarters, he'd played with the servants' children as if he were one of them. It was a good time until he got mad at Wari, the son of one of the gardeners. He slapped Wari and got slapped in turn as the boy lost his temper and hit back. Mother got rid of Wari and his whole family, turned them out onto the street with only what they stood up in. After that the other children avoided him.

There was one good thing about being officially a man; he could leave the compound whenever he wanted as long as he took a bodyguard with him. This wasn't something he minded, not with vashlar from the hills and streeters from the Nattar making such a good business of selling careless sons back to their families. He changed his clothes, went back to the affiliate's court to pick up the two men who usually guarded him, and one of their sons to stay with the horses, while he walked along the waterfront and looked at the ships coming in from all round the world, then settled to watch what was happening.

Sitting on a bitt, listening to the strange tongues and picking out words he knew from his language lessons, smelling the pungent odor of spices and oils being loaded and unloaded, watching the swirl of oddities moving on and off the ships tied up at this busy port, wondering who they were and what their lives were like when they were home—this was one of his favorite things to do when he was feeling restless and uncomfortable like today.

The Kurrin Compound was a walled house surrounded by other walled Houses of the High Merchants of Nikawaid, built on the high ground at the northeast rim of Nishamin and surrounded by a moat filled with water from the river Nisherikaw. As the hooves of his mount clattered hollowly on the bridge that led to the rest of the city, Lyanz caught a strong whiff of moat stench. He grimaced. That meant the Merchant's Association would be having another set of meetings to argue about funding a clean and which of the local Burnmasters they should hire for the job. And that meant his father's temper would grow so brittle that anything could set him off. Not that he exploded or anything, he just became grimmer and grimmer and cut no slack at all, not for anyone or anything.

Lyanz left the horses and the watchboy at a livery stable near the Great Temple and walked along the street called Mukkad because of all the shrines and monasteries along it. Since it was one

f the safest streets in the city, there were also some very unsa-
red Houses of Discretion there and streetwalkers were thick on
he ground. His guards always enjoyed this part of the trip.

Until he neared the turn that led to Shipper's Way, he enjoyed
imself. He strolled along taking pleasure in the warmth of the
fternoon and the exchanges between the guards and some of the
/omen who leaned out the windows of the houses or offered in-
itations from alleys. Then he saw Kyodal sitting on the walkway
n the far side of the street.

His brother was wearing the brown sackcloth robe of a Maratha
nonk; his head was shaved, his face gaunt and smeared with dust
et more serene than Lyanz had ever seen it, his eyes focused on
omething only he could see.

Lyanz looked over his shoulder. His bodyguards hadn't no-
iced. They were watching a woman leaning from a second-floor
vindow; she'd popped the catches on the thing she was wearing
nd let her breasts tumble out. Right now she was shaking her
houlders and saying things that made Lyanz blush. He looked
)ack at the monk, wondering if he'd made a mistake. He hadn't
een his brother for almost four years.

Though Kyodal was nine years older than him, had been a man
or as long as Lyanz could remember and worked hard as any
;rub-thumper to learn the business and please their father, he'd
tlways had time for his little brother. He explained things, he
hought up stuff to do, he taught Lyanz how to kick-fight and
hrow knives, how to climb walls and swing on ropes, how to do
tll kinds of things their mother would have fainted over if she'd
:nown about them.

Now look at him. Gone to be a monk. How could he! Begging
n the streets, getting peed on by dogs and kicked by horses and
:ursed by storekeepers, rousted by city guards . . . Lyanz wanted
:o turn away, pretend he hadn't seen his brother. Then he felt
.ick. Then he got angry at himself. "Sah Sirsh!"

The bodyguard swung round. "Yes, Sah Lyanz?"

"You two wait here. I'm going across the road." He scowle
when Sirsh opened his mouth to protest. "Don't argue with m
There's no traffic out there, just walkers. You can see me fin
from here." He didn't wait for a response but ran across the roac

"Kyo, why?" Lyanz fumbled in his belt pouch, pulled out a gol
zar and dropped it in the bowl. "I wish you'd come home. I mis
you."

Kyodal took Lyanz's hand, held it a moment against the sid
of his face, the smile gone and sadness in his eyes. Then h
sighed and released Lyanz. He laid a finger across his lips an
shook his head to show he was under a vow of silence, then dre
his hand through the twisted curve that was the Blessing sign.

It was dismissal.

Lyanz trudged back across the street, called his bodyguard
away from the woman still teasing them and marched on to th
waterfront, determined to finish what he'd started though thi
meeting had spoiled the day for him worse than his father's in
difference.

[3]

Ulla the servingmaid knocked on the door to Lyanz's bedroom
pulled it open and stuck her head in without waiting for an an
swer. She giggled as he snatched at his trousers and held then
in front of him. "Sah Lyanz, your father says he wants to see yo
in his office fast as you can get there."

She slammed the door behind her and went off, still giggling

"Oh kaf! Why now? What am I . . ." He dropped the trousers
went into the dressing room. Maybe some cold water would help

Lyanz knocked at the office door and waited for an invitation t
enter. He didn't want to annoy his father. Not after this morn
ing. And not after what Sirsh must have reported to him abou
Kyodal.

"Come."

Lyanz went in, bowed. "Father."

"Sit down." Saretal clasped his hands on the worktable. When Lyanz was settled, he said, "The repairs on the *Kisa Sambai* are finished and she is being fitted out for a voyage west. The divinations have been done and the day of leaving is appointed, one month from today. I was wrong to be so abrupt this morning. You have not yet had opportunity to learn the fundamentals of trading. To remedy this you will sail with me on the *Sambai*. Be prepared to be away from Nishamin for one year. When we return, you will begin intensive lessons on the preparation of the records that must be shown each year to the Servants of the Shadoshan. And you will learn how to deal with them when tax time arrives. Kah Muali assures me that your grasp of mathematics is admirable, though your facility with languages is somewhat less so. I will expect you to improve your performance as we spend time in port on this voyage. Do you have any questions?"

"No, Father."

"Then, Marath Alaesh bless you and send you calm sleep."

Lyanz lay in bed staring at a ceiling covered with shifting shadows from the leaves of the tree outside his window as the wind blew the clouds in for the coming storm. "It's because I saw my brother. I'm the only son he's got now and he's afraid I'll catch whatever got into Kyodal."

He grimaced, changed his thoughts to a more pleasant subject. Halfway round the world. Chierim. Yosun. Lim Ashir. Cypresta. Tyst. He rolled the names like mints in his mouth, tasting strangeness and wonder and infinite possibility. The Great Ports on the Western Trade Way.

Chierim. Yosun. Lim Ashir. Cypresta. Tyst.

When he finally slept, those names echoed in his dreams.

4

The Mages of Nordomon and Nyddys

By the secret calendar of the Watchers, events dating from the 7th day of the summer month called Pendarmis, the fourth month in the 735th Glandairic year since the Settling.

MAHARA OF KALE

[1]

Half a dozen wide flat drums hung on the walls between th torches that lit the round room at the top of the Mage's Towe the leather of their heads tattooed so thickly that little of the orig inal hide was visible. They were named for the Mages whose ski made those drumheads, each Mage murdered by his successo despite his attempts to avoid this fate. Zehirl the Great. Mueda Keyn. Faraza. Burgu. Hasrem Rell. Sitoon Kaa.

They buzzed and rustled as the sweet, sickly halitus of bloo rose from the grooves carved in the black stone floor where th Mage Mahara worked a Summoning, dancing the intricacies o the maze in soaring, twisting leaps, his bare feet slapping th stone, strong high-arched feet nearly as wide as they were long Each short sharp slap struck on a stress beat of the chant, crack ing through the powerful rumble of his voice.

"Mutecessis," he sang. Splat of foot on the bellowed *mut* and the marginally lighter *ces*.

> Mutecessis muteceyan
> Vero vero ver'm'heyan
> Gorun gorun onosirmal
> Mutecessis mutehaymal

Round and round he leaped and capered, the beat of his feet a drum song of its own, supporting and lending the power of his body to the power of the chanted words.

He was a Rhudyar of Kale, a Red Dyar the color of drying blood, with eyes as dark as bitter chocolate. Around his neck he wore a miniature dagger on a silver chain, a dagger that jolted and swung with the twists of his body. Naked otherwise, written over every inch with the tattooed blue lines that mapped his power, he danced the path between the grooves until he reached the heart of the maze.

There were two hexagrams etched into the floor, one outlined in silver, the other in blood, this one incomplete. Mahara stepped inside the second.

"Tamamalaaaa," he cried, slashed his finger with the silver dagger and completed the barrier with his own blood. When that was done, he held up the finger, stared at it till the wound closed and like the hexagram he too was whole.

The drums hummed as his resonant basso once more filled the room. "Gaaaaym, Gorrrun. Gaaaym, Gorrrun."

Mist rose inside the silver lines, flowing from one meaningless shape to another until it coalesced finally into a twisted creature all the more hideous because it mocked the form of the man who stood before it.

Mahara clapped his hands, the sound drawing the shadowy eyes of the other to his.

"Let it be said: The night sky has strange visitors and the day sky deforms.

"Let it be said: The Watchers scurry about with the desperate rush of ants whose hill has been kicked flat.

"This is my question: What brings the Watchers out from their holes?"

The creature shuddered with each word and when Mahara finished speaking, it hunched over, hugging itself for several minutes before it answered him. Its voice was hoarse and breathy; some of the words gurgled in its throat like phlegm it was trying to expel. "Thee Sett-ling approaches. Thee Time of Chaos comes upon Glan-dair and Io-mard."

Mahara stroked his throat with his healed forefinger, gazing at the creature but not really seeing it. He could smell power gathering. He couldn't quite touch it, not yet, but he would. His certainty was as solid as this tower he'd bought with his teacher's blood. Once again he considered the questions he wished to ask. They were limited to three, then the spell would dismiss the Answerer. And he had already spent one of them.

"Let it be said: The Watchers are scattered, the Watchers are searching.

"This is my question: For what do they search?"

"Thee Chaos Drums have wak-ed. Thee Watchers take thee Chaos Drums from thee hid-den places and look about for a boy here, a boy there. Has to be thee right age. Has to make thee little drum speak when thee drum doth touch him. Thee boys are thee candidates. May-be Hero."

Mahara scowled as he picked through the flurry of questions these paired answers had spawned. There were fragments in the Books about the Settling and the upheaval in both worlds when Iomard swung close and lay upon Glandair, but they were airy speculation, gossamer nonsense, as useful as a dried-out cobweb. The details of that time, the hard facts he needed, those were only recorded in the vaults of Cyfareth University and in the minds of the Watchers. He had access to neither.

Before their recent stirring, the one thing that had brought those fusty scholars out of their dens was a Mage of the Dark Path who dared to touch a Watcher. The Mage in question found to his astonishment that those crabbed and ink-stained hands could wield enormous power when it was a question of defending themselves or their kind. Mahara knew all this for he'd seen such a harrying and he'd seen the remnant the Watchers left, a thing whose heart beat and lungs breathed though there was nothing left to look through its eyes. He viewed the Watchers with wary contempt. To have so much and not to seek more? It was madness.

"Let it be said: The Watchers search for the Hero.

"This is my question: What is this Hero that they are so desperate to discover him?"

"It is not what hee is, it is what hee will be. Hee will be thee Pole of Power through which all magic flows. That of Iomard and that of Glandair. It will be drawn into him and hee will be as a god." The creature shuddered and melted away as the spell's compulsion ended with the end of the third answer.

[2]

On the roof of the tower with nothing but sky above him, Mahara flung his arms wide and opened his mouth in a great SHOUT. "All! I want it all! I WILL have it ALL!"

When the echoes quieted and the night's silence returned, he drew it around him like a cloak, leaned on a merlon and gazed out across the moon-silvered Yuskova Plain, the high plateau that stretched across Kale from the feet of the Dislir Dags to the low savannah along the coast. It had once been the sum of his ambitions to rule that Plain and all around it, but now . . .

At long last he knew his true heart's desire.

The first thing he could remember wanting was enough food and a place to sleep where he'd be warm and bugs wouldn't bite him. He achieved that when he tried to rob a wrinkled ancient and discovered that a Mage has defenses that don't rely on steel or muscle. He followed Sitoon Kaa to his lodging and pestered him till the old man hired him as a servant and eventually bowed to what he saw in the boy. Sitoon Kaa bent Mahara over a bench and took the needle to his buttocks, giving Mahara a blue power-knot, then he began the first of the many lessons that made Mahara a Mage in his own right.

It wasn't enough.

He wanted wealth and freedom and got those when he killed Sitoon Kaa and acquired all the old man owned including his skin, which Mahara cured and stretched across the drum he'd made for it. The Drum Sitoon Kaa.

That, too, was not enough.

A little while ago, he thought he wanted Kale. Now he knew that Kale would not satisfy him, that nothing less than the Apotheosis of the Hero was big enough to hold him content. *To contain all power within himself, to rule absolutely. . . .*

He stared across the moonlit plain and let himself dream a while.

[3]

Unlike the bare and immaculate Summoning room, the quotidian workroom of the Mage's Tower was crowded with the acquisitions of each Mage who had taken possession of the place. Ancient books were piled in heaps in the corners, the bottom volume crumbling gradually into dust indistinguishable from the thick gray layer felted over every available surface; bottles with indecipherable labels that contained what had once been powders but were now rocks harder than the glass wrapped around them were stacked in corners or lying on their sides half under shelves rising from the floor to the shadowy ceiling. Alchemical glassware sat on those shelves, along with scraps of leather, crystal bowls for water scrying, bronze mirrors, ivory spell-knives, sable brushes standing point upward in ceramic mugs, strings of chant-beads, rolls of paper, tools for bookbinding, cakes of black ink, crusted jars of gold and silver paint, red paste for painting and making red inks and the remnants of all the things that the Mages had found useful across the centuries that this tower had existed.

Spiders haunted cracks and crannies and the interstices in the vaulting of the ceiling, hatched from spider lines so ancient that their bodies were more clots of magic force than flesh, but there were no mice or rats down here nor anything else with red blood running in its veins save the Mage himself.

It was a huge space, not in the tower itself but dug out of the heartstone of the mountain, with long slanting shafts to bring light from outside and mirrors to focus that light where it was wanted. After he claimed the tower, Mahara cleared an area large enough to move about in, rooted through the piles and shelves for those things that suited his own needs and left the rest to the spiders and the dust.

Gilding dust motes and turning webs to threads of silver, shafts of light flooded the worktable, made the wet ink of the hooked and slashed Kale cursive glisten like polished coal against the creamy surface of the Yosun seapaper Mahara used for notes and calculations and drew liquid shimmers from the face of the mirror that lay at his elbow.

In the mirror a man and a boy walked along a built-up road paved with broken white shells; papyrus reeds grew thickly in the stagnant water standing in the ditch beside the road.

"Uyuz! There's another of the vermin. Let's have your name and where you're from. . . ."

Mahara took the pen from the ink pot and shook several drops onto an ivory saucer. He bent down, blew at the ink until it unraveled into strings of glyphs.

He read the words under his breath so he would remember

them, then he inked the pen again and pulled a sheet of paper in front of him so he could copy the glyphs before they melted into shapeless blobs.

He wrote:

Uyyum Tikkirt, Watcher, of the city called Yosun. Chulluk Harf, Hero candidate, of the village called Kagit attached to the Paper Collective called Koy Iltihak. First Destination: Lim Ashir. Final Destination: the University of Cyfareth.

Five boys so far. And the Watchers and their candidates were all moving west, toward the ocean. All heading for Nyddys and Cyfareth. He stroked his throat with the tip of the penholder. That could complicate matters. He took another sheet of paper from the pile.

He wrote:

Any Hero candidate who is killed is effectively defined as not-the-true-Hero. An outcome most useful in identifying that individual.

The mirror was keyed on the Chaos Drums. These were much like the drums hanging on the wall of the Summoning room, but smaller, their diameter the length of a man's hand, and with no tattooing on the drumheads. When he saw a Chaos Drum for the first time and noted that resemblance, it called up a memory. The tower drums had begun whispering not long after the first Watchers appeared.

He wrote:

Are all drums kin and some merely more vocal than others?

He wrote:

It is necessary that I control access to the location of the Apotheosis. So far my attempts to determine this location have produced little beyond a single negative. It will not be on Nyddys. This means I must search the mainland. Symmetry suggests a lo-

cation near the western border of Nikawaid, but such a reading has a very low incidence of accuracy. To deny others of the Dark Path access to this place wherever it is, it will be necessary to gain effective control of the whole of continent Nordomon.

HUDOLETH OF CHUSINKAYAN

[1]

The small white houses of the scholar's village at Kingakun University were built on terraces carved from the chalk cliffs overlooking Lake Mizukor, the walls constructed from the excavated stone, the roofs made of curved tiles glazed a bright blood-red. Miniature orange and cedar trees grew in red ceramic tubs and made patches of dark green against the white walls. Red and white and green with the bright blue lake below—an echo of the quadricolor ensign of the University.

The houses were joined by a web of paths with bronze rails and posts between the walker and a plunge into the cold water of the lake. The paths curved and recurved, the slopes kept gentle for the aged legs of the older scholars. Scholar and Mage Hudoleth was what counts for young in that company so she had one of the lower houses with farther to climb when she went to teach her classes on symbology and chant. On stormy nights sometimes the spray from the lake blew high enough to grow icicles on the patio railings in the winter and drape them with waterweed in the summer.

Hudoleth was Myndyar, Golden Dyar with soft silky skin the color of day-old cream; her face was delicate and narrow with a vertical crease between graceful arched brows that one of her teachers had called swallow's wings not long before she poisoned him and stepped into the rank his death freed for her. Her hair was smooth and black, coiled into a simple knot that suited her better than the more elaborate styles favored by High Banyakor Court fashion the past few years.

A month after Mahara had his epiphany, on a bright, warm morning with only a few shreds of cloud in the sky and a brisk wind blowing whitecaps on the waves, Hudoleth sat in her study looking down at a small white bird with iridescent blue feathers on its breast. It was pinned to a board, its wings stretched wide, its body cut open to expose the beating heart and the liver.

When it was finally dead, beak slightly open, delicate talons curled into knots, she turned her shoulder to it and opened her Daybook.

She wrote:

Mahara has left his tower.
It is certain that I will have to confront and defeat him—sooner or later—the timing will be important.
He is greedy, sensuous and amazingly ignorant but nonetheless dangerous, for his defects of knowledge and discipline seem to re-inforce his grasp on power rather than diminishing it as one would expect were he a more ordinary man. Desire drives men hard and trying to turn them aside from their goals can be like blowing on an avalanche. One must first dig traps for his feet and throw mirages before him to distract him. I must think on this.

The room was filled with light though the glass and silver lamps were not lit and there were no windows because the Scholar Magicians of Kingakun would tolerate no avenue through which their practices could be overlooked. Polished silver mirrors hung everywhere, shaped to catch and amplify the light brought to them along mirrored shafts cut through the stone of the walls. Between those mirrors were silver cages with small bright birds in them. The birds were beginning to sing again after their silence while the Mage had been seeking answers in the entrails of one of their number.

She wrote:

The Hero search has begun.
In my mirrors I have scryed nine Watchers on the roads and a

dozen more in Nikawaid; already four here and three in Nikawaid
have found Hero candidates and are moving toward our coast.
There have been rumors for years of a mountain valley where the
Watchers maintain a training ground for those they take into
their service: The Kunhatakin. Apparently these whispers have
more basis in truth than rumors usually do. If they weren't so
touchy about being overlooked and so—shall we say, militant
about discouraging such spying, I would have more to work with.
Cursed Traditionals. They turn up their noses at the Scholars of
Kingakun and save their loyalty for Cyfareth at the other end of
the world. I call them traitors. Traitors to their own.

She tapped the end of the penholder against her nose. I need
time without interruptions. And a secure base. Hm. One of the
retreat cottages might do. There shouldn't be anyone at the Finger Lakes this time of year. The Great Minds of Kingakun don't
like heat and dust. . . .

[2]

The Scholar's Garden was a carefully cultivated wilderness with
each plant and object in it chosen after much thought by the University Gardener who knew every theory about growing things but
had never set hand to dirt, leaving the execution of his concepts
to the plebeian fingers of the Semmer who sharecropped the University farms, small, shy dark folk who'd drifted up from the Semmerta Islands south of Chusinkayan, hoping to escape pirate
raids, killer storms, erupting volcanoes and the other upheavals
endemic to those parts.

Hudoleth paced along one of the paths, the hem of her white
robe brushing the carefully placed leaves into new patterns, her
fingertips resting on the arm of the man beside her, her head
tilted as she listened to his grave pronouncements.

". . . seems possible that Scholar Johinna has come up with an
interesting and perhaps useful connection between the little
gods and the Great Ones. It has long been evident that what com-

mon folk have always called the little gods are discrete lumps of magic force animated by those aspects of perversity and obstreperousness that exist in the soul of the common man, he who has no discipline of mind or spirit."

"Mmm," Hudoleth said.

"Yes. It is the Scholar's contention that the Great Gods differ only in that they are larger agglomerations of that force and are shaped—one might say created—from the hopes and dreams of the most elevated of our species."

"Interesting indeed. A theory that calls into question our origins. If we were not created by the Great Gods, then how did we come to be? The political ramifications of this should also be taken into consideration before such a theory is, ah, spread beyond those few who have heard it and who are, of course, sufficiently learned to understand the necessity of intellectual freedom. The University is to some extent dependent on the good will of High Banyakor. You will remember that the Emperor claims direct descent from Tayo Sugreta the Great and Merciful. Any line of thought that calls into question the Being and Attributes of Tayo Sugreta might be considered treasonable. And the result of that . . ." She let the last word trail off into a gentle sigh.

"You are quite correct, Scholar Hudoleth. This is not for common chatter. No indeed. It might do damage to the young minds we are here to shape and encourage. I shall have a word with the Chancellor and arrange to have Scholar Johinna's explorations contained within tight limits. Let us turn to a happier issue, or so I hope it prove. You had a request you wished me to present for you?"

"You are most gracious, Scholar Kazatoreth. I have hesitated to speak of this before, because I do so enjoy the bright and happy minds of my students, but I have been working too hard on my own studies—it is a fault I do confess. I am very tired and I have been, ah, not well for some weeks now." She stepped away from him and allowed herself to droop gracefully, her dark head like a flower too heavy for its slender stalk. "I would have you request a space of time, a retreat, perhaps till winter's end, in which I can meditate, recover my strength and return to my duties renewed in vigor and purpose."

"Of course, of course, it will be done immediately. You should hear before evening of the Chancellor's decision."

When he left her, his short fat feet were moving so quickly he might have been said to run if he had ever done anything so active in all of his pampered life. And she would have laughed if one of the Semmers hadn't been a short distance off, clipping dead leaves from a bush. She neither liked nor trusted them. Sly schemers. Lazy and stupid. Vengeful. Spies for whoever stooped to buying them. And if you didn't watch them closely, they attracted little gods like rotten meat brought flies. Sugreta forbid those pests ever finding a home anywhere at Kingakun or Imperial Banyakor.

As she walked, sedate and grave-faced, toward the arched gate, she could almost see the visions passing through Gasbag Kazatoreth's head. Her illness—perhaps she was pregnant with an Imperial bastard? Influence. Accusations of treason. The pressing table. Himself the meat between two iron sheets and stones being added one by one to the top of the sandwich until he was only a smear in the middle. And he'd given her the ammunition from his own mouth because he wanted to impress her with his intellect and worm his way into her bed so he could play belly brother with the crown. What a fool.

Head bowed, arms folded, hands hidden inside her wide sleeves, she passed through the gate and moved with calm dignity along the cliff path, heading for the Scholar's Village and her own house.

OERFEL OF NYDDYS

[1]

The main conference room in Tyst's Grath Hall was both shabby and grand, with splendidly carved panels of the dark wood imported from the coastal mountains of northern Faiscar, the floor a mosaic map of Nyddys, its tiny chips of stone collected from the length and breadth of the island. The panels were dry and dull, with a film of dust on them and the mosaic was scratched, with many chips missing.

Oerfel Hawlson sat in the corner of that room, his pen scratching over sheet after sheet of paper as he used the shorthand he'd invented to take down a record of what the men and women sitting around the conference table said as they debated fees and the list of repairs presented by the Presmun appointed to the Port of Tyst. Oerfel was a long narrow man, an Ivory Dyar with translucent blue-white skin that had a tendency to redden and peel whenever the sun touched it. What hair he had left, a fringe that ran from ear to ear, was a dull brown, that particular shade that seems to turn eyes aside so that it is seldom actually noted as a color. His mouth was thin, a pale brown line straight as a taut string connecting the deep grooves that ran from the edges of his nostrils to his chin.

Mahara has been a busy lad. I like to see a man taking his work seriously. The ends of his mouth twitched in a fleeting, humorless smile. Another ship went to the bottom yesterday, with three Candidates who won't be a bother any more. And sweet Hudoleth is swatting them like flies. Working for me, though she doesn't know it yet and won't, I hope, for a good long time.

With Cyfareth breathing down his neck, suspicious of those storms and alerted to the possibility of Dark Work, he had to be more circumspect than his rivals, but it was time he emulated them and got busy dealing with the Candidates already here.

Very carefully, oh yes. And not just because of the Watchers and Cyfareth. Mahara and Hudoleth don't know that there's a third in the game and I'd like to keep it that way. Hm. Everything would be easier if I could do something about Cyfareth. Not yet. Not yet. May those priss-faced snoops be damned to Tanew's lowest, dankest hell! The time would come when Cyfareth would be on its knees before him, but until then he had to work through the delicate twitchings of Chance and surrogates like his esteemed patron Broga Clebranson, the chief boar at the city trough. Boar, boor, bore, he thought. A man of many parts and all of them horrible.

"Hawlson, if you'll read back that last but one objection."

"At your service, Ryn Broga. If I may be sure I have the right one, the objection by Rynnat Crebachswyf?"

"Yes, yes, that's the one."

"Hem-hm. 'I don't see why it is necessary to lay a new course of stone on the breakwater. This is summer and waves in summer storms don't come near the top as it is. What it's about is obvious, Presmun Jobyn's brother owns a quarry over in the Dreyals somewhere, nepotism, that's what it is, wasting public money to pay off his brother's debts.' Do you wish more of the record read out, Ryn Broga?"

"No. By agreement of the Whole, we wish the objection and all matters concerning it excised from the record before today's deliberations are entered in the Daybook."

With a flourish of his pen, Oerfel drew lines through the several statements involved, including Broga's last. "It is done, Ryn Broga. The material has been removed."

The tedious arguments began again.

Once again Oerfel abstracted most of his attention from the meeting.

Hero, he thought. I need a Hero of my own. A puppet who'll dance when I pull his strings. The Watchers are right. Pick them young and train them the way you want. Thirteen, fourteen at most. Good-looking. Charm. Good with games. Good with weapons. Good with horses. Not stupid, but certainly not overly bright. I want a leader, not a thinker. Or rather someone who looks and acts like a leader. Hm. Should be well connected, to the Tyrn's line if possible. Plenty of bastards to choose from. One thing that boor is good at, siring bastard sons. Time to start looking about. . . .

Broga Clebranson tapped the sounding block with his rod of office. "Let it be written, the meeting of the Grathal of Tyst is concluded. All matters left incomplete will remain on table till the end of Foolsreign. Let it be written, the Lesser Council will reconvene on nine Choomis at the beginning of the Second Watch. Stand all for the dismissal. Councilor Brother Noglyd, speak the words."

Councilor Brother Noglyd, Representative of the Religious, cleared his throat. He was a small twig of a man with an orator's training, capable of projecting his deep baritone voice to the back corners of an auditorium; in this smaller room it boomed loudly enough to stir the dust on the paneling. "May Dyf Tanew the Omnipotent and All-Merciful bless our going and our labors for his people. So let it be."

[2]

The last day of Foolsreign was cloudless and hot. The sun glinted off the painted roofs of Tyst and turned the dust kicked up by thousands of feet to gilded motes that danced through the streets and floated above the viewing stands.

Children ran everywhere, throwing handfuls of colored paper cut into tiny squares; a few of the more enterprising had eggs they'd painted with iodine, hair dye and whatever else they could get their hands on. Streams of little gods followed them, packets of mischief that sent awry everything they touched.

As Oerfel followed the Tyst councilors across the square, carrying Broga's blankets and cushions and a covered basket with a wine jar and glasses, meat rolls, iced foolscakes, and damp nap-

kins in a small porcelain bowl, one of those eggs caught him in
the back of the head and splattered over his neat black robe. Behind him he heard giggles and hoots, but though he was shaking
with rage, he didn't turn to curse the thrower, just continued
walking, the yellow goo sliding down his back. When he reached
the elaborate fountain in the middle of the square, he backed into
a niche, checked to see that he wasn't being watched, then used
a minor clean-spell to rid himself of the egg. He stayed there a
moment until he had better control over himself, then he hurried after the councilors.

The Cyngraths of the ruling council of Nyddys, the Grathals
of the city council of Tyst, Dyf Tanew's High Priest Gwan Ar-
belson and his Brother aides, Soror Ubain of the Order of Healers and her Sister aides, the wealthier merchants and those
Broons and their families who'd come to town for the five days
of Foolsreign were all moving into the shade of the awnings
raised over the viewing stands, carrying rugs and pillows and
whatever they considered necessary for their comfort.

Oerfel helped Broga arrange his cushions, spread the lap robe
over them and settled the basket beside him, then he took his
own seat up with the servants on the highest tier, the wall of the
building at his back, his head so close to the awning that it
brushed the canvas. He'd arranged to sit at the end of the bench;
the thought of being squashed between two stinking celebrants
nauseated him.

He took a sip of water from the bottle he'd brought for himself and settled to endure the discomfort and boredom of the
next several watches.

For an interminable time nothing much happened except
the occasional crash or yelp as a little god got busy; groups of
men stood around muttering in low tones or broke into loud
arguments, gangs of children chased each other shrieking and
laughing, latecomers yelled at people who'd spread into their
purchased seats. All around him people were gossiping, com-

plaining, yelping, laughing, eating, drinking, a clanging cacophony that brought migraine ripples to his eyes, watery shimmers like the wings of draigflies caught by sunlight. He shut his eyes but they were still there and his stomach churned until he was afraid he was going to vomit on the people in front of him. Groping inside his robe, he brought out one of the bits of bindroot he'd twisted into turnip leaves and tucked into an inner pocket. He tore the leaf off it, popped the bitter fragment into his mouth and chewed at it.

A tweekhorn sounded and the noise around him stilled suddenly as the servants leaned forward to get what view they could under the front edge of the awning.

Beggars came dancing along the street, singing the praises of the Fooltyrn, crying out for alms and collecting a shower of red and green and gold boiled sweets as they thrust their bowls at the folk on the lower benches.

Oerfel spat the cud into his hand and dropped it to the pavement, took several sips of water to wash the taste from his mouth and cut the burn of yellow vomit rising in his throat as he watched the capering beggars. Those were the children of rich merchants and Landbroons, dressed in silken rags; the dirt on their faces was dusted there with their mother's sable eyebrow brushes and their scars were painted on. The city guard made sure none of the genuine poor slipped through to join the procession.

He'd been one of those poor children when he was a boy, peering past a guard's leather sides, seeing beauty and joy he knew he'd never taste for himself. He was not a beggar child; his father was first mate on a trading ship, his mother had a popular sweetshop, so he'd never gone hungry or cold and he was always neatly dressed with proper shoes and a clean white shirt every third day. But from the moment he began to learn the ways of the world, to understand the barriers between him and that bright shining life he could watch but never enter, desire had filled him, an ching need to destroy those barriers and take for himself what he knew he deserved. Desire made him a Mage.

I have other dreams now, he thought, perhaps not better dreams, but at least these I can realize.

Tumblers followed the beggars' dance, acrobats from the Tyrn's court, some bounding and wheeling along the pavement, some making and breaking towers that walked, three, four men high, some flipping each other in an extravagance of motion, limber forms contorting into impossible shapes, the white paint blanking out their faces so all that was left to catch the eye were those mercurial bodies.

Then soldier clowns came marching to the rattle of their drums.

Then painted boys in horsehair wigs and pretty gowns rode by on produce carts pulled by other boys in horsehead masks, prancing and cavorting, shaking the horsehair tails they'd strapped to their narrow buttocks.

Then a tweekhorner marched by alone, dressed in white, face and hair painted white, the only color to him that golden tweekhorn from which he drew alternately transcendent fanfares and ludicrous squawks.

And last of all came the Fooltyrn himself, riding in the traditional lifeboat on wheels pulled by four ancient bony horses with tinsel tacked here and there about the harness.

This year the Fool was an immensely fat man, dressed in billowing ruffles made from flour sacks bleached white, with the Fool Face painted in the middle of his puffy countenance, his hair stiffened by lime into ragged spikes.

The Royal Fool was also royally drunk, waving his tinsel scepter through elaborate swoops, dropping it repeatedly so one or the other of the exasperated escorts who actually did the driving had to jump down and collect it.

As the mutilated boat rattled past his stand, Oerfel slipped another bit of root in his mouth. Through the haze of pain he was pleased with himself; Broga had left the choice of the Fool to him and this was his little joke on the world. The beggars might be fake, but the Fool was really a fool.

He leaned against the wall of the building behind the stand, his eyes closed. The nausea had passed and the dizziness, but he felt as if he were swimming inside his skin and knew that his hands would be trembling if he took them from his pockets.

The tweekhorn blared again. He winced as the sound cut into his head.

What it announced was the Foolsride, the wild race through the streets of Tyst, the sons of Broons and courtiers riding bareback on young stallions from the Tyrn's half-broken herds. When the tweekhorn fell silent, he could hear the war screams of the horses and the cheering of the Tystans standing in the side streets or crushed back against the buildings or leaning from upper-story windows—then the thunder of hooves as the first rider turned the corner and came racing past the stands.

There was a gasp, then silence under the awning.

Pricked by curiosity, Oerfel forced his eyes open and watched the boy in the lead.

He was riding lightly, superbly, balanced on his thighs; his eyes were shining and he was laughing between the words he sang to the stallion. A golden boy, glowing in the sunlight, tanned, his body oiled and naked but for a twist of cloth about his loins.

That's him, Oerfel thought. That's my Hero.

5

The Siofray Mage

By the calendar of the Domains of Iomard, events that begin on the 17th day of Thairin, the fourth month in the Iomardi year 6531, look back to an interval beginning on the 2nd day of Antram, the third month in the Iomardi year 6530, then return to 17th Thairin in 6531, the 718th year since the last Corruption.

[1]   6531

When the Dyar Watcher interposed between Dur and that girl whose magic and mystery had called to him across the Veil between the worlds, when the Window was slammed shut in his face, Dur leaped to his feet and went careening about the cavern, howling with rage and frustration.

In the corner where she was away from the light so he wouldn't see her sucking on her muscar jug, Fanach heard him and sat up. "Dur, what . . ."

He halted his tantrum and stared at her, noting that her speech was carefully crisp, but that she couldn't force her sodden mind to frame a real question.

"Not your business," he said. He would have said more but he still needed her. He put the rage away from him, waded into the dark pool and let the water close over his fever-hot body.

It was only one more frustration of all the frustrations that had worked to bring him here. . . .

{ 2 } 6530

The Domain patrol attacked shortly before dawn on the morning of the second day after Dur and his band of scurds had returned to their home camp with the loot from a series of raids on the Minor Domain of Mionmiol.

Dur was in his hut on the mountainside above the narrow canyon, stretched out on his blankets, so deeply asleep the mountain could fall on him and he wouldn't wake. He was exhausted from the long, tense ride home. With Mionmiol patrols spread out like swarms of ants hunting for them, he had to spend his vitality with a lavish hand, wiping away the tracks of the horses and the herd while he kept a Sight watch scanning for armed riders. And when they reached camp with their backtrail clean, he had to set up the no-see shield round the mouth of the canyon. Working the Pneuma Flow like that stripped more vitality from him than the long days of hard labor in the fields when he was a daroc boy.

He was up here alone because his men got antsy when they watched him work a major spell, and life was easier in the days that followed if he stayed away till the memory of his capering and chants had faded a bit.

The horses the band had brought with them and the small herd of tribufs were grazing with the other livestock. The weapons, clothing, flour and other food they'd collected were piled in heaps on the floor of the communal cabin they'd raised beside the hot springs near the back end of the canyon. Five men snored on bunk beds, a sixth man was in the cookhouse, trying to get the fire to catch so he could start making breakfast and a seventh was out at one of the sulfur springs, dipping bandages in it, preparing fomentations for his wounded leg.

Fifteen riders swept down the valley, led by a dark-eyed Seer who flung fire at the building so that it went up with a roar, catching the six men inside before they had a chance of getting out. One of the patrol pinned the wounded man at the hot spring with a short lance and the whole thing was over as quickly as that, the loot back in the hands of its owners and the scurds who'd stolen it dead.

Except for Dur. The sudden surge in the Flow and the ripping asunder of his no-see shield jolted him from sleep.

He ran.

He didn't stop to reason it out, he simply obeyed the panic that seized hold of him and fled into the hills.

When he couldn't run any longer, he flung himself down on the oozy earth of a mountain meadow and lay panting until his mouth was so dry that the pain drove him to the bank of the tiny stream, where he lay and drank until he was sick and brought most of the water up again.

He washed his mouth out, drank again, more slowly this time. Then he shifted himself to a weathered boulder and sat with his bruised and bloody feet dangling in the icy stream.

When he was fourteen he ran from the Domain where he was a daroc's third son, ran because they were going to geld him, brand him and burn out the places in his mind that let him handle Pneuma, burn out his magic. He ran with only the clothes on his back and a small sack of food and every Siofray hand against him.

"Thirty years," he said aloud. "Nearly thirty years and I'm back where I started." Once again he had nothing except the clothes he wore. Not even a blanket or a knife. He moved his feet in the water. Not even a pair of boots.

Cautiously he touched the Flow. It was clean at the moment, no jangles, so he drained off a tiny trickle and painted it over his body like a second skin—a magic skin that he could use to mimic the form and feel of one of the larger beasts that lived in these hills when the Seer came looking for him.

Domain Seer. She'd read the Flow, smelled out the knots he'd put in it and used them to trace the knotter. In an ironic way it was a compliment. He and his band had done enough damage to the Domains to win the interest and time of a Power. Not too shabby for a runaway daroc boy and a collection of misfits.

Food. He had to find something to eat. Feed the vitality and the vitality feeds you. What Grinneal used to say when she sat watching him eat, waiting for him to take her to bed. She expected vigorous service for teaching him how to tap the Flow and what he could do with it.

He moved along the bank until he found a place where a tree had fallen across the stream, stretched out on it, careful to keep his shadow from touching the water, watching fish swim by below him, waiting for the right moment. . . .

The back of his neck prickled.

Teasing the magic skin into a bear's form and feel, he dropped to hands and knees, thrust his face against the water and drank as if he were a beast, then he crawled through the brush and into the trees.

The tickling probe lingered a moment; he fought down panic and concentrated on making bear moves to reinforce the image.

The probe left.

He continued the lumbering crawl and a moment later the tickle was back.

It left once more and this time didn't return.

The next few days he kept life in himself with roots and raw fish, worms and grubs as he made his way slowly through the mountains. Twice more the probe touched him. He played wolf and cougar for it and the Seer moved her gaze on, satisfied with what she'd sensed.

On the fifth day of his run, he came across a stone boundary marker, slid his fingers over the incised letters. Domain Eolais. We stayed away from Eolais because it was too close to camp. Hm. The House will be out of the hills . . . I think Eolais is built

on the bluffs above river Anyar . . . but there'll be herdgirl camps
. . . or herds . . . I can ride a tribuf if I can't find a horse. And live
off its blood. Better than worms. Just about anything is better
than worms and grubs.

The magic skin counterfeiting a deer, he crept forward cautiously, expending vitality he couldn't spare to move in an irregular pattern from brush clump to brush clump watching warily
for any sign of herdgirls in the area.

If Domain herdgirls saw him, they'd come after him to find
out what he was. And after they rode him down, all it would take
was one look at his mismated eyes and they would know. Brown
and green, geld and brand. He wasn't the first to run from the
knife. Or the last.

The horned cayochs they rode instead of horses got part of
their food from graze and browse, but the larger part of their diet
came from coneys their riders trapped for them. If they caught
him, those riders would treat him like the coneys, cut him up and
feed him to their mounts.

Half an hour after he started the stalk, he smelled water, snaked
through the brush at the top of a hill and looked down into a
stock-cistern with a stone rim built around it and a waterwheel,
which was used to transfer water from the cistern into a flume
that led into a smaller pond a short distance off.

Beyond the cistern there was a small stone blockhouse. A lanky
yellow dog dozed restlessly on the flags in front of the door and
a thread of smoke came from the chimney. Herdgirls worked in
squads of three. Two would be out with the tribuf herd and one
left behind to do laundry and cooking and any repairs needed on
the gear.

Hot food. Real food. I'd almost forgot.

Behind the blockhouse there was a stable and a fenced turnout
with three cayochs drowsing near a feed box. He watched them
twitch loose skin and shake their long heads, startling swarms of
flies into flight.

Stealing those cayochs would alert the Seer searching for him, but if he rode them hard enough and pulled a skin of Pneuma over them like the one that shielded him, he could keep clear, he was sure of it. And get to sanctuary. He closed his eyes for a moment and dreamed of the Sanctuary Isles where the Seers were blocked by knots and swirls in the Pneuma Flow, where they couldn't *see* him, where he'd be free of them. Finally free.

He had more raw power than any single Seer, but they had knowledge and training. What he knew he'd stolen by eavesdropping on the Lynborn when he was a boy; he'd added the dribs and drabs he'd picked up from hedge witches, outlaw wizards and Grinneal, an outcast Seer willing to teach him and risk a flogging for a year of his services in bed and out.

He could take a minor spell and twist it and turn it and expand it enormously, but he didn't know enough to create his own spells and until he did he was vulnerable. When he thought of that ignorance, deliberately imposed on him by the Lynborn Seers and the Traiolyns who ruled the Domains, he was filled with rage. The boy Dur's rage was hot and helpless, but it had turned cold these last years when he was an outlaw and a leader of outlaws. Scurd, the Lynborn called him and scurd he was.

There was a certain satisfaction in hurting the Lynborn and their Domains, but it wasn't enough. Fleabites would never be enough to cool the cauldron inside him. He wanted the Domains crushed, the Lynborn Siofray bowing to him as he'd been forced to bow to them.

Not bow. No. Lie with his face in the dust while they walked on him.

For his soul's sake, for his pride's sake, they had to eat dust and feel the weight of him marching across their backs.

The door to the blockhouse opened and a thin girl came out, a towel tied about her waist, a bowl filled with meat scraps held in both hands. She set the bowl on the ground on the far side of the steps and went back inside. The yellow dog uncoiled himself, jumped down and began eating.

The day was almost over; in the west the sun was beginning to slip away. The girl would be leaving with the dog soon, heading for the herd to take her turn at watch. The place would be left empty until the other two came to eat and sleep. Not for long. Maybe long enough.

Raid the blockhouse. Food, waterskin, knife, rope, blankets, tack for the cayochs. Crossbow, bolts, any weapons he could find. Whatever else looked useful.

Saddle one cayoch, lead one. Don't stop till I reach the River-ines.

No. Don't stop till I reach the Isles.

A short time later, the girl rode away with the yellow dog trotting after her.

[3]

He went through the blockhouse dumping everything that looked useful onto a blanket from one of the beds. He tied the ends to make a bundle, scooped stew from the pot simmering on the stove's warmplate into a deep, lidded bowl, tossed in a spoon, snapped down the lid, then carried his gleanings to the stable. His belly cramped at the smell of the stew, but he couldn't stop to eat, not now.

He used a touch of Pneuma to freeze the two cayochs so they wouldn't try to kill him. Their front claws were formidable and they had tearing teeth like a dog's. When he had the saddle and headstall on one of them, halter, leadrope and pack on the second, he mounted, rode to the fence post where he'd left the bowl of stew, collected it, then left the corral, the cayochs docile under the Pneuma bond.

He dropped the waterskin into the cistern, jerked it out full and dripping.

A shout. Two riders racing toward him.

He tightened the Pneuma knots, twisted the cayochs into a flat-out run, heading south, out into the rolling grassland. They'd come back too soon. Prophet's Tears, too soon.

Reckless in his panic, snatching from the Flow with a lavish hand, he laid a rope of Pneuma around the legs of the pursuing cayochs, threw them off their feet into a squawling, struggling tangle.

With the start he'd won for himself, enough to take him out of sight, he turned east, and as he fled toward the uplands ahead, he wiped away the scent and clawmarks of the cayochs' feet; herdgirls and their dogs were the best trackers in the Domains, but they needed some sign to guide them. He scoured the earth behind him and left nothing, no tracks, no scent, not even a bent stalk of grass.

He could feel the Seer sniffing round for him.

A flare of triumph. She was looking at him. No. Not at him, at the land round him. She still couldn't see him. But she was scanning. . . .

Ah. Of course. Searching for a clue to identify the place she was seeing. At first he thought that wasn't going to be easy, one patch of grassland was much like another, then he remembered the brands on the cayochs and cursed his own stupidity. He'd meant to spread a Pneuma skin over the beasts to hide them too, but he'd forgot.

Another flare. She'd seen the Eolais brand.

The Flow throbbed. She was calling.

Another presence. Anger. Contempt.

The Eolais Seer.

All he could do was ride. Out of here out of here out out . . .

As it passed a tangle of thorny, stunted drach trees, the cayoch stumbled, blatted its distress and squatted, nearly throwing Dur over its head; then it rolled, trying to catch his leg and crush it.

He kicked free from the stirrups just in time and flung himself from the saddle.

The cayoch on lead sidled closer, black lips lifting to bare the tearing teeth, eyes narrowed, ears tucked tight against its head.

Dismayed at how quickly his knot spell had frayed, Dur slipped a tap into the Flow and teased out enough Pneuma to reinforce and retighten the knots.

When he had them docile again, he glanced at the sky.

Not so quickly, after all.

The moon wasn't full but she was swollen enough that the Prophet's Fan was visible and she was almost down to the horizon in the west. At this point in her cycle, moonset was well past midnight. He'd been riding and erasing his signs of passage for more than two straight watches.

I can't go any more, he thought. Just as well the cayoch crashed on me. Rubbing at his back—the muscles were jumping and pain like a toothache moused up and down it—he turned in a slow circle, looking for a likely place to camp.

Nothing better than drach thicket anywhere in sight. Shelter from the wind. Shelter from wandering eyes. It'll do.

He poked his toe into the ribs of the squatting cayoch. It groaned, but came back onto its feet. Fingers hooked in its halter, he led it and the packer over to the nearest tree, tethered them there. He stripped off the gear, gave them some water and a few mouthfuls of grain from the pack.

They grumbled at the grain, lifting their black lips in cayochan sneers that set him laughing until another spasm of his back cut off his enjoyment. He flattened himself against a tree, spread his legs and stretched. Ahhh, that felt good. He rubbed his shoulders against the trunk, the thorny limbs shaking about him. Have to set out snares before I hit the blankets. They need meat if they're going to keep working this hard. I need meat. No fire, though. Can't afford a fire.

He retrieved the stew bowl from the saddle ring where he'd tied it, found a seat far enough off so the cayochs couldn't reach him if the knots slipped again and began spooning up the chunks of meat and tuber. The herdgirl was a good camp cook. Even cold the stew was tasty. Best meal he'd had in days.

As he ate, he brooded over the next day's ride.

Have to keep away from roads. And watch for travelers.

The Domains were small round here, but there were a lot of them and much less freeland than in the Hill Country. And every Domain would be warned and waiting for him.

He finished the stew, used a fistful of dead leaves to scrub out the bowl and clean the spoon. He tied the bowl back to the saddle ring and searched through the pack for the coil of thin cord he'd tossed into it. He cut some lengths of cord, fashioned nooses, cut forked branches from the drach trees and went hunting for signs of a coney run so he could set up his snares. With a little luck there'd be meat in the morning for the cayochs.

[4]

When the cayochs finished tearing into the coneys he'd brought them, the sun was clear of the horizon. Each time he looked to the east, Dur cursed himself for oversleeping and fought down the urge to get out of there at top speed, ride the cayochs into the ground, kill the stupid beasts if he had to, just get out of there, get away. Get away . . .

He saddled the second cayoch and put the other on lead. Then he carefully rubbed his hands over them, coating them with a fine layer of Pneuma, a magic skin of no-see. Working slowly, carefully, rigidly disciplining his panic, he renewed his own overskin, strengthening the places worn thin by time and internal tempest.

The Seers were still watching, waiting for him to make a mistake. Three of them now.

Three Seers. Hunting him.

Hunting a male and a worker of magic.

Why was that so important now and not before? It was nearly thirty years since he'd run. They'd had plenty of chances to hunt him down before this. And with a lot less effort.

He only got away the first time because no one really cared that much. Just a half-grown daroc boy with maybe a little talent he shouldn't have had.

He remembered all too clearly the Historian of Domain Gruam riding past the field where he was working. She brought her horse to a halt and stared at him for several minutes, then rode on without speaking. An hour later, the patrol came for him and took him to the house. He remembered the examination and the girl making notes. Always notes, the steel penpoint scratching and scratching, tinking against the stone ink bottle, scratching some more. Enough notes to fill a book. His name. His parents' names. His height. His weight. That he had one green eye and one brown. The scars on his body. On and on.

That night his mother hugged him, handed him a sack filled with biscuits and bacon, all she had to give, told him to run and never look back.

Still running, Mama. He could see her as if she walked beside the cayoch, square and strong, burnt dark by the sun from working in the fields beside his father. Faded brown eyes as if someone had taken them from her head and washed them in harsh soap, leaching away the color. Coarse black hair. Scarred, twisted hands, with fingers that wouldn't close into fists because of the chalk disease in her joints that grew worse every year. She never talked much, never sang as some of the women did, but when she smiled at him she found a fleeting beauty.

He'd never seen her again, never tried to see her. Best she knew nothing. Domain Gruam's Seer would see the truth of that and let her be.

He could see her clear. Could see her set her hands on her hips and click her tongue at him. "You're in a mess again," she'd say.

"I know. I settled for what I could get. You told me to reach as high as I could. I forgot to do that."

"You can do it still. Just don't forget this time."

"No." He frowned at the twitchy round ears of the cayoch. "I won't forget. . . ."

[5]

By nightfall the land had changed. Hummocks like horripilation on winter skin rolled away to the horizon on every side of him. The ground was dry and barren with drifts of pebbles in between the tufts of short, sun-dried grass. He'd reached the Comconair, the high plain between the two lobes of Continent Saffroa.

He eased his feet from the stirrups, drew his legs up and managed to stand in the saddle and turn slowly, peering through the gloom, looking for seeps or patches of shoum.

The seeps were marked by a darkening of the green around them and a circle of turbils, spindly trees that rose higher than the rest of the vegetation.

Shoum patches were the best, though. Shoum were succulent growths with water cells like miniature bottles spread throughout stems thick as a man's wrist. You could strip the skins and feed the pulp to horses and cayochs and suck the bottles in the stems to quench your thirst. You couldn't live on one shoum patch for long, but it was enough to keep a man going.

If he could find shoum. The plants were a pale green, a color that should jump from the tan and faded yellow of the sand and sun-bleached grass, but they grew low to the ground and, in this light, were almost impossible to pick out. He strained to see. Nothing. No turbils, no shoum.

Then the cayoch on lead snuffled, moved forward three steps and lowered its head to gnaw on something.

Dur looked down and started laughing so hard he nearly fell off his perch. Under his nose, a patch of shoum. He drew his sleeve across his face, lowered himself carefully and swung from the saddle.

Lips drawn back from its tearing teeth, the cayoch lifted his head and curled its snaky neck round. Dur felt the change in the reins, looked up just in time to punch the beast in the side of the head as those teeth came at him.

The cayoch jerked his head back, watched Dur from narrowed eyes, waiting for a chance to strike.

"Prophet's Teeth! Slipped again. I will dance a damsir on the day I boot you in the rear and jump for a boat." He tightened the Pneuma knot until the cayoch's eyes glazed over, then he caught hold of the bridle and led it to the shoum patch where the second cayoch was munching happily.

In the days that followed he worked his way cautiously across the Comconair. Because it was so barren and dry, there were no Domains, not even any freeholds, only Scribe trails and trade roads. He stayed away from those and from the few waterholes, depending on shoum and turbil seeps for water, roots and snares for food.

By the time he reached the Broken Lands at the eastern edge of the Comconair, his flesh had melted off his frame and his two cayochs were racks of bone, their skin hanging loose from their spines.

There were no shoum patches in the Broken Lands, that long downslope between the Comconair's high plateau and the Eastern Plains, and no seeps, but there were dozens of places where water bubbled up, ran a few strides and vanished in the broken rock. And thickets of wild tachta plumtrees everywhere. The plums were starting to turn purple, still unripe but with enough sweetness to move the weary cayochs into a trot whenever they smelled plums on the wind. On the evening of the second day in the Broken Lands, Dur led the cayochs round a tachta grove and saw water bubbling from under the tangle of roots.

He drew in a long breath, let it out and smiled. He was looking at the source of the river Droa Croab.

[6]

He woke with an aching head, a sour, musty smell in his nostrils
and a soreness at his wrists and ankles. He was tied and blind-
folded and the ache was because someone had knocked him cold
while he was sleeping. I thought I was safe. That far in the back-
country, I thought . . .

Soft scuff of feet, the smell of an unwashed body.

"Awake are you?" The voice was harsh, the syllables slurred.
Dur recognized the accent—one of the ashog hunters out of
Creoch on the Droa. A rough hand jerked his head up, held a cup
to his lips. "Drink, fool, or I pour it down you neck."

Dur sputtered as he swallowed and at the same time realized
what he was swallowing. It was raw batta, that white fire made
from whatever the stillman threw in the pot; when he was
younger he'd got drunk on it once and swore off for life because
it blinded his Sight.

He tried to stop drinking but the Ashogger popped his jaw,
forced his mouth open and he had to swallow or drown.

" 'Nough. Don' wan' to kill you off, you worth too much alive."
He lowered Dur's head onto the rough sacking, checked the
binding on his wrists and ankles. "Whoo-ee, them Lynborn want
to get hold a you. Got any idee how much they say they'll pay for
your hide with you in it?"

The Ashogger moved away. The creak of a door. Gone outside.
Outside what?"

Ashogger. So. Probably a drying shack for keeping the rain off
the ashog hides and strips of meat. There wasn't any meat here
yet or he'd have smelled it.

He didn't have to try touching the Flow; the batta muffled his
Sight as effectively as the blindfold did his eyes. He pulled gent-

at the binding on his wrists, testing the knots. No joy there. The Ashogger knew his bends.

Dur lay still and concentrated on relaxing his muscles. His wrists were tied with cord rather than rope and that was going to make it harder, but with a little luck he was sure he could work free of that binding. His hands were deceptive; they looked big, but his thumbs were unusually limber. He could fold them nearly flat against his palms and slip most bonds with a minimum of wriggling.

The door creaked again.

Dur went still, let his thumbs drop into their usual place.

The Ashogger had his boots on this time. The heels clunked on the floorboards. He caught hold of Dur, lifted him with a light grunt of effort and dumped him over a meaty shoulder, then carried him outside.

His captor heaved him facedown across a saddle, tied him in place with a few quick half hitches. Again he used cord, not rope. He slapped Dur on the rump. "Fastest turnaround I ever made. Don't you worry now, little wizard, I'm not turning you over to that clutch of bitches till I've got you and me both safe from their cheating. You're gonna bring me double what they think they gonna pay. I know 'em better'n you, daroc. I know their pinching ways. Hoy! I am gonna enjoy this better'n my first jug of batta."

All that morning Dur heard the *thud thud thud* of those booted feet as the Ashogger walked ahead of the horse, moving at a steady lope as if he could maintain that pace forever. And perhaps he could.

Ashogger. I'd swear he was Lynborn before he turned hunter. Yes, one of the surplus males that wandered away from the Domains because they'd lost too many mating battles. And he knows about batta, what it does to the Sight. Not a stupid man, not when he was cool and in charge.

Not good enough to make it as a breeder, but too ruttish t
hang about the Domain. Run off as a troublemaker, no doubt
I'd better be careful what I say. Get his rage going, let that figh
training take over, I'm a dead daroc. Blood in his eye would blin
him to gold.

Around mid-morning the Ashogger stopped to feed and water th
horse. He poured more batta down Dur, then went whistlin
about the camp, fixing some tea and boiling some strips of drie
tribuf. He didn't bother feeding any of either to Dur.

"Enough coin to buy a good-sized freehold, that's what you are
little wizard." He lifted Dur's head, eased the blindfold back an
checked his eyes to make sure he was properly soused. "Gotta tak
good care of you, Seers won't buy dead meat. They say they wil
but the price goes down so low 'twouldn't profit me to bring yo
in. So we don't feed you till we stop for the night. Don't wan
you getting sick on me and strangling on your spew before I snif
what's happening."

Dur was barely conscious when darkness caught up with ther
and the Ashogger stopped for the night. His head felt as if it ha
been stuffed with raw meat, he'd wet himself and hadn't messe
his pants only because his gut was so empty. He was about as mis
erable as he'd ever been and more helpless than a newborn babe
He couldn't even stand when his captor yanked the knots loos
and let him slide off the horse.

Dur let himself drowse till he heard the whistling, honking snore
coming from the direction where the Ashogger had flung him
self down for the night. Then he began tensing and loosening hi
muscles, working up a good sweat after a while, but doing it s
silently he hoped his captor wouldn't wake and notice. His hand
were swollen and numb; even with his trick thumbs he had n

chance of slipping the cords that bound him. But he might be able to work the batta out of his system.

Tense and relax ... supper a lump in his belly, breathing through his mouth, his throat so dry he could barely drag in the air. Sweat in his eyes, stinging, salt sweat in the corners of his mouth.

He was working so hard he didn't notice when the snores stopped.

Tense and relax, tense and ... There was an explosion of pain in his head, then nothing.

Dur woke bellydown across the saddle again, the horse clip-clopping along the river road. He could smell the water and old droppings from other horses that had passed this way. They must be getting close to Creoch. At the moment, he couldn't bring himself to care.

The Ashogger's voice drifted back to him. "That wasn't a kindly thing to do, little wizard. Trying to steal your good self away from me like that. We'll have to do something about that. Oh yes we will."

The horse's gait changed as it left the road and moved into much rougher going. At first Dur noted this as just one more misery, but after a time he dredged up enough vitality to wonder why they'd detoured like this.

Before he could flog any answers from his deadened brain, the horse stopped moving.

He let his head hang limp, his cheek against the stirrup leather.

Leaves rustling. A grove. Yes. Tachta plums, he could smell that sour sweetness of the fruits.

Feet walking about. A crackling sound. Glug of water being forced from a skin. A hand grabbed Dur's hair and jerked his head up and around. The Ashogger forced the mouth of the jug into Dur's mouth and drained the last of the batta into him.

More footsteps. Going away.

Dur listened intently until he could no longer hear his captor, then he struggled with the muzziness in his head and tried to think.

Get rid of the blindfold.

He began rubbing his face across the stirrup leathers, searching for something that would catch on the filthy cloth and help him ease it off.

Catch, slip, catch, slip, leather burns on his face, his stiff and straggly beard itching as if it were thistle fuzz grafted to his skin. Catch, slip, each time loosening and shifting just a little . . .

He shook his head. The blindfold fell off. He could see.

The horse was an old bay, hard used but with a few good years left in him. The Ashogger had left him haltered and tied to one of the trees, a pan of water wedged between two roots where he could reach it easily enough but be unlikely to kick it over. There were some broken grain cakes nearby and several bushes within reach. The horse was nibbling at the new growth on a bush, twitching his skin and swishing his tail to drive off the flies that were crawling all over Dur also.

Dur rested, blinked the sweat from his eyes and drove his mind to considering why the Ashogger had left him and the horse in this grove.

The jug.

A fly crawled on his nose, the tickle maddening, distracting him until he managed to shake it off.

Empty.

The horse nosed at the bush, couldn't find more tender ends to browse on, shifted position and sucked up the last drops of water, then began munching on one of the grain cakes.

Ashogger knows what batta does to the Sight.
Control.

A pair of squirrelmonks ran about the branches of a nearby tree screeching at each other. Their cries drilled into his head and shut his thinking down until they calmed again and dropped their noise to the occasional chitter that mixed with snatches of song from the small brown donnbirds that nested in the grove.

Yes.

The wind rose, a warm damp wind that wrung sweat from him, sweat that soaked his clothes, ran down his arms and dampened the ropes that held him. The rustle of leaves grew louder as the wind grew stronger.

Going for more. Stillers in the area.

Why leave me?

Ah. Treasure. Doesn't trust the stiller. The reward must be a great one.

That thought burned through him. Even if he got free from this one, he couldn't trust the Riverines because those greedy merchants would sell him without a qualm. For a moment he despaired, then he ground his teeth and began patiently working with his hands, even though they were still swollen, pressing his thumbs inward, easing them out-joint so he could fold them on his palms, rubbing the cords against the horse's girth, working them hair by hair along his hands. . . .

When the Ashogger returned, Dur had bit through his lower lip and was almost unconscious from the pressure of blood in his head because his struggles had unbalanced him and he was mostly hanging off one side of a disgruntled horse—and he was very close to ridding himself of the cords.

"Hoy! Little wizard, look what you gone and did." The Ashogger cut the ropes and eased Dur onto the ground. "Fan, bring that water and get over here."

A moment later a woman bent over him. She wasn't old, but her hair was streaked with white and there were deep lines in her face. She wore her hair in a Scribe's braids and had the weathered look of a Round Rider, but that had to be wrong. Dur gnawed at the thought. A Scribe wouldn't be taking orders from a stinking Ashogger. And Scribes didn't leave the Guild. Unless they were thrown out.

She bathed his face. The water was cool against his skin. Soothing. He began to think more clearly. She was renegade or reject, but she had the training. If he could reach her . . .

She bathed his wrists, then spread ointment of some kind over the rope cuts and bound them with strips of cloth. Have to be careful, he thought. Don't mess with her when the Ashogger's around. But smile at her when he's not looking. Get her to think about me. To pity me. And if the Ashogger leaves us together, tell her what's waiting for me. Work on her . . .

The Ashogger came over with a cup of batta. "Hold his head up, Fan."

"Troc, you shouldn't feed him that, it could kill him."

"Hush now, baba, little wizard here is tricky and if we don't keep him muzzed up, he gonna do bad things to us. He's daroc, you know, raised to be tough."

"But . . ."

"Don't fuss me, Fan. I don't like that."

She cringed and moved away.

Dur gulped the batta, trying to spill as much as he could from the corners of his mouth, but Troc was too canny to let him get away with that. He used the edge of the tin cup to scrape up the spilled batta and made Dur drink that too.

Later that night, after Fan had fed him, Dur watched blearily as Troc made himself comfortable, his back braced against a tree, his ankles crossed. He sipped at his tea and contemplated his captive with visible satisfaction and a small frown. "I got you, wizard, but how I'm gonna keep you is puzzling me. Ev'body and his dog is out looking for you, and them, they ain't gonna respect nobody's rights."

"Sanctuary Isles." Fan came from the darkness, walking with too much care. She looked sideways at Troc, tried a shaky smile to soothe his irritation. "You should take him"—she pointed at Dur—"to the Sanctuary Isles. Seers can't see into that place and them that live there don't hold with messing in other folk's business." She coughed, wiped the back of her hand across her mouth. "Isn't much back and forth between Isles and Main, so it's likely they wouldn't know about the reward and won't sneak up on you, knock you on the head and take him away."

Troc cleared his throat, spat to one side. "Long way. Gonna be hard to hang on to him and keep him alive."

"You know the Domains. How likely is it that the reward is fool's gold set up to catch the fool who believes what he hears?"

Weary, head buzzing from the drink, Dur closed his eyes. She was making his arguments for him. He wondered why. What had driven her to this point? How did a man like Troc get his claws in her? What did she do to make the Scribes repudiate her? She wouldn't be here if they hadn't.

He let the questions drift away. The answers didn't really matter. If Troc agreed, this pair would take him where he wanted to go. All he had to do was stay mildly drunk and let them do the work.

[7] 6531

Dur looked at the drowsing woman curled protectively about the jug of muscar. After a year of living with her he knew the answers to most of the questions he'd had about her, knew the fears and the pain she plunged into the bottle to escape and knew she'd never have the strength to face them.

She could walk between worlds and, for all his own power, he could not, but he could add that power to hers, make a Bridge out of her and ride her like a half-sound horse across the Veil and into that other world.

For that he would keep her alive. For a while longer, until he knew whether he'd need that gift or not.

He still didn't know why she'd decided to stand aside and let him kill Troc. She'd watered the batta to hide what she stole from the jug. Reasonable enough. Troc would have beat her to bloody pulp if he'd found out. Was that why she didn't warn him when she realized that Dur was faking the stupor? One day he might ask her. Or he might not.

He turned away now without disturbing her and walked across to the nearest of the workrooms and the books left there by other Mages and magic workers. That was another thing she could do. Teach him languages so he could read what was written in those books. Something was going to happen here and on Glandair. Something important. He wanted to be ready to use it, and to use it he had to know what it was.

6

Lyanz at Work and Play

By the secret calendar of the Watchers, events dating from the 13th day of Pedarmis, the fourth month in the 736th Glandairic year since the last Settling.

[1]

Lyanz Kurrin woke when he felt a change in the motion of the ship. It was still dark but he rolled out of the hammock and groped around for his clothes, then stood a moment sniffing the air that came falling down the tubes. It reeked with the briny, dead-fish stench that meant the *Kisa Sambai* was easing into the harbor at Tyst. He scrambled into the cutoff trousers and the sleeveless shirt he wore on board and went out to see what Tyst was like.

When he reached the deck he looked cautiously about for his father but didn't see him. Grinning his relief, he headed for a spot in the bow where he could watch the ship creep toward her anchorage.

High Sailman Karp thumped him on the head and elbowed him away before he got his foot tangled in a rope sliding along the deck. "Watch it, fuz."

Lyanz hooted, jerked his thumb up as he skipped backward a

few steps. Hands caught him again. Tarash the anchorman shoved him aside and stumped past him, a sour scowl on the small part of his face visible over the prickly hedge of his whiskers.

Unperturbed, Lyanz moved on, threading through the busy sailors. He had more freedom than most passengers because he was the Owner's son and he took all the advantage of that he could get away with, but he was pleased when he made the bow without further mishaps. He swung up onto the rail and sat with his legs dangling as the last of the sails came down and towing cables were tossed to the pilot boats waiting just ahead.

Tyst was built on hills, a bumpy rambling sort of town, rising on both sides of the river that flowed into the bay. The roofs of the houses were painted red, blue, green and even purple and the doors and shutters he could see matched the roofs. Some distance beyond the city, there was a huge stone pile with a curtain wall and pointed silver caps to its towers, caps that caught the early sun and flashed a blinding brightness into his eyes.

The harbor was busy—four other merchanters big as the *Kisa Sambai* and dozens of smaller coasters and fishboats. In the clear, cold air of the early morning he could hear the creak of cart wheels, the clatter of hooves, the snorts and squeals of draft horses, the rushing lilt of the Nyddese speech as men and women dickered for the loads of fish and shellfish, ordered the ladesmen here and there, greeted each other, cursed and got cursed for clumsiness or carelessness.

A hand closed on his shoulder, jerked him from his perch on the rail and his father's voice sounded in his ears, low and harsh and terribly contained, an anger in it Lyanz had learned to dread on this long trip. "I thought by this time you would be conducting yourself like a man, not like the servant scum you ran with before your brother, cursed be he and all his get, left my house and renounced my name. Mother's boy, you will learn to be a man if I have to break and reset every bone in that too pretty body of yours. Do you hear me?"

Lyanz rounded his shoulders and stared at the planks of the deck. "Yes, sir," he said. "I'll try to do better, sir."

"Before the watch is done, we will be talking to the Tyst Port Master, the Presmun as they call it here. Say 'Ryn Presmun' when you address him. If that is necessary. You will not initiate conversation at any time. I will expect you to remember everything that is said and be able to repeat it to me later. According to your tutor you're quite capable, though you've shown little aptitude so far. Remember also that you are my Heir. I will not have a business it took five generations to build destroyed by your ignorance and ineptitude. I have been patient because you are young, but my patience is at an end."

"Yes, sir. I understand, sir."

"Go below and get yourself properly dressed. Meet me on deck and we will go ashore."

"Yes, sir."

It never changed. He was always like that. Cold voice that cut like knives and the kind of words you use when you're talking to strangers, not your own kin. No more feelings than a stone. It was no wonder Kyodal ran away.

Lyanz slouched back to the black hole someone with no sense of irony had called a cabin, alternately envying his brother and hating him for getting out and dumping this on his shoulders.

He was sad when he thought how excited he'd been when he learned he was going with his father on this trading voyage. He'd found out soon enough once they left Nishamin that it was going to be a misery and mostly duller than spit. The *Kisa Sambai* was one of the bigger merchanters, but there wasn't all that much space for getting away from anyone and it wasn't long before he felt like a dead fish being pecked at by an angry gull. Pick and peck all day, every day. Nothing he did was right or even intelligent.

He was the only son left. He had a duty to his family, but ahh, those meetings with officials and the bargaining with traders off the other ships in port or the local merchants! They were so miserably, mind-numbingly dull.

He washed himself and got dressed in the cleanest of his two suits, the long gray tunic with the high collar that he hated, the narrow gray trousers that folded into black knee-high boots. When he went on deck again, his dark blond hair was slicked back from his face to show off the single ruby stud in his left ear, the marker that told those who knew Nikawaid that he was the Heir.

His father glanced at him, nodded, then tapped the rail beside him. Lyanz stood there through the last maneuvers of the towboats as they brought the *Kisa Sambai* alongside one of the wharves that lined the inner curve of Tyst Harbor. A small group of men were waiting for them.

[2]

Saretal Kurrin bowed stiffly. "Presmun Jobyn, I'm honored that you come yourself."

The Presmun was a short, broad man with a short, broad face so red it looked raw, short-fingered thick hands and brown hair streaked with gray that the sea breeze had tossed into a pointed tangle. He returned the bow, hands crossed over his ribs. When he straightened and spoke, his voice boomed out over the noise around them as if he were so accustomed to talking over it that he'd forgot how to speak naturally. "How could I do less for one of the great merchant families of Nikawaid? Welcome to Tyst, Kurrin of the House of Kurrin. Should there be anything we can do to make your stay more pleasant and profitable, you need but ask."

With Lyanz following a step behind, the two men walked together along wharves toward the Port Offices, trading elaborate compliments and using them to maneuver through unspoken negotiations. When they got to the Presmun's office, Lyanz would be formally introduced, would be expected to present himself modestly, smile and be silent. It was a dance that never seemed to change. When they stopped at Chierim, it was interesting for a while because that was the first time he'd been in on a business conference, though trying to understand a language he'd only studied made his head ache and he'd missed so much that was unspoken that the session with his father after the meeting was a torment.

He suspected every trading voyage after this would go exactly like this one and that he was going to hate being a shipping merchant; whenever he thought of taking over the business after his father decided to retire, he had a cold lump in his stomach. If his father ever did. Lyanz could see himself as a doddering old man with his father a crunched-up ancient beating him on the back and shoulders with his walking cane.

He wrinkled his nose, looked wistfully at the bustle around him with all the noise and laughter, shouted insults, greetings. Half a dozen men squatted in a circle at the mouth of an alley with piles of coins before them, rolling dice with quick sharp gestures. A female cat trotted past, teats swollen with milk, a mouse dangling from its mouth. A large bird landed on a bitt, tossed up and caught a long, whippy white-bellied fish it had been carrying in its beak, working it around until the fish aligned itself properly so it could be swallowed.

Lyanz wrinkled his nose. Poor ol' Presmun. When Father gets through with him, he'll slide down easy as that fish. He sighed. It wasn't even fun to watch Saretal Kurrin operate, not any more. I can't do this. Not all the rest of my life. Holy Flying Alaeshim, I can't . . .

He followed his father into the office, bowed politely and smiled when he was introduced, then set himself to gathering in all the information he could from the exchanges that followed, information about local merchants, about the Tyrn duties that would have to be paid on all goods imported into Tyst, what new laws and regulations had been instituted since the last time his father had passed by. He listened to the Presmun's not so subtle steering toward those merchants who'd sweetened his salary, assessing the man and his weak points, how far he could be trusted, what he was likely to try on for himself. This trip had been a lesson in the grubbier side of all Dyar, whatever the color of their skin and whatever language came out their mouths.

[3]

"I am pleased, Lyanz. You've done well this time. Your tutor was right. You are clever when you want to be." Saretal Kurrin was actually smiling. Lyanz felt a warm glow building inside, though he was surprised that his father was willing to acknowledge how much Lyanz had got from the conversation. He knew he'd got nearly as much when they stopped at Cypresta, and his father had just grunted when he finished and sent him off.

"There is more to being a successful trader than what you've seen thus far, however. The thought has come to me that I've kept you too tightly bound to my side. You need to acquire the feel of a city other than Nishamin. The rest of the day is yours. Explore Tyst. Discover what you can about how these Nyd-Ifor think. If you find yourself in difficulties look about for one of the city guards. He'll be wearing a helmet of leather dyed red with a long tail of white horsehair hanging from it. Give him your name and House and have him bring you here. Morrer's Inn. Remember the name. You do have more common sense than your brother, I'll grant you that. By now you should know what I want you to look for in terms of trade. Beyond that, though, simply talk to people and seek to feel comfortable with their oddities. The more you understand about the people you deal with, the more profitable those dealings will be." Saretal Kurrin held out a small purse, heavy with coin. "Change your clothes before you go. Be back here by nightfall and tell me what you've seen."

{ 4 }

Lyanz pushed his hands in his pockets, leaned against the shop wall and watched two men riding toward him along the main shopping street, the one called Syopoor. The men were City guards in black and crimson tunics with short-handled maces clipped to their belts and alarum horns on cords and the leather helmets his father had mentioned with the long tassels of white horsehair that flowed across the crowns and hung down their backs. They were lean, fit men, riding with an easy arrogance he'd have given his back teeth to acquire—as well as that cold, intent gaze that saw everything and focused on nothing. Nobody was going to cut them down, with words or anything else.

He watched them until they vanished around a curve in the street and thought about following them to see if they were going somewhere or just patrolling, but a street vendor's cart came trundling from the building next to the one he was leaning on. It was heaped with steaming meat pies and chunks of some kind of bird mixed with onions on wooden skewers. His stomach cried *food* and he fished inside his shirt for one of the coins his father had given him.

Chewing on one meat pie with another tucked into a pocket of the loose shirt he wore, Lyanz strolled on, enjoying the color and noise of the street. And the freedom. No bodyguards following him about, flirting with whores, complaining of sore feet and hauling him away from anything that looked interesting.

A small plump man sauntered up and began to walk beside him. He grinned at the pie, but didn't speak for several minutes. Finally he said, "A visitor to our fair city, are you?" He had a cheerful voice and a thick Nyddese accent.

The accent made it difficult for Lyanz to puzzle out what he was saying. The Presmun was used to speaking carefully for visiting traders, so he was easy enough to understand, but this was a local nobody who probably couldn't care less about foreign traders. "Uh," he said, being polite, but giving nothing away if this turned out to be one of those diddlers or rogues featured in half the tales the sailors had told him.

"I expect your pa's a Captain, or maybe a passenger on one of the ships tied up t' Port.

"Uh."

"Got a son jus' 'bout you age 'nd one couple years younger. Good boys, but th' do like they bits a blood 'n' guts. Evah see two real good dogs goin' at it to d'cide who's best?"

"Uh, no."

"You like dogs?"

"Uh, yes."

"My Lougat, t' one that's your age, he went out, earned his own money and bought hisself a pup." The little man turned a beaming smile on Lyanz; his eyes were a washy blue and very round and he looked guileless as the pup he'd been talking about. "You like to see Lougat's pup? 'S a wonder, he is. I swear t' dog can almos' talk."

"Uh . . . thank you to tell me that. I . . . uh . . . must go to Father back. He . . . uh . . . for me is waiting."

"Hoy! You speak Nyd-Ifor almos' good as born. Smart boy. And so polite." He clicked his fingers, shook his head. "But not truthful. No. Look at me. Do I look des'p'rate, boy? Like I gonna jump you bones?"

Lyanz felt lower than a slime toad, but before he could say anything, Sailman Karp was suddenly there with them, tapping the man on the shoulder. "Scap off, trash, afore I yell for a guard."

The man whipped round. When he saw Karp, his face changed, went ugly for a moment, then he scuttled off down the alley they were just passing.

"You watching me?" Lyanz scowled because that sounded whiny. He pulled the back of his hand across his mouth and turned his glare on the sailman.

Karp shrugged. "Your old man he told us to keep an eye open if we happen to see you." He nodded at a woman across the street standing in the shadow of an arcade. "I was talkin' to her. She told me dough-face who was talking to you, he runs a string of boys in this kennel down by South End and word is he does offshore supply too. What I'm saying, you see him again, you yell for guard. Hear?"

"Yeah. I hear."

Lyanz watched Karp cross the street and move into the shadow under the arcade. He sniffed, dug out the other pie and went on down the street, his gaze more intent now as he tried to take in everything and figure what it meant and how it could be used to sell things to these folks. Karp was for sure going to tell about the man and what happened, so Lyanz knew he had better have an extra-sharp report on the rest of what he'd come to see if he wanted to keep his father's approval.

It was a busy street, people all around him. Children playing, chasing each other, working, carrying packets at a trot, darting in and out of the shops, begging, child thieves snatching whatever they could get their hands on. Women with string bags stuffed with goods they'd bought from the shops along the street, some of them with toddlers leashed to leather belts. Women sweeping the walkway in front of their shops. Women gossiping in groups. Other women like the one that Karp was fooling around with, dressed in red, with square metal plaques on thongs around their necks. Men hurrying along, intent on getting somewhere fast, driving carts, others standing in clumps talking and gesturing, their arms swinging wider than Lyanz was used to, their faces sweaty and red with the beer they were drinking and with all the shouting exchanges, all the talk.

Talk. These Nyd-Ifor talked while they were walking, while they were shopping, while they were working. Probably even when they were asleep. Words everywhere, filling the air, the shops, the carts. Everywhere.

After a while his head got so tired of trying to puzzle out what they were saying that he didn't listen any more and drifted along with only his eyes working—and surprised himself because after he'd stopped straining to decode the sounds, he began understanding more of what was being said, picking up a word here, a word there as he relaxed into the rhythm of the language.

Two more city guards threaded through the cart traffic, riding with the insolent ease of the first pair. One of them didn't have the horsetail on his helmet though his outfit was the same, from the two maces to the black and crimson tunic. He wasn't much older than Lyanz, probably fifteen, maybe sixteen, yet he had that look and he rode with the same ease as the other man.

Fascinated, Lyanz drifted after them, watching the young one and wondering what it was like to be a guard and have people get out of your way like that and turn nervous and honest when you went past. He grinned as he saw a short, thin man go slipping into an alley and a drunk straighten up and pretend he was looking at belts on a table in front of a clothing shop. A woman in a red dress stepped into a doorway. Beggars called out nervous greetings but the level of noise went way down as the guards rode past.

As he followed them, Lyanz didn't pay much attention to where he was going; by the time the two riders tied their horses to hitching rings and went inside a gaudily painted sweetshop, he was thoroughly lost. The building had three floors and the windows of the floor above the shop were hung with red curtains. A freckle-faced blond girl was leaning on the sill, her arms crossed, her eyes moving over the street below. She saw Lyanz hesitating in front of the shop and waved to him. "Whyn't you come up and see me, pretty boy? Give you a good time."

His face got hot and he scuttled away, hearing sniggers and comments behind him in so thick an accent that he couldn't understand the words. He didn't really have to, though. He dived down the first side street he came to and hurried along it till he left the laughter behind.

When he looked about, he saw he was in one of the poor parts of town. These Nyddese didn't seem to know about square corners on any of their streets, but the ones in here were the worst of all, like the tracks of a drunken spider, narrow and twisty, climbing up and over the low hills of the backside of the city, cutting across each other in a maze of intersections. The buildings were tall and weary, leaning on each other, and the wood they were built from had the stench of poverty in every fiber. The only well-kept structures were the dozens of small temples scattered along the ways, one every few steps or so it seemed to him. A sad-faced angular god was carved in low relief above the doorway, sitting cross-legged, arms to the sides of the narrow body, elbows bent, palms up. From the left palm dripped what looked like teardrops, from the right a scatter of plum blossoms. And the little gods cavorted in a tangle of strange shapes around his pointy knees. Lyanz frowned, realizing for the first time that he hadn't seen a single little god since he'd set foot on this island. That was odd. Back home there were swarms of them, breaking things, getting underfoot at the worst times. Cook was always complaining about them. Maybe Nyddese little gods didn't like strangers.

The streets were filled with children, some the pinkish pale of the Nyd-Ifordyar but there were also many mixes with skin colors of all shades from the dusky red of Rhudyar to a bleached gold of those that were part Myndyar. As far as he could tell, none of them were more than five years old. He put that together with what he'd seen on Syopoor Street and decided that the older children must be working or begging in places where money was less tightly held than here.

He squinted at the sun and tried to get his bearings, but he was thoroughly turned about and the buildings were too close to let the shadows show him direction. He wasn't all that worried, though, nor was he pushed for time, so he rambled on, uphill and down, round the curving streets, keeping an eye out for anything that might interest his father though he didn't expect much from this area.

The adults moving about among the hordes of children

watched him sometimes with frowns and sometimes with a disturbing speculation in faces that were squared off and odd looking to his eyes. After his first brush with local attention, being noticed like that made him nervous. Trying to look at ease, he walked faster.

When he went round a curve of the street and over the crest of a hill, he found himself looking down at a roughly circular open space surrounded by more of the tall creaky tenements. At first he thought it was the city dump, but it turned out to be a market of sorts, crowded with buyers. There were improvised stalls made from waste lumber, handcarts propped up with goods laid out on open tailgates, woven grass mats thrown down with piles of stuff on them, the piles sometimes higher than a man's head.

He plunged into the crowd, finding it hard to believe the rubbish people were haggling over was worth anything. Rags. Old clothes. Teapots with broken spouts and missing lids. Cracked and chipped china, platters, plates, bowls, ewers, pisspots, mugs and other lumpish pottery whose use Lyanz couldn't even guess at. Day-old produce, limp, spotted with mold and mildew. Heaps of rusty tools. Leather pouches, broken bridles, a saddle so old that Lyanz suspected its tree was fossilized. Horseshoes. Bits. Girths. Used knives, the steel tarnished and rusty, even a sword or two. Chains. Ropes. Heaps of nets gray with age, mostly rotted and torn. Piles and piles and piles of everything under the sun with a swarm of people picking over them, against all odds finding items they were looking for, bargaining at the top of their voices.

The clamor in the market was incredible, the noise held in and bounced back by the facades of the tenements. There was the smell of mildew and rot, ancient sweat, dust and grease, and most of all, unwashed bodies.

Several of the older children he'd missed in the streets were in here. Thieving, according to the merchants—a big part of the noise came from their howls and screams as they warned these young Tysters away from their goods. Lyanz was cursed and threatened, got the butt of a staff shoved into his ribs. His nerves were jangled by the noise and he was furious at being treated like a good-for-nothing lowlife. For a while he was too angry to let himself be driven away by a bunch of local streeters who didn't know who he was and that his father was worth more than the lot of them. Soon though, his head started to ache and the smell made him sick to his stomach. He forgot anger and looked about for the exit.

Lyanz was working toward the gate when the man who'd jabbed him with the staff let out a blat of outrage and came racing from his stall after a boy who was strolling past, a thin wiry youth, darker and different in the face from the Nyd-Ifor around him. The youth skipped ahead of the stallkeeper, hooting and taunting him by dancing along just out of reach. Lyanz followed them, relishing the fury of the man who'd given his ribs some serious bruises; he found that he didn't care at all that the Tyster boy had probably stolen something from the stall.

A second stallkeeper, a small man with a pinched narrow face blotched with large irregular sunspots, darted into the aisle and grabbed the collar of the dark youth's shirt. Without stopping to think, Lyanz started running, elbowing people out of his way; he came up behind the man and flung himself at him, knocking him off his feet and jarring him loose from his hold on the young thief's shirt.

Lyanz scrambled to his feet and took off for the gate, still exhilarated by what he'd done—but with a cold bolus growing in his stomach as he thought about his father's reaction should he get caught. Hands grabbed at him, but he slipped them all and kept scrambling until he burst through the gate and went charging up the slope beyond.

When he was over the crest of the hill and most of the noise behind him had died away, he stopped, pulled his sleeve across his face to wipe the sweat away, then looked around.

He hadn't seen these buildings before, not any of them. There must have been more than one gate to the market and he'd come out the wrong one.

"Thanks, cra. How c'm y' do it?" The youth came from the shadows and stood in front of him, head tilted to one side, hands clasped behind him so he looked like a harbor bird contemplating a stranded fish.

"That jinj he bang stick off me." Lyanz closed a hand into a fist and snapped his thumb off the tip of his nose. "Kot him."

"Huth! You off a ship?"

"Yes. Father he buy sell." He glanced at the sky. Though the sun had slid behind a thick layer of clouds, he could tell it was about ready to set. It was time he was getting back to the Inn and he hadn't a clue which way he should go. "Uh. Where harbor?"

"Y' lost? Huth, cra, won't point, easy to go round 'n round in the' bothrin and ne'er c'm out. C'm on. Me, I'm Talgryf. Gryf f' short. You?"

"Lyanz. Come out of Nikawaid, me."

"You go round a lot?"

"No. This first sailing. Lots more coming." He made a face.

"Hulla? You don' like? Me . . ." Gryf grinned, circled his arms and pulled them in as if he were hugging the world.

"Sailing good, other no good. Tie to father, go round listen to talk talk talk, yamma yamma yamma, can't figure out meaning." He flattened his hands against his ears, moved his head side to side. "Talk talk talk head hurt, got to listen or father get mad."

Gryf shook his head, punched Lyanz's shoulder. "Gotcha. We both in the family business. My pa he's a thief, Ma she worked the Curse Lay in Kale till that got too hot and she stowed away on a coaster and jumped ship in Tyst. She's dead, since three years ago. She was Rhudyar. Folks say I look like her."

"Uh. Thief. Hard learning?"

" 'Spose so. Gotta know all about locks and how to climb walls and how to fake people out so they don't know you're there. Shee! Pa would kill me for fooling around in the market like that if he found out, but I wanted a good knife and now I got it."

Lyanz chuckled. "My pa too. Rope end on backside."

Not hurrying overmuch, they walked through the busy, crooked streets of what Gryf had called a bothrin, silent some of the time, the rest of the time talking in a way that Lyanz had never known before. Friend to friend. Equals.

Gryf touched his arm. "Likes of me they don't want in these parts. The guards they drop loop on us and we spent a cold, sore night in jail. You go that way." He pointed. "Morrer's Inn is just a couple streets over, anyway you can smell harbor from here when th' wind kicks up some."

Lyanz hunched his shoulders and clasped his hands behind him. "Back in jail, me. My pa, the sailmen doing guard . . ." He lifted a hand with his fore and middle fingers raised and pressed together, the others held down by his thumb. "Ti' ta', the one t'other, can't tell apart."

Gryf shrugged.

Lyanz could see the Tyster boy didn't think he knew spit about jails or the way guards really acted, but didn't feel like arguing. He looked round, saw a shop a few doors down with a brass lantern hanging from the sign pole. A chandler's shop. He pointed. "I get loose tomorrow, say round mid-morning, maybe we meet there, go look at ti', ta' and t'other?"

"Might do." Gryf looked past Lyanz, made a face. "Gotta go." He took off running as another pair of guards came riding toward them.

[5]

Lyanz passed his hand over his hair a last time, wiped his palm down his side and knocked on the door.

"Come." The word was sharp-edged and slid through the panel like a knife.

This is not going to be good. I better dance real fast. Lyanz opened the door and went in.

The session went better than he'd expected. He started with the incident with the procurer, telling it calmly and objectively, a lesson learned without much pain, then moved on to a careful listing of his other observations, watching his father's face lose its hard edges as he talked.

". . . and I thought of something that might be a useful addition to the trade, Father. When we went through the market at Yosun the day you met with Bahar the Spice Merchant, I saw piles and piles of salt-glazed pots and plates and the like. I don't know what price these were bringing, but the buyers seemed to be peasants and day laborers so I imagine it wasn't much. Most of these utensils here in Tyst are metal or wood. There isn't much clayware at all and, from what I saw in that old goods market in the poor section, what there is seems to be used long past the point when most people in Nishamin would throw it out. What I thought was, if Kurrin House bought up a load of Yosun clayware, stowed it as ballast or something like that so it wouldn't take up room from more costly items and brought it over here, mightn't there be a small but useful profit in the exchange?"

"Ha!" His father leaned forward, slapped his palms on his knees, his face more animated than Lyanz had ever seen it, even in anger. "Good work. A possibility worth investigating. You're getting the eye for this, Lyanz." Saretal Kurrin got to his feet. "We're dining tonight with members of the Tyst Grath, two men, one woman. Observe them. We will discuss them when we return. You need to learn how to pick up indications from even the briefest of meetings as to how such folk will act when the time comes for closing a deal."

When they were in the hall and walking toward the stairs,

Saretal Kurrin set his hand on Lyanz's shoulder. He cleared his throat and when he spoke he was carefully facing the newel posts of the stair just ahead. "We'll be at Tyst for another three days. Since you have shown your ability to handle yourself adequately on your own, you will be free until dinner those days. Use the time to continue learning the city. I will be pleased if you can discover other potential markets, but not disappointed if you don't."

Lyanz flushed, reached up, brushed his father's hand, just a brief touch. "Thank you, Father."

That night, when he was curled in his blankets and turning the day over in his mind, he had very mixed feelings about what he'd done. He glowed with pleasure whenever he thought about his father's approval, but his interest in the business was a sham and he didn't know how long he could keep up the pretense. And he was filled with anxiety about what would happen when that truth emerged.

After a while he made himself stop thinking about it and began puzzling about one of the Tysters at the dinner—a skinny twist of a man with washy blue eyes and a sour turn to his mouth. He was the one who met them at the door. Every time Lyanz glanced his way, the man was staring at him. It made him feel very nervous.

He turned onto his back, stretched his legs out, relishing the room to spread. If he tried that in the ship, he'd be on the floor. Wonder if Gryf will show up tomorrow? Hope so, it's going to be fun if he does. . . . He fell asleep in the middle of plans that even he knew suffered from a lack of hard information.

7

Hunting the Hero

By the secret calendar of the Watchers, events dating from the evening of the 13th day of Pedarmis, the fourth month in the 736th Glandairic year since the last Settling.

{ 1 }

When the Myndyar boy came into the private dining room, slim and nervous behind his father, Oerfel nearly lost command of himself. Candidate! You couldn't miss it, even without a Chaos Drum to mark him. But a strange one. Disconcerting. The boy was empty, utterly without magic. Nothing there. Not even the touches that the lowliest cretin possessed.

As Oerfel bowed and walked beside the two of them, escorting Saretal Kurrin and his Heir to the places of honor waiting for them, he could barely feel the boy's presence.

The meal began with the usual round of toasts and speeches in which the speakers contrived to say nothing at all, but charmingly and with as much wit as they possessed. Oerfel ate stolidly his milk-poached fish, dry toast and thrice-washed salad greens, drinking occasionally from his carafe of distilled water. He'd taught the Tystgrath cooks his needs and limitations and they were careful to abide by his instructions since he explained in simple forceful words about the spell he'd "bought." Every pang he felt from miscooked food would rebound on them threefold. A few miserably dyspeptic nights had been admirable tools to convince the cooks of the time of the truth of his claim and since those early days his meals had been prepared with more care than the Tyrn's.

He kept glancing at the boy as he ate. He knew this was foolishness, but he couldn't help it.

He had a lot to think about. Why hadn't the local Watchers tagged him as a Candidate?

A moment's consideration gave him the answer. The children of Nikawaid Trading Houses were isolated behind the walls of their Compounds. The fierceness with which South Nikawaid Clans protected their privacy was notorious across the length and breadth of Nordomon. Then there was the long voyage. Three months at sea and in foreign harbors.

Why didn't Mahara take note of him? The answer to that lay in another question: Why is this the first time I realized that a Candidate was moving so close to me I could have stumbled over him outside any door? Fork suspended, the morsel of fish congealing on the tines, Oerfel stared at the boy. He was more elusive than a dayfly and like a dayfly one wouldn't be aware of him until he landed on one's nose. It was as if he weren't quite real. I wonder if he would be visible to a scryer's search? I'll have to see. And soon.

Those questions settled to his satisfaction, he brooded over that odd emptiness he felt in the boy. It wasn't something that would be apparent to anyone but a Mage of considerable power like himself, of course, but to him the anomaly was as loud as a scream.

By the end of the meal he reached the uncomfortable and disturbing certainty that all the other Candidates—those he, Mahara and Hudoleth had killed and those few that managed to reach the two training grounds—were all set up as false targets to conceal the presence of this boy. Lyanz Kurrin was the true Hero, the one born to contain the total magic force of two worlds.

No wonder he had no magic of his own. He was merely the vessel for that power—the means that the gods, whatever they might be, who rode the turbulent forces that flowed from Iomard to Glandair and back again had created to accept and redeploy what would otherwise burn through both worlds and destroy all life on them down to the smallest of seeds.

In order to draw that power to himself, Oerfel had to kill this boy and put Anrydd in his place. The first ravages of that immense force would be lethal to anyone but the true Hero, but in his dying, Anrydd would draw its teeth. Oerfel could fold the chastened power into himself and survive the process.

Kill the boy. As soon as possible. Before he was recognized for what he was.

This decision made, Oerfel shaped a collecting lens from air and from the heat of the candles that lit the room and gave an ear to the conversation at the Honor Table while he brooded over what he was going to do about this Candidate. The House of Kurrin was important to Tyst and any attack on Saretal or his son would stir up so much trouble he'd have to put his plans on hold and get to work smoothing things out. Watchers were thick on the ground here so he'd have to be wary if he wanted to keep his shroud intact. And he most certainly did. The Watchers might know there was a Mage on Nyddys, but they didn't know who he was. And not knowing, they couldn't act against him.

Ah! Leaving on the noon tide tomorrow.

Good. With all the storms Mahara has been stirring up in the Halsianel Sea, he's ripe to take the blame for this one. Only drawback, once I do this, he'll know I'm putting my finger in the pie. Hm. Have to work it the sly way, big show with little power expended, keep him guessing. Keep them all guessing. Shouldn't take that much force to scuttle a ship if I do the shaping right.

Oerfel sipped at his water and watched the boy fidget. He col-

apsed the ear and pulled his extensions back behind his shields—
and was interested to see that the boy relaxed immediately. Like
an empty jug, he resonated to magic without having any in him.

When Broga rang the bell at his elbow, Oerfel got to his feet
for the ritual blessing and dismissal, concealing his impatience
behind the bland mask he had cultivated over the years. He
wanted this business over with. He wanted the boy feeding the
sharks in the Halsianel Sea, he wanted this Candidate's bones
rolling around with the bones of all the others that Mahara had
sunk there, but he had to wait until the ship was far enough away,
until he could get at his workroom without anyone seeing him.

The thought came to him that if he waited too long, the boy
would slip away. Hudoleth had missed him in Nikawaid and Mahara had had two chances at him, at Yosun and Lim Ashir, and
had been blind to his presence. If I miss, he thought, if he gets
away from me . . .

[2]

There was no Tystgrath meeting on the following days. On the
third day after the dinner, Oerfel labored all morning in the
Grath scriptorion, turning his notes into Formal Nyd-Ifor and
overseeing his scribes as they copied his entries into the Daybook
of the Acts and wrote the reports that would be sent to the Tyrn-
house Recorder and to the University at Cyfareth.

His mouth tightened when Loghu's pen dripped and laid a blot
across the lines; his voice was a whisper filled with rage when he
reprimanded the scribe. Loghu's job was protected because Broga
was his patron so he just shrugged and used a bit of rag to soak
up the blot. The scriptorion positions were sinecures where the
Grathals of the Tystgrath tucked their more hapless relatives so
they could get the town treasury to support them rather than having to do it themselves.

Oerfel moved on, willing his fingers to relax into an ordinary
curl, the rage-heat building and building in him until he feared

he would explode like a puffer fish brought suddenly from the bottom of the sea.

He stopped behind Camgol, snorted and slapped the man sharply on the arm. "I told you, concentrate! You left out three lines. Do it over." He took the sheet of paper away and tore it in half. "Do you want me to explain why to the Rynnat Crebach-swyf?"

Camgol hunched his shoulders, reached into the paper slot for a new sheet and began recopying the page.

Around and around the room he paced, hands locked behind him as he inspected the work, a burn in his stomach as he saw how carelessly it was done. Around and around with needs and fears knotted round that boy, that beautiful terrible empty boy, needs and fears whispering in his head, time creeping past, measured by the sun pouring through the markhole, its bright circle crawling across the floor from mark to mark. Around and around until he could no longer stand to look at the sloppy work the copiers were doing and went back to the Daybook to do the entries himself.

When the bells of the Temple rang the Noon Peal, Oerfel's hands trembled so badly he could barely replace the cork in the ink bottle. Soon, he told himself. Just get through the rest of the day. Out on the open sea there's no way he can survive. No way. Once I set the storm on that ship, he's dead.

Hands folded on the top of his writing table to mask the shaking, Oerfel sat on his tall three-legged stool and watched the four scribes clean off their tables as they got ready to leave for the day. For once he was glad to see them leave even though they'd got only half the work done.

Taking extra pains because he wanted to be out of there so badly, he set the scriptorion in order, locked the door and paced through the maze of corridors at the back of the Grathhouse, his eyes fixed on the floor, his hands clasped behind him. He wasn't given to casual conversation at any time and he emphatically didn't want to have to talk with anyone today.

He reached the wharves in time to watch the masts of the *Kisa Sambai* bloom with sails as she slid past the breakwaters at the mouth of the bay. And he smiled. I'll be with you come midnight, and that's the end of it.

[3]

The Grand Temple of Dyf Tanew rose at the border between the bothrin and the more respectable streets of Tyst. It was used as a reference point for directions because its spires with their icicle eaves and swirling silver caps and its square bell tower were visible from most points in the city, though not from the twisty narrow streets at the heart of the bothrin. The tenements were too high there and too close together to offer more than a thin jagged river of sky.

When he had returned to Tyst from his solitary studies at Kingakun University and elsewhere, Oerfel had rented a set of rooms in a tenement on the comfortable side of the bothrin in the shadow of the Temple, but he was careful to do none of his spells or other magic there. Being a secret man and one who fixed his eyes on distant years rather than the day in which he was living, he wanted no taint on those rooms to guide the Watchers to him, nothing to tell anyone that he was a Mage.

Beneath the Temple were crypts that no one had visited for a thousand and a thousand years, crypts where ancient Tyrns were buried, Tyrns who lived so many Settlings ago that no one remembered who or what they were or why their bones were in those ossuary jars. After watching patiently to see whether those rooms were as undisturbed as they seemed, Oerfel established his workroom in one of the largest.

He scrubbed the floor, ruled a pair of six-pointed stars on the stone flags and carved the grooves with such care that the figures took seven months to finish. Then he melted silver and ran it into the grooves. When the metal had cooled he rubbed it with jeweler's rouge until the surface of the stone and the silver lines shone mirror smooth.

He spent the next three years carving the ward staffs, rods a man tall and as big around as a man's arm. When they were finished he shod the ends with silver and set them in holes he'd drilled at the points of the two stars. He did this with such care because he was invading Dyf Tanew's house and needed to shield himself from the god's notice.

Should it become necessary, a Mage could command a god. It was one of the marks of what he was—that and his knowledge that gods were essentially just discrete lumps of the force that flowed between Glandair and Iomard, given awareness and volition by the beliefs of their subjects, shaped into what they were by the best and worst aspects of mortal beings and by mortal expectations. Gods were capriciously generous, jealous of their rights, often lazy and very easily distracted. Dyf Tanew was more cunning than most and inquisitive, given to poking about when anything caught his interest, but he was no real danger even in this, his own House. Dyf Tanew would dance to Oerfel's call if the need arose. For a while. A very short while. And Oerfel would have to drop everything else to achieve the necessary intensity of focus. Better to deflect the god's attention and rejoice that it was so easy to do.

As soon as he dared, Oerfel crept into the Temple, unlocked the door to the crypt stairs and ghosted along the underways, the eye of his mind sweeping the maze of corridors around him, his bare feet soundless on the dusty flags. He carried a large waterskin and some rags; all else he needed was stored in his workroom.

The silence in the corridor was suddenly broken by the *tik tik* scurry of rat feet; the vermin who took refuge in his workroom fled as they heard him coming. He grimaced and felt a headache starting in his temples. He loathed those rats, but to keep them

way he'd have to arrange a trickle feed of Pneuma in the room
nd that would be setting out an invitation for the Watchers.
'hey'd been hunting for him. He could feel them sniffing about.

He lit half a dozen candles, took the twig broom from behind
he door, swept the floor, grumbling to himself as he eased the
ebris out into the corridor. Everything had to be perfect and it
lways took forever to get the place and himself ready for work.
Vould be nice if he could simply snap his fingers and set a golem
o cleaning up, but he didn't trust anyone—or anything—to do
he work right.

He lit the candles around the large mirror with the blackwood
rame, which was one of several mirrors that he had acquired in
dainamin; if he had paid for it, it would have cost more than his
our years of study at Kingakun. The Myndyar of South Chu-
inkayan were the only ones who knew how to make plate glass
nd silver the back to make a mirror, and that secret stayed in
he families and behind the clan walls. Oerfel approved of this
oarding of knowledge. Used as they were intended, mirrors
ould be dangerous things in the hands of the untrained. Or
hey could be debased into baubles and trinkets, a distressing triv-
alization of something beautiful.

He tipped blue powder into a bowl, wet it with a mouthful of
vater and stirred it round till the paint was ready. Then he
tripped off his walking clothes, shook them out and hung them
n wall pegs. He dipped his hands into the thick blue paint,
vorked it into his hair until it stood out in stiff spikes. He washed
.is hands, thinned the paint some more, took up the stencils that
.ad cost him so much time and effort and began marching the
lesigns along his legs and arms.

When he finished, he set the stencils aside and took up the
rush again. Standing before the mirror, he carefully painted
nto his face the spirals, dots and jags that concentrated his
ower for him. He drew three wavery waterlines from his chin,
lown his neck to his navel, the middle line first then the two

outer ones, pulling them in at the base till they met at his navel.

That done, he inspected himself carefully in the mirror, then walked in meditative circles while he waited for the paint to dry. Time he needed was slipping through his fingers, but he didn't let himself think about that. It would be done. Yes, it would be done. All wound up waiting to go. Requiring only a word to set the winds whirling. It would be done. It would.

He moved his arm and watched the stenciled fish wriggle with the shift of muscles and skin. Dry enough not to smear.

All around the room a dozen wide, thin drums sat on pedestals that brought them navel-high. He moved three of them inside the largest of the hexagrams, set them in a triangle with one point toward the Halsianel Sea. He took six fat black candles from one of the closets, set them just inside the points of the star, a finger's width from the carved staves, touching the wick of each to life as he settled it onto the spike made ready for it.

He had already chosen his chant, lines from an epic poem in a version of Nyd-Ifor so old that no one now could read it other than a few scholars at Cyfareth University, and they so old and decrepit that no one bothered to listen to them any longer. The words sang of a great storm that sent many a ship to the bottom of the sea. True poetry had a power like a true mirror, greatly beyond that which was apparent. It sang in the blood and shaped the Pneuma in ways that ordinary words would not.

He stepped into the hexagram, touched the inlaid silver line with his toe and took his place at the heart of the lines of white light. Letting his lips go loose like a horse twitching its skin on a fly-filled morning, he shook his head, then threw it back, opened his mouth wide and let a hoarse roar pour up and out of him. The thighbone he used as a drumstick woke the drums to life, *toom toom ta toom toom toom ta toom toom toom ta toom*, one then two then three, ending with the drum nearest the Sea. Round and round he danced after that, tapping the drums one after the other until the sound filled the small room. *Toom toom tooom*

Candlelight glistened on his blue-painted skin, sweat gathered in the blue spikes of his hair, ran down his face, dripped from his chin and nose. *Toom toom tooom.*

Eyes glazed, he sang:

> Arva iluch ched   vin ven dar uswed
> goyn mallu a melt   a goyryt dias sed
> ac ail yed goreu   ac aitorm a vereu

On and on he went, threading through the part of the poem where the sailors fought the tossing water and the tearing winds, where lightning walked from mast to spar to deck, on and on until the spell was wound up and only waited the triggering word to lose those winds he'd gathered and start the lightning strutting about the ship that was his target, House of Kurrin's *Kisa Samai.*

He stopped the dance, threw back his head, screamed, "BAEDD HAU!"

He felt the winds slip from his hold like the reins of a runaway horse and dropped wearily to his knees. The storm was on its way. It wouldn't actually reach the ship for at least a watch, but that was good in its way; it would pick up strength from the water as it moved, multiplying its force until nothing built by man could stand against it.

After a moment he got to his feet. He spoke the word that lulled the silver wires and turned them quiescent, snuffed the candles and put them away in the closet, poured water into a washbasin and began scrubbing the blue paint from his body and his hair.

4]

Derfel woke confused, at first not understanding what had roused him from the exhausted oblivion he'd sunk into the moment his body touched the sheets.

He sat up, rubbed at his eyes; they were gummy and his throat sore from breathing through his mouth as he slept. His face was raw from the stiff brush he had used to get the blue paint off, the skin on his arms itched as if he had a rash.

Crude raw force.

As if an animal had its teeth in the magic flow, twisting it and rending it.

Scrambling his head, churning his stomach.

He dragged himself off the bed and stumbled to the commode, poured water into the basin and splashed it onto his face. He spent a moment leaning over the basin until he became aware of images forming in the water. Hastily he broke away. Nothing in this place. *Nothing* that would link him with magic.

The shock cleared the dregs of sleep from his mind and body. He dressed hastily, slipped one of the small mirrors he used for scrying into a pocket, listened a moment to the beat of rain and the howl of the winds outside and got his thickest cloak from the chest.

It was a miserable night. The streets were empty; even the beggars who usually slept in doorways were gone.

Head down, clutching the cloak about him, Oerfel made his way to the backyard of Saloua's eatery. He lifted himself over the gate and opened the door to a small, sturdy grain shed beside the chicken run. He had found for himself a number of niches like this throughout the city and used them when he didn't need the paraphernalia in his workroom.

He snapped his fingers, produced a small blue-white globe of foxfire and set it bobbing gently in midair, then slid the mirror from its leather case and called up the image of the *Kisa Sambai.*

What he saw was debris scattered over the water heaving into enormous waves. The boy was astride a spar, hands clamped on a tangle of ropes wrapped around it, his face contorted with fear. Oerfel started to smile, then swore as a woman was suddenly standing on the water beside the spar. She caught hold of the boy,

fted him and vanished. "I don't believe it. An Iomardi Bridge.
Where . . . why?"

His hair was dripping into his eyes and onto the mirror, dis-
orting the image. He drew his sleeve across his face, pushed the
air back and smoothed it down with the palm of his hand, then
e shook the mirror and set it on his knee. "Hero. I can forget
he others. He's the one. Yes. That's sure now. If he pulls help
rom Iomard, who else can he be?"

He slipped the mirror back in its sheath and put it in his
ocket. There were dozens of questions he needed answers to,
ut not tonight. Not until he was rested and had thought about
his some more.

8

Growing Pains and Other Problems

By the secret calendar of the Watchers, events dating from the 17th day of Pedarmis, the fourth month in the 736th Glandairic year since the last Settling.

[1]

Cymel watched her father ride away on Black Prifolt with Bay Dawnsy on the lead rein and Prifolt held to a slow plod because the gelding on lead had cast a shoe and Ellar didn't want him to go lame. They were heading for Old Goff's smithy and it'd be milking time before he was back. She was just a week from her tenth birthday and old enough, Pa said, to hold house by herself for a half day.

What he hadn't said was he'd be watching her, but she knew that well enough, so it'd be tighter than when he was home.

Shaking her head, she fetched a pitcher and took water to the bell bush she'd planted on the slight mound where she'd buried Cyswe's broken body and the few scraps of fur and bone that were all that was left when Noswe ran away up the mountain. Her eyes stung with tears; she missed them so much. Pa wanted to get her some more kittens but it just didn't feel right.

She scrubbed at her eyes and went inside to deal with the

kitchen, which needed mopping again. Seemed like as soon as she got finished scrubbing those tiles, they were filthy once more.

By mid-afternoon she was seated at the writing table in the study, trying to solve the math problems her father had left out for her.

The days were getting hot in the afternoon and the soft breeze coming through the open window was trying to put her to sleep. The words her father had written kept blurring her eyes. She wrinkled her nose and read aloud, "If a farmer has three cows, and two of them give two ystocs of milk a day each and the last only one ystoc because she is going dry, and if it takes one ystoc of milk to make a single round cheese, how many cheeses could the farmer make in one week if he used half of each day's milk for making them, and how much milk would he have left over?"

"Oh, that's easy."

She looked up, made a face. " 'Lo, Breith."

Round midwinter last year, Breith had worked out a way they could talk to each other, not just watch what the other did. Cymel was annoyed that she hadn't figured it out first and madder than mad whenever she thought about him getting snotty and not telling her how he did it. After all, she'd started looking at Iomard a long time before he even had a notion to try it.

There was a round place in the air and in it she could see him sitting in his favorite place, atop the flag tower; she could tell where he was because she could see the crenels and merlons behind him. "Want me to show you how to work that problem?" he said with that smirk that shouted how smart he thought he was.

She turned the paper over and put the pen back in the holder, a widemouthed jar filled with round lead pellets. "No. Pa'll know and he'd just set me more of the stinking things. How'd you get in here anyway? I thought we had wards set to keep lookers out of the house."

"Well, there are spots where they're getting thin and a couple of places where they're just plain gone. You'd better tell your pa about that. He should maybe reset them."

"So how come you're not in school?"

He scowled at her. "Nosy Norit."

"You don't need to call names. I was just asking."

He fidgeted for a moment, then looked away from her. "I called my history teacher a liar and a mushwit. Well, he was. The stuff he was teaching, it just wasn't true. But the Brother who runs the place, ol' Holy It's-so-because-I-say-it-is, he didn't want to hear from me so I can't go back till I apologize to Brother Hollow-head. And Da's mad and Mum's upset and Mam was looking at me like I should crawl under a rock or something till she had to go upriver on business, and I'm stuck inside the walls till she gets back."

Cymel scratched at her nose. Lots of times she thought she'd cut off her big toes or have all her teeth pulled if she could get away from this farm and have someone besides her father to talk to. Because Pa didn't like anyone knowing anything about them but his friends from Cyfareth, she couldn't even go visit with the girls on the farms down the hill. Not that they were much anyway from what she'd seen when she went to market with him, but still . . .

"Well, will you? Apologize?"

"If Mam says, I suppose so." He made a face. "She can be awful convincing."

"I still don't understand how come you have two ma . . . scat, you!"

Mouse wiggled its whiskers at her and fluttered its ears as it gave the pot a shove and sent ink running in black streams over her lesson papers. That particular little god had been hanging around her for years now, making her life miserable, and during the last few months he'd gotten even worse. Nasty thing. She slapped at the creature, but it vanished before her hand reached it. She grabbed at the papers, shook the ink off them and fanned them out on the table to dry, then set the ink pot back on its base.

"What was that?"

"Little god. They're all over the place. You mean you never saw one?"

"I don't think we have any on Iomard."

"You don't know how lucky you are. They're the worst pests in the world and all you can do is hope they get bored and go away, because mostly you can't catch them and you can't drive them off or keep them out of anywhere they want to get." She glowered at the spot where Mouse had disappeared. "You want to wait, I've got to go get a rag and mop this mess up before it stains the wood."

"Well, actually, the reason I'm here, I asked Pa about your mother, what she was like and what happened to her, and he said he'd find out what he could, that you had a right to know."

Cymel pressed her fist against her mouth, swallowed, swallowed again, the ink forgotten.

"Fa went over to Scribe's Hall. He's looking through the records there. That's not easy. He took me over there a couple of years ago and showed me rooms and rooms and rooms of boxes full of papers from all over the Domains. He's really good at finding things in all that. Your aunt Corysiam says he's better than most Scribes. He found a bunch of stuff." Breith held up a paper roll. "I . . ."

His form wavered and Cymel felt warning prickles, the ones that were like being lightly whipped by nettles; they meant that the Pneuma Flow between the worlds was about to turn to a flood. When that happened, Breith couldn't reach her, even a Walker couldn't move through that kind of mess. "No! Breith, read it. Hurry!"

"Cym . . . get . . . ack . . . you . . . ater."

The round place in the air rippled and vanished.

"Why didn't you tell me right away?" she wailed. "Wasted all that time . . ." Angry tears blurred her eyes. She slapped her hand on the desk right in the middle of one of the ink puddles, splashing herself and ruining her shirt. She didn't care. "Mushwit? You're the mushwit! Stupid, horrible boy!"

She looked at the mess on the table, sucked in a breath and went for a wet cloth to wipe it up.

[2]

The low-hanging sun was making a pretty play in the shimmers of dust the late summer winds were raising over the peaks as Cymel climbed up the mountain, heading for the durbaba pool. Her father had asked her not to go far from the house when he wasn't around, but he was due back any minute now and she couldn't stay inside any longer. Briefly she missed the cats again because they always went with her when she was out like this, but she pushed the thought aside and trudged along, muttering one of the poems her father had made her memorize.

After she brushed the sand and debris off the tree trunk, she stretched out on her side, her head propped on her hand, and watched the mama durbabas working together to round up the babies and tuck them away for the night. The babies were treating this like a game of tag, ducking and darting about and having a great time. Her eyes stung and she looked away.

"Hey, Cym. I'm back."

She brushed surreptitiously at her eyes, swung round and sat up. The talking window was hanging over the stream a short distance downslope where a clutch of boulders kicked up lots of foam and noise.

"Yeah. I see you are. Can you get closer? I can hardly hear you."

"Right. Just a minute."

The window blinked out, reappeared at the foot of the trunk. "This better?"

"Yeah. Hunh, you look . . . I dunno."

He made a face. "Mam got home and took my skin off for being so dumb. Scande! I hate her lectures, she knows how to make me squirm and feel like the slime off the bottom of a rock."

"Know what you mean. I'd lots rather Pa took a switch to my legs than talk at me and look disappointed." She chewed on her lip. "You never explained how come your father gets to have two wives at the same time."

"He doesn't. Mum is Mam's wife, Da's their Seyl."

"That sounds weird."

He snorted. "No weirder than your pa being off by himself without a clan to keep him. Though I will say it isn't usually the thing for a sister to marry a sister. Mostly it's a way to bind clan to clan. But Mam Fori and Mum Yasa got in a quarrel when they were little, and I don't know exactly how—they don't talk about it—but Mum got blinded then. So when Grandmam Sayargam died and Mam got to be head of the Family, she married Mum so she could take care of her. And they both chose Da to be their Seyl. Anyway, Mum's the one who birthed me and Mam's the one who birthed my baby sister Bauli, who's going to be family head when she grows up because she'll be the oldest girl. Mum takes care of us while Mam runs the House and the business. We're one of the biggest trading families along the Rivers. It works out just fine. All *you* got is your Pa and that dinky farm."

"Pa's a Watcher and I'm gonna be one too, that's lots more important than your dinky smelly ol' riverboats."

Breith made a rude sound, then the window winked out.

Still angry, Cymel jumped to her feet and went plunging downhill, running from all the bad feelings she didn't want to think about because, if she did, she'd have to curl up and howl.

[3]

Outside the wind was whistling round the corners and Cymel could hear crashing and thudding noises as branches broke away and slammed into the buildings or other trees. She lay on her stomach in front of the fire, reading one of the books that the last visitor from Cyfareth had brought her and trying to ignore the words forming in her mind as her father sat at the table writing in his journal. She liked being in here with him in the evenings, but the intrusion of the words she couldn't help picking up was beginning to feel like an itch that wouldn't go away no matter how much she scratched it.

Ellar Yliarson wrote:

We continue to suffer the backwash from Mahara's weather dealings—mostly windstorms up here in the Dreyals. There has been little snow and no rain in the Vales and the crops are suffering from the lack. The days are also unseasonably warm and the beasts are uncomfortable because they're starting to grow their winter coats. Does anyone know how many ships Mahara has sent to the bottom of the Halsianel Sea? I have watched at least ten of them foundering and counted twice that many Candidates drowned. It seems he is adamantly opposed to any boy reaching the Vale of Caeffordian, whether he is of Kale or Tilkos or Faiscar.

I know we of Cyfareth have often discussed and disagreed among ourselves as to whether there is a Mage on Nyddys. I was among the unbelievers, but no longer. I have felt him stirring. I am certain that the Mage is indeed male. The aura I have brushed is unmistakable. Unfortunately that disqualifies only half the population of Nyddys. I cannot locate him or determine who he is. He is a very careful man and seems content to stand in Mahara's shadow.

Cymel sighed and turned her book facedown on the rug. She pushed up until she was sitting with her back to the fire. "Pa, am I going to be a Watcher like you?"

Ellar eased the pen into the holder, blotted the last page he'd written, folded his arms and contemplated her, looking over the top of spectacles pulled down low on his nose. "Now what made you ask something like that?"

"Oh, nothing much important. I was talking to Breith today and he said some stuff. Well, I started wondering about what I was going to do when I got older."

"Iomard is a very different place, Mela."

"I know. But still . . ."

He rubbed his hand across his mouth, then pulled his head back so the lamplight glinted off his spectacles. "I don't know, Mela. That's the truth. You don't need to fuss yourself about that, you've a home here as long as you want it."

She could see that he didn't want to talk about it. A year ago, even a few weeks ago, she'd have let the whole thing drop, but the day had rubbed at her and rubbed at her until she felt raw all over. "Why don't you know, Pa?"

He was silent again for several minutes and she could feel something harsh and strong working in him that made her want to take back the question. But she couldn't. It was out there, hanging between them.

"All right, Mela. No, I don't think you're going to be a Watcher."

"Why, Pa? Because I'm a girl?"

"No. There are women who are Watchers. It has to do with temperament, Mela. You're too much like your mother, you wouldn't be able to stand aside when . . ." He didn't try to finish the sentence, just shook his head, the glass in his spectacles gleaming like moons.

"I don't understand."

"All right. Suppose you saw Orog Dyrysson with a spear standing over the durbaba pool, and you knew he meant to go fishing for durbabas just for the pleasure of killing them. What would you do?"

"What would anyone do, Pa? I'd try to make him stop. I'd push him in the water or throw rocks at him or something."

"Very like your mother. If you were a Watcher, you would watch and write down what you saw. Because you would've sworn an oath and the other Watchers would see to your paying the last price if you broke it."

"But that's not right, Pa. If you can do something to help people who need it, you gotta do it."

"Writing it down is doing something, Mela. And there is a very good reason why that is all we do. If a Watcher is attacked, he can defend himself, but he must not interfere with other people's lives. It is sometimes very hard, Mela, and we have bad dreams. It would be so easy to tweak life a bit here and a bit there, like Beda Orriswyf when she makes your dresses, so it would lie smooth and comfortable. And it would feel so good. But do you know what we'd be after we walked that road a while?"

"No, Pa."

"Monsters, Mela. In trying to make the world perfect, we'd kill it dead. That's what Mages do and why they can be so dangerous, especially now."

"Maybe I'm going to be a Mage, then."

"No!" The word exploded out of him and the anger in it frightened her. "No," he said more gently. "I can't tell you what you will be when you come into your full gifts, Mela, except it'll be something strange and wonderful that doesn't have a name yet."

"All right. But *why* not a Mage?"

"A Mage is hunger without an end, Mela. A Mage *needs* more than anyone else and uses people as if they're scraps of paper he can throw away when he's finished with them. There is an odd thing about Pneuma; you'll find that out after you've studied it longer. It seeks out emptiness and fills it. Because of that and the hole his endless hunger eats in him, a Mage controls more of the Flow than any other single being alive. We Watchers can block and turn away attack from Mages, but only because we are many and can link together to counter that power. It's why I worry when you go outside the wards. That Siofray Mage . . . if you ever see him again, call me the minute it happens."

"I said I would. You don't have to keep telling me." Cymel

laced her fingers together, opened her hands out and gazed at the zigzag the inside of her fingers made. "Pa, did you watch Mama get killed?"

"Yes." He hesitated a moment, added, "Your Mother was Siofray, Cymel, and the attack was on Iomard. Even if I'd had the right, I could not have done anything to help her."

She couldn't look at him and she couldn't stop herself from saying, "You watched her get killed and you didn't do anything."

"Yes."

Leaving her book open and facedown on the rug, Cymel got to her feet. Before she got to the doorway, her father reached for the pen and opened his journal; she could hear the scratching of the nib and the black words began shaping themselves in her mind. She pushed at them, scraped them from her mind as she stumbled toward the stairs, ran up them and finally flung herself facedown on her bed.

[4]

A hand touched her shoulder.

She jerked away.

"Cymel." Corysiam's voice, not her father's.

She rolled onto her side, looked up into her aunt's face. "He just watched," she said. "He didn't even try to help. Did you know that? Did you know?"

"Of course I knew, Mela."

"Don't call me that. That's what he calls me. Call me Cym."

"All right, Cym. I'll call you brat too. Horrid little snot nose. Listen to me. Your father swore an oath and he's a man who keeps his word. That's not something to be despised. It's why I've never been angry with him."

"I'm not a brat! I just don't—"

"Think of it this way. If it hadn't been for you, he'd have killed himself when Doeta died. He'd have found peace then. You owe him ten years of suffering."

"I thought you were nice. You're not nice."

"No. I'm not. You aren't either." Corysiam chuckled, sat down on the bed and lifted Cymel onto her lap. "Makes us a pair to scare the world." She rubbed Cymel's back and rocked back and forth, holding her against her soft warm body.

Something broke inside Cymel and she started crying as if she'd never stop.

"Remember this too, Cym," Corysiam went on. "Your father isn't a Walker and his magic doesn't reach to Iomard. There was nothing he could have done even if he had broken his oath and tried."

[5]

Cymel dreamed.

Huge waves were crashed around her. She could hear screams and shouts. A ship was breaking up, going down. At one moment she seemed to be standing on something that heaved and tilted under her, at the next she might have been a bird circling overhead, fighting the drive of the chaotic winds.

A boy was on a spar, riding it like a bucking horse, hands clamped on a tangle of ropes wrapped around it. His head was turning, there was terror, but also a frantic anxiety in the set of his body. He seemed to be looking for someone, calling out for someone, though his voice was drowned in the roar of the wind.

Even bruised and battered, his face contorted with fear for himself and that other person, he was astonishingly beautiful, a glorious golden boy. To the watching Cymel he seemed to glow like the sun in the center of that dark and terrible storm.

Then the boat went under. At the same time a huge wave picked up the boy and his spar and cast him away.

Cymel woke, knowing she *had* to rescue him. She just had to. And she couldn't go to her father. She couldn't bear to make him say again that he couldn't interfere. Corysiam!

Without bothering to pull her robe over her nightdress, Cymel ran down the hall to the guest room, flew inside and shook her aunt awake, babbling about the ship and the boy. "Help me," she cried, "help him."

"Hnnnh . . . whaaa . . . who . . ." Corysiam fumbled with the covers and tried to sit up. "Cymmy, slow down, let me wake up."

"There's no time, he's going to die. We *have* to save him. We *have* to." She caught hold of Corysiam's hand with both of hers, the urgency growing inside her till it ate everything away. She squeezed her eyes shut and willed her aunt to DO SOMETHING.

There was a twisting, wrenching sick feeling; it vanished for just an instant and she felt cold hardness under her feet, then it was back, worse than before—as if her skin were being turned inside out and her bones wrenched from her body. Then it was gone and her hands were empty and someone was shaking her, slapping her face.

She drew in a long shuddering breath and cautiously opened her eyes. She and Corysiam stood on sand with wind hammering at them and a gray, wild ocean stretching to the horizon in front of them.

Corysiam slapped her again, no gentle tap. Her palm stung and brought tears to Cymel's eyes. "Cymel! Do you hear me?"

Cymel lifted her hand to stop a second slap. "I do."

"Well, you better listen hard. You forced the Bridge to this place. Now you have to anchor me. Dig your feet into the sand, make yourself feel as heavy as you can, do whatever you did before and concentrate. Think about the boy, don't stop thinking about him. Do you understand?"

Her hands shaking, Cymel looked away from Corysiam at the heaving water. All she'd done was *want* something terribly. She didn't even know why she felt like that, but it was still there, that urgency, and she knew it wouldn't go away. "No," she said. "But I'll do it."

She turned her back to the wind and kicked at the sand until there was a hole big enough for her to crouch in. The sand was cold and wet, but that only made it easier to dig the hole, then scrunch down in it, wrap her arms around her legs and concentrate. Heavy, Cory says. Heavy. I'm a rock in the stream. I'm rooted deep and the water can't move me.

Her shaking stopped and even her nightgown was too stiff and rockish to move in the wind. That gave her yet more confidence and she thought about the boy. His form leaped into her mind as clear as if he were stretched in front of her.

She kept chanting the words over and over. "Heavy heavy, save him, heavy heavy, save him." Over and over. Somewhere in the middle of her chant she felt a terrifying pressure that threatened to drive her into the ground. Her nose started to bleed and her throat squeezed tight, but she didn't let those things distract her. "Heavy heavy, save him," she droned. "Heavy heavy, save him."

The pressure vanished and that was harder to ignore than when it was there. She concentrated and chanted, letting the words narrow her focus until there wasn't anything else but *heavy* and *save him*. No storm no sea no sand blowing into her nothing but the boy and the need to save him.

The weight came on her again, but it was lighter this time. She heard the sound of a hand slapping flesh and her face stung, then from way far away someone called, "Cymel."

A short time later, more words came, shouted at her. "Let go! It's done. Let go! Stop it, Cymel!"

When the meaning of the words finally got through to her, she sighed and opened her eyes. She was tired. So tired. Cold. Shuddering in wind that felt as if it were scouring her flesh from her bones.

Arms closed round her. Corysiam was lifting her, cuddling her against her soft cushy breasts. There was the wrenching twist and a layered darkness full of eddies and flows that took wild leaps. For an instant light banished the dark; she saw walls, part of a tower, stone flags paving a courtyard. Then they were back in the darkness and this time they landed on the walk outside her house, right by the steps and the needle tree that grew there.

Her father stood by the door, yellow lamplight spilling past him. He was so angry he was shaking. "Bring her in, then. I want that boy out of my house, and I don't want to see either of you here again."

"Stand aside, then."

Cymel was half asleep. Corysiam was up the steps and through the door before Cymel understood her father's anger and what he'd said. She lay quietly while Corysiam carried her into the front parlor, but when her aunt tried to set her down on the divan and step back, she wrapped her fingers in the thick wool nightgown that Corysiam was wearing and wouldn't let her move.

"Cym, baby, your father has the right to say what he wants. This is his house. Let me go."

"No. Pa!"

Ellar Yliarson came to stand grim-faced in the doorway. "I will not have you put in danger by some rush of sentimentality or other foolishness. I want both of them out of my house and I don't want you arguing with me, Cymel."

"Pa, you've got it all wrong." She paused; her head was swimming and the room kept going odd on her. "Was me that did it, not Aunt Cory. I forced the Bridge, it wasn't her."

"What are you talking about? You're a child. You can't—"

"I did. I swear by Mama's soul, I did it. And I'm not crazy or stupid. I know what I did. I had to save that boy. I just *had* to."

His shoulders slumped and he looked as tired as she felt. "Why, Mela?"

"I don't know. I had this dream and I just knew I had to do it. So I did. Where is he? I want to see him."

"On the window seat in the back parlor."

Using her hold on Corysiam's nightgown, Cymel pulled herself onto her feet. She swayed and the room swam around her, but her strength was rapidly returning. She left her father staring at her aunt and went down the hall to the back parlor.

Her father had got the boy out of his wet clothes and into one of his own nightshirts and had tucked a blanket around him. In the light from the lamp on the writing table, his skin was a brownish-gold and his hair was soft and thick and the color of sunlight. He was about the same age as Breith, but Breith was earth and stone, rough and unformed, while this one was all air and glory.

Behind her she could hear her father and Corysiam arguing, but it was just ordinary mad, not that cold fury that had frightened her.

"She's got to be taught how to use that power." That was Corysiam.

And her father said, "Not on Iomard, thank you. She belongs to Glandair. And I *am* teaching her. Simple exercises. She's a *child.*"

"Did I say she doesn't belong here? But she needs more than baby games. She needs a disciplined and ordered lessoning on how to control and direct that power. Otherwise she'll be a danger to herself and everyone around her."

"Not on Iomard. I won't have my daughter turned into a Siofray matriarch with all their ignorant arrogance."

"So you turn her into an ignorant Ifordyar hedge wizard to be sucked into the backwash when your Mages march on each other. Or she could turn Mage, have you thought of that? It's there. If you won't see that, someone must stop her from setting her foot on that road."

"If you or anyone else tries to go off with her, I'll evoke the self-defense codes and stop you with whatever means I have to use. And she's no Mage. She will never be a Mage."

The fire had burned low but the heat from it felt good on the side of her face. The wind rattling the windows and whistling round the corners made the room into a place as warm and cozy as curling up under a stack of quilts on a winter morning. Cymel got to her feet and closed the door on the argument, then went back to kneel beside the sleeper.

The boy opened amber cat's eyes. "Who?"

"I'm Cymel Ellarsdottar. What's your name?"

"Lyanz of House of Kurrin. My father . . . the ship . . . what happen—" He pushed up, looked around. "Where?"

"Was your father on that ship with you?"

"Yes."

"I'm afraid he's drowned, then. The ship had gone under before my aunt and me, we found you."

"Drown . . . say again, I not speak Nyd-Ifor so good."

Cymel wrinkled her nose, glanced at the door. I hate this, she thought, I wish Pa'd stop arguing with Aunt Cory and come help me.

But that wasn't going to happen. She sighed and began explaining again, speaking slowly and clearly, willing Lyanz to understand her so she wouldn't have to do it all a third time. When she finished, she knew he'd got it because he rolled over, turned his back to her and pulled the blanket up over his head.

She didn't know what to do. He didn't seem to want anyone there, but she didn't like to leave him alone. She pushed at her straggling, wind-knotted hair and felt a lot older than she had when she got out of bed yesterday morning.

9

Jealousy and Loneliness

By the calendar of the Domains of Iomard, the 3rd day of Cuggos, the fifth month in the Iomardi year 6533, the 720th year since the last Corruption.

[1]

Breith dropped onto the end of the bench and sat with his legs splayed out and his hands in the pockets of his school tunic. Moggie and Trosc were on the other side of the room and wouldn't look his way even if he called their names, which he wasn't about to do. Since the muga with the history Brother, they'd avoided him like he had some disease they didn't want to catch.

Tel wasn't here and he wouldn't be in any of the other cadres. He was an Ascal brat, not Siofray; he was over here being schooled in Valla Murloch because his father was some sort of government muck who got kicked out and had to run for his life. You'd think he'd know what standing up meant, but no, he was just like the others, letting Gloy jerk their strings and playing smile games with the Brothers.

Stinking Gloy. I thought he was my friend. Now he acts like I'm some sort of scurd who sneaked in when the Brothers' backs were turned. Da was right. Couldn't rule the run in his own age track so he comes prancing round us.

Somehow, knowing all that didn't make Breith feel any better. He stared at his feet, waggled the toes of his boots while trying to pretend that he didn't care about being treated like he wasn't there.

A harsh and all too familiar voice broke into his unhappy musings. "Sit up straight, gar! Tuck those feet under."

Without waiting to see if his commands were obeyed, Brother Bullan stumped through the rows of benches to the lectern at the front of the room. He was big. All over. Every way. All his gestures were wide and swooping. His arms outdid other men's legs, there were rolls of fat about his chin and neck and his belly was a barrel of hard fat and muscle. In Breith's exercise classes, when Brother Bullan was stripped to his loincloth and should have lost some of his bulk with the folds of his thick brown robe removed, he seemed even bigger, nothing less than a force of nature as he came whirling by Breith and the rest in the class, yelling the count of whatever exercise he had them doing.

Brother Bullan brought the measure stick down hard on the lectern, the sharp crack cutting through the buzz of conversation that eddied around Breith without touching him.

"You all know why you're here." His voice boomed out, big as the rest of him; it made Breith want to pull his head down between his shoulders to protect his ears. "But I have to make this speech to all the cadres in your year, so you're going to pull yourselves up and listen without squirming. Hanas!"

A rotund boy from one of the shipbuilding families, Hanas jerked out of his droop, a squeal startled from him. He turned red and kept his eyes forward, ignoring the grins of the others around him.

"If you go to sleep on me, you'll run the wall till the hooters fly. What're you grinning about, Gruat? You straighten out, or you'll be trotting right behind him." He crossed his arms and leaned into them, the lectern groaning under the weight pressing down on it. "Anyone asks you, you're Cadre Boig. I'll repeat that. Cadre Boig. If I ask you, you'd better get that name out fast, or I will make sure you don't forget it again."

He paused, ran his eye over them. "On this day your general education ends and your training begins for the Seyl Games. To look at the lot of you now, doesn't seem likely that any woman with a trace of taste or the sense the Prophet gifted her with would choose any of you for her Seyl mate. It's my job to whip you into shape so you make a good showing and don't disgrace your school.

"In case you were asleep in your history classes, let me tell you that in the Domains, the Challenge battles are blood games. Nothing organized about them. A highborn son comes marching up to a Domain Hold, bangs on the gate, calls his challenge and either kills the resident Seyl or one of the lesser highborn men in the Hold or he gets killed. In the Riverine Confederation we are rather more civilized. Our Seyl Games are neither blood matches nor merely physical posturing. In addition to the series of duels in which you show off your strength and agility, you will be expected to play in credible fashion one musical instrument, preferably two, write and declaim your own poetry, exhibit the minor graces of holding household and polish up any special talent you own that would help you distinguish yourselves from the rest of the Gamers. Ennock! Drop that and sit up straight. That's better.

"In four years you will enter your first Games. By your tenth Game you have to be chosen and Seyled or you'll be sealed out of the High Rolls. To spur your enthusiasm for my lessons, I'll be taking you to visit a bachelor hostel and a worker village so you'll see what you face if you fail at the Games.

"For the rest of the year we will lay down the basics of your Games training. In Holy Fainachtrim you will attend a Seyl Game as observers. Next year you will begin intensive study in your particular specialty, whatever that turns out to be. However, we need not talk about that at the moment. When I call your name, come up and receive your schedule of classes. These are not open to dispute either as to teacher or subject. Consider your schedule in effect the moment you leave this room. Aanal-Edro, Daol na. Move it, Daol, I've got four more cadres to deal with after you lot. Asthmon-Andred, Grios na . . ."

[2]

Breith ambled down Front Street, inspecting the blisters from the hilt of the split wood rapier Brother Bullan made him jab over and over and over again at a canvas sack in the shape of a man's torso. Brother said his skin would harden after a week or so, but it was going to be a pain and a half until that happened. Breith thrust his hands in the pockets of his school tunic and brooded over what he was going to do to that last-year student with the empathy of a rabid polecat who was running mat training and took a snickering delight in every thump Breith got as he was learning how to fall. Gorta na Fasar-Menal, the creep. Something really gruesome like maggots in his shoes or itching powder in his shorts. Breith could think of a lot worse things, but Mam would have his hide if he even came close to doing them.

Despite his bruises—and Gorta the creep—he was rather pleased with himself. And with the fact that most of the work, aside from the training, he was supposed to do on his own. No more sitting in stuffy classrooms listening to a teacher droning on about this or that, though when he let himself think about it, he wasn't looking forward to the performance aspect of some of his classes. Standing up in front of gnors like Moggie and Trosc and declaiming verse was an ugly thought. Or trying to get his fingers in the proper place on the frets of a lute while they sniggered at his efforts.

He wasn't so sure how he felt about the reason for all this. Knowing what was coming in a vague sort of way was one thing, actually getting ready for finding a mate changed everything. It made him itchy. A tribuf at the meat market, paraded, poked and prodded before being bought and slaughtered. Da didn't seem to mind, except he hadn't gone to the Games. He was a runaway daroc from some Domain or other, working on the riverfront when Mam . . . Breith moved his shoulders. It made him feel odd thinking about his parents that way.

He felt even more uncomfortable when he caught sight of his father a short distance ahead of him, standing outside the Nuach-Turaim papermill, talking to Scribe Corysiam and a tall, lanky girl he'd never seen before. He shuffled his feet, wondering if what he was thinking was written on his face. Sometimes it seemed to be when Da was climbing his frame for some dumb thing he'd done.

A sharp sting on his shoulder broke him from his thoughts and he jumped back. He'd stepped into the cross street without thinking, and now he saw he'd nearly walked into a small herd of cut tribufs being driven to the stockyards, the noises they made lost in the roar of the steam-driven chippers in the mill. One of the herdgirls had flicked him with her whip. She looked at him with the usual Domain contempt for Riverines, then forgot him as she went back to her job, growling and whistling at the beasts, using her whip to keep her section close herded and moving where they were supposed to go.

Breith watched the black mass clump past him and decided that the Domain they were from must be having money troubles, because it was early in the year for a drive and the tribufs were gaunt from the overwintering, their hipbones standing up like the ends of a ladder and their ribs visible through the stubble on their sides. Their horns had been docked, some of the stubs still had bloody scabs, and their long black hair had been sheared off for Domain spinners and weavers.

Three riders followed at the end of the herd, a Lynborn Bantar from the Domain followed by two Lynborn ridos there as her bodyguard. Breith stared at them, wide-eyed. They had muscles in places where he didn't even have places and looked like they could pick Brother Bullan up and toss him back and forth without even raising a sweat. They wore loose black shirts inside a harness of black leather strips ornamented with silver studs and wide black trousers tucked into hightop boots. They were armed with sabers and longbows.

The Bantar glanced his way as she rode past, her eyes sliding over him with the contempt the herdgirl had shown. Then those eyes widened, the nostrils of her beaky nose flared. She swung the horse toward him. Startled, Breith stepped back.

"Mirra!" It was his father's voice, a roar filled with anger and warning that broke through the noise around them and brought the Bantar's head snapping up and around. Malart flung up both hands, fingers extended and slightly curled.

The Bantar started a gesture to the two ridos, but there was a flare of yellow light from Malart's fingers so intense that it brought tears to Breith's eyes.

The woman froze. The two ridos slumped in their saddles, eyes closed, faces emptied of expression.

"Breith, come here." Corysiam's voice. "Quickly."

He could feel the tingle of concentrated Pneuma and circled cautiously around it.

His father stood on the walkway, his face straining, his arms held out stiffly in front of him, yellow light streaming from his fingers. Breith turned toward him.

Corysiam's voice was harsh with urgency as she called to him. "No! Don't distract your father." She touched the girl's arm. "This is Amhar, follow her. We'll catch up with you later."

"But . . ."

Amhar grabbed his arm. "Come on, your father has enough to deal with. You can help by getting out of sight."

Heavy braid bouncing on her shoulders, her fingers digging into his arm, the young Scribe took Breith through a web of back streets he'd never seen before, despite all the time he and Gloy and the others who used to be his friends had spent running around in the city. He had knots in his stomach from worrying about his father; he wanted desperately to help, but how could he be sure that running like this was the right thing? He let her haul him along because he didn't know what to do.

After about ten minutes of hurrying down narrow dusty streets and around corners, she turned into a small family tavern, passed through the taproom without so much as a nod and took him into the back court where there were a number of dusty tables set under trees that were just budding out with new leaves.

She pointed to a chair, pulled out another and sat down.

"What was that about?" He scowled at her. She was only a few years older than him but she was treating him as if he were a child and he didn't like that. Her face wasn't exactly pretty but it had features of a striking cleanness and clarity, as if they'd been carved from a tight-grained wood with a very sharp knife. Her arms and legs were long and he thought they were too thin, but she was stronger than she looked.

A finger tapping on the table, she ran her eyes over his face, then nodded. "You look a lot like your father."

"Yeah, Mam and Mum say so, but—"

"He ran from the Domains, didn't he?" She laughed at his offended look. "You needn't answer that. It's obvious. The Bantar was some kind of kin and she recognized you from your resemblance to your father. Which meant that you were her property. They're supposed to leave runaways alone if they come across them in the Confederation, but they don't always. If that Bantar had tossed you to one of the ridos and he'd got out of the city before the guards could take him, there's not much anyone could do about it. Not going to start a war over a braysha boy."

"You know it all, huh?"

"More than you, braysha boy."

"My name's Breith. Breith na Faobra-Yasa."

"And I am Amhar ait é Iobhai out of the Scribe House at Gabba Labhain on service to the Scribe House at Valla Murloch."

"Ait é Iobhai. That's not a Riverine name."

"My grandmother was like your father. She ran," Amhar said. "She got a place with the Scribes and we've been Scribes since, but she didn't see the need to tie herself to anybody, so she didn't. She passed her name to my mother and my mother passed it to me. And I'll pass it to my daughter should the time come when I feel like having one."

"Least you don't have to go round setting yourself up like a tribuf fattening for the market."

Amhar shrugged. "When you're old enough to know what you want, you can worry about what you have to do to get it." She looked past him, smiled and got to her feet. "See you round," she said and walked away, her body moving with a vigorous grace that made him feel like a looby who could barely keep from tripping over his own feet.

Though he didn't want to, he couldn't help turning to watch her—and he saw what she'd seen, his father and Corysiam standing in the doorway that led into the court.

The two Scribes left and his father came across to join him at the table. He took Amhar's chair and sat staring down at the table, saying nothing until Breith couldn't stand the silence any longer.

"Da, that Bantar. Amhar says she must be kin. Was she right?"

Malart's hands clenched, then opened again. He lifted his head, stared past Breith. "Yes." The word was almost a whisper. Breith knew his father wasn't Riverine because of talk he'd picked up playing with affiliates' children. But he hadn't guessed that Malart was Lynborn not daroc.

Malart touched his tongue to his lips, but still didn't look at Breith. The way he was acting made Breith feel itchy, but the questions in his head itched worse, so he kept his eyes fixed on his father, willing him to answer.

"Her name is Mirrialta ait é Mullach-Tiolan. She was a cousin, fostered at Domain Tiolan." Malart got to his feet. "Wait here. I'll be back."

Sitting in this walled court with not a breath of air stirring, Breith felt like a coila being roasted for Ascension dinner. Sweat plastered his hair to his head and ran down his face to sting his eyes, drip off the end of his nose and his chin. He watched the drops splat into the dust on the tabletop and wondered what his father was doing, and why they didn't just go home.

That was the first question he asked when Malart came out of the tavern with two mugs of cider.

Malart set them on the table, pulled his chair out, pushed one of the mugs across to Breith and took a long pull at the other. He wiped his mouth. "Partly because I want to be sure we can get to Urfa House without being intercepted. Mirrialta has the Sight, though she's not very strong and I could always blank her, even when we were children. I'm drained, Breith. I couldn't light a match right now."

"But . . ."

"Why would she bother? Because she's a vindictive loit who carries every slight she's ever imagined engraved on that stone where her heart should be, and she repays each one over and over again. Unfortunately, she's also quite clever. Before the day's out, she'll know who I am now and where to find me. I can defend myself, but you and Bauli . . . you'd be her targets, not me. She's good at attacking where it would hurt most. Why did it have to be her bringing in that herd? She hasn't been to Valla for years, since before you were born actually. She doesn't like cities. . . ."

"Da, how come . . . ?"

"Why am I on her hate list?"

"Yeh."

"Because she wanted to wed my eldest sister, who was heir to

Tiolan. She was close to getting what she wanted, but I saw her with a daroc boy and what she was doing to him—he was just a baby. . . . I won't talk about it, you don't need to know those kinds of things, but it was bad enough that I had to tell my sister."

He paused, took a long pull at the cider, then went on with his tale, speaking slowly as if the words were being pulled from him. "When our mother the Traiolyn looked into what I said, she was furious. At me because I brought the whole mess up and at Mirrialta because she could disgrace the whole Lyn if what she did came out. She ordered Mirrialta back to Lyn Mullach. That Domain is just west of here. Fever country and poor land."

He shook his head, looked grim. "Mirrialta couldn't fight the exile, but she did what she could to punish me. She'd been spying and found out I had the Sight. She tried to get me cut, written out of the family book and reduced to daroc. I ran before the ruling, so she got that much revenge, but it wasn't enough to satisfy her. Now that she knows I'm alive and prospering, she won't rest until . . ." He emptied the mug, then sat staring gloomily at it.

Breith drew in a breath to ask his father to tell him about the run and how he got to Valla Murloch and how he met Mam, but before he could say anything, he heard faint chimes coming from somewhere above the table. "What's that?"

"Corysiam." Malart got to his feet. "She's got word to your Mam and seen Fori heading home. A Scribe has to be discreet, Breith. They aren't allowed to interfere in disputes in the Domains or between the Domains and the Confluence. So you won't say anything about this."

"No, Da."

"Come on. It's time we went home too."

As he hurried along the twisting lanes, trying to keep up with his father, the strong feelings that overflowed from Malart scratched

along Breith's nerves. Malart didn't like being reminded of the
fears and hardships of those old days and he was fiercely angry at
the chance meeting that had disturbed his comfortable present
with visitors from that past. Catching the infection, Breith found
that the small houses with their plaster walls, the flat red-clay tiles
of their roofs and the worked straw blinds in the windows were
beginning to look strange, unwelcoming. And the people in the
lanes were like that too. Looking at him and his father out of shut-
tered eyes. Even the children.

By the time they turned onto River Road not far from Urfa
House, Breith was almost as angry as his father. That Bantar had
stolen something from him. He didn't know exactly what it was,
but he could feel the hole it left in him and he was pretty sure
he'd never get it back.

The gates were closed and Gateward Neech had his son in with
him, the young man armed with a crossbow and a pair of spears.
When he saw them, Neech worked the levers and opened the
gates a crack, just enough to let them through.

As the iron bar thunked home behind them, Neech called
down, "Seyl Malart, Cay Faobran waits in the library."

As they walked to the business wing of the House where the
library and the offices were, Breith thought that the whole population of Urfa, all the third- and fourth-degree kin, all the gardeners and house servants, all the clerks and the cooks and the
stablemen, everyone inside the walls were standing in shadows
watching him and his father walk along the gravel path. They
were discreet about it, didn't hang about staring, but it put knots
in his stomach.

He stopped at the base of the stairs that led to the side door
of the public wing and watched his father go bounding up them.
When Malart reached for the door latch, he said, "Da, whyn't I
go have a bath and do some of my studies, huh? You 'n Mam 'n
Mum, you don't need me there."

Breith felt a flood of relief that wasn't his own. Malart turned his head, nodded. "Don't go outside the walls. You understand why?"

"Yeah. I won't."

【 3 】

Though the sun was near setting by the time Breith left his room, the breeze blowing through the crenels that circled the tower roof was a hot breath out of the south and the stockyards, carrying with it the stink of tribuf herds in the fattening lots, a reminder he didn't need right now.

House Urfa was built right on the river with the other Trading Houses on the hills around the perimeter of the city proper with its scattering of factories, mills, shops and the small houses of the independent workers. Though the town center wasn't more than a dozen marks away, usually it was quiet here with the wind following the river out of the north.

Breith stretched out on the hot red tiles of the roof, his chin resting on crossed forearms, his eyes closed. Sweat coiled from his hair and ran down his face, popped out on his back and arms, soaking his shirt.

Below him in the Gatehouse, Neech and Young Neech were talking. The sounds of their voices floated up to him though he couldn't make out the words. Behind him in the courts of Urfa House he could hear the chatter of maids, the deeper voices of the men servants and clerks, an occasional whinny from the stables. Gath was barking at the squirrelmonks again and one of the stable dogs was taking that for a challenge and barking back at him. With all those familiar and comforting sounds around him, it was hard to remember that there was a Bantar from the Domains out there who wanted him gelded and land-tied to a life of hard labor. Or dead.

He was still mad at Gloy and irritated by the way Moggie and Trosc and Tel had been acting, but he didn't want to hurt them, he didn't even want to rat on them to the Brothers and get them chewed out for incivility. How anyone could hold a grudge for over seventeen years, longer than he'd even been alive, was something he just didn't understand.

He put that aside and considered briefly the talk going on in the library. Looked like he mightn't be going to school while the Bantar was in Valla Murloch. She couldn't stay here all that long, but maybe she could hire a fist or two to do the job. From what Tel said his father said, it didn't take much gelt to buy a thumping. As Amhar said, he was only a braysha boy who had to catch a bride for himself to mean anything, not an Heir like his baby sister Bauli, so even if what's-her-name ah Mirrialta sprung for a snatch, it wouldn't cost her more than the price of a few tribufs.

If anyone had asked him this morning what he thought about taking a month or two off from school, he'd have said, Oh yeah, when do I start. Now that he contemplated such a thing in reality, he didn't like it at all. Moggie and Trosc would get way ahead of him in the fight training, and being stuck here inside these walls was going to get real old real fast. He wiped the sweat from round his eyes, rested his head on his arms again. At least there was one way he could get out without sticking his head in a trap.

He pushed himself up and scooted across the tiles to sit in the shade of a merlon, his arms draped over his knees. A moment's concentration and a fistful of magic force opened the talking window onto Glandair.

Cymel was sitting on the log by the durbaba pool; from the way the shadows puddled about the trunks and the sharpness of the sunlight on her face, it was about noon where she was. Breith's brows drew together. She usually noticed him as soon as the window opened, but today she was gazing somewhere else so intently she didn't even know he was there. He fussed with the window, turning and tilting it so he could see what she was looking at.

It was a boy about his age, or maybe a year or so older, a golden boy with hair that glimmered in the sunlight and skin as smooth as polished metal. His eyes were a dark amber, neither brown nor yellow but somewhere in between. His face had the same clean-edged features as Amhar had, but while she was not pretty at all, he was beautiful in a way that caught the breath. Beautiful in Cymel's eyes too, that was obvious. He was running at one of the trees; as he neared it, he leaped, caught hold of a limb and pulled himself up with a neat quick twist of his body. He rested a moment, a sheen of sweat on his face, and lines of weariness that made him look older for a moment. When he had himself together again, he pulled himself up till he was standing on the limb and reaching for the next one.

He vanished quickly into the heavier foliage. Breith picked up the rustle of the leaves as the boy worked his way higher into the tree, then he saw a flurry of movement in the leaves near the top of the tree, heard a series of cracks and rustles as the climber broke away a number of smaller branches so he could look out across the forest.

Cymel tilted her head back, called, "Can you see anything yet?"

"I can see the road, or at least part of it. Um. The double bend and the place where it crosses the river. That's the place you dreamed about, isn't it?"

"Can you see the ferry?"

"Sort of. It looks like a black biter crawling on a blue thread."

"It's moving?"

"Uh-huh. Too far away to really see who's on it, but I don't think it's more than one person. Maybe your father coming back from Cyfareth. He said he should be here by suppertime."

Cymel chewed on her lip. "What about the road?"

"Nobody on it, not even a cloud of dust. So maybe it was just a nightmare. Or maybe your monster will be along tomorrow or next month."

"But why did that dream come today?"

"Don't ask me, I don't know anything about this magic stuff. Ow!"

"Huh?"

"Ants. There's a whole swarm of them up here and they think I'm food. Yow, that smarts." The leaves shook again as he started down.

Breith concentrated, shifted the window closer to Cymel. "Mela, who's that?"

She twitched, looked around. "Oh, it's you. His name's Lyanz. The ship he was on sank and I saved his life."

"Huh?"

"Never mind, I'll tell you 'bout that later. He's been staying with us for the past week—which you'd know if you bothered to show up."

"I thought I'd wait till you got over your snit."

"I don't have snits. Just you acting like a grunting boch and getting your nose out of joint."

"Well, if you don't want to hear how I was nearly kidnapped and carried off with a collar round my neck . . ." He rushed the words out as he saw the boy she called Lyanz drop to the ground and crouch by the roots, beating at himself, trying to get rid of the ants still clinging to him.

"Hah! Trying to make yourself look important!"

"No. It's true. I'm stuck here in the House and I'm not going to get to go outside the walls for maybe a month because one of Da's kin from the Domains has got a major hate for him. If she gets me out of the city and in the Domains, I'll be chained to a hoe for the rest of my life and worse."

Cymel stared at him, eyes widening. "You're serious. This isn't a game."

Lyanz came walking over, stopped at the root end of the trunk, leaned on one of the root stubs and raised his brows. "Who that?"

Cymel made a face. "Lyanz, meet Breith. He's on Iomard, we talk back and forth."

"Iomard?"

"Oh. I forgot. Most people don't know about Iomard. It's a whole other world somewhere else. I don't understand much where it is, but I can look there and Breith can look here. And he figured out a way we can talk."

Up close, though he didn't seem all that healthy, Lyanz was even better looking than he was running at the tree, and Breith could see that Cymel thought so too. She was smiling at him like an orphan puppy. He could almost see her wagging her tail. He glared at Lyanz. If he had any consideration, he'd go off somewhere and not stick his nose in where he wasn't wanted.

He was about to say so when he saw Cymel turn and lean tensely forward, staring intently at something downslope. He extended the focus on the talk window and saw a twisty black funnel cloud roaring straight for the pool.

Cymel's long black hair began writhing as if it were snakes instead of hair and small lightnings popped off the ends. She put her hands up to touch it, squeaked as the lightnings bit her fingers.

"Mela! Listen. Hit the Pocket, you know, like when we played Hide the Mouse. Now! MELA!" That wasn't just a whirlstorm, it was an attack; he could smell the malice and the magic churning round it. He hunched closer to the window, willing her to hear him and remember. "Mela. The Pocket. Pull it round you. Mela—"

The window shivered into shards, the shards melted and all he could see was a pair of hot yellow eyes, staring at him, commanding him. "Come," a voice said, a musical contralto. "Come to me."

He forgot Cymel, forgot everything, the eyes filled him, there was nothing inside him but the yellow glow of those eyes.

He got to his feet and went down the stairs, stumbling, clumsy. But that didn't matter.

He moved along the walkway that connected the tower to the wall and went into the gatehouse. Neech and Young Neech were frozen, staring at nothing. He tripped the lever that unbarred and cracked the gate open, then climbed down the ladder, the voice whispering in his head, the eyes burning before him.

When his foot touched the ground something knocked him aside, sent him tumbling end over end.

He woke from the spell, his hands throbbing from gravel burns and his head one huge ache.

His father was standing at the gate. It was closed, the bar down. Malart had his hands up as shield and weapon. White fire was flaring between him and the woman outside, geysering into the sky.

Breith heard a scream filled with frustration, then the flare vanished and the woman was gone with it. Still shaky, he got to his feet. "Is she dead?"

Malart turned, set his back against the wrought-iron rods of the gate. Lines were graved deep in his face and his skin was gray with weariness. "No," he said. "She Walked." He closed his eyes. "I didn't know she was a Walker."

"Is that bad?"

"It's more trouble than I need right now." He pushed away from the gate. "Come on, we'll go to talk to Mum Yasa. I hope her gift is working."

"Da, I need to look at Glandair again."

"Maybe later. And after this, never without someone close by to yank you loose when Mirrialta tries again."

"I *really* need to look, Da. Cymel, she's in trouble, it could be bad."

"Not now, Breith."

The weary impatience in Malart's voice silenced Breith as

nothing else could have done. It brought back too clearly how close his brush with disaster had been and how much his carelessness had cost his father. There isn't anything I could do anyway, he told himself. Either Cymel heard me and pulled the Pocket over her or that thing got her. It's over by now, whichever.

He squared his shoulders and marched beside his father toward whatever Mam and Mum had waiting for him.

10

The Mages Plot and Worm Their Way Toward Their Goals

By the secret calendar of the Watchers, events beginning on the 1st of Pumamis, the fifth month in the 736th Glandairic year since the last Settling.

MAHARA OF KALE

[1]

The Kad Mermi field was a long oval of grass like shaved green velvet with tall, freestanding columns of glossy white marble ten feet apart around the outside of the oval. Black silk banners hung from several of these columns and black silk pavilions rose between them, furnished with backless chairs for those who wished to watch the game without tiring themselves by standing too long. On the field the six riders of the two teams flung their horses into twisting turns, shoving them against each other, trying to take out the horse as well as use their long-handled hooks to catch one of the loops on the Mermi-ball, flip it up and send it through the eye of the goal. The Prince's Men were battling the Temple Dragon, the prize a jeweled egg, a gift of the Olch Omir.

The sun was blinding hot on this end-of-summer day; the air

vas still, the banners on the columns hanging limp against the tone. The thudding of the hooves, the *hunhunhunh* of the horses' breathing and the creak of the saddles, the *tink tunk* of he metal parts of the bridles filled the stillness, merging with the quiet murmurs and tepid applause of the spectators.

His matte black robes, shaven skull, dark mahogany face with the tracery of blue tattooing making an effective show against the austere white of the column he'd posed himself in front of, Mahara stood apart from the courtiers in their pavilions. In one hand he held a clacker, in the other a black silk fan which he flicked back and forth to stir the air. From time to time he pulled a white handkerchief from his sleeve and mopped at the sweat beading on his head, dripping from his nose and chin.

Across the way, the Second Prince, who was refereeing the game, leaned across his chair arm, spoke a few words to his Stentor, who translated them to a noise-cutting bellow.

"BLOT! KAN HISHIR. TEMPLE DRAGONS."

One of the riders cursed, but lifted his hook and acknowledged the call.

The First Prince's supporters, the Tavushmen, painted their faces with heavy maquillage that turned them into white masks and made a change of expression difficult if not impossible. Their hair was braided into elaborate loops, and they wore earplugs set into lobes which stretched into flesh loops—carved jade discs or gold medallions for the most part. They carried short, elaborately carved wands and used them to underscore what they considered witticisms or ironic comments on the scene. They sat inside the pavilions on their carved stone chairs while slaves walked treadmills to blow ice-cooled air around them. They drank iced juices that the serving slaves brought them, the slaves all dark Rhudyar like Mahara, boys and girls between the ages of eight and twelve, taken from the slums of Yosun and Lim Ashir, bought or netted off the street by the Olchun procurers. The ice was far more expensive than any of the slaves and treated far more tenderly.

"BLOT! BADEM SOMERT. PRINCE'S MEN."

Fingers touched Mahara's wrist in a feathery caress then were gone. "This must be terribly boring for one who has seen demon wars." Pika Mar's voice was a musical alto, unusual in a court where most women cultivated a whispery, childish treble. She was the Third Prince Zulam's favorite and, according to one of the many rumors that blew about Aile Kuvvet, the reason that he had not yet taken a wife.

Mahara closed his fan and tapped her wrist with its ivory sticks. "No indeed, O Maytral Mar. The black horses on the green grass and the skill of the riders make an honest and joyous image that no demon could come close to matching."

"GOAL! THE ORNEK SEFER ZULAM. PRINCE'S MEN. THE SCORE IS TIED. TEMPLE DRAGONS TWO GOALS. PRINCE'S MEN TWO GOALS. THE FIRST TO SCORE AGAIN WINS."

Mahara languidly waved his clacker. The sharp crack of wood hitting wood merged with the polite clatter of other clackers as the Tavusher courtiers applauded the point.

On the sidelines, scorning the pavilions and the dainties offered by the slaves, the Savachemen who considered themselves the Third Prince's party whistled and shouted their approval, breaking their noise to suck the bloodred wine from wineskins with the hair left on them.

Mahara despised their deliberately slovenly dress, their straggly facial hair and their dreadlocks. He found their attempt to imitate the world he'd escaped from, the filthy, murderous streets of waterfront Lim Ashir, stupid and often pathetic. Unfortunately he needed the Third Prince as his figurehead, so he had to smile on the Savachemen and listen to their burble with an appearance of appreciation.

"And would you like to be out there with them, O Mage?" Her perfume was disturbing, blended as it was with her own odor, a musky scent strengthened by the heat of the sun. Her beauty had claws, but that danger was part of her allure.

Mahara patted at the sweat on his face and knew it wasn't only heat that brought it out. "O Maytral Mar, I am content to follow the sumptuary laws of the Olch Omir, may the hot breath of Great Rueth envelop and protect him. The black horses of the Agirsade are not for such as I."

"For one with such power at his fingertips, you are a cautious man, Mahara of Kale."

He heard the barbs hidden in her words and knew what she was after. He wasn't ready yet to succumb to her lures, but the thought of what might be ahead roughened his breathing for a moment.

There was another roar from the Savachemen as Zulam blocked a Dragon and knocked the Mermi-ball loose from his hook.

"BLOCK FAIR. THE ORNEK SEFER ZULAM. THE PRINCE'S MEN. BLOT ON BADEM SOMERT CANCELED."

Mahara slapped his clacker, called out, "Oh, well-played."

With a throaty laugh, Pika Mar drifted off.

Mahara paid her no attention, kept his eyes focused on the game, though he found it boring beyond belief.

"Such an extravagant passion for doing." The voice was languid with a touch of contempt in the vowels.

Mahara turned slowly. The maquillage made faces so similar that it was as if they all wore masks, but he had no difficulty recognizing this Tavushman—the Ulvit Kenar nin Metazor, leader of the Tavushmen and unofficial head of the First Prince's unofficial secret police. Mahara bowed with careful restraint—too much effusion would be taken as an insult—and, as he lifted his head, glanced behind the courtier. Yes, the Ichuged was standing a step behind Kenar, her eyes dark smears behind the thick folds of the veil draped over her head. Magic sniffer. Reputed to be one of the most sensitive around. Well, the only game being played here was the one out on the grass. "Sefer Ulvit," he said. "I am honored by your notice."

"Hm. Perhaps. You seem eager to join the Third Prince's following."

"A tower can be a lonely place, Sefer Ulvit. I find Zulam and his young men agreeable company. They waken in me some of the youth left long behind."

"Youth is a time of ambitions and overreaching, Tower Mage. In these environs such things are, hm, small we say, discouraged."

"I will remember your august advice, Sefer Ulvit." Mahara bowed again, face and voice both gravely serious; a reputation as a dull pedant was considerably more useful than a claim to cleverness. "Pleasure is one thing, politics another entirely and something I endeavor to stand aside from. As one mentioned earlier, I am a cautious man. Indeed, it is a necessary part of a Mage's education that he learn most thoroughly his limitations."

The Ulvit tilted his wand, touched it to his forearm then swept it through a brief arc in one of those meaning-laden gestures that Mahara loathed because he couldn't read them. You had to have been born into this world to know all the things that were left unsaid.

Mahara bowed again and waited blank-faced as the Ulvit and his attendant Ichuged moved away. He'd just been warned off the Third Prince. He'd expected that but not so soon. The Olch Omir must be losing hold and the maneuvering of his heirs growing more vicious. Which meant a Mage would have to be very wary indeed of any obvious entanglements. He focused on the game, struggling to deal with his boredom and his impatience, because he knew more than one of the Savachemen were watching him.

If they only thought it through, they'd see that an overt connection with the Tower Mage would be a disaster for Zulam.

Contact should be secret and subtle. What he had been doing till now was setting out flags to let the Prince's managers know he might be interested. It was time to pull back and let the real string pullers practice their art. The Ulvit and his kind. Faceless ice-blooded string pullers.

Sitoon Kaa had shown them to him when he was still learning the craft. *The Olch Omir,* he'd said, *he's all show, and most of those who call themselves the Born, they're masks for the ones who work behind the curtain. But the show is necessary and the puppeteers know that. They will preserve that facade in any way they deem expedient. I never forget the puppeteers. You think because I'm a Mage with power enough to turn them all to ugly garden ornaments, I should just ignore them and do what I want. You won't believe me now, but you'll learn. I'm only one man and I have to sleep sometime. If I want peace, I live by their rules.*

Mahara waved his clacker as another of the Prince's Men scored a goal. The team was named for and sponsored by the First Prince, not Zulam, but it was his showcase and part of the power game he was playing. Or so Mahara hoped. He didn't want a great deal of intelligence in the man he'd chosen as his mask. A moderate mind coupled with immoderate ambition was what he hoped for and from all appearances what he would get.

The First Prince and Prime Heir didn't need him and wouldn't let him near; Takrib shared the Omir's distrust and rabid dislike of all those who played games with the Pneuma Flow. He was also deeply into the Tavush faction, with little interest in war or conquest. Second Prince Kameer was far too intelligent and too indolent for Mahara's needs. There was a further obstacle—their mother. The Byrin Anna Mishada was a formidable woman and the one with the best chance to block his schemes.

"Good game, hah?" The words were spoken in a deliberately roughened voice and the accent of the streets. The speaker was the younger son of the Rueth Paz, Mankafa the Holy, the highest official in the royal Temple. Being one of the Born, his skin

was normally a pale mahogany, almost rose-pink, but today he
was flushed red from the sun. His brown beard was straggly, the
straggles twisted into wispy dreadlocks. His hair was bundled
into a single long braid that reached halfway down his back and
was suspiciously thick considering the thin crop on the top of his
head.

Mahara bowed. He was seriously annoyed to be accosted publicly like this, but he didn't let it show. "It is indeed," he said. "A
powerful and subtle use of power and skill to achieve a temporal
goal. You can liken it to the maneuverings for influence in the
world of the merchants, the application of carefully judged leverage in the form of coin and the rivalry among the sellers. I—"

"Ah. Yes, most interesting." The Savacheman pushed past
him, hurried around the rim of the playing field to join a group
of his friends.

Not amused by any of this, Mahara left his post by the column
and began threading through the pavilions and away from the
field before another Savacher came blundering up in another stupid attempt to compromise him and leave him no option but to
accept a role in the Third Prince's faction.

[2]

The High City of Aile Kuvvet was built on the concentric rings
of a terraced flattop mountain across the river from the lowly
trade city Lim Ashir. It was an old city, the terracing done so
many Settlings ago that even the books in the workroom under
Mahara's Tower had no mention of the Mage who carved the
mountain or the men who built the core of the Cherai, the House
of the Olch Omir. The road that led from the curtain walls of the
Cherai spiraled downward, enclosed in lacy pierced stone walls
with bronze spearpoints marching along the top course, points
whose three edges were honed razor sharp. The bronze strap that
linked them had a diamond-shaped cross section with the edges
also kept sharp enough to slice a thought in half. At each level

there were Ring Gates and guards; anyone without a gech was not allowed onto the level, a gech being a square of bronze stamped with the number of the house where the bearer lived. Born or Elevated, slave or free, without a gech no one passed through a Ring Gate.

Mahara had inherited a house in Aile Kuvvet along with the Tower. It was one of the lowest of the rings, and years of neglect had turned the gardens into a wilderness of weeds and wild growth and infested the walls with vermin of every sort. The roof had leaked, and many of the rooms were filled with mold and broken furniture. Until he'd reamed it out and patched the leaks, the pipe that connected with the aqueduct and supplied water to the house was corroded and so filled with moss roots and other clogs that only a trickle got through and that the color of sepia ink. He'd set up a brace of golems in the kitchen to do cooking and cleaning for him. Slaves were spies, all of them; he wanted no one watching him in his own home. He cleared out a few rooms for his own use, one to sleep in, one to study in and one apart from the others where he could entertain any visitors he might have. He left the rest of the house to molder away as it had been doing for the past forty years.

He opened the creaking gate, pushed past the overgrown plantings along the path to the house, starting scurries in the tangle of weeds that choked the gardens and flutters overhead among the branches of the ancient trees. He smiled as he picked his way along the broken flags of the path. This jungle annoyed his neighbors so much that they sputtered when they spoke of his house, yet none of them had the spine to complain either to him or to the WatchWard of the city. Every time he walked this path, he enjoyed thinking about them. It was one of the small moments that made life in Aile Kuvvet endurable.

Mahara dismissed the golem, poured some distilled water into his silver scrying bowl. The lens spell he'd established in one corner of the room outside the circle of wards siphoned cold air from deep inside the ice caverns of the Dislir Dags and brought it curling round his neck. He settled into the coolness with a sigh of pleasure, then sat in his armchair sipping at the tea the golem had brought on the tray along with the bottle of distilled water.

Behind the carved ivory screens on the ventilation outlets up near the eaves of the workroom, he could hear the rustle and twitter of the mudswifts that lived in the walls and the patter of mouse feet. The wards kept them out of the workroom and away from the books he'd brought with him from the Tower; other than that he didn't care what they did. Besides, he was accustomed to the small sounds of the resident vermin and found them relaxing.

He set the teacup aside, used the napkin to pat his lips dry, then leaned over the wide, shallow scrybowl and summoned the vision of one of the Tilkos men he'd been tweaking into setting up a conspiracy.

In the Bowl, the Image with Sound

The Parshak Gurra Rasidal wore an exercise tunic, a dark red garment that left his arms and legs mostly bare, the hem hitting him about mid-thigh. He was a light Rhudyar and kept his fashionable pallor by wearing hats and gloves whenever he ventured outside. Tilkos pride in birth was a fierce thing and any hint at dark blood was a cause of shame, an insult that brought a duel to the death.

The long narrow room was silent except for the scrape and stomp of Gurra's feet as he lunged and darted at the target, the point of his slender sword tapping with accuracy and restraint each point he meant to hit. He was slight in build but well muscled, and the sword practice he was engaged in at the moment showed his formidable speed and control. Also his discipline and determination.

Mahara watched him for several moments, then moved the point of focus to check the room and its surroundings. The Stanca was a warren, the compound large as a small city, so Gurra was seldom alone anywhere, just here in this decaying salle and in the cubicle he was assigned as a bedroom. He belonged to the cadet branch of Family Rasidal, all of them pensioners and hangers-on with little say in the life of the Stanca. His resentment at his poverty and the lack of any opportunity to use his abilities was a bitter thing.

Tilkos was a satrapy of Kale, conquered long ago, plundered, used as a dumping ground for Born Kalesmen who were too inept or too corrupt to ride the waves of preferment in Kale. Tilkose faced a ceiling on their ambitions because all the top posts and the most lucrative positions were reserved for the Born from Kale.

Mahara twitched a towel from a peg, used it as the core to form a simulacrum of a Rahza called Whan, one of the mountain bandits who preyed on caravans moving back and forth between Kale and Tilkos. He'd used Whan himself as willing pawn several times when Gurra joined hunting parties led by the Rasidal or Rasidal Minor. Other times he'd evoked the man's form as a golem to carry information meant to prick the Parshak's ambition.

"El Parshak."
Gurra whirled, sword up, point out. He dropped the point when he saw who it was, but kept the sword in his hand, ready for use at the slightest threat or even at something he took as an insult. "Whan. How did you get in here?"
"A good thief is silent and elusive as a shadow. I am a good thief. I also give value for value. You sent me to look upon the border forts. I am here to tell you what I saw."
"Ah!" Gurra waggled his sword at a mat rolled up and pushed against a wall. "We'll sit over there. Where we can watch the door."

"Well?"

"The fort at the Parma Bight is rotten. The Bashar is a Born and a drunk, his Aide is Born and selling everything in the place that's not nailed down, with just enough sense to let the guard detail have shares in the rake-off. They'll put on a good enough show when the Olchar tax farmer walks off the ship from Lim Ashir with his half-dozen pikemen, but you put out a finger and touch that show, it'll go foof! like an overripe puffball. This is the softest target and the one that will gain you most."

"Go on."

"The fort at Buyegil is in better shape, the Born Bashar is simply lazy, not corrupt and not stupid. He tolerates more indolence than another would, but he is a careful man and otherwise maintains the discipline. Perhaps because he sits in the middle of Tilkos and knows he is not loved."

Mahara smiled. Tonight, while Gurra slept, dreams would play across his mind's eye, visions of taking the tax money for himself and his growing cadre of rebels, buying arms and favors with it.

Gurra would do it. He was intelligent, filled with rage and ambition. A natural leader, born to be a conspirator.

Losing coin was one thing the Olch Omir could not ignore. He wouldn't be gentle about looking for the guilty, nor would he listen to pleas when the Tilkose were forced to replace the stolen money, to pay their taxes twice in one year. Which would bring recruits by the handfuls to Gurra's Secret Legion. They'd stir up more trouble, the Olch Omir would send in more troops from Kale, and so the spiral would go until there was nothing left but open war.

And I will keep the rancor hot here in Aile Kuvvet. Hone the army on Tilkose bones, take Faiscar then Nikawaid. And when that's done, Hudoleth, you're mine! His smile widened. And Nordomon, you're mine. Then I wait until the Hero shows his face. When he does, ahhhhhh.

HUDOLETH OF CHUSINKAYAN

[1]

The evening was warm and silky, typical of early autumn on the shores of Lake Mizukor. The sky was marbled with clouds, dry clouds with a full moon riding through them.

The Emperor had decreed an evening of lights and verse in honor of the end of summer and Hudoleth was one of those favored with an invitation to the Garden of Fair Words. The honor had cost her two days and more coin than she wanted to think about. Various functionaries of the Court had offered to gift her with the robe and the flowers for her hair, but such largesse had strings she didn't want binding her. Bad enough that she had to take the Emperor's offer of a suite in the Women's Quarters and handmaids to help her prepare herself. There was no way to refuse the Emperor's gifts though she could and did contrive to ignore the subtle bindings that came with them.

Like all the other guests, both men and women, she wore a long narrow robe with silver leaves and flowers embroidered on the heavy white silk. The women wore silver flowers in their hair, the men wore circlets of silver leaves. All carried Garden of Fair Words fans, some spread, some folded, white silk tassels swaying gracefully below their carefully positioned hands. These particular fans were carried in no other place and on no other occasion but an Imperial invitation. In the language of fans at Court, a tilt was a question, a flick pointed out the subject of the question, the answer perhaps a fan spread with the embroidered side out, the silver lacing laid on the lips. Or a combination of other gestures, according to the inclination and ingenuity of the respondent.

Fireflies in glass bubbles hung from the limbs of trees which were beginning to drop their foliage. Fires in blackstone stoves added warmth and a reddish glow. Incense pots rested on them, sending up braided threads of perfumed smoke. Scattered along the paths were small blackstone tables with brushes standing point upward in porcelain jars, the already prepared writing ink in squat cups beside them. Small sheets of paper were piled beside the pots, weighed down by water-polished stones taken from the stream that twisted and fell through the garden so that its limpid musical burbling was everywhere without being oppressive.

The guests walked the paths in pairs and groups or alone. No one spoke because it was not *yesah* to speak at the Emperor's own party before he himself broke the silence and authorized general conversation. *Yesah* was that vast and complex system of manners and obligations that governed Court life, never written but known in all its details by those who lived in the Palace, a compound of courts and residences more than ten miles across, housing the judiciary, the headquarters of the secret police and the vast warren of the Civil Service in addition to the living quarters of the Emperor. It wasn't a city, though it was larger than many, but more like a stage on which a cast of thousands played roles that had been laid out for them centuries before.

Grim behind her obligatory smile and downcast eyes, Hudoleth walked the paths alone. For more than a year she'd risked being sniffed out by the Emperor's Niosul as she whispered through his dreams, turning his mind away from her. Then she'd got too busy watching Mahara, flushing out the Candidates, arranging accidents for them and the Watchers traveling with them, stirring up rebellion in the Grass Clans north of Nikawaid, the thousand and a thousand things that kept her mind churning and wiped away all thought of the volatile little man who ruled Chusinkayan. To call a Scholar of Power to his bed, to control her comings and her goings, to have her bow to his whims and titillate his appetites—she could feel the frisson of pleasure that went through him each time he contemplated this.

If she wasn't very careful tonight, he'd touch her shoulder and whisper the invitation and she'd have no choice but to move into the Women's Quarters here.

The one small area that offered her a shadowy safety was that he could imagine no one refusing him. He wouldn't believe that she found his person distasteful, his habits loathsome and the splendid rooms where he'd settle her as his current favorite more like a prison, so anything she tried in order to prevent that offer, to turn his attention from her to one of the other women here, would not wake the suspicion that mingled with the blood in his veins and the air in his lungs.

She walked alone along the winding path, eyes half shut as if she contemplated the beauties of the night and sought for words to capture them, but she was looking at the other women, searching for the one most apt to deflect the Emperor's interest. She knew none of them. They were years younger than she was, daughters of the Court not the University. That made them harder to assess, but without a certain degree of charm and wit they would not have been summoned to this gathering. Beauty was necessary but not sufficient to gain entry to the Garden of Fair Words.

When she saw the tall girl, she knew this was the one. There was a careless confidence to her though she was perhaps the youngest of the women here and far from the prettiest. When she moved past one of the stone stoves, the red light that the coals cast upward emphasized the strength in the bones of her face and for a moment she was almost ugly, then two steps later, in the muted light of the moon and the fireflies, she had an extraordinary beauty that had nothing to do with prettiness. She walked beside an older man, though visibly not by her choice, and though she offered courtesy, she ignored the sly insinuations of his fan-speech and carried her own fan folded, fan-mute as she was mouth-mute.

He will take delight in taming her, Hudoleth thought, and felt a sour pleasure in the images brought up from memory. She walked onto the rustic bridge and stood leaning on the rail and gazing into the moon-silvered water while she completed her preparations, her fan unfurled and held flat against her cheek, a sign that she was musing and did not care for company.

A boy playing a flute stepped from the doorway and danced a few steps till he stood at the head of the stream where lampions hung from standards cast a rose-pink light on the marble flags of the floor where the Emperor would stand and declaim his couplet.

When she heard the flute, Hudoleth clicked her fan shut and hurried to the declaiming floor. Robe lifted so the grass wouldn't stain the silk, she dropped to her knees and bowed her head. All around her the other guests did the same.

The Emperor came through the door followed by one of his Niosul, the magic sniffers charged with keeping him safe from the snares of the Pneuma. The thin, tall figure was wrapped from head to toe in layers of black gauze, that dark veil a convention that meant the Niosul was not there, that she should be ignored as if she were a shadow, not a living being.

The Emperor was a short, slight man of late middle age. When he began losing his hair, he had his head shaved and refused to wear a silver garland to disguise the nakedness of his skull. There were heavy pouches under his eyes and deep lines running from his nostrils around the corners of a full-lipped mouth. He wore a heavy cotton robe, wrinkled and frayed around the edges. His feet were thrust into crude wooden sandals like those that peasants wore when they worked in the fields.

His voice when he spoke was trained, flexible, a deep, burring baritone that turned the competent but uninspired couplet into music. That powerful voice filling the garden, he sang:

> *Harvest moon, a silver sickle reaps a pallid cloud*
> *To weave for dead summer's corpse her winding shroud.*

The fluteboy brought to him a glass bowl blown so thin that it seemed a breath would shatter it. He folded the paper with the couplet written on it into a small pyramid, set it into the bowl, then with his own hands carried the bowl to the stream, placed it carefully on the water then straightened to watch it go floating off, the first of many bowls as each guest declaimed his own verse and gave it to the genius of the stream. He turned and scanned the faces looking up at him.

Looking for me, Hudoleth thought. She saw the Niosul stir uneasily as she slipped a faint sheen of glamour across the girl she'd chosen, something so subtle it might have been a part of the girl's natural charm. Then she dulled and aged her own appearance, drawing round herself a cloak of NO, DON'T-LOOK-AT-ME and I-AM-BORING.

It scratched at her soul to have to do this. Her beauty had always been important to her in more ways than the obvious. It was a source of strength and certainty. She tended it as if it were an object apart from herself, using her control of her body to maintain the velvet perfection of her skin and the tone of her muscle so that no wrinkle marred her face and no splotch adorned the backs of her hands, though she'd recently passed the fiftieth anniversary of her birth.

The Emperor stretched out his hand to her, smiling. At first she thought the constraints imposed by the presence of the Niosul had weakened her contrivings, but the smile wavered and there was an uncertainty in his eyes as she stepped into the light of the lampions.

"Welcome to the Garden, Scholar. We wait with great eagerness to hear your variation on the theme."

"You honor me beyond my deserts, O Blessèd of Sugreta."

Behind her smile she was furious. This was another wound she owed to the Emperor and she promised herself that he would suffer horribly for it.

With a studied wave of his hand, he dismissed her and extended his arm to the glamoured girl. "Walk with me, Daughter of the Lily, and tell me your thoughts upon this theme."

Hudoleth took what solace she could in the sudden apprehension in the girl's face, then she too moved away from the declaiming floor. The couplet she'd prepared at home required a little work to turn it to the theme, but not much; as she'd expected, the Emperor had chosen harvest and death of summer as his paired thoughts. He had a regrettably conventional mind even in his debaucheries.

By the end of the evening she was exhausted, barely able to set one foot before the other; maintaining that trickle drain at such a low level that it was hidden by her aura but at sufficient strength to be effective was like standing tiptoe on one foot for ages. It had to be done and she did it.

And she'd won her game. The Emperor's mind had been turned away from her for another space of time and she could get on with her real work.

[2]

Wet hair wrapped in a towel, wearing a much-washed cotton robe tied loosely at the waist, her face glistening with moisturizing cream, Hudoleth wrapped a potholder about the handle of her kettle and poured boiling water over the leaves in her steeping pot.

While the tea was steeping, she fetched an apple from the cool room in the pantry, peeled and quartered it, cut away the core and set the pieces on a plate beside a small pile of iced wafers. She straightened, moved her shoulders and smiled. So good to be alone in her own place. She could feel her elbows coming out from her sides and her muscles loosening, relaxing, her whole body humming.

When her face was patted dry, her hair combed out, and the tea was ready, she took the tray into her workroom and set it on a small, round elbow table beside her armchair. The cages that hung from the walls were empty. She wasn't planning any harus-pication this day. No blood, no mess, just mirrors.

Between bites of apple and sips of the tea, she polished her glass mirror and set it on its stand, then she leaned back in the chair, flexing her toes and moving her head between sips to fluff her still-damp hair. For a moment she shut her eyes and entertained the thought of forgetting this whole business and settling into her spot at the University. Then she laughed at her foolishness and sat up. "An invitation to ossification."

Her particular gifts lay in the subtleties of the Pneuma Flow and one of the most cunning was her way of looking through distant eyes. Where wards would blank all ways of scrying, when she slipped into the mind/body of a bird even the most sensitive of traps ignored her presence.

Because she had used the mudswifts in the walls of Mahara's house before, it was easy to find a mount and take the bird up to the carved ivory screens that blocked the outlet of the duct.

The wards were quiescent, the room empty, filled with shadowy darkness. Night still lingered over Kale though dawn was near enough to rouse the swifts. Mahara usually worked during these dawn watches before the midday heat in Aile Kuvvet sucked the energy from everything including him.

Hudoleth moved from swift to swift until she looked through the pierced ivory into Mahara's bedroom. He lay on his stomach with the corner of a rumpled sheet pulled across his body, wearing only a tracery of blue lines on his mahogany flesh. His breath came even and slow and he smiled as he slept, contented about something.

She dismounted and returned her consciousness to her own workroom. Annoying. So much time lost to the whims of the Emperor and the necessities of her teaching schedule. Without such constraints Mahara would be using these days to the last flicker of the time candle. She hated him more intensely at that moment than she'd ever hated anyone.

A restlessness seized her as she looked at the apple going brown on the plate and the tea gone tepid in the cup. There were thing she had to do and none could be done here. So much flux in the Pneuma Flow would start noses twitching in every corner of the University. She knew her colleagues all too well. They raised snooping to a fine art.

She touched her hair. Still wet. It'd pick up dust until it was stiff as plaster. At least the stink of the Palace was off her, though she'd have to wash again when she returned. She pushed the chair back, got to her feet and went to get ready.

[3]

Ugly as a pimple on a courtesan's face, a nameless volcanic island rose near the southern shore of Lake Mizukor. Hudoleth ran her boat up onto the coarse black sand of the only beach, tied the bow rope to a bronze ring set into an upthrust of basalt.

Shifting the straps of her backpack and settling it more comfortably, she began the long difficult climb up the narrow path to the rim of the cone, muttering imprecations under her breath and envying the Iomardi Walkers their ability to step from world to world and back again, covering vast distances with a pair of short strides.

At the rim she had long ago fashioned a working floor, basalt polished flat with inlaid pentagrams of silver wire. It had been months since she'd been here and the place was fouled with bird waste and windborne grit, but she'd expected that and prepared for it. She broke a spelled egg and a few gallons of seawater came crashing across the floor, washing the debris into the cone, flashing to steam as it struck the lava far below.

She dropped a cushion into one of the pentagrams, then stripped and spread cream on her face and body against the ravages of the sun. From the backpack she took an ivory tube removed the wax stopple and upended it. What looked like several tangles of silver wires fell on her knees, but when she shook the biggest tangle it became a long tunic made from silver symbols bonded together by tiny silver links. She stood, smoothed it down, wincing as the sun began to heat the metal. She unrolled wide filigree bracelets and clasped them about her arms and slipped on the power rings, and last of all, smoothed and spread the filigree silver fan. Her power suit, she called this. It did for her what Mahara's tattoos and Oerfel's paint did for them.

Cautiously she settled herself on the cushion, the silver tunic falling like a tent around her.

Her narrow hands swaying in the air before her, turning and twisting the fan so that it caught the sunlight and danced reflections off the stone around her, she chanted a wordless song that changed imperceptibly into the old tongue of Chusinkayan, the tongue before time.

"Oda, Akuma," she sang, her rich soprano filling the crater before her.

"Oda Akuma mai yapuur." Command in the words, the fan held level, slicing through the heat waves rising from the black stone.

"Ida shi anata shi." One hand beckoning, the other holding the fan upright before her face.

"Ida shibar wijiti." Her voice grew louder; the power that rose to fill her also filled the words. The fan danced through a flat figure eight, the other hand twisted and turned through a series of gestures.

> *Anata yi ida hanuur,*
> *Anata kai kus ida shuur.*

As the last words hung in the air, a shimmer formed in the second pentagram but did not solidify until Hudoleth uttered the final command.

"Doë rhu Alaeshin!"

The shimmer bulged and warped, went through a final convulsion. A winged bull's body with a horned but human head and a broad, heavily muscled human torso stood in the heart of the second pentagram. This was the Alaeshin, the Messenger of the god Kamkajar, worshiped by the nomad tribes of North Nikawaid, the Grass Clans who roamed the vast, cold prairies spread across the top of Nordomon. Or rather, it was a demon forced to assume the outer appearance of an Alaeshin.

"I am. What else do you require, O Mage?" The false Alaeshin's voice was a basso grate, as if the rocks he stood on were speaking for him.

"You are to appear first to the shamans then to the chiefs of these Grass Clans. The Dmar Spyonk. The Nagar Burrik. The Snop Kra. The Ser Turuk. You are to say to them that they have been chosen by He Who Walks in Fire to punish the sins of the corrupt. You are to say to them that they are to ride round the fingers of the Kush Kurum mountains and by sword and fire bring all souls there into the service of God. You will say these words to each shaman and each chief three times. You will speak them and leave. Three days later, you will return and speak again. Three days after that, you will say to them a final time. When you have said the last word to the last chief, then you are dismissed to your own place and free of further requirements. This I require of you, O Akuma."

"And so shall it be."

"Ja-DA!"

The instant she spoke the release syllables, the false Alaeshin vanished.

She lifted her head and laughed aloud. "Ah Oi! Mahara, I too can hone an army. We shall see. Oh yes, we shall."

OERFEL OF NYDDYS

[1]

Anrydd Barbranson gan Lusor.

   Mother: Prydda, daughter of Ymborth, the wealthiest of the Tys merchants.

Official father: the Cyngrath Barbran Canithson gan Lusor ɔm the Broony of Lusor.

Actual father: according to well-established rumor, the Four-ɛnth Tyrn, Dengyn Tyrn Feallson.

Current residence: Barbran's suite within the walls of the ɪrcalon—there are two other sons and a daughter residing with ɩn.

Oerfel looked at what he'd written, rolled the sheet of paper to a spill and tapped it against his chin. I have to get closer, he ɔught. I have to learn the ins and outs of the boy.

He looked around him at his workroom, at the shadows danc-g on the walls, cast by flickering candle flames in the lamps he'd ɪng with his own hands, at the silver lines of the hexagrams, ɪlled and quiescent now but still producing a glimmer or two response to the light, at the half-seen cabinets and compart-ents filled with jars and boxes, bundles and scrolls. This was ɪs home far more than the room where he slept. He had every-ing he needed close to hand. Moving away from here was going make life much harder for him. But at the moment he had no ɪoice.

He pushed the Daybook aside and ran a soft cloth across the ɪce of a scrying mirror, then tuned it to Brownt Oedranson, the ɪrrent Secretary to the Cyngrath in Carcalon. Oerfel's mouth ɪrled into a tight smile as he saw the skinny old man splashing ɪter over his face and blinking bleary eyes while behind him a ɪoman yawned and turned over in a rumpled bed. Oedranson ɪd a weakness for slatternly whores expert with small whips and ɪe kind of paddles that headmasters used on unruly boys, a ɪste he had to keep very quiet about, or the scandal would blow ɪm from his office. Not having a mistress, but the kind of woman ɪ favored.

The room was on the top floor in one of the tenements on the ɪuth side of the bothrin, twenty minutes' ride from the east gate ɪ Carcalon. Oedranson kept a roster of guards bribed to let him

in and out of the wicket without reporting his wanderings, b**[**
he wasn't going to make it back this night. Oerfel watched hi**[**
toss a small money pouch onto the bed, push the door open ar**[**
go out, his riding boots in his hand, his feet shod in felt slipper**[**

The stairs went round and round an unroofed airwell at th**[**
center of the building, lit only by the moon and starlight. Th**[**
railings were in fair shape, though polished dark by the hands **[**
countless men leaving bedrooms and going swift and silent dow**[**
the steps. Oedranson's pale pink tongue fluttered between h**[**
lips. He blinked then slapped his own face with his free hand, tr**[**
ing to jar himself into sufficient wakefulness to get down tho**[**
stairs and into the stables where his horse should be waiting f**[**
him, saddled by the ostler the Directress hired to take care of suc**[**
things.

.He reached for the railing.

Oerfel whispered a word.

Oedranson's hand passed through the wood as if it were on**[**
a bar of shadow.

Oerfel whispered again.

An invisible fist thumped against Oedranson's back and h**[**
toppled headfirst into the airwell.

He screamed all the way down, but Oerfel blanked the mirr**[**
before he hit. He wanted no taint of magic when the Tyrn's me**[**
came to claim the body and stifle the scandal.

It was begun. Tomorrow he'd be offered the position, Brog**[**
would see to that, and by the end of the week he would be Se**[**
retary to the Cyngrath and installed in Oedranson's suite in th**[**
Grath Tower at Carcalon.

He closed his eyes. His head was starting to throb again. H**[**
knew why. From this moment on, he'd have no rest. Everythin**[**
was planned but he knew how delicate such schemes were. **[**
breath of air could shatter them. He would have to keep adjus**[**
ing the flow of events, fiddling with this, fiddling with that, a**[**
ways watching.

Which reminded him. That boy. Saretal's son.

I don't dare let him grow up. The forces protecting him will rengthen with every year he finishes alive. The whirlstorm lissed him. That's twice. No more storms. What now? Get him It of those mountains and here in the city. The Watcher . . . llar Yliarson . . . a poet . . . hm . . . once I'm settled in as Secretry to the Cyngrath, I can start a fad for his work. Yes. Dengyn yrn pretends to culture. A Festival of Poesy with Yliarson and few others specially summoned to the Presence. His daughter a child and he doesn't seem to have a wife, so he won't leave er on the mountain alone. The boy either. And once they're ere . . .

He wiped the mirror again, slipped it into its padded case and ut it in his pocket. After sitting a moment, head in hands, he ose from the worktable and moved about the room, gathering ems he expected to need in the next several weeks as he estabshed himself at Court and began to spin the web of influence e'd need to keep himself safe and start the long process of shap-ng his pseudo-Hero.

His head was throbbing, the migraine well established, but he idn't dare chew any bindroot until he'd sealed off this space and as on his way back to his room. He was incapable of concen-ration and focusing at the moment, but the spell was in place, ll it needed was the triggering phrase. He snuffed all the can-les carefully, took each from its holder and laid it on the stone loor. Even if some faint stray coal eluded him, stone wouldn't urn.

One by one the lights went out until all that was left was the aint glow from his dark lantern. He slid the handle of the bas-et over his arm, lifted the lantern from the table and went slowly rom the room. Once he was outside, he whispered the trigger-ng syllables.

The door vanished. All that was left to the eye and to the ouch were the stones of a wall.

He touched the pseudostones with the tips of his fingers an for a moment felt bereft, then he shut the slide of the dar lantern till only a thread of light came out and he went gropin along the corridor, passing the dusty crypts, hearing the scuttl and chitter of the vermin in the walls.

History and a Journey

By the secret calendar of the Watchers, events beginning on the 30th of Pedarmis, the fourth month in the 736th Glandairic year since the last Settling.

[1]

Cymel loosed her grip on the Otherplace and let the Pocket collapse, turned with a grin to Lyanzy who lay with his face in the leaves, his body shuddering. His misery hit her like a slap in the face. For a breath or two she didn't understand, then she realized that the storm sounds had taken him back and he was losing his father all over again.

She wanted to do something, but she couldn't think what, so she got to her feet and looked at the mess the storm had left because she didn't want to look at Lyanz.

The whirlstorm had unraveled and the air was very calm and quiet. No birds were flying and the small furries were in their burrows too frightened yet to go back to their usual scratchings and gnawings. There were trees down all around the stream, though none had fallen into the durbaba pool.

The adult durbabas were coming out of their hiding places; the children were still tucked away. As she watched, one of the little ones darted past a female and did a tail-switching dance out in the middle of the roily pool. Cymel laughed aloud at the agile little swimmer—then she remembered Lyanz and felt guilty for being happy.

Then irritated. Why not enjoy being alive? She'd just kicked a Mage in the face, hadn't she? Let Breith brag how he wanted, *he* hadn't faced down a Mage and made him eat his ol' big wind.

She brushed herself off, bent down and put her hand on Lyanz's shoulder. "Come on. We better get back to the house and behind the wards. I dunno what's going to happen next."

"Go 'way and lea' me alone. Don't need you. Don't need anyone."

"Be like that."

Angry and hurt, she marched off down the path. She'd saved his stupid life, that's all.

Halfway down the slope, as she put her hand on the trunk of a conifer ripped from the ground and flung down across the path, meaning to vault herself over it, Pneuma caught in the wood nipped at her. Residue from the whirlstorm. Weariness dropped over her suddenly, so heavy a load she was almost sick with it. She looked up. The sky was a roil of currents and curds, like being inside something's stomach and watching half-eaten food churning away. She pressed her hand to her mouth and hurried on. It was hard to breathe and the pressure was making her head hurt.

Something caught at her ankles and she fell flat.

When she pushed herself up she heard twin high-pitched giggles and saw the little god Mouse and the mantis-bug god bouncing in the air in front of her face, pointing their skinny fingers at her and laughing at her. She swatted at them, missed and fell over again. They swung in a wild sort of circle dance above her and made her so mad that without thinking about it, she mindslapped at the little gods, then crouched on her knees, startled as they went squealing away, ki-yipping like dogs that had been whipped.

She got wearily to her feet and trudged down the slope. Tears flooded her eyes and she gulped and snuffled as she walked, not because she was still scared from the storm and not because Lyanz was such a gudge, but because seeing that pair of little gods reminded her again of Cyswe and Noswe and she missed them even more than she usually did.

[2]

Lyanz reached the house in time to see Cymel go dragging up the stairs. Hand on the wall to steady himself, cursing the weakness he'd felt since Cymel and that aunt of hers had pulled him from the storm, he lurched along the hallway to the small room Ellar Yliarson had set up for him.

It was humiliating to be rescued over and over by a girl four years younger than him. Cymel was a good kid, but she was spoiled worse than his sisters and fell into snits twice as fast when he didn't keep feeding gratitude to her as if he were holding the bottle for a nursing kid.

He pulled his boots off and stretched out on the narrow bed, lay staring at the ceiling, his hands clasped beneath his head. He was angry and full of grief. His father had started to like him and now that was all lost. The thing he wanted most he'd never get— his father telling him how proud he was that Lyanz was his son and Heir. Couldn't happen. His father was dead.

This miserable wart of a house. He hated it.

These people, they were nothings. Poor, not even a house-keeper. Cymel did most of the cleaning and cooking and she got mad if he didn't help. And got mad when he did because he did things all wrong. Why should he know how to peel some stupid tuber? That's what servants were for.

He wanted to go home.

He wanted his mother and his sisters and his cousins and the rest of the people who had been around him all of his life, and he forgot how lonely and restless he'd been since his brother left the house. He wanted his horses and his rooms and his city where even in summer it didn't get so cold at night that he froze if he kicked his blankets off. He wanted to be in a place where his head didn't hurt all the time from trying to figure out what people were saying and then having to dig for words to answer them. He wanted to hear the rapid, slurry Nikawarish that was like silk to his ears.

He wanted his father back.

He wanted him not to be dead.

The horror of that night came back to him again and, for the first time since he'd waked in this place, he cried over his father's death—cried himself to sleep.

[3]

When Cymel woke, the sky had settled and the shadows were long outside, the sun low in the west. Her eyes were gummy but most of her headache was gone. She lay in the bed stretching and yawning until tickles running along her legs drove her from under the covers and onto her feet. She had work to do. And better to do it than lie around feeling sorry for herself.

On her way to the kitchen Cymel looked in on Lyanz. He was curled into a knot, sleeping heavily. She chewed her lip a moment, but shut the door carefully so she wouldn't wake him. Pa wanted him taught to do chores, but she was just as happy he wouldn't be around when she started getting ready for supper. He complained all the time, got in her way and never did anything right. It was hard to see how anyone could mess up peeling tubers, but he'd managed it, leaving more tuber on the peel than he ended up with in the pot.

She fetched wood from the box in the pantry, opened the oven's firebox and made up the fire again. She fetched the tray of rolls she'd left in the coolhole and set them out to do a last bit of rising while she waited for the oven to heat up enough. After that she moved the crock of stew from the hotsand where it had been cooking slowly since morning, lifted the lid and gave the rich ubbly stew a good stir, then settled it on a cookplate to finish off while she went out back to the garden to fetch greens for a salad.

As soon as she stepped through the kitchen door, she saw wilted plants thrown everywhere and heard a little god giggling. It was sitting on a fence post making faces at her, not Mouse or its mantis friend, but another one. This one was bigger, almost the size of a cat. "Pest!" She picked up a plant stake, threw it at it and thought about mind-slapping again, but decided she'd better not. She suspected Mouse and the mantis god had rushed off to their big brother or whatever it was and the little god was here to make her sorry she'd done it.

There wasn't much left in the garden, just a few onions and some lyt-leaf still fresh enough to be usable. She dropped these in her basket, stuck her tongue out at the little god and went back into the house.

She was just shutting the oven on the tray of rolls when she heard movement in the front of the house and her father talking to someone. She checked the stew, then ran along the hall.

"Pa, did you see the whirlstorm? It came right at us, but I played Hide the Mouse with Lyanz and it—Little Noll, I didn't know you were coming!"

Noll grinned at her, cupped his hands and pulled them out away from his face, signing that his smile was as big as the reach of his arms because he was so glad to see her. She always forgot he was mute, but it didn't matter anyway because he didn't need words to say what he wanted people to know.

He was half a head shorter than she was but something like three times as wide, with massive shoulders and powerful arms. His legs were shorter than his arms and bowed so that he swayed back and forth like a kick'em toy when he walked, but he could ride anything with four legs on it and mesmerize bird or beast into purring contentment. Even the little gods seemed to like him and they didn't like anybody.

Ellar hung his cloak on the peg and gave Cymel a hard hug "Yes, I saw the storm. Where's Lyanz?"

"Sleeping. He was upset."

"Leaving you to do all the work, if my nose is telling me right The bread smells good, little cook."

"Oh! I'd better . . ." She freed herself and ran back to the kitchen.

Ellar and Little Noll followed her and came in while she was shifting the tray to a slightly cooler level. She eased the oven door shut and turned the latch, glanced at Noll, then looked into the stew pot. The stew needed stretching. She put the lid back on the pot, went into the pantry and down the short ladder to the coolhole. Behind her she heard the creak of the pump handle and the gush of water, then her father's voice came muffled through the door.

"Mela, while you're in there, bring out one of the crocks of cider. It's been a long, thirsty ride."

Whistling breathily a happy little tune, Cymel tumbled half a dozen tubers into a small handbasket, crooked a finger through the handle on a jug of cider and hurried up the ladder to the kitchen. It was so good to have her father back again.

Ellar was standing at the sink washing the greens for the salad. "Little gods back, hm?"

"Was a new one." She sniffed, unlatched the oven door and checked the rolls. "Done done done." She took a pair of potholders, brought the tray out and dumped the rolls on the cooling rack. Then she went to the table, pried the waxed stopper from the neck of the jug and filled the glasses her father had left on the table. "Big as a cat."

"Hm. Might not be all that new, Mela. Soon now they're all going to start growing bigger."

"Mouse hasn't." She piled the tubers on the table and went to the block for the paring knife so she could peel them; she meant to quarter them and pop them into the stew. "It and the Bug, they messed with me when I was coming down the mountain. They were the same size as always."

"Mela, when you get a moment, I'd like you to write all you can remember about Mouse, Mantis and the new one. We don't have enough history on the little gods."

Noll tapped her wrist, took the paring knife from her and picked up one of the tubers. When she protested, he shook his head and started peeling, his short clever fingers revolving the tuber and using the blade to spin off a long coil of skin.

Cymel giggled, got another knife and sat beside him, whittling her way round another tuber. "All right, Pa. I'll do it after supper. Did you find out what you wanted at University?"

"I think so. Leave the rest of those to Noll, Mela, and go wake Lyanz. I need to talk to him."

When Cymel brought Lyanz into the back parlor, her father was sitting at the writing table with Little Noll's saddlebags by his elbow. Little Noll was perched on the window seat, his short legs crossed on the cushion, his hands resting on his knees, the sunset pinking one side of his face, the other side lost in shadow. It was still light outside, though it wouldn't be much longer. The windows were braced open, with extra wedges to hold them against the strengthening wind.

Ellar stood. "Lyanz, if you'll come sit here. There are some things I have to tell you."

"Pa, is this going to take long? Because if it is, I'd better go shift the stew to the hotsand." Cymel said this, hoping he wouldn't just dismiss her.

"We'll wait," Ellar said. "You need to hear this too."

When she got back, Cymel shoved a hassock over by Little Noll, perched on it, her eyes shifting from her father's face to Lyanz's and back.

"We went to Cyfareth to fetch this." Ellar untied the thongs and laid back the flap of the saddlebag. He took a small flat drum from the bag and set it on the table between him and Lyanz. "It's called a Chaos Drum. It's very old and very precious. Perhaps the oldest made thing on all of Glandair."

The little drum had been painted at one time, but the colors had faded and only a ghost of the design was left. It looked like old bones dug out of the earth, like dead leaves from a year long gone. As soon as he'd taken it from the bag it began humming and buzzing. Ellar watched a moment, turned his head. "You see, Noll? Already."

Cymel shivered. The power in that thing made her skin crawl.

Lyanz scowled at the drum. "So? What mean that to me?"

"I want you to take it. Hold it. Just for a moment."

"Why?"

"I'll explain later. Please."

As soon as Lyanz touched the drum, the buzzing turned to a steady throbbing like the beating of his heart. He almost dropped it. "Alive."

"In a way perhaps it is." Ellar took the drum from him and put it back in the saddlebag, slowly, methodically retying the thongs. "There are drums like this in many hands, but as I said, this is the oldest, the pattern for those others. They only come awake during the Settling and they only speak when touched by a Candidate."

"Me? Thanks for honor, not interested. I want go home. I ask you find out ships to Nikawaid. Well?"

"There are no ships bound for Nikawaid in Tyst harbor and even if there were, any ship you set foot on will be sunk as fast or faster than the *Kisa Sambai*. You were supposed to drown when she went down. The Mage who sent that storm also sent the whirlstorm this afternoon. The one that nearly killed my daughter along with you."

Lyanz went a greenish-cream color, clutched at the arms of the chair. "My father . . ."

"You can't go home, Lyanz. As soon as you're away from land, either the Nyddys Mage or Mahara will sink the ship. Even if you escaped them and made it back to Nishamin, the Mage Hudoleth would burn your house down to get you, kill everyone around you to get you."

"No! You lie. Why you say these things? I don't believe." Lyanz jumped to his feet, struck at the saddlebag, knocking it onto the floor. "No! You play games on my head. It is you make drum act like that. Why?" He rushed to the door, reached for the latch. Lightning leaped from it and stung his hand. He turned and ran the length of the room to stand staring out one of the windows as he fought to control himself.

Ellar got to his feet, picked up the saddlebag and set it on the table. He returned to his chair and waited, hands folded, face impassive.

After several minutes, Lyanz trudged back. His face was drawn with the weariness that kept overtaking him since Corysiam Bridged him from the sea. "Why me? I have no gifts. Maybe a . . . shom . . . um a . . . a craft . . . a way of seeing behind charms and spells. My father . . . my father say it stupid trick, no use but to make fool of me." He sighed, lifted shaking hands and pressed them against his eyes.

"That's one thing I can't tell you, Lyanz. Why you—or why any of the other Candidates are chosen. The drum doesn't choose either, it only points out Candidates and announces the coming of the Settling Chaos. That's why it's called the Chaos Drum."

Lyanz lifted his head. "Others?"

"Yes." Ellar contemplated the backs of his hands for several minutes. The quiet room was filled with the rustle of leaves, small scratchings and clucks from the chickens, a blat from a distant calf and other noises from the farm animals. Finally he lifted his head and started speaking, his voice grave and serious, his words coming slowly so Lyanz would be able to understand what he was saying.

"Two Candidates managed to reach Sanctuary in Chusinkayan. And three are here on Nyddys. Not counting you. Two from Nyddys. And one from Tilkos who managed somehow to escape the notice of the Mage Mahara, probably because he was busy elsewhere. Mahara has sent at least ten ships to the bottom of the Halsianel Sea and has arranged the deaths of something like thirty boys in Kale along with the Watchers who were with them."

"Why!" The word was a drawn-out wail.

"Because one of the Candidates will be the Hero and these Mages want what the Hero will have. To explain that, listen. There are two worlds, Iomard and Glandair. I expect Cymel has told you about Iomard. Between these worlds there is a . . . well, call it a membrane . . . whose thickness changes. It's like ice over a pond, thin in autumn, thick in winter, though it's never completely gone. About every seven hundred years the two worlds come very very close till in a way they're both in the same place. The Flow begins and gets stronger and more chaotic every day. The Flow is magic, Lyanz. Iomardi magic comes to us, Glandair's magic crosses to them. We Watchers call this the Settling. It's a strange time. The little gods grow bigger and turn mean; they don't just play tricks, they try to hurt and maim. The Great Gods walk the earth. There are storms and earthquakes, volcanoes are born and spout rivers of molten stone, cracks open in the ground and swallow whole cities. Oceans rise, lakes go dry. The folk of each world can see the others like ghosts wandering across their land and ordinary people who don't watch where they walk can take a wrong step and find themselves lost on a world that's nothing like their own. Siofray come here, Dyar go over there. Mages and sorcerers, witches and wizards, even hedge magicians who can barely glamour a copper coin to silver, they all grow more powerful. The more they have, the more they want.

"The Hero is the one who will return order to both worlds, who will draw into himself the magic of Iomard and the magic of Glandair. For a while, he will be more powerful than the gods.

More powerful, Lyanz, than Marath Alaesh and all his Messengers, more powerful than Dyf Tanew here. When the Chaos Drums start speaking, we Watchers hunt you Hero Candidates out and try to get you to Sanctuary before the Mages kill you all, because they intend to take the Hero's place and receive the Hero's gift."

Lyanz stared at the saddlebag, his face pinched.

Cymel watched him and was glad she was a girl. She'd picked up some of what her father had said from the reports he wrote in his Daybook and his arguments with Corysiam, but she'd never had it all together like this. Storms and volcanoes and the earth cracking were frightening, but she couldn't get all that worked up about them since she'd lived through storms and had never seen the other things. The little gods getting bigger and meaner, though—that was the really bad news.

She glanced at the dark fireplace, remembering the Iomardi Mage who'd called to her over two years ago. She wrinkled her nose and thought about Breith instead. He hadn't said much lately because they were arguing, and then there was the storm, but maybe that Mage over there would go after him like the one here was after Lyanz. She chewed on her lip, wanting to look over to Iomard and make sure Breith was all right. She didn't know if she could, however. Even though the sky had settled down and the flows weren't so knotty, she was afraid to try it. A thought struck her. "Pa, what about Breith? Could he be a Candidate too? Will that Mage you-know-who try to kill him?"

"No, Mela. The Hero is always Dyar, not Siofray. It's just the way it is. Breith will be fine. He's got his family to look after him."

Cymel got to her feet. "Well, I'd better go see about supper. Don't be much longer, will you?"

In the kitchen she shifted the stew back onto the heat. The pieces of tuber were still hard so that they would have to cook a while. She touched the rolls. They were stone-cold. Too bad. They'd have to eat them that way.

She wrinkled her nose at the limp greens her father had left in the sink. No good for a salad. Maybe if she cooked them fast with a bit of fatback Pa had traded from Dyrys the time he'd butchered a hog. Cymel bustled about, trying to get the meal together and wondering what was going to happen next.

[4]

Little Noll came back two weeks later with letters from Cyfareth too important to trust to birds.

Cymel was tired and bad tempered. Breith was ignoring her and Lyanz had gone beyond gudge and was almost as nasty as that little god who seemed be living on the fence to the kitchen garden. And her father's body walked around the house, but his mind was a dozen other places; he ate when she put food in front of him and she thought he got some sleep, but mostly he was up in the Watch tower where she wasn't supposed to go.

He came down when Noll got there and went into the back parlor to talk to him.

Ellar opened the kitchen door and stepped in. "Mela, where's Lyanz?"

"In his room, I think. Sleeping probably."

"Bring him to the parlor, will you? And I'd like you there too."

"All right, Pa."

Lyanz wasn't sleeping. He was sitting on a stool and leaning into the room's single window, staring out at the oak grove behind the house.

"Lyanz."

"What?" He didn't bother looking at her.

"Get up off your snit and come to the parlor. Pa and Little Noll want to talk to you."

"I don't want to talk to them."

"Who cares what a gudge in a snit wants? Pa said bring you

and bring you I'm gonna." She shoved the door hard enough to make it bounce off the wall and marched into the room.

He was up, kicking the stool away, and out of the room before she reached him, leaving her standing like a fool with her hand out.

"Tsah! His mum should've . . ." She sucked in a breath, let it out and followed him.

"Lyanz, my colleagues at Cyfareth have been working out how best to keep you alive and get you to Sanctuary at the Vale of Caeffordian. It won't be all that bad. You'll have the other boys for company and teachers to help you prepare for what's coming. And lessons in sword and bow and hand work. Arrangements have—"

Little Noll leaned forward, snapped his fingers to get Ellar's attention. *Someone coming,* he signed.

A moment later Cymel heard the sound of hooves on the rutted lane that led to the house; the sounds stopped, then there was a tantara from a horn.

Ellar got to his feet. "That's a Tyrn Messenger. I wonder . . . Wait here, all of you. I have to go see what he wants."

Cymel heard her father's voice, a pause, then the sound of hooves again as the Messenger rode off, and moments later the sound of her father's feet in the hallway. He was walking slowly, as if the Messenger had given him something that troubled him.

When he came into the back parlor, he was holding a packet made from a sheet of parchment folded in half then folded in thirds with a red blob of wax holding the ends together, a large seal pressed into the center of the blob.

He set the packet on the desk, took the glass chimney from the lamp and turned up the wick. A snap of his fingers fired the wick. As soon as it had stopped smoking he replaced the chimney. Then he broke the seal and read what was written on the inside of the packet. He clicked his tongue and shook his head. "This makes a problem. Mela . . ."

"Pa?"

He dropped the parchment on the table and frowned at her. "I don't want to take you to the Tyrn's Court. The brood that swarms there is corrupt in ways I hope you'll never know. Vicious tongues. If I weren't sworn to Watch, I'd sweep that sty clean." He passed a hand over his mouth, shook his head. "Just as well I wasn't born to be a Mage."

Cymel brushed aside all that and got to what was worrying her. "Why do you have to go, Pa? Is it trouble?"

"No trouble, Mela. Someone has talked the Tyrn into having a Festival of Words at Court a day or two before Foolsreign begins and he's summoning poets from all over Nyddys, me being one of them. And even if this is worded as an invitation, Mela, when the Tyrn calls, all you can do is saddle up and go." He picked up the parchment again, held it closer to the lamp. "We'll be traveling in comfort at least. The Tyrn Barge will be at the landing at Cesayl on the 23 Pumamis and I should be prepared to be on it with such of my household as I mean to bring with me. Four cabins are reserved for me. 'All expenses will be paid from the Tyrn's Purse.'"

His face creased with worry, he let the sheet fall again and turned to Lyanz. "This is about you, Lyanz. Dengyn Tyrn is far more interested in the chase and killing things than the skillful turn of a phrase. Joke at Cyfareth is that he'd outrun a stallion in rut to escape a recitation." He took off his glasses, pressed thumb and forefinger against the inner corners of his eyes.

"Pa, you think it's the Mage again?"

"Mela, yes, I do. He has missed Laz twice with his storms, now he's going to be setting up something else."

Cymel rubbed at her nose. "Pa, why don't you call Aunt Corysiam and have her take Laz over to Iomard to visit Breith? The Mage couldn't get at him there, could he? She said Dyar magic couldn't get through the Veil and she already Bridged him through Iomard to get him here, so it shouldn't be all that hard."

Lyanz slapped his palm on the chair arm. "Toh! Don't talk about me like I not in the room. If your aunt take me from sea to here, why she not just take me home? No ships to sink that way. Then family hire our own wizards and let the Mage try breaking through wards."

Ellar gave Cymel an angry glance. She could tell he wished she hadn't opened her mouth. "It sounds simple, but it's impossible. When you get a good look at answers that seem sweet and easy, you'll generally find that things you need to know are being ignored or left out." He tapped his fingers on the table, his eyes half closed as he thought over what he wanted to say.

Cymel straightened her legs, massaged her knees. Her father's way of slowing conversation down because he was turning over every word in his head before he let it out of his mouth sometimes irritated her so much she sputtered when she spoke. She refolded her legs and waited to be told why she was wrong.

"You didn't know what you were doing when you forced that Bridge, Cymel. Once Corysiam knows Laz is a Candidate, she won't Bridge him again. You see, until one becomes the Hero, every Candidate's life force is bound up with Glandair. If the break with Glandair hadn't been so short, Laz might have died." Ellar turned to Lyanz. "Consider how you felt when you woke, Candidate, and how you've felt since."

Lyanz shivered. "Get better?"

"Yes. You should be back as you were in a month or so. If I can keep you alive that long. Noll."

Little Noll sat up, looked alert.

"Cyfareth's arrangements are no good now. Timing's wrong. Lyanz will have to come with us to Carcalon. I'll be tied in knots of protocol and won't be able to keep any kind of watch on him there, and leaving him here would be like staking him out for wolf bait. I want you to take Prifolt and pony Dawnsy so you can switch horses and ride without stopping to Cyfareth. Tell Alder Mechin the problem, ask him to send Diawad and Cadarn to Carcalon, not here."

"Pa . . ."

"Yes, I'll take your help too, Mela. But your training has just begun. Experience is also important. And one of the things you need to know is how to blend so that the whole is greater than the individual strengths. You've started that with Corysiam . . . hm . . . if I could trust her, I'd ask her to come and stay with you, just take Laz with me. She's been trying to get you away from me since the day your mother died. Never mind. That has nothing to do with the problem."

He reached for a sheet of paper, dipped a pen in the ink bottle and started writing. "This is a note to Dyrys. I'd like him to watch the farm while we're gone, send a farmhand up to milk the cows and feed the stock. I want you to go that far with Little Noll, Mela. Have Dyrys lend you a pony for the ride back. He can pick it up later. Then we'll have to pack. There's just enough time to get ready before we have to be at the Barge Landing."

[5]

Lyanz could feel Cymel's eyes on him as he leaned on the rail near the front of the sailbarge. He watched the dirty brown water of the dredged area near the wharf at Cesayl pile up and curl round the bow and felt the wind called up by the Weatherwoman teasing the hair at his neck. She was going to cling to him like a starved tick until this visit was over and that thought made him itch all over.

The barge was the biggest boat on the river, longer by half than the *Kisa Sambai*, though its stubby masts made it look like a dwarf to Lyanz. It was shallow draft too, not much space under the double line of cabins. Ellar had the first cabin on the port side, Lyanz's was next, then Cymel.

Across from Ellar there was a poet from Dadeny in the north, lanner Corbswyf. Ellar said she wrote bloody epics and battle les. On the ride down from the farm, he'd passed some of the me telling them about the other poets summoned to the Feast f Words.

Across from Lyanz was a short, broad man with a bald head nd copper-colored moustaches that he kept waxed and twisted p like the horns on one of the Kurrin silkgoats. Kennig Goerayson. He wrote murmurous pastorals and religious poems.

Across from Cymel was one Chwant Fyffson, a little brown ian with squinty eyes and a turned-down mouth that looked as our as if he'd been drinking vinegar. He wrote rollicking lumerjack and sailor songs.

The next room down was a dining room that took the whole dth of the barge. Beyond that were six more cabins, but these ere empty. Ellar was the only one who'd brought family with im.

With the Weatherwoman keeping the sails filled, the barge egan gathering speed, gliding along with a kind of ponderous cceleration that sent the much smaller fishboats and peddlers' raft scurrying out of the way. He grinned as a sail skiff no biger than a flea ignored the horn and hauled its net in just in time glide out of the barge's path, the two fishermen making curse igns at the crewmen yelling down at them.

After they rounded the first bend and left the village behind, he river traffic cleared away and Lyanz watched the countryside istead. It was very different from the land around Nishamin. The ountains were jagged and bony, with patches of white wedged among the black peaks. Despite what these people called a rought, the fields and slopes were lushly green in a way that outh Nikawaid never achieved, even in the wettest days of early pring. The sky seemed closer too. This was an intimate kind of nd; it closed in around you and you could never see for very far any direction.

Deceptive too, he thought. A puppy with poison fangs. Win-

ter. He shivered. He didn't like being cold and suspected he w:
going to be very cold indeed if he managed to survive till wint
and snowfall. He'd never even seen snow until this trip and as f;
as he was concerned he would just as soon give the experience
pass.

Four more days till Carcalon. Those were Carcalon's silv
roofs he'd seen flaring in the sunlight when the *Kisa Sambe*
came through the harbor at Tyst. He thought about Gryf an
wondered if he could manage a visit. Maybe if Cymel came alor
and those two shiks from what was it . . . ah . . . Cyfareth. Ho
Alaesh! I hate this.

[6]

Cymel bent forward to blow the lamp out, but she straightene
again when she felt the scratchy sensation that meant Breith w:
about to make the talking window.

"Mela, where are you?"

She hopped onto the gimballed bed and pulled a quilt aroun
her shoulders as the bed rocked gently under her. "Travelin
Tyrn's Barge." She thought a moment of all the things she coul
say and decided they needed more explanation than she wante
to bother with. "Pa's going to read his poems at a Festival. Yc
all right? You been gone a long time."

"I couldn't do spit for day on day on day, couldn't even go ou
side the walls till I was about ready to chew my way out I was s
bored. And Da was working me all the time, taking me throug
control exercises till my head was spinning, and Mum took ov
when he got tired. And when I wasn't doing magic, this Scrit
girl was giving me lumps teaching me how to fight barehand."

"How come?"

"Like I started to tell you, there's this cousin I didn't know
had. Who I wish I didn't have. . . ." He went on to tell what ha
happened from the time when he felt the whip cut on his shou
der.

"Wow, that's weird, Breith. You really mean she wants to steal ou away from your folks, clip you and make you spend the rest f your life with a chain round your leg?"

"That's what Mum and Mam and Da all said. And Amhar too. er grandmother ran off from the Domains, so she knows what ney're like."

"Well, what's she like?"

"Two, three years older than me, a whole head taller and a ton eaner." He rubbed at his forearm, made a face. "And fast. Vhoo! So what was that storm about?"

"The Nyddys Mage was trying to kill Lyanz. Because Laz is omething called a Candidate." She scrunched up her face. Looks like I'm going to be stuck minding him."

"Last time you seemed to think he was the cream on your erries."

"Did not!" Cymel sniffed. "He's a lazy snob. Turns up his nose t the way we live and is useless at doing any kind of work. You oing back to school?"

"Mam says yes. Mum doesn't say anything and that kinda wor- es me. Did I tell you about Mum's Gift?"

"Nuh-uh." Cymel swallowed a yawn. It had been a long day and ne was tired, but she didn't want Breith to go; even if he always nded up making her mad at him, he was her friend, just about ne only one she had.

"Well, when Mum has one of her spells, she sees the might- e. You know, like three, four paths that are what's going to hap- en next week or next year. Sometimes even four or five years n. The spells don't come all that often, but so far as I know, she's ever been wrong. Sometimes she won't say what she sees, be- ause she's afraid she'll change things too much and make bad hings happen. Which makes me kind of nervous."

"But you don't know if she had a spell. Maybe she didn't."

"I can tell, Cym. The air turns funny around her. Like heat rip- les. Anyway, I'm supposed to go back to school day after to-

morrow." He made a face. "It's all about learning how to figh
and make nice so I can get some girl who wants a Seyl mate t
pick me."

Cymel giggled. "Charm school for boys? Here it's girls who g
to those. Pa keeps threatening to put me in one if I don't lear
to mind my manners." She sighed. "He spent three whole day
warning me about the nasty things people at the Tyrn's Cour
are likely to say to me because I'm part Iomardi and not pure Nyc
Ifor."

"Eck. Sounds just like the Domains from what Da an
Amhar've told me. What're you going to do?"

"Stay out of it as much as I can. Laz has this friend in Tyst tha
he wants to visit and Pa says that's all right if we take a couple o
guards with us. Hunh! You needn't look at me like that. I kno
they won't want us along, but Laz isn't stupid even if he is a snitt
gudge. Did you know, the biggest place I've been to is Osgotow
when they did the census and the Tyrn's Clerk had to write dow
our names. Osgotown has more dogs than people. There's les
than a dozen families and only six houses not counting the Tow
Ha—" A yawn broke through the last word. She blinked. "Hal
Breith, you mind? It's been a really, really long day, and tomor
row morning early, Pa's turning me over to this poet Hanne
Corbswyf so she can teach me how to curtsy and stuff like tha
We both going to charm school, heh?"

[7]

Mid-morning on the fourth day after the barge left Cesayl, it ne
tled up to the docks at Carcalon. The sun turned the silver roof
into white-hot glories and a short distance farther along the rive
the painted roofs of Tyst were like a garden of bright flower:
Lyanz remembered the morning the *Kisa Sambai* came into th
harbor and those roofs were shining at him. His father was aliv
then and all the sailors. His face grim, Lyanz waited for Ellar t
tell him what he wanted him to do.

12

Poetry and Power Plays

y the secret calendar of the Watchers, events dating from the 5th day
Foolsreign in the year 735 to the 3rd day of Foolsreign in the 736th
landairic year since the last Settling.

1]   735

On his fifteenth birthday, the last day of Foolsreign in the year
35, Anrydd Barbranson stood across the writing table from the
Cyngrath Barbran Caṅithson gan Lusor, younger son of the
roon of Lusor, and learned that what he'd suspected for years
as true and that the time of reckoning for that old sin had come
own on him. Gan Lusor was not his father and had no inten-
on of maintaining the pose any longer.

Anrydd picked up the sheets of parchment that took away his
irthright and gave it to his younger brother. He read each word
owly though Barbran gan Lusor tapped impatiently at the table.
he language was difficult, archaic, the phrasing cryptic, but the
meaning of the whole was clear enough.

When he finished and looked up, Barbran gan Lusor said,
Sign it."

"Why should I?"

"If you don't, I'll see you branded as a bastard, have you thrown

out of my house, and I'll cut off all support. Not a penny more
only the clothes on your back. If you do, I'll keep my own coun
sel on this matter and make you an allowance until Caria
reaches his majority. That will give you eleven years to arrang
your life. But understand me clearly. If you do anything to brin
disrespect on my name, I will drive you from Nyddys entirely
Don't have any illusions about going to the Tyrn for help. H
never has and never will acknowledge his bastards. Make troubl
and he'll have you strangled and dropped down a well some
where. Sign the waiver. I will allow you to use the name this las
time."

Anrydd took the pen, dipped it in the inkwell and scrawled hi
name. Then he walked out of the room, filled with silent fury—
silent because he knew just how much Barbran gan Lusor hate
him. He was a constant reminder that the Tyrn had diddled hi
mother, that Barbran had let his honor be bought for a dowry an
preferment. As he strode through the halls in the wing of th
Palace where the Grath Suites were, Anrydd swore he'd get eve
for this humiliation. He didn't know how or when, but it woul
happen. Or so he told himself over and over.

To work off his anger and cool down enough to start plannin
his revenge, Anrydd went to the Practice Court, took a woode
sword from the Armorer and went out to practice with one of th
mudans, figures made from canvas and wood with wooden sword
clamped to their single arms; they were mounted on spring
swivels and had a habit of whirling about to whap the unwary
He went at the mudan wildly in the beginning, picked up a col
lection of bruises on his arms and a bleeding knot on his head
then settled to working patterns on the mudan, getting into th
rhythm of its swings and sways until he stopped thinking an
dropped into the continuous present of the body. And was fille
with a warm aching joy that was better than sex, better than any
thing he knew except those rare times when he was riding an
he and the horse worked as one being.

2] 736

Two months before his sixteenth birthday Anrydd was alone in the Practice Court working out on the mudan, bleeding away his rage at insults he'd suffered, and insults he'd had to ignore or turn to jokes. He finished his flurry with a combination that had the dummy whirling and bowing at the end in a way that amused him. He stepped back, grinning, wiped the sweat from his face and bowed in mock courtesy.

As he heard a laugh behind him, he spun around, the wooden sword lifting.

The man who stepped from the shadows, hands raised in the Peace sign, was the Captain of the Palace Guard, Toc Ubanson gan Goolad, third son of the Broon of Goolad, a man of medium size, the bony features of his face contained within a dark line of brows that almost met and a short pointed beard. "Would you care to have a rather more responsive opponent?"

Anrydd's face went hot. Words churned in the back of his throat and got stuck there. That invitation was an enormous compliment, something he wouldn't have dared to dream of. Toc gan Goolad was the Tyrn's Champion and had been for longer than Anrydd had been alive and aware. "Y-yes, Morryn Toc," he managed. "I would like that."

3]

Derfel sat in his office high in the Grath Tower. His windows looked out over all of Carcalon and the fields beyond though he seldom bothered with the view. Sheets of paper with the layout of the Festival of Words and the living arrangements of the summoned poets plotted on them were strewn across the polished surface of his worktable. He was checking to make sure that Ellar and his household were placed in the rooms he'd chosen. He intended to keep well away from Ellar and that irritating child of his. He liked his anonymity and meant to maintain it as long as he could.

He glanced at the scry mirror lying at his elbow. Anrydd was working with the horse that Toc gan Goolan had given him, a compact sorrel with a light mane and tail, walking him in wide circles, trotting a few strides, moving into a canter then back to a walk. The boy was doing nicely, consolidating his position at Court with only minimal help from Oerfel's nightwhispers into the ears of those who could advance his career and widen his influence. Oerfel was more pleased with his choice each day that passed. Anrydd was a charmer, a schemer and a natural leader— and he bore grudges with the patience of a cat at a mouse hole.

Things happened to people who annoyed him, though only Oerfel knew the truth behind those accidents.

A Broon's son training for the Guard mocked him for his birth and for signing away what should have been his birthright. Anrydd laughed and told him he'd earn his own respect, he didn't have to rely on his father's name because he wasn't a gormless know-nothing who tripped over his own feet. The Broon's son lost his temper, but Anrydd just laughed some more, danced round him a few times, then walked away. Two weeks later the Broon's son tripped on something, went tumbling down a flight of stairs, cracked his ribs, broke his collarbone and both legs and was sent home to recover if he could. Oerfel had sniggered for days over that bit of machination.

He patted a yawn. He'd been so busy these past days and nights that he'd got little rest and less sleep. His headaches were more frequent and his digestion was shot. His plans were well laid, though, and once he'd dealt with that Hero-in-Embryo, he could relax and continue grooming Anrydd to gather power as his proxy and in the end to enter the Empty Place, take the inflow of Power and filter it through his body so Oerfel could safely absorb it into himself. First Nyddys, then Nordomon and the Empty Place, finally the taking of the Power.

He was contemptuous of Mahara and Hudoleth because they were planning to take the Hero's place themselves. Ignorance, that's what that was. That rush of Pneuma would be so over-whelming it would scrape volition and understanding out of the vessel it filled only an instant after the inflow began. It was afterward that it would be accessible to a properly prepared Mage.

A tap on the doorjamb interrupted Oerfel's daydream. He touched the mirror and the image vanished, then he looked up. One of his undersecretaries stood in the doorway. Berfan, Oerfel remembered after a moment's thought.

"What is it, Berfan?"

"The Musician's Guild, they want a By-Appointment Certificate since the Festival comes before Foolsreign. With the Tyrn's Seal."

"Their representative is here?"

"Yes. Cerion Cerd and two apprentices."

"Bring him in and stay here. I want full notes of the negotiations."

[4]

Anrydd led Sernry into the turnout and began wiping him down. "What a beauty you are. And you know it, huh? Yes, you do. Yes, I know, you'd like to go on and on. Dumb horse. You like to work. Well, who can blame you? All those eyes admiring you."

"He's looking good."

Anrydd shook out the old blanket he'd used for the wipe-down and grinned at Toc gan Goolad, who was sitting on the top rail of the turnout's fence. "He's a smart one, Morryn Toc. Makes me work to keep up with him."

"Going to put him in the Foolsride?"

"No. He'd probably win, but that's a chancy run at best. Besides, I've already taken the crown twice. I don't think it would be wise to try for three in a row. Best let someone else have a turn."

Toc nodded. "You've an old head, young Anry. I've noted that. If you want a position in the Guards, I'll sponsor you."

Anrydd stumbled to the pump, blinded by the sudden eruption of all the ambitions he'd kept suppressed the past year. He took the bucket from its hook, set it under the lip and began working the handle of the pump, letting the effort burn off the excess of excitement. As the water cascaded into the bucket, he looked up, smiling broadly. "Yes," he said. "Yes! Thank you, Morryn Toc."

"Good. I'll get Secretary Oerfel working on the papers, and come The Birthday, you'll be Cadet Anrydd. What about the jump match—have you thought about entering him there? I'm seeded in the Honors Round. Riding Arian. I know you could take the Intermediates."

Anrydd wiped his hands along his sides, took the bucket over to Sernry. "Thought about it. Might do." He stood stroking the horse's shoulder as the beast drank. "Last I heard, they hadn't settled the judge roster."

"Malyndar gan Varnais has changed his mind. He'll be head judge. Rhaf gan Ymfross and Hamdin gan Ilaffson got hold of some bad meat the other night. They picked up a Dispensation from the Secretary, left for Difyrhau this morning on a coaster, gone to drink the waters, get their strength back. They won't be on the panel; their slots have been filled with . . . shall we say more temperate men."

"That does change things."

"Thought you might see it that way." Toc swung off the fence and strolled away, vanishing behind the end of one of the stables.

Anrydd leaned against the gelding and smiled at the ground. His luck was holding strong. Those two dronns—may their bellies rot and their teeth fall out. If he could have managed it, he'd have slipped some clyfigg into their tea. Wouldn't have killed them but would've made them feel like death. No way to do it without leaving a trail that'd lead right to him. And now he didn't have to. Rumor said that the Tyrn and the Heir were coming to watch the Meet. Good stuff. "Right, Sernry, that's enough for now. Let's go inside and I'll find some oats for you. Tomorrow we start getting you ready to jump."

[5]

In the Hall of the Thousand Lamps, Anrydd stood slouched against the wall, half hidden by the folds of the arras. Barbran gan Lusor and Anrydd's mother sat in chairs in front of him, his brother and sisters perching on hassocks by their knees. He didn't want to be here, Barbran didn't want him here, but for his pride's sake, he had to show his face at this stupid Word thing, so here he was, about to be bored out of his mind by a clutch of driveling poets because the Tyrn got a bug under his skin about culture.

The famous thousand silver lamps of the great room had been polished and filled with pine-scented oil, the silver thrones had been polished till they gleamed like water. A dark purple carpet had been rolled across the mosaic floor with its coiled dragons flying about the representation of Nyddys Isle. The chairs along the walls were filled with the Broons and their families, with the Cyngrathmen and their families and the other courtiers who mostly lived off the Tyrn's Purse. Like his mother and Barbran, they wore their best silks and velvets and enough jewels to light the place without those thousand lamps.

The room was filled with the buzzing of whispers and the echoes of those whispers. The huge tapestries that hung from the walls were meant to cut those echoes and divert the icy drafts that curled round the baseboards, but they didn't do all that good a job. The hangings shivered in those drafts; the lamplight picked out areas of bright color and glinted off lines of gold and silver wire couched in with the embroidery threads. Behind the throne a flag hung flat against the wall, a pale blue ground with the green device of the House of Denarys appliquéd upon it.

The Denarys claimed descent from the Tyrns who lived in the days when the epics were written and most folk pretended to believe it, but Anrydd had picked up enough gossip to know that the Denarys were upstarts who'd grabbed the rule about four centuries before by force of arms and grafted themselves onto the old family by persuading a half-blind old aunt of the former Tyrn to adopt them.

As he stared at the flag behind the throne and thought about the Heir whose uncertain health was one of those items of gossip, vague notions that had been drifting in his head during the past year grew clearer. It would take time, work, lots of careful planning and discretion, but he had time and he knew with a sudden and passionate certainty that he could do it, he could take the Tyrn's place as his birthright and see to the repayment of all the slights and insults he'd had to eat this past year. He moved half a step away from the wall and looked around the room. A lot of second sons of second sons here with nowhere to go and nothing to do but fool around and pry what coin they could from their reluctant fathers. He knew some of them; time to start meeting and judging the rest. Connections. Toc's loyal. Have to keep him sweet. Won't be easy. He's sharp. Hm . . .

A blare of tweekhorns broke him from his reverie and he looked toward the great double doors.

Two hornmen dressed in cloth of silver, with silver-plated busks and half-gloves, paced slowly along the purple strip, blowing a fanfare to announce the incomers.

A light wizard followed, exploding spheres of light from the tips of his fingers, creating a kaleidoscope around him of brightly painted air.

The first of the next four walkers was a tall chunky woman with shoulders like a wrestler, dark red hair streaked with white plaited into heavy braids and pinned atop her head. She wore a black tunic and a long black skirt with neither jewels nor paint to add even a trace of charm to her heavy features.

Then came a thin, sandy man. He might have been well enough looking when he was young, but he'd probably never been a handsome man and the years had dealt harshly with him.

His abundant light brown hair had threads of gray in it. His face was clean-shaven, but deeply lined, especially around the mouth and eyes. He wore a black tunic and trousers, black boots soft with age but polished to a high gleam. As he passed Anrydd, he turned and looked at him. Despite the gold-rimmed spectacles, there was a sharpness to his gaze that Anrydd found disconcerting.

Whoever you are, he thought, I don't want any part of you.

The third was a short, broad man with a bald head and copper moustaches that were waxed and the ends twisted into horns like the cusps of a crescent moon. He too wore black, but he'd had one ear pierced and from it dangled a heavy silver ornament with free-moving moonstones swaying in the openings.

The fourth was another little man, a rack of bones awkwardly bound up in a leathery hide. His black tunic hung on him in ill-fitting folds. His face was tanned dark, his blond hair bleached almost white, his eyes narrowed to squints, his mouth dragged down at the corners as if he'd spent the morning drinking vinegar.

They followed the hornmen to a bench set beside the throne dais and sat down on it in the same order they came in. The poets, Anrydd thought. This is not going to be a lot of fun.

The buzz of whispering around him got louder until another pair of hornmen played the Tyrn's Fanfare. There was a rustle of silk, a creak of leather, scattered thumps and scrapes as those seated along the walls rose to their feet.

When they appeared, these hornmen wore cloth of gold and gilded busks. Their faces and hands were painted gold and their tweekhorns glistened gold in the lamplight.

Then the Tyrn came walking in, the Heir two paces behind him.

My father, Anrydd thought. They say you put the print of your face on me so that even an idiot would guess my parentage.

The Tyrn was a big man, but not a bulky one, with a lean vigor giving strength to a face and form that might otherwise have been too pretty for strength. His hair was a lion's mane, dark amber, thick and springy. His neatly clipped moustache and beard were a shade darker, outlining a wide, sensuous mouth. His eyes were a brilliant blue. He was dressed simply, his tunic and trousers a dark green with hints of blue in the shadows. His only ornament was a heavy gold chain, its square links set with emeralds. He wore riding boots, polished and soft, the natural brown of fine leather.

Behind him his Heir was a pale and pitiful copy, bony rather than slim, tired and listless, his eyes a faded blue, his face expressionless, his thoughts—if he had any—carefully hidden.

Anrydd eased back into the shadow of the arras. The Heir was his own age, born only a month after him. A small twist of fate and that could be him out there, his life laid out for him, everything he wanted ready for him to reach out and take it. No insults. No waiting. No having to court or seduce those whose support he needed. Anrydd watched his half brother walk past and hated him with everything in him.

Dengyn Tyrn strolled with leonine ease along the carpet, paused at the foot of the stairs leading to the dais and smiled at the row of poets. "I'm pleased you were able to come to our impromptu festival. You honor us. No, no. No need to speak. We'll hear your splendid words in a moment." A wave of his hand, then he ascended the stairs and settled himself on the massive silver throne.

The Heir stepped silently up the stairs and took his seat.

Anrydd moved farther into shadow till he stood in a niche between two of the tapestries, his arms crossed, his shoulders against the wall. At least this one time he had a better place than his half brother; he didn't have to look interested in the poems. He glanced at the Heir's blank face. Hunh, maybe that feeble little worm gets off on poems. Somebody must have talked Dengyn Tyrn into holding this thing.

At a gesture from the Tyrn, the Court Stentor stepped forward, banged the butt of his Staff on the Silence Plate, sucked in a long breath then brayed, "Hanner Corbswyf presents her poem 'The Raid of the Gleddol.' "

The big woman rose from her place on the bench and stepped onto the silver circle raised two handspans above the floor. She stood silent for a moment, her arms stiff at her sides, her hands closed into fists. When she began her recitation, she chanted the lines in a rich and powerful contralto, the words flying all the way to the back of the room.

> *Renan's Host goes thundering*   *to Daddeny lost to Gleddol*
>
> *Rigor and right proclaiming.*   *Destiny has him in thrall.*
>
> *Sing I the song of the burning*   *Purple sails wreathed in red fire*

[6]

Cymel moved her shoulders. Her skin felt itchy and her ears tingled. "Someone's watching us," she said. "I think we should wait for Diawad and Cadarn to reach Carcalon before we go out from behind the walls. I don't like this."

"You here. And your father would not have given me this"— Lyanz touched the Pass he'd shoved into the breast pocket of his tunic—"if he not think it was all right."

"I suppose." She followed Lyanz down the narrow lane behind the Palace wing where the Chamberlain had stowed them, then along the wall to one of the east gates. Lyanz held up the Pass and the gateman let them through.

Outside the wall was a more or less flat, open field where a throng of people were busy getting ready for the Foolsreign Fair, some putting up poles and stringing lines of toothy flags from tip to tip, some raising canvas pavilions and setting up booths, others scurrying about doing enigmatic things that seemed have no purpose, though they looked pleased to be doing them. Others were leading strings of horses, pack mules with rolls of fleece piled higher than the mules were tall. Others brought in herds of sheep, hair goats, grunting porkers. And yet others led bullock teams, yearling bulls and heifers.

So many people.

Cymel felt confused and strange and annoyed at Lyanz, who went along easy as a lamb in a herd; he was used to crowds and didn't seem to notice that even the air he breathed was being used by dozens of other folk, nor did the noise of them make his head ache, nor did the smell of them make his stomach do flip-flops. She was beginning to be glad her father had kept her up on the farm all these years.

"Laz! What you doing here? I thought you were on your way back home."

Cymel swung around. The speaker was a thin, wiry boy whose black eyes glittered in a face with jutting cheekbones, a nose with a hump in the middle and a pointed chin. His skin was an odd reddish-brown and his hair only a few shades darker.

"Wait there a moment, I gotta do something." He plunged back into the crowd and Cymel saw him run up to a tall, skinny man with a bald spot that glistened in the sunlight.

"Gryf," Lyanz said. "I think we have to go to Tyst to meet with him."

Cymel wrinkled her nose; she wanted to say, I knew that, but she bit her tongue and stayed silent.

Gryf came running back, bonked Lyanz on the shoulder with a bony fist. "M' da had me working, dipping purses, y' know. I hadda hand off what I'd got and tell him I was taking a break. Hoy! I thought you upped anchor and headed home."

"Storm," Lyanz said, his face going dark. "Ship go down, I get pull out. Her." He jerked a thumb at Cymel.

"Ahh. Y' da?"

"Drown."

"Shoo, I was all tore up when my ma got wipe out with the fretchy fever. If m' da went . . ." He shook his head, then slid his eyes round to Cymel. "Talgryf," he said. "Call me Gryf."

"Cymel," she said. "My father's Ellar Yliarson. He's here for the poetry thing."

"You a witch?"

"Huh?"

"Well, Laz he says you pull him outta that storm."

"Not me really, my aunt. My mum's dead too, she got killed by wild men."

"Ah. Laz, you going into Tyst? I've got to stick round here till Da says it's time to go home."

Lyanz glanced toward the painted roofs glowing in the afternoon sunlight. His mouth tightened. Cymel suspected that he didn't really believe her father about the ships and the Mage, so she was glad that Gryf was pulling at him enough to keep him from ditching her and heading for the wharves. "So what's to see here?"

"Whyn't we go look at the horses? Broon Siffyl from over to west coast ship a bunch of his best colors round the Heel. Saw a piebald I'd lift in a hair's breath 'f the rope didn't scare the marrow out m' bones."

As Gryf led them through the throng of carpenters and merchants setting up for the Fair, Cymel brooded over what he'd said. When they reached the horse sheds, she edged closer to him. "Your da makes you steal stuff?"

"Well, yeah. Learning the family business, I am. 'Sides, he's got the rheumatism in his hands, so he can't do the dips he was used to. Tyrn's Law, they cut the first finger off you get caught second time. So he mostly runs scams and fences stuff these days and I do the hand work."

"Oh."

"Over there. Look. There's the paint. You ever see a prettier thing?"

[7]

Anrydd covered a yawn with his hand. As the first lines thundered out, Hanner had engaged his interest despite his low expectations, but she'd gone on and on, his enjoyment dribbling away until he wanted to cheer when she stepped down. He glanced around the room, watching faces, noting who looked disgruntled or restless. The Tyrn's half-closed eyes were moving subtly from side to side. It was an awakening and a warning. The man wasn't the fool he seemed.

The Court Stentor banged the butt of his Staff on the Silence Plate. "Ellar Yliarson of Cyfareth and Peak Farm presents his poem 'Dance of the Dead Wife.'"

The sandy man stepped onto the Speaker's Round. The light from the lamps dealt more harshly with him than they had with Hanner, picking out the gray in his hair, painting black shadows in the lines of his face. When he spoke, his voice was powerful but rough with a bitter edge.

> 'O Belovèd,' she sings who dances
> Among brown dead trees winter bared,
> Through wind-blown leaves that cling
> Where chance does fling them.

[8]

As the sun began to settle behind the black peaks of the Southern Dreyals, a team of bullocks hauled a scraper over the last bits of a level patch of ground in a ring of hills, stirring clouds of fine white dust that coated everything and made Cymel sneeze. Behind the scraper another team pulled a sod wagon. Once the ground was prepared, the grass rectangles were laid down, pegged in place and watered so the roots would take hold.

Lyanz and Talgryf were a short way off talking with a clot of stable boys and horse handlers. She'd hung around the outside of the group till she got tired of being ignored. That lot were as bad as Orog Dyrysson and his gang of stupids. Though she'd thought of marching back into Carcalon, she stayed where she could still see Lyanz; she'd feel horrible if the Mage got him just because she was off in a huff. It wasn't a hard thing to keep track of him. He was half a head taller than most of the others and that bright gold hair and dark gold skin made him easy to find. Gold hair, gold eyes, gold vanity. T'huh!

Below her on the flat the last of the turfs were laid in place and watered. She watched, fascinated, as a moment later a swarm of men moved onto the grass, carrying poles, panels painted to look like bricks and pots with boc hedge in them, green and bristly and clipped square. In the remnants of daylight they turned what had been waste ground into the most elegant of jumping courses. Their neighbors and the villagers had jump meets at Summer Solstice, laid out on a catch-course, using field fences, streams and hedges for the obstacles. It was odd to see such a pretty course created so quickly where nothing but weeds had been a short while ago.

Behind her a horse screamed. She jumped to her feet and swung round, hand over her eyes, looking for Lyanz.

The crowd around Lyanz had scattered. For a moment she didn't see him, then she saw a crumpled body on the ground and knew it was him.

Several horses were out of their stalls, running and rearing, screaming challenges, their hooves tearing up the wild grass in the walkway between the sheds, striking down dangerously close to Lyanz. Pneuma glittered like a halo round all of them. The Mage had done something to them to drive them wild. They were avoiding the body as much as they could, not because of any respect for human flesh, but because a soft, rounded body offered dangerously poor footing. Sooner or later, though, one of them would kick him again, break his head perhaps or stamp his ribs through his heart and lungs.

She trembled on her hill, terrified and frustrated. Running down there wouldn't help, pulling the Pocket wouldn't help. She closed her hands into fists and mind-slapped at the horses, mean-

ing only to drive them away from Lyanz. But she was too new a
this and had no way of measuring how hard a blow she gav
them, so she was startled to see three of the horses drop and th
rest stand shivering, heads down.

Talgryf reached Lyanz before she did, went to his knees besid
him. He thrust his fingers under Lyanz's chin to find his pulse
looked up as Cymel dropped beside him. "I think he got clipped."
He touched a thin crooked line of blood oozing through th
blond hair. "He's alive, but he's going to have one thumper of a
headache."

"We've got to get him away from here. The men who own
those horses . . ."

"You're not supposed to move 'em when it's a head thing." Tal
gryf lowered his voice to a whisper, a thread of sound that barely
reached her ears. "You do that?"

"Yeh. But don't tell."

"No way."

"All right. But we really, really have to get him away from here
before something else happens."

"Look, you better go get my da. I'll talk them off him till you
get back."

"I don't dare leave him. You don't understand. You fetch your
father."

"They're going to blame him and me 'cause we weren't
s'posed to be here. Those are prize horses, worth more'n I'd see
in ten years dipping."

"So hurry up."

Talgryf squeezed slick as butter through the crowd of angry
horse copers converging on the sheds. Cymel watched until he
was gone, then she settled Lyanz's head on her thighs and prepared to defend him. Words now, not magic. She didn't dare
show Gift, it'd be the same as confessing she'd been the one who
did in the horses.

9]

n his niche, Anrydd bent one knee, then the other, tightened and
oosened his muscles as the Court Stentor banged the Silence
late and cried, "Kennig Goefrayson presents his poem 'Dyf
anew's Lament.' "

Lamplight shining off his bald pate and turning the thumb-
vide strip of hair that reached from ear to ear into hot copper
oils, Kennig stepped onto the Speaker's Round. His waxed
moustache jerked and circled as his bass voice rolled out so deep
nd strong the lamps trembled and the shadows they cast made
trange shapes on the mosaic floor.

> Oh Belovèd, see how my eyes overflow when I behold my sweet
>   teeming land
> Where the cities of painted roofs are filled with faithless
>   friends
> Where the lords of river and mountain spend their substance
>   in base display
> Where fathers deny their sons and wives dishonor their vows
> Where sellers cheat on weight and worth and buyers steal
>   without a moment's pause.

10]

"He didn't do anything," Cymel said. She was talking as calmly
as she could to the men cursing around her as they tried to lead
their still-shuddering beasts back into their stalls. Though she'd
feared it, the horses on the ground weren't dead, just in serious
trouble; they were beginning to twitch and try to heave themselves up. Men with slings and the help of several big plow horses
were working to get them back on their feet.

"Ask your handlers. He was just talking about the horses like
anyone would. Then one of them breaks loose and kicks him in
the head." At first she thought no one was listening to her, but
though none of the men said anything, now and then their heads

would turn and she would meet angry eyes. "Look, his father i an important trader from Nikawaid. House of Kurrin. Lyanz i visiting us awhile; we're here because my pa was one of those th Tyrn called to Court to read his poems. And he's a lector at Cy fareth University. Why would we want to hurt your horses Maybe it was one of the little gods. Pa says they're turning mean."

Still no answers, nobody paying attention to them—but sh relaxed a little as she felt the hostility dissipating. She looke down at Lyanz's head. Her trousers were wet with blood trick ling from the wound. She touched the bump gently, keeping he fingers away from the break in the skin. She couldn't feel an bone shift, not like the time when she and her father took Buh win and Bucochy down to Dyrys's farm so his bull could service them, and Cyswe sneaked after them and the bull kicked him i the head and killed him so quick the hair was still standing u on his back. The bones in her cat's head had moved like th pieces of a broken plate stuffed into a sack.

She bit her lip. Poor little things. She still missed them terri bly. Noswe disappeared one night and all she found later wer some bones, a tuft of black hair and a lot of wolf tracks. She ha a feeling the little gods were responsible, but there was no wa of really knowing what had happened.

She looked up and nearly fainted from relief as she saw Tal gryf hurrying around the end of the sheds into the open spac where she sat.

He dropped to a squat beside her. "Da and Jibby are bringing a litter," he said. "They'll get 'im to the gate and the Tyrn's me can take him on from there. He still out?"

"Yeh. But he's breathing easy and I don't think any bones ar broken."

Talgryf leaned closer, whispered, "You know what this is about don't you?"

"Uh-huh. You want to come in with us, I'll lay it out."

"Better not. They don't like my kind in there. Maybe you could ome to the gate round sunup? I'd really like to know he's all right nd how come."

She just had time to nod, then the others were there, ready to ft the boy onto the litter.

11 }

> . . . *sails fill with moonlight and mist*
> *And the sea heaves under me*
> *Never a man so blessed.*
> *And never a man so free.*

As the mellifluous voice so at odds with Chwant Fyffson's our visage rose to a triumphant shout, then dropped to silence, stirring in the arras behind the Poets' Bench caught Anrydd's ttention. A servant slipped round the edge of the hanging and vhispered in Ellar Yliarson's ear.

The sandy man's mouth tightened and his hands closed into ists, but he simply nodded and sat where he was. If something ad gone wrong with his household, which is what it looked like, omeone else would have to take care of it. He was trapped here until the Tyrn dismissed them all. Like me, Anrydd thought and wallowed his impatience.

There was a reception after this, but with a little maneuvering, he could collect some like-minded second sons and slide way for some more congenial fun. Build your web, he told himelf. Bind these little flies tight and suck them dry. He was a man how, sixteen years and counting. By the time he left the teens behind, he should have fiddled a high post in the Guard and eeled in a heap of men who owed him favors and thought him a friend. He looked at Dengyn Tyrn and nodded. Yes. You're my model, Father. What you've done, I can too.

{ 12 }

Oerfel groaned and hauled himself off the floor where the back-bloom off the slap-away spell had flung him. His head throbbed and his throat burned so badly that for a moment he didn't re-alize he was bleeding, face and hands cut by shards of the bro-ken scry mirror. He could have been killed if he hadn't felt the onrush of the heat and pushed his chair back.

He took a dustpan and a small broom from a closet, swept up the shards and tilted them into an iron box. He closed the lid, took a second mirror from a locked chest, located a pair of tweez-ers and began easing the bits of glass from his flesh. He was fu-rious, but he didn't allow that to hurry him or put a tremble in his hands. With four Watchers haunting the place, he didn't dare show up in public with that stigmata on his face.

Muttering heal spells, he pressed his thumb on the cleaned cuts, mended the flesh cut by cut. The tedious process hardened his rage. A child. An untaught baby did this to him, not out of skill but raw impulse unmitigated by any control.

The only satisfaction he got out of this mess was the memory of seeing a hoof catch that slippery Hero-to-be in the head. At least he'd finally got that done.

He used the mirror to check his face, nodded with satisfaction. The healing was done and done well. He drew a hand down across his face to bleed off the excess Pneuma. Then he willed the mirror to show him the Hero.

"Tanew's Teeth! Not again."

The boy lay on a litter being carried toward Carcalon, the girl walking beside him, her hand on his chest. His eyelids twitched, opened a moment; his eyes were glazed, unfocused, but he was alive.

13

Raid

*By the secret calendar of the Watchers, events dating from the 1st of
Choomis the Tax Month, the sixth month in the 736th Glandairic
year since the last Settling.*

{ 1 }

On a warm autumn evening in the Fort at the tip of the Parma
Bight, the tax farmer Vergo nye Sivice was finishing the evening
meal with the man who ran the Parma Fort, the Sul Bashar Davul
nin Meftun. In a room opening on the Sul Bashar's private garden, they reclined on divans and supped on light soup, roasted
pilich (a meaty waterbird found only in the salty inlets), fresh
baked bread and frozen sorbets. It was too hot and muggy for anything heavier, though the arrival of the Olchar taxman merited
a High Meal.

Parma Bight was a long, narrow finger of water thrust between
two mountain ranges, the Ascarns that marked the easternmost
stretch of Faiscar and the Dislir Dags at the northeast border of
Kale. The banks of the Bight were mostly sea marsh, and the only
connection to the interior of Tilkos was by a highroad on stone
piers that one of the past Mages of Kale had created for the convenience of the Olch Omir's tax collectors.

Small dark folk lived in the marshes, trapping six-legged tim-sah for their bright-colored skins and collecting the resins of the kauch tree. They had their own language and guarded their ways with a fierce pride that saw insult in ignorance. Between Marsh steel and Marsh magic, not many strangers who went into the swamps came out again.

Vergo nye Sivice wrinkled the nose that was the bane of his life because it lacked the regal hook of his highborn kin; he'd inherited it from his merchant mother and felt it marked him as lowborn and was the reason his climb into favor had been so slow and unpromising. At the moment he had the tax concession in Tilkos, but he had hopes of stepping to a more honored post if he did well. "Sul Bashar, does it always smell like this?"

Davul nin Meftun waved his fan at the sticks of incense standing in the sand bowl. A moment later he slapped at his neck with a meaty hand and shifted his bulk on the divan, snapping his thumb against the bell to bring in one of the serving slaves. He didn't worry about his nose or anything else. He'd been in this post for fifteen years and knew he wasn't getting another unless a miracle happened. He didn't believe in miracles. "This is the pleasantest time of the year. The air's almost dry and the water's low in the Marsh. Come high summer you use your sword to cut your way through the stink. As it were."

The slave came in, slid her eyes round to nye Sivice as she dropped to a squat and waited for orders. Vergo ignored her. She'd been hanging round him since the ship landed because she had hopes of using him to get out of this place, but she gave him the grues with those matte black eyes and hair, that green-brown skin that looked more like tree bark than anything that belonged on a woman's body.

Davul grunted, tossed her a small wood chip with his sigil on it. "Go boot that hedge wizard of yours out of the sack and have him redo his off-spells. The weeros are getting past them, one of them bit me on the neck. I don't like that." He glared at a small black speck that had landed on his arm, smashed it with the edge of his fan and brushed it off him. "And tell Shiv to chip some more ice and bring up a bottle of kanyak."

When she was gone, Davul shifted on the divan to face nye Sivice. "I can let you have six men to add to your pikeguard. They've got no polish and couldn't do parade if you beat on them for a month of Ruetha fetes, but they know the ins and outs of the hill country west of here. Bandits are thick as lice and the Tilkose are restless. I've had news of two assassinations and four attempted. Been 'changing messages with other Sul Bashars in-country; main suspects are younger sons with fire in the blood over the Born from Kale running Tilkos. I have a cote with a good bunch of message tullins. I'll send a brace of them with you. If you run into trouble on the way back, loose a tullin with a message in its leg quill and I'll get relief to you."

"Who pays for those men?"

"You weren't told? You do. And for any damages they do while they're in your command." Davul shrugged, his massive shoulders rolling with the gesture. "It's custom. Been in force longer than I've been here. And not a bad deal either. It's tricky dealing with the exiled Born and angry natives."

"I'll take one man and you can keep the tullins."

Davul raised his brows, then splashed a finger's width of kanyak in his bubble glass. "Your call. Give you a list, you can pick your man in the morning. Don't ignore him when he warns you about something. You don't know Tilkos. You make a mess, I have to stir myself and clean it up. And with that on your record, you'll be lucky the Omir doesn't send you to count paper slaves and water use in the marshes north of Yosun."

[2]

Gurra Rasidal flexed his arms, moved the muscles on his face to resettle the black leather mask. He stood in a long line snaking about the courtyard, one of the seven guards to the Stanca Steward who was responsible for handing over the coin for Family Rasidal. Other years he would have been itching for a fight, anything, anyone, some way to retrieve his pride after this craven capitulation to Kale and its rule and the low rank and poverty that rule condemned him to. Now he watched with satisfaction as chest after chest was carried to the tax table, the coin inside counted, then placed in the larger chest behind the taxman.

Other years.

Not this one. This time I've got more important business than tavern brawls. His plans swam in his head as the group he was in crept forward.

Meet tonight with the others for last-minute fix-ups.

He'd got permission to hunt jabbuz in the Ascarns with Riza bar Aslayeh, which had raised some eyebrows. Even if Riza was only a third son, his father was head of Family Aslayeh, which was one of the richest and most important in Tilkos, not counting the Born, of course. Riza was four years younger than Gurra, half blind, a clumsy rider and hopeless with a sword. With all that, he was on fire at the corruption he saw everywhere around him. Sometimes Gurra wondered what was going on in those milky eyes, whether Riza was as easy to manipulate as he seemed or too clever to show he noticed what Gurra was doing.

Three days' ride to Hanuf's farm in the hills to meet with the others who'd be away from home with excuses much like his. Collect the extra horses for the long ride south. Horses, mules and stores. Riza had supplied most of the coin for this, but they'd all squeezed out what they could.

Five days' hard ride south.

A two-day detour to pick up that swampie shaman Whan had promised to supply to cover their traces from scrymen in Kale. He'd said he might be able to get an Ash of marshmen to add to heir numbers, but Gurra was skeptical. If he did manage that, hough, the little beasts would be useful indeed, especially if one or two of them got killed. Leaving the bodies behind would turn he search away from Tilkos. Didn't matter. The Sul Bashar wouldn't be expecting trouble before the taxman and his gold reached the Fort. Even with that last detour they'd be ahead of the taxman and his guard by at least two days.

Gossip said this new one only had six pikemen from Kale and a scruff from Fort Parma to guard the chests. The old one brought a full Ash of pikemen from Kale and ten old farts they were, wily as a harfox sniffing round a henpen. No getting close to them. And he picked up five scruffs from the Fort. These he kept under hand; he knew how bribable they were. Cornered, they'd fight like rats and that was all he wanted out of them. Old man was crazy and clever and tough as a root and in his day no one even thought of lifting the revenue chest. Wonder what happened to him, why he's not back.

Hm. Taking the Parma Fort. That's still chancy. We'll need luck to pull it off. Maybe . . . No. Best to stick with the plan. Take the Fort and wait for the taxman to ride into the trap. Kill them all and burn the place down.

Winter was on the way. Next month was First Snow Seimis. By the time Kale got round to taking action, the passes in the Dislir Dags would be closed. With the Fort taken out, the Bight would turn into a death trap.

Whan told him the marshmen were restless. Someone was preaching a holy war. Whispering it, anyway. That left Chierim as the only door to Tilkos. Let the lowlanders face the Omir's men if he got around to sending them. High Tilk could wait for the invaders to wear themselves out. Gurra smiled and dreamed of a free Tilkos—a Tilkos where he'd be the one with power. Not those useless Born from Kale. And not empty-headed fops like his cousin, who was head of Family Rasidal.

When they reached the Counting Table, he shifted position so he could see the taxman.

Low blood. Look at that nose on him. Fat, greedy hog. Probably clever, though he looked stupid as a lump of clay. If his looks were true, he wouldn't be here; this is too rich a plum for fools to pluck. Tight in the fist or he'd have more men with him, but the ones he did bring looked tough. Definitely better to catch him when his guard was down. When he thought he was safe and could relax.

The coins from the Rasidal coffer flickered through the taxman's plump fingers as if he were a hedge wizard palming sweets. Coins wrung from the work of Rasidal cousins, artisans and clerks and from the sweat of the rustais, and most of it going to buy face paint for the Born in Aile Kuvvet. And we let them take it and we lick their feet for our pains.

Gurra watched the coins vanish into one of the ironbound tax chests. You'll buy swords and men, crossbows, quarrels and war charms. You'll bribe the Born to put their own heads in the noose I hold.

One watch later, Gurra was heading south, mounted on an Aslayeh gelding with two mules on a lead rope, Riza beside him on a gentle white mare who looked half asleep but managed to cover the ground at a respectable pace.

[3]

Whan emerged from the shadows, moving with the peculiar gliding walk of a mountain razh on his own territory, touched his brow with his fingers when he saw Gurra Rasidal. "You look ready for the business."

"Yes. The shaman?"

"Waiting. Got the swampies too. Twelve. Waiting for us over at Roundloaf Hill, which looks down on the Fort. You get 'em n, you can forget about 'em. They'll take care of their business. 'ime they leave, won't be no Fort no more."

4]

'our days later, shortly after sunset, a line of mules and weary iders came down the trade road and stopped before the gate of 'ort Parma. The sole guard looked hazily out the gatehouse winow, belched, collected his wandering wits and rang the bell so he slaves could work the windlass and raise the gate for them. le leaned on the sill scowling at the riders below. The taxman oming back meant Sul Bashar would be getting on their tail to marten up and look right till the Kaleman was gone. He cratched morosely at a weero bite.

Two men lifted crossbows and put bolts through his throat and ody. He died before the glamour dissolved and the raiders harged into the Fort.

5]

n his workroom Mahara watched with satisfaction the scene in he scrybowl as fires began licking at the walls and the structures nside the Fort, the dance of the flames discovering then hiding n darkness again the sprawled bodies of the guards along with hose slaves who stumbled between raider and defender and died of bad timing. In the calligraphy of the dead were two small dark igns, marshmen left behind to mark this as their work. Gurra and is band were well away and effectively masked from the Sight of the Omir's Warseers, and Mahara had scrubbed away all smell of his own interference.

The bell at the front door jangled discreetly. It was long past noonset, little more than a watch left before dawn. Who would come calling this late?

Mahara wiped away the image in the bowl and took a look at he figure standing in the shadows of the entranceway.

Pika Mar.

She was heavily cloaked and her form padded to make her seem an older, chunkier woman. A clever woman in her way, but like the rest of the Born who lived on Kuvvet's mountain she was so isolated by the artificiality of the Court that she could do things of monumental stupidity—like coming here this time of night when no one moved along the terraces. The Ulvit Kenar's spies wouldn't be fooled for more than twenty seconds by that disguise.

And not only Kenar's spies. The Byrin Anna Mishada, the mother of the First and Second Princes, and her bitter enemy the Uchin Anna Desimet, mother of the Third Prince, both had men watching him, as did the Ulvit Zahir, who ran the Omir's Guard. And Sorum Sopa, Chief of the Merchant's Guild. And at least two wizards from the Warmagic Guild. Watching them maneuver for the best vantage amused him when he wasn't busy with other matters.

Feeling mischievous, he glamoured a golem with the form of a beautiful woman and sent it to open the door.

"It's wonderfully cool in here, Mahara. How do you manage that?" Pika Mar had removed the cloak and rearranged herself for display. In the lamplight she had a vivid glow that made mere beauty irrelevant. She knew that and smiled as she invited him to sit beside her.

One look at what she'd worn under that cloak told him she'd come with a more ordinary sort of seduction in mind. And he had a mind to accommodate her.

"Is this wise, Maytral Mar? I would not wish to bring harm to your patron. A Mage is a chancy acquaintance." As he spoke, he tapped his forefinger on a block of wood set into the wall, the call plate for the activated golem.

"I walk my own road, Mahara most wise, and favor whom I choose." She changed position slightly in the chair, her body, moving through a subtle serpentine curve that put a catch in his breath and woke a brief surge of fear as he felt control of the situation starting to slip away from him.

He reminded himself that she was a bribe, a scented sack of gold coins. A commodity the Third Prince was using to buy his interest. "You honor me, Maytral Mar."

"Yes. I do." She held out a hand and smiled as he lifted her to her feet. "I require you to pay homage, Mage."

14

Dreams

By the secret calendar of the Watchers, events dating from the 7th day of Choomis, the sixth month in the 736th Glandairic year since the last Settling.

[1]

Inside the gur, a dome of leather stretched over bent wooden braces, the fire in the brazier was ripe, reduced to gray coals with patterns of red crawling across the surface. Rinchay Matan stirred them with the bronze rod chained to one of the brazier's three legs, and when she was satisfied, she dropped jeglin powder onto the coals. She hunched over the shallow bronze bowl and sucked in the acrid threads of smoke that twisted upward as the powder burned.

Jeglin was a mix of grasses and roots, dried in the sun and pounded into a fine gray-green powder. It was a soul walker, freeing the mind from the constraints of the body. There was smeygo in the camp of the Dmar Spyonk, smeygo leaping from man to man, and she needed to find the soul roots of that madness.

Babcol was the first. A hand and a thumb of days ago he crept from his gur while his wife and baby son slept peacefully in their furs. He took his war club and slipped out to the kakar herd, care-

ully circling the two boys on night watch, then he screamed the
war cry, threw himself on the kakarn as if they were enemy raiders
and lay about him, killing five of them before his brothers got a
rope over him and pulled him down. The women of Dmar had
saved the best of the wool and were tanning the hides; the men
had set up smoke frames to save the meat for winter and were
cleaning the bones for tools, but it was still a sad loss of clan
wealth.

Two dawns later Tompao ran for skyedge, arms out to embrace
the sun, broken words tossed behind him, his ears closed against
the shouts of his kin.

The third and last so far was the boy with no wits. He had no
name because he could not speak other than a babble of nonsense, and no more than the herd dogs did he understand the
speech of others. He tore off his clothes and fell on his belly, moving along on elbows and toes, hissing like a shake.

Rinchay Matan drank deeply of the smoke, then let herself fall
back on the pile of skins.

Her soul swam in darkness, falling and falling, spiraling down
through an endless sunless place until her soulfoot touched
ground and the darkness grayed around her.

She stood in a black, white and gray land. A short distance
south of her, a tangle of pale roots hung from the black sky, the
soul roots of those who slept in the gurs of the clan camp. She
walked toward them, the gray land flowing liquidly under her
feet.

A beetle gnawed at one of those roots, a thin, wispy rope that
looked too frail to support its weight. The beetle was a harsh red
with black spots on its shell. Its legs were a metallic purple, an
evil color that hurt Rinchay's eyes and made her stomach lurch.
As she closed on it, the creature grew larger and threatened her
by kicking its feet and snapping its feelers like kak whips.

She walked firmly toward it, eyes fixed on it, never looking
away. And as she walked, she sang:

I don't fear you, soul eater.
I don't fear you, dream stealer.
I don't fear you, filth of the earth.
   My feet are iron
   My legs are horn
   From my sex flows power
   In my navel is the world.
You should fear me, seed of evil
You should fear my iron feet
You should fear my iron hands
You should fear my iron heart.

The beetle's movements grew quicker; it turned its hideous head and spat at her. The spittle hit and rolled off her shield of knowledge, the knowledge of her power against it. It did not touch her soul flesh at all. She kept singing and set her hand on the thorny leg.

The spines pierced her flesh but she ignored the pain and set her other hand on the edge of the carapace. It was honed like a knife blade and it cut her flesh, but she ignored the pain and twisted what she held until the beetle cried out and fell away from the soul root.

She stamped on it until it was stamped into the gray earth and all its evil colors had vanished.

Twice more she did this. There was a yellow-green and orange-pink louse with bright blue legs and a flea that was all colors and none. She freed the soul roots of these vermin, stamped the colors away, then she searched the roots for their eggs.

These she stripped away, setting them in piles upon the dead gray earth. She summoned fire to her mouth and breathed it on them and, when they were black ash, scraped with her feet until the ash was mixed into the soil and part of it.

Then she set her bleeding hands to her own soul root and climbed in pain and weariness back to the gur where her body slept.

* * *

Before she could begin the muscle patterns that would throw off the effects of the jeglin smoke, she felt a Presence enter her dream. She went still, frightened but ready to struggle free if it was Mugh the Nightworm come to eat her out from the inside.

The Presence was shapeless at first and painful in a way she hadn't experienced before, but as it assumed shape and she saw what visited her, awe warmed through her.

Alaeshin. Messenger from God.

Broad wings spread wide behind the heavily muscled torso, and four great hooves were planted on the stuff of the dreamland. Huge eyes in the heavy, blunt-featured face fixed on her. The mouth opened and rumbling words came forth: "You of the Grass have been chosen."

She couldn't move, but she gathered herself sufficiently to shape acceptance/abasement/obedience into a ball and thrust it toward the Alaeshin.

"The Dmar Spyonk have been chosen."

She waited, coating more submission onto the surface of the ball.

"He Who Walks in Fire says to you, go forth and punish the sins of the corrupt. He Who Walks in Fire says to you, ride and walk and drive your herds before you around the fingers of the Kush Kurums. He Who Walks in Fire says to you, bring those souls who have fallen away back to the service of Me. By Sword and by Fire bring them back. Thus is it spoken, thus shall it be."

The Alaeshin went and Rinchay slept.

On the next day, she took down the gur, packed the hides, tied the curved wooden poles to the pack and walked over the hill, along the stream and back to the camp of the Dmar Spyonk.

In the morning she went to the place where the three in smeygo were bound, inspected them and knew her work was good, and better than good because the boy with no wits heard her words and the knowledge of what she said was bright in his eyes. She ordered the three unbound, and those who kept watch there bowed in honor of her power.

In the afternoon she took the hide from one of the smeygo killed kakarn and began flensing it so the leather could be worked and turned into boots and other gear.

The Pai-gor who ordered the going of the Dmar Spyonk and who was also her uncle came ambling to her gur when the sun was high and hot and even the dogs were sleeping. He squatted beside her, watching her hands sometimes, sometimes staring off at the horizon.

"I had a dream last night," he said finally.

"Is it so?"

"An Alaeshin came to me and said thus and so." And he told her what she herself had heard.

"Ah," she said. "I had a dream of Alaeshin also."

"Could be wind in the gut," he said.

"Once."

"You think it comes again?"

"Best to wait and see. Comes twice, send to ask Nagar Burrik, Snop Kra, Ser Turuk. Behind, beside, before. A holy war will need many hands."

"It is so."

"Comes three times, best to pack up and go."

"Ah." The Pai-gor got to his feet and walked away.

Rinchay shifted the hide on her knees and continued working

[2]

Three days later, when the Alaeshin came a second time into the dreams of Rinchay and her uncle, Rinchay plucked the leaves of sibse grass and wove query drans with two lobes and a knot, added the totem sign of the clan and brought them to the Pai-gor. He chose three youths of the clan, gave them ponies and sent them to Nagar, Snop and Ser.

In two days all three were back and each brought with him a second dran to show that the clans beside, behind and before had also been visited with dreams.

On the next night the Alaeshin came a third time.

Thus were they summoned to holy war by Kamkajar the Merciful and Almighty, the Parter of the Seasons, Who scattered the seeds of life with his golden right hand and reaped them when they were ripe with the scythe in his black left hand. And the four clans at the headwaters of the river Higaherikaw folded their gurs and drove their herds before them around the end of the mountain range called Kush Kurum, the Comb of God, and into the northern Kays of Chusinkayan.

[3]

Hudoleth held up the crystal rhomboid, its polished facets catching the light from the western windows and breaking it apart. "This month we will consider crystal, not as instrument but as sign—an aspect of the craft used for the manipulation of the Pneuma. The Watcher Commentaries stored at Kingakun are our best source for the historical development of crystal craft and I will expect you to become familiar with the Index, but for this year I will allow secondary sources unless you formulate a thesis that has not yet been investigated. Though not impossible, this is unlikely, so don't waste your time. Or mine." She tapped the tips of the fingernails on her free hand against the tabletop, the small ticks loud in the tense silence.

"Contemplate this crystal." She turned it again and small rainbows danced on the wall. "Observe how the light is captured and changed, how you can see the control of—"

She broke off as the door to the Seminar room swung open and an Imperial Messenger walked in. He carried a piece of parchment folded into thirds, a wax seal holding the ends together. He bowed, turned the packet to the vertical so she could see the seal.

Hudoleth set the crystal on the table and sank to her knees. Raging inside, she lifted her hands higher than her head to receive the missive.

When the Messenger was gone, she rose to her feet. "You will pardon me," she said. "Contemplate the crystal while I read what is here." She took the missive to the window.

The Emperor's image had to be removed without being broken; the custom was to hold the wax over a candle flame since fire was clean and a translation to a higher state, but she was too annoyed and too impatient to take that extra step, so she snapped a spark into the seal and melted the wax away.

The parchment was folded about an Imperial Token, the words on it elegantly written by the Court Scribe. It summoned her to an intimate evening in the family quarters of the Palace. Her back was to her students so she permitted herself a tightening of the lips. The watches of daylight and dark were limited in number and she needed to sleep at least two of them. Each time she added an additional puppet to her theater she had less time to regulate the life she kept on view to the world, yet for her plan to unfold at the proper rate, she had to add to the players. Everything was so delicately balanced right now, she needed most of her attention just to keep the puppets dancing in order.

Mahara. The name was a bitterness on her tongue. He had his tower for a retreat when he chose to return there and none of the distractions that were driving her toward a recklessness she knew would be fatal. It wasn't fair. Just because she was a woman. She pushed the thought away, folded the parchment into a smaller packet and tucked it in her sleeve, turned and walked back to the table, her face a smiling mask.

"By necessity, our seminar will be shortened today. Doubt not that I will arrange it so you will have the whole of the time due you in this skill rank." With a polite three-finger point, she indicated the most advanced of the students. "Seeker Rikajes, give us first-level speculation on the manipulation of the Pneuma in which you employ the symbology of the crystal's ability to turn and focus light."

[4]

Bathed, perfumed, dressed in her formal robes, Hudoleth bowed to the DoorKeeper and presented the Token.

The fat old eunuch took the ivory square, inspected it, grunted with satisfaction and waved her in. He dropped the Token in an ivory box, then tapped a small hammer at a set of chimes, playing a simple tune on the bronze tubes.

A moment later one of the maids who did all the work inside the private rooms bowed before Hudoleth and led her through the entrance maze into a small side room with a padded bench, an elbow table with a pitcher of lemonwater, a goblet and a dish lamp filled with scented oil.

The maid bowed again, and in the obligatory high, whispery voice that seemed to deny that she spoke at all, she said, "Someone will come soon." Hands folded, eyes fixed on the floor, moving with tiny steps so her silken skirts fluttered around her ankles, she backed from the room. She was young and very pretty, but that was true of all the lesser servants allowed inside the Inner Wall.

Getting through the outer barriers to the private quarters of the Emperor was always tedious, but it was necessary to accede to the pace set by custom and the master of the dance.

In the ballads of the sheynsingers and tales told round winter fires, Mages waved a hand and went where they chose with a terrible arrogance. Her mouth twisted in a bitter smile as she thought how wrong they all were.

A Mage was solitary by nature and necessity and, by that solitude, made vulnerable. One ant could be crushed, but if hordes and hordes of them kept coming, they would strip the meat from the bones of the strongest man. Mortals swarmed like ants. What was the point of ruling a ruin, which was all that would be left if she unleashed her power to seize what was not offered.

The Emperor's mind was like quicksilver, running here, running there, blowing with the wind, changing as the wind changed.

The daily rule of Chusinkayan was firmly in the hands of the clerks and the Grand Council. The Emperor was symbol and glue, essential to keep the Kizoks from tearing each other and the country apart in their scramble for the seat he planted his fundament upon. Ten Kizoks for ten Kays, the irregular pieces that locked together to form the puzzle of Chusinkayan.

Playing the Kizoks against each other and the Grand Council and the clerks against them all was so easy after his years of practice that he was left with time on his hands and no natural gifts to occupy his mind—a mediocre mind, cunning rather than intelligent and with less curiosity than any other person she'd ever known, even the half-wit who swept the walkways of University housing.

He had quickly grown bored with the girl she'd used to draw off his attention and turned that flitter-glitter mind back to her. Four years ago it had seemed easier to let the man bed her. She'd expected that once his curiosity was satisfied, he'd drop her as capriciously as he'd pursued her and turn to new games to rub away his boredom. That hadn't happened. And she didn't really know why.

Nearly a full watch after she'd been left in the waiting room, the Guides came for her and took her into the family reception room where she passed the evening bored out of her mind, creating intricate, colorful magics for the entertainment of the Imperial family, closely watched by three Niosul.

[5]

The vast bedroom was empty except for the shadowy Niosul who knelt in the corners of the room, fine black veils billowing in the drafts stirred by ceiling fans that turned in massive silence, powered by the sturdy legs of Semmer slaves walking and walking the treadmills in rooms cut into the thick walls. The Imperial bed was the size of a barge and raised on a high dais; it loomed over her as she knelt and waited for the Emperor to enter the room.

She had been stripped and given a full body search, then dressed in white silk. Her long hair hung in a glistening black fall, spread over her heels and swirled around her on the tiled floor, arranged in precise curves by the serving maid who had dressed her for presentation. The mirror she had brought with her lay on the floor in front of her knees, catching the light from oil lamps that burned behind acid-bitten glass, a soft light that pushed aside the darkness with gentle hands and helped to conceal the always-present Niosul.

She heard him come in, bowed low until her brow touched the tiles and loops of her hair fell forward, curtaining her face. His bare feet padded and squeaked across the marble tiles, the sound diminishing as he climbed the velvet-shrouded stairs to the bed.

In the halo of the magics she'd been summoned to provide, the Veil cast over the reason for her summoning, she'd laid down small caches here and there in this room with charms woven into them, subtle knots meant to turn his mind without alerting the Niosul to what was happening. There was one of them in the padding of the bed and she smiled to herself when she heard the creak as he sat down. Slowly, subtly, she extruded a thread of Pneuma far below the threshold of the Niosul gift of smell and released that knot. He would feel the warmth rising through him, tickling into his head, but that would only please him because he'd link it to arousal and consider it a sign that the night would go well for him.

And it would. Oh yes.

"Why the mirror, Scholar?"

The words were permission to straighten and speak. She composed her face and lifted her body. "It is a gift and not a gift, a special delight I have prepared for you," she said. "It is a gateway that I pray you permit me to open."

"Explain."

Smelling the magic on her and knowing her power though they were not among the select few who recognized her as a Mage, the Niosul in the four corners of the room hissed a wordless alarm, but the charmed heat in his brain would not let him listen to them.

Hudoleth lifted the mirror, held it out so he could see the dancers, woman-shaped fire demons veiled in crimson and gold tissue and dancing their heat with a compelling eroticism that had stirred even her when she'd shaped them to her will and watched them perform. "At your word, O Mighty One, I will bring them here to dance for you and at your word I will compel them to obey you in all things, and I will bind myself to your welfare in that what comes to you comes to me also so you may be assured there is no danger in this."

The hissing from the Niosul grew louder and the senior Niol rose to her feet and took a step into the room, the weight of her disapproval increasing with the extension of her silence. She stopped when the Emperor raised an impatient hand.

"The bond," he said. His words had a breathless rush that sent a flush of triumph through Hudoleth. "Make it." He shifted the hand he was still holding vertical into a scoop, summoning the Niol. "Come here. You may touch me, your hand on mine. Measure the bond as it forms. Tell me if the Scholar speaks true."

[6]

Hudoleth knelt beside the door and tried to ignore the tides of pleasure that coursed through her body as the Emperor reacted to the fire demons, who were tireless in their invention and sang to him in their fire-touched voices an endless stream of flattery. Because she needed to devote only the smallest fraction of her attention to control them, she passed the rest of the time using the mirror to view the progress of the Grass Clans as they continued their march into Chusinkayan.

15

Dyf Tanew Walks

By the secret calendar of the Watchers, events on the 4th day of Fools-reign in the 736th Glandairic year since the last Settling.

[1]

In his tower aerie Oerfel listened as an undersecretary droned a long and tedious report about the fees and garnishes due this particular year and the amendments that the Cyngrath proposed to the lists.

When the undersecretary finished, Oerfel nodded. "Admirably complete," he said. "You have the lists?"

After the old man had crabbed from the room, Oerfel pulled open one of the drawers slung under the top of the worktable and looked into the mirror concealed there, watching grimly as the girl whose raw power had come so close to killing him walked through Carcalon's Tyst Gate. She was alone for once, a small, vulnerable figure—to the eye only. Oerfel had no intention of trying anything with her. Never again. Whatever forces raged in her, they were beyond his control. She was a sport. A mongrel creature who shouldn't exist.

He pushed the drawer shut, scowled at his agenda and tapped the bell to call in the next person waiting for him. This new position gave him the access he needed, but he missed his workroom in the Temple and the freedom he'd had once his day at the Tyst Hall was finished. He looked up, smiled sourly. "Yes, Monitor?"

[2]

As Cymel walked through the city gate, she saw Talgryf kicking at gravel on the footpath beside the road into Carcalon, his body a knot of rage and frustration.

"Gryf!"

He swung round so quickly he almost kicked himself off his own feet. "Mela. How is he? Is he all right? Nobody would tell me anything or let me in to see."

"What Pa said. He said to tell you Laz is going to do just fine. He does have to stay in bed a while more, though, so Pa's arranging for you to come visit him after Foolsreign is over."

"Oh." Talgryf dropped into his usual slouch, ran fingers through his shoulder-length black hair. "Good. So where you going?"

"I dunno." She started walking backward along the road as she talked to him, not sure where she was going, but away felt good. "First thing, I wanted to tell you about Laz, then more than that, I was just getting itchy shut up in there. I don't see how people can live like that."

"Foolsreign is lots of fun . . . hey!" He caught her arm and pulled her onto the walkpath as a group in from one of the Broons came riding along the road. "You want to watch out for that lot, Mela. They think they own the world and the rest of us are fleas they can stomp on."

Cymel made a face at him. "Nobody stomping on this flea."

"Hunh. Maybe not, seeing who your pa is. Me they wouldn't even bother to stomp, wouldn't even see me." He waved his hand at the hills where flags like bright-colored teeth were whipping in a breeze that barely touched the two of them down on the path. "There's all kinds of stuff going on over to the Fair. You want to go see? Or if you don't feel like going over there after what happened to Laz, we could walk over to Tyst and look round there. I got till sundown to fool round. My da says I only have to work mornings and evenings this Foolsreign, 'cause that's when the Tyst guards are thinnest on the ground."

"Uh . . ."

"I told you before. Don't you remember?" It was his turn to swing round and walk backward on the path, watching her with a funny look on his face. "Well," he said after a while. "Maybe you don't wanna go round with me. We're no-count folk outta the bothrin. Thieves, my da and me and all my fam'ly. Since I dunno when that's the family business. Like I said."

"I forgot, that's all. Laz being kicked like that knocked everything out of my head. Hm. I never knew anyone who worked at thieving, just some clothead boys who poach and tear on the edges of Broon lands. We're mostly freehold up where I live, but the Broony of Ysgorf is just the other side of the river. The hunting's better on the slopes but Orog and the ticks who run with him think it's fun to tease ol' Ysgorf's groundsmen. When they get caught, which happens at least once a season, their pas pay the fines and whale on their backsides, but they don't ever learn. I expect what you do is different."

"Yeah. I get caught with someone's purse, it's twenty good ones with the cat the first time, then branding, then a finger off each time after that. Five fingers and I'm hanged."

"Ay!"

He grinned at her. "Won't happen. Me, I'm good." He lifted his hands, spread the fingers out. "See? All there."

Cymel stared, fascinated by the kaleidoscope of color and activity swirling around her.

The Foolsreign Fair had exploded into activity since that first day. The road from Carcalon to the fairgrounds hadn't many riders or walkers, but the road from Tyst was clogged with clumps of people going and coming.

The Healing Sisters sat on the left side of the lane to the Fair Gate, begging bowls by their knees, singing their hymns and blessing all who passed by. The Teaching Brothers sat on the right, silent by rule, slapping their clackers in the ancient rhythms of suppliance and thanksgiving.

Children ran everywhere, laughing and shouting, shaking their fool-on-a-stick dolls, the small tinny bells wired to the crudely carved heads tinkling in a kind of continuo underlying the more sporadic noises of the crowd.

Inside the Gate, acrobats, their faces white ovals, glitter paint about their eyes, red mouths like bloody gashes, went flipping and whirling about.

Three people high, two towers circled in a vertical dance, the girls on the topmost shoulders waving bright silk ribbons. Round and round the towers turned, then there was a rattle of a drum, a flirt from a tin tweekhorn. The towers fell apart, the girls whirling over and over, caught by their partners, whirled over a last time, landing feather light, arms outstretched, red mouths smiling. A clatter from the drum, a blare from the horn, and all six flew about in twisting leaps and tumbles. Then the girls took collecting bowls and walked through the crowd, whistling the imperious pay-me of the street player.

There were dancing dogs and fortune-telling birds. Fire-eaters and jugglers whose patter came with an ease that matched the casual flip of their hands. There were street singers and dancing dogs. Cookshops and sweet vendors. Other vendors sold wine in throwaway clay cups and beer cooled by ice magicked from the mountains by the Tyrn's Own Wizard.

A woman with a round sweaty face, her hair tied up in a scarf, was breaking up sheets of foam candy with a wooden mallet and twisting the bits in squares of wax paper. Cymel bought a sackful for herself and Gryf and they wandered on.

There were country folk in linen and leather, and Broonkin, the men in slashed silk shirts and sueded leathers, women in long dresses trimmed with fur despite the heat of the day, wearing twisted silver headdresses with gauzy veils or turbans of feathers, or dozens of other absurdities that made Cymel and Talgryf giggle and point.

They watched puppet plays and rode the flying swings, watched spice sellers and perfumers playing the chaffering game.

Finally, when the afternoon was drooping to a close and they were weary, sticky, near sated with wonders, they went to watch the jumping at the horse show.

The place where four days ago Cymel had watched the scraper working and the sodders laying down the grass was now a lush green oval with viewing stands on both the long sides. The jumps were a series of weathered limbs set at various heights, a tree laid flat with a water splash on the far side, three waist-high hedges and a pair of brick walls set at a wide angle to each other, the whole a carefully manicured and condensed version of a hunt ride in the Broons. She and Talgryf had climbed up the back side of the eastern stand and sat on the backrest of the top row, their feet hooked round one of the uprights.

Talgryf poked Cymel in the ribs and grinned as a clumsy bay went down in the splash and dumped his rider in the mud. "Know that 'un," he whispered. "Rhona, she's a whore, she says he likes slapping women and . . ." He blinked and didn't finish what he was saying.

Cymel pretended to ignore him, though curiosity was churning in her belly. Her father wouldn't ever talk about this kind of thing or lots of other stuff she wanted to know, and he wouldn't teach her scrying so she could find out for herself. And she was annoyed because she couldn't figure out a way to get Gryf to explain what he was talking about.

Down on the green, the Stentor cried: "ANRYDD BAR-BRANSON, RIDING SERNRY."

The horse was a burnished sorrel with a cream-yellow mane and tail, the rider a boy a little older than Lyanz with much the same kind of golden beauty, though he was pure Ifordyar while Lyanz was pure Myndyar. Cymel had seen him here and there in Carcalon, mostly in the middle of a clump of boys his age or in the court under her window playing with swords.

Talgryf poked her again. "You wanna see good riding, watch this 'un. This is the gamp who won the Foolsride two years running and nobody does that."

As he spoke, Anrydd rode at a quick walk along the grass. He looked easy and relaxed, sat the saddle as if he were an extension of the beast.

The pace quickened as horse and rider neared the first jump. Sernry's ears were up, his dark eyes intent, and he was making small whuffing sounds audible even up where Cymel and Talgryf were. The beast was enjoying himself as much as the boy. His hind legs tucked up, he cleared the tree limb with room to spare, landed on stride and moved swiftly toward the second jump.

The round was quick and neat, with no refusals or hesitations, and only once did the horse even tick one of the jumps. He landed a bit short at the splash and kicked up some water, but that fault wouldn't count much against him. Anrydd seemed only along for the ride, but there were many in the stands with knowing eyes and they gave him the whistle tribute when he rode out the finish gate.

The Stentor stepped forth again. "THE HONOR'S ROUND. TOC UBANSON GAN GOOLAD RIDING ARIAN."

Cymel had seen him, too, usually with Anrydd. "Captain of the

Palace Guard and Tyrn's Champion," said Gryf. "He really is the best rider on Nyddys. You watch. You'll see just how good Anrydd is because he's almost as good as this 'un."

Cymel made a noncommittal sound and glanced again at the sky. It was filled with whorls and flows of Power, so much so that even the un-Sighted were growing nervous. Down on the green Arian was snorting and resisting control by the Champion, whose face had gone grim as he fought to acquit himself credibly. He turned the horse in a small circle first in one direction, then the other, then he began the round, pushing hard, riding the jumps as swiftly as he could. Cymel could see his mouth moving. He was talking to Arian, not cursing the beast, as far as she could tell, but soothing him, piling endearments on his nervous head.

He finished. It wasn't a beautiful round, or a flashy one, merely quietly competent.

Around Cymel there was a collective hiss as breath held for the length of the round was let out again.

Then she was being pummeled by Powerflows stronger than anything she'd come across before. It felt as if her skin were coming off and her insides were boiling. She bent over, clutching at her middle, trying to hold herself together.

Songbirds and raptors, wild tullins and colos, birds of all sizes and colors soared through a spiral overhead while the sky tore itself apart; pieces of blue fell and writhed in midair, chaos looking for shape. . . .

And finding it.

Dyf Tanew stood straddling Carcalon, his huge eyepools fixed on the City and the Fair.

Cymel straightened and stared as the immense head turned slowly from side to side.

A moment later the figure bent and lowered a hand the size of a river barge into Carcalon, a hand that passed unrestricted through the stone walls. The god straightened and stepped onto the green of the jump course. Fire leaped up around him, translucent flames that licked out through the crowd on the stands, the people frozen where they were by fear and awe.

Cymel shivered again as Power surged through her as if the flames were real, the heat real. The hair stood out from her head and her mouth dropped open in a silent scream. Beside her, Talgryf was sitting stiff and still as if he were paralyzed. She reached out, touched him. Raising her arm was hard work; it was as if she were trying to lift one of Bucochy's calves. And touching him was like touching stuffed leather; his skin gave under her prodding fingers, but there was a heaviness in him that she couldn't move.

There was one other who had dragged himself free of the spell or whatever it was.

Anrydd rode through the gate and onto the green, his sword raised in salute, the fire playing around him, the slanting sunlight glowing on his hair and turning the sorrel's coat molten, giving the man/horse combination a physical beauty more than human.

The god cried out, a huge cry that rolled like thunder across the land, then the image melted back into the air and the spell was lifted from those who watched.

Sernry reared, bugled a challenge, then Anrydd brought him around and rode him at a controlled trot from the arena.

Cymel caught hold of Talgryf's sleeve and tugged at it. "Gryf, let's go. You've got to get back and I do too."

Gryf blinked, stretched and looked around. "Hoy! That was something, wan't it? Yeah, time to get before this lot starts waking up and going goolie." He grabbed the top rail, swung round and began climbing down.

Cymel followed.

As soon as they were on the ground together, they started running, leaving behind the rising uproar at the jumping green.

At the Tyst Gate, Talgryf touched Cymel's arm. "See you tomorrow? Same time?"

"If I can. I think that'll be all right." She watched for a moment as he went trotting off, then held up her Pass so the guards could see it. When they opened the gate, she trudged back into Carcalon.

[3]

Oerfel stood a moment at the window in his tower office, staring at the place where the god had manifested himself and where he'd caught a brief glimpse of Anrydd's salute.

Amazing, he thought. It couldn't have gone better if I'd planned the whole thing. What a clever young rogue my Hero is. And how good his instincts are. You'll be Tyrn first then Emperor of the World, which is what that fool in Chusinkayan calls himself, but for you it'll be the real thing until you take the Flow and filter it for me.

He crossed to the worktable, shut the ledger and slipped it into a drawer. Time to get ready for another interminable evening while Dengyn played powergames with his Broons and pretended to relish the blatherings of those cursed poets.

16

Amhar Walks, Breith Watches

By the calendar of the Domains of Iomard, the 17th day of Sakhtos, the eighth month in the Iomardi year 6533, the 720th year since the last Corruption.

[1]

Breith threw the mooring rope to his father, then followed Amhar over the side of the sailboat and helped drag the boat up onto the sandy slope of the beach on the western side of Troman Bay. They were near the mouth of the bay and could look out on the blue-purple rollers of the great ocean south of Continent Saffroa. Past the grassy dunes he could see a hand's width of the tops of several trees. Willows, he thought, from the look of the pale green leaves and the thin withes that draped in the beginnings of graceful curves, willows growing along a stream that emptied into the bay a few sailmarks down the coast.

Though they were going to have their lessons and picnic on the bank of the stream, they couldn't pull up there. Beyond this point the shore was too marshy, with swordgrass, quickmud and hordes of black biters.

Breith took the roll of grass mats that Corysiam handed him, tucked them under one arm, looped the coil of thin rope over his other shoulder and started trudging up the unsteady slope of the nearest dune, following his father, who was carrying the food baskets with the water barrel strapped to his back. The wind off the bay was chill, but the sky was cloudless and the sun glared down hot enough to start sweat coiling down his face and back.

They were all the way out here because it was beyondlaw to teach magic to a boy even in the Riverine Confluence, with serious fines and a flogging as penalties, and what they were going to try couldn't be hidden behind House walls like the other exercises he'd been doing and the Window to Glandair. Despite that danger and the anxiety that went with it, Breith was enjoying the trip. It was good to get out from behind the House walls, to work with his father. He loved his Mam and his Mum but sometimes they drove him scandabug with all the things they expected from him.

Amhar came running up the dune and stalked along before them, staff in her hand, her eyes on the ground, watching for vipers and scuttlers with poisonous bites. Corysiam followed behind Breith with her bag of books and her herb kitchen.

With nothing but the heat and the sand that kept slipping away under his boots to distract him, Breith started thinking about school. He'd missed so many days they wouldn't take him back into Cadre Boig; Brother Bullan had set his heels in and just plain refused. If he went back now, he'd be down a year and in with a bunch of first-years, looking stupider than Gloy running with a lot of babies like that. He kicked at a clump of grass, sneezed as it popped a load of pollen all over him. As he wiped his sleeve across his face, he thought of Cymel floating down the river with that Lyanz, cool breezes, fun stuff to look at and a party at the end of the trip. If I could just Walk, he thought. If I could just step across and—

"Breith, stop dreaming and get along."

He sighed and walked faster.

[2]

Malart sipped at the lemonwater, then sat holding the cup on his thigh. "The last Corruption," he said. "Cory, I've taken the date match your sister's husband worked out as a point of search and I've hunted out the scrolls for those years in the Repository. Did you know how little there is? Some years don't even have birth lists. Those records that are there say nothing useful. Nothing.'

Corysiam shook her head, irritation written on her blunt features. "T'k! I must say I'm not all that surprised, Mal. I suspect the Domains wiped out the unorganized Riverine settlements and purged the Scribehalls of all records except for the genealogical ones—and from what you said, maybe some of those too. Could be some of the Domain leaders had blotches on their birth records that they wanted to remove."

"Hm. You Scribes should train historians and set up some sort of long-term society like the Dyar Watchers. All you're doing now is accepting and storing what the Domains give you and you only get the picture they think you should see. Do you know how much I want to read those Watcher Archives, how much I wish I were free of responsibility and could tease you into Bridging me across so I could spend the next five years just reading?"

A corner of Corysiam's full mouth twitched up, then the half smile was gone. "I know," she said. "A History Runda—I like the idea, Mal. Our Priom would never sanction such a deviation from tradition even if the Sinne Council considered allowing it. They're all afraid of change. Best not even bring it up."

"I wasn't thinking of anything official."

"I know. I've been talking with this one and that. I think something might be done. Ellar is willing to be as much help as he can, but he has cranky elders to deal with also. One of the things he suggested is to send some of our apprentices to Caeffordian Vale to train with the Hero Candidates. He says the Watchers in the Vale are quite interested in gaining information from us. They share your passion, Malart." She smiled. "Unlike most Siofray, who couldn't be less interested in what happened yesterday, let alone seven hundred years ago."

"Foolishness."

"So it is." Corysiam set her cup beside her on the roots of the willow where she was sitting. "But right now it's time for lessons, not talk." She leaned back against the trunk and looked from Amhar to Breith. "I'll defer to Malart on the research, but I will say that I've never heard of a male Walker, no matter how proficient he was at handling Pneuma Flow. This seems to be a quality that belongs strictly to Siofray women. I don't understand why." She paused for a moment, frowned at her feet. "I might talk to Ellar about this; the Dyar are better at such investigations than we are. I'd like to know . . ." She sighed. "Never mind, that's beside the point. Amhar, you're close to Walking. I want to see if Breith can follow you. Breith, this isn't something you can learn, at least not past a certain point. Either you can do it or you can't. Your visualizations are so strong and your Mum's talent is so rare, there's a chance you could be the first. I want you to watch carefully with your mind's eye and your body's eyes. Do you understand?"

Breith shivered with the intensity of his desire. "Yes," he said when he could talk.

"Amhar, see that patch of sand where the grass is thin? Clean it off completely, no twigs, leaves or grass roots. Don't stop till you have a circle whose width is about half your height. That is your anchor. Smooth it with your hands till you know it as well as you know the palms that are doing that smoothing. Lick the sand off your fingers so you know the taste. Put your head down and smell the sand until you know its scent. Listen to the sound of the wind in the leaves, the rustle of the dead things it blows along the ground. You know the theory, show me you can do the practice."

Amhar bowed and touched her forehead with the first two fingers of her left hand. Her eyes slid round to Breith and he felt her reluctance. She didn't want to do this in front of him, but she didn't protest, just stalked over to the chosen place and began preparing it.

Corysiam leaned down to talk with Malart while Amhar was busy with the anchor. Breith couldn't hear a word they were saying, only the murmur of voices half lost in the rustle of the leaves. He could feel the itch from the Pneuma tickling through the hairs on his arms so he knew either his father or Corysiam had set up a filter to keep their conversation private. He wrinkled his nose with disgust and decided to watch Amhar instead. It was satisfying in a squirmy sort of way to see the girl who'd put him through so many painful exercises set to work by *her* teacher.

He hadn't had the intensive teaching Amhar had spent years at, but he could see why she'd want to know intimately the site she was going to be stepping from and then back to. The notion that one could get lost on the other side and not be able to find one's way home gave him the grues. So he watched very carefully as she worked. If by some chance he had the ability to Walk, he'd be doing much the same thing soon.

[3]

"I know the anchor." There was an acerbic edge to Amhar's words. "Shall we do it?"

Breith wriggled where he was sitting, fought to control his excitement. He felt a small sting and looked down. An ant was walking on his arm; his wriggling had startled it into nipping him. He brushed it hastily away. He didn't want to miss any of this. So many distractions. His father watching. Maybe some of the same things Breith was feeling, his father was feeling also. A wondering. A wanting. Corysiam was there, stronger than he knew she could be. She was a Bridge as well as a Walker. That must be why Amhar came to her. Or was sent to her. A Bridge could carry others with her when she Walked from world to world. Safety net for Amhar if she walked across and couldn't get back. Safety net for him too. He hoped. He tried to believe that he would be able to Walk, but there was an empty spot inside him where certainty should be. He had tried things before that he simply could not do, and there was always that moment when he called on his will and his power and there was nothing there.

Corysiam got to her feet and crossed to the anchor patch. "Right. I'll step across first. I want both of you to watch the patterns of the Pneuma Flow that move with me. Watch and think about creating those patterns yourselves." She stepped into the circle of sand. "The first lesson, of course, is to look where you're stepping. I'll target Ellar's farm this time, because you both have looked over to that place and are already familiar with the area about the house. The two of you, look across to Glandair and watch what I do."

Corysiam vanished in a whorl of forcelines.

Breith struggled to sort the pattern as quickly as he could, then he looked across to Glandair.

The Scribe was standing on a familiar walkway, in the shade of the needle tree beside the house's front door. At that instant, a man came walking round the corner of the house. He scowled at her, his mouth moving. It was a simple Look not a Window so Breith couldn't tell what he was saying, but it seemed reasonable that he was asking what she wanted. Ellar must have hired him to take care of the stock while he and Cymel were gone. Breith's mouth pruned up. And that Lyanz.

Corysiam made a wiping motion with her hand. The man turned away and went back round the house. A moment later she was standing in the sand circle, swirls of Pneuma fading around her.

Amhar tapped her brow in a perfunctory salute. "What did you do to him? If you don't mind explaining."

"I took memory from him and I'm not going to tell you how, either of you. A hair too strong a touch and you'd turn a brain to mush, something worse than murder because at least death brings an end to suffering." She rubbed the side of her forefinger across her chin and looked thoughtfully at nothing for a moment. "Actually, this is no big problem. It simply gives you more data, Amhar, before you attempt the crossing. Hm. I want a place I know well enough to avoid complications. There are difficulties in stepping across into a place where you have no physical experience, some of them connected to the Pneuma and some to the reactions of the Dyar if they see you pop out of midair in front of them. They're a hasty lot, with a tendency to strike first and question later. First steps should be kept simple. And safe. Amhar, Breith, come here. Take my hands and Look with me."

Breith blinked and felt a little dizzy as he tied into a power he hadn't imagined before. Even his father's strength paled before this compelling Flow.

The scene opened before him.

A mountain valley surrounded by high angular peaks, black stone with snow tucked into the cracks and hollows. By comparison the mountainside that Cymel played on was a gentle place.

The lower slopes of these mountains were dark with conifers with the occasional lighter accent of an aspen or oak. Dozens of small streams tumbled down the scarps to join a narrow rushing river more white water than dark. The valley itself was serpentine, following the curves of that river. There was little brush and much grass and clover, good grazing for the herd of horses and a herd of what Cymel had called cows, beasts rather like tribufs but with much shorter hair and different coloring.

The scene shifted slightly and moved past the herds to some fruit trees growing around low wood buildings, unpainted and weathered to a pleasant silvery gray. There were three boys and a man doing exercises that looked all too familiar, though he knew that Dyar didn't have anything like Seyl-mating. Cymel had been rather shocked at what he'd told her, which considerably surprised him. He bit down on his lip. He didn't want to keep thinking about Cymel. He was annoyed at her. She was too much involved with Lyanz no matter what she said. Then he was annoyed at himself for letting his mind wander. Stupid. Focus. Listen to the Scribe.

". . . Vale of Caeffordian, where the Watchers have their Sanctuary. If you remember, Malart and I spoke of the Vale earlier. I have acquaintances there, but I'd best ask permission before I step over. Watchers are a mild and peaceful lot, but you don't want to startle them or cause them to view you as a personal threat."

She swam the point of view over toward a man that Breith hadn't seen because he was standing in the shadows just inside an open door, frowning at the boys who were doing their exercises with a lack of enthusiasm that Breith felt a great deal of sympathy for.

Corysiam brought sound to image and spoke. "Taymlo."

The man came forward. He wore a rough brown robe with a cowl pulled off to lie in folds on his shoulders. His square face was as hard and expressionless as if it had been carved with an axe from a pale, hard wood. His eyes were lost in the shadows of the ledge of his brow and the thick woolly eyebrows that grew there. As he stepped onto the flags of the practice court, his mouth curled briefly into what might have been meant as a smile. "Scribe." The voice that came through the window was far mellower than his appearance promised.

"I'm training a possible Walker. An apprentice Scribe. May I bring her there?"

"Why here?"

"Safety."

"The question is, whose safety? We would rather not attract the notice of the Nyddys Mage."

"I think you'll soon have no choice about that. There is a Hero Candidate on Nyddys and not one of yours. The Nyddys Mage has already tried three times to kill him and has done considerable maneuvering to keep him away from the Vale, but he has survived all that and will be coming your way soon."

Taymlo scowled. "How do you know this?"

"And why don't you? As to the first question, remember my relationship with one of your colleagues. As to the second, you should have been notified about the boy. I suspect the Mage has intercepted the carrier birds. If you wish, after the training session is finished, I'll step to Cyfareth and inquire."

"Hm. I'll consult with the others about that and get back to you. Meanwhile, I don't want you upsetting the boys. That should be no problem if you stay away from the halls and the practice grounds. Any area where you can't be seen from the grounds will be acceptable. And finish your Walking in not more than an hour. Lessons will be over and they'll have free time. As I said, I'd rather they weren't disturbed by things they are not ready to understand."

"As you wish. May the Pneuma bless you."

She shifted the Window away, set it swimming through the orchard and around behind a high, thick thorn hedge planted to keep the animals away from the fruit trees. There was a wind coursing the length of the Vale, its passage marked by the bending of the grass and the swaying of the trees, but the day was bright and sunny, the sky bluer than on Iomard.

Breith watched carefully as Corysiam examined a patch of short leafy stems that looked like lawn clover; her nostrils flared and her eyes moved rapidly from point to point. He tried to imitate her, though he couldn't tell if he was getting anything like the messages she was picking up. He drew back a bit, examined the Pneuma lines about her body so intently that he was startled when she gave a soft exhalation and straightened.

Corysiam freed her hands and stepped from the sand circle. "So," she said. "I will cross again alone. Focus on the Pneuma patterns, Amhar. Watch them carefully, see how they change when I will the step from the anchor to the place I visualize. As soon as I am in place, you view the landing area, will the crossing and come to me. Malart, would you bring me a glass of lemonwater? This is tiring business."

With his father's hand on his shoulder, Breith watched Amhar shiver, then do a few of the relaxing exercises she'd taught him. She gathered herself, her face intent, she stepped . . .

And landed beside Corysiam, staggering, the color in her face washed out to a greenish pallor. She fell forward on her hands and knees and all she'd eaten at lunch came spewing up. Even after she was empty, her body continued to convulse.

Corysiam dropped to her knees, caught hold of Amhar's shoulders, pulled her upright; she whipped a handkerchief from her sleeve and wiped the girl's face. "First time can be hard, I know. But you made it, and going back won't be so bad. It'll never again be so bad." She took a flask from her belt pouch and held it out.

Amhar took a mouthful of the water, spat it out to clear the taste of the vomit from her mouth, then she drank again. After a moment she lowered the flask. Watching through his Window, Breith could see her color coming back.

Corysiam rose to her feet and stepped away from her. "Can you go back on your own?"

"Yes. I've got it. I just have to make myself do it." Amhar drew her arm across her mouth, took another drink from the flask. She got to her feet and stood swaying a little until she'd got her balance again, then she turned her back on the pool of spew and stood with her eyes closed. The lines of her face sharpened until they had even more clarity than usual. Without opening her eyes, she brought her arm up and held out the flask. "You'd better take this. I think I should have my hands free." Her voice was hoarse and her hand shook a little.

Breith watched intently, trying to tease out the complex lines of force as Amhar stepped from Glandair and a second later was standing in the circle of sand. He could still feel nothing inside and he was afraid he never would. Malart's hand was warm on his shoulder, the fingers biting into his flesh. His father was expecting him to be disappointed, he knew that. And he knew from the strength of the grip that his father was ready to support him, whatever happened. He felt a flush of warmth, a love that he was too ashamed to speak of but that spread through his whole being. He looked up and smiled at his father, then touched the hand on his shoulder.

When it was his turn in the circle, he opened the Window to Glandair, glanced nervously at the landing spot, then looked into Corysiam's eyes.

She smiled and beckoned.

He planted bare feet in the sand, feeling it, knowing it, and willed the step to the other world.

Nothing happened. What he could see of the Pneuma Flow coiling round him was not at all like the pattern both Amhar and Corysiam had produced . . . so effortlessly.

He tried twisting the Flow, forcing it to curl and curve into the pattern he remembered, but he couldn't see behind himself and the curves were incomplete. He couldn't make them come. He pulled back within himself, tried to find the rest point his father kept talking about, the point of maximum leverage. The point from which his true strength flowed.

He wanted it too much.

He couldn't let go.

To let go would be to give in to the fear that might be what was crippling him. If he didn't give in, maybe . . .

He felt the swirl of the Pneuma. With a rush of excitement he thought the jam might be breaking.

Then he felt a body brush against him and knew the only thing that had happened was Corysiam returning from Glandair.

"It's enough." Her voice was quiet in his ears. "Breith, there's no shame for you because you can't do this. Think of it this way.

ou'll never bear a child. And why? Because you have no womb.
he capacity is not in you. This is the same thing. The capacity
not in you."

He turned his head away, his eyes tight shut to keep in the tears
e didn't want anyone to see. Maybe the capacity wasn't in him,
ut he could do so many other things that it didn't seem right
at he couldn't do this. And just because he was male not fe-
ale. It wasn't *right*!

"Come on, Breith." There was strength in his father's voice and
entered into him, gave him ease enough to open his eyes and
ep from the circle. He moved over to the baskets and the things
attered around on the mats, began collecting the dishes and
e refuse, busying himself so he wouldn't have to look at the
thers.

Behind him he could hear Amhar arguing with Corysiam. The
rl wanted to Walk again, but Corysiam was adamant.

"I'm tired," she said. "And it is a bad idea to cross over so many
mes packed so closely together. Walking drains you and affects
our thinking, almost like chugging down successive bottles of
ine without stopping to let it settle. You think you're alert and
oing just fine, but you'll end up spattered all over the Between,
oul-lost and very dead."

"But—"

"Tomorrow, girl. Not before. And not inside Valla Murloch.
ry getting sneaky and you'll learn what it means to be slapped
own by a Master. You hear me?"

After a moment of stubborn silence, Amhar sighed. "Yes,
cribe, I hear."

As Breith shifted the baskets to the ground and began rolling
p the mats, his head started to throb so painfully he couldn't
ee what he was doing. His skin itched all over and his knees
urned to jelly, dropping him hard onto the ground. Beside him,
Malart grunted as if he'd been hit and went down too.

Breith forced his head up and opened burning eyes.

The willow withes were whipping about wildly; erratic wind blew grains of sand and other debris across the open space; the sky was filled with whorls and Flows of Power. . . .

Then it tore itself apart; pieces of blue fell and writhed in midair, chaos looking for shape. . . .

Great winged figures of the Prophet's Messengers grew from the chaos and hovered in a vast ring above them, long, narrow hand touching long, narrow hand, long, narrow feet brushing the horizon. Then they *sang*. A wordless wondrous song that filled the sky and eased into Breith's bones, waking in him a vast amorphous hunger and at the same time healing his grief about his failure to Walk.

A few minutes after the Messengers appeared, they vanished.

Breith sighed, rubbed at the back of his neck. "What does that mean?"

He wasn't talking to anyone in particular, but his father answered, "I don't know. I think it might be a sign that the Corruption—"

Corysiam touched his arm. "When it's just us, call it the Settling, Mal. I am coming to dislike the other term. It reminds me too much of the power of the Domains and of the cantairs." Her face twisted together so her mouth went sour and her eyes nearly vanished as her brows came down. "And of the Sinne Council. They're getting so rigid that anything that stinks of a little thought is smashed before it can flower." She pulled her hand across her face, wiping away the sourness with it. "Breith, you and Amhar be very careful who you talk to about this. And you too, Malart. I'm not telling you to stay away from the Archives, but be very quiet about what you're doing."

"It's got that bad, Cory? Slionn hasn't made any difficulty about letting me see whatever I want."

"Slionn lives in her own world and takes note of the outside only when it intrudes on her. It is going to intrude on her soon.

'm afraid. I've heard rumors that the Archives will be closed to
utsiders within the year."

Malart shook his head, then went over to the water barrel,
lipped his arms into the straps. "Help me with this, Breith. It's
ime we were heading home."

· 17 ·

Scattering

By the secret calendar of the Watchers, events dating from the 4th day of Foolsreign in the 736th Glandairic year since the last Settling.

[1]

Covers kicked back, the sheets damp with his sweat, Lyanz lay on the bed, being miserable. He was awake but his head was throbbing, especially around his right eye, which felt as if someone had rubbed rocks in it. He had a dull pain in one shoulder worse than a toothache and a vague nausea hovered round his middle, intensifying whenever he moved his body. The Healer had assured him he wasn't going to die, but at the moment there wasn't as much comfort in that as there might have been.

He was alone. The Healer's Aide had looked in on him an hour ago, told him to behave himself if he wanted to get off the bed any time soon, filled the water carafe on the bedtable and left him to his aches. Lyanz turned his head to stare at the wall and grumbled to himself about Cymel running around having fun with Gryf and leaving him to rot. If she'd been on the job as she was supposed to be, this wouldn't have happened and it'd be him at the Fair with Gryf and her tagging along.

The air went suddenly cold. Frightened though he didn't know why, grunting at the pain, Lyanz pushed himself up and thrust his legs over the edge of the bed. When his good eye cleared, he saw a strangeness like a curve of pale pink-gray light passing through the wall and sweeping toward him. Before he could get to his feet, the light closed around him and held him. Heat tingled through him and he felt suddenly filled with vitality, the pain in his head vanished, the pain in his shoulder was gone, the blurriness in his eyes was gone, the nausea was gone.

The light moved again, passed through him and through the wall behind him.

Lyanz sat on the bed, blinking.

The air was filled with an effervescence that stirred the hairs on his arms, tickled his nose and made him sneeze. There was a faint smell too, rather like grass wet by rain after a long dry spell.

He pushed the nightshirt off his shoulder. The bruise was gone. The place where the horse's hoof had torn his flesh was closed up and there wasn't even a scar to mark where it had been. He touched his eye. No swelling. He pushed the bandage off his head and felt around for the slash that the side of the horseshoe had cut into his scalp. Again there was no cut and no scar that he could feel. He slid off the bed. No dizziness. An ache in his legs that had nothing to do with pain—it was just an urge to run and run and run till he'd run off the overflow of vitality.

He got dressed, smoothed his hair back and went out. The Healer and Ellar were going to have a fit, but he couldn't stand the thought of staying in that tiny room another minute. He galloped down the stairs, enjoying the free movement of his body, went swinging around a corner and found himself face-to-face with Cymel.

"Laz!"

Jigging from foot to foot, he scowled at her. "Look like *you* have good time."

"Well, I did." She stared at him. "Dyf Tanew."

"Huh?"

"There was Stuff," she said. "The God came. He bent over the Palace. He touched you, didn't he?"

Lyanz blinked. "Something."

"Where you going?"

"Somewhere. I dunno."

"Don't you ever think! You go loping around on your own and you-know-who puts his thumb on you and smashes you into goo."

"I can not stay no more. Walls push at me."

Cymel sighed. "I know. Walls everywhere. Just round the corner from this bunch of rooms, there's a bit of green and a fountain and nobody much goes there. But I better leave a note for Pa so if he comes in he won't worry. Have you had anything to eat? I was talking to one of the cooks' boys this morning and he showed me round the kitchen. Hoo! That's a big place. Like a cave. Anyway, he said if we wanted some extras anytime, just come see him."

"Not hungry. Need more . . ." He waved his arms.

"Yeh. I know. Walls. Tomorrow won't be so bad. Pa got Gryf a Pass so he could come in and see you."

Lyanz followed her back up the stairs. "But tomorrow is last day of Foolsreign. Maybe we all go into Tyst, huh? Gryf say the parade is much fun and Foolsride is wild."

"Maybe. I'd kinda like to see that." She crossed the landing and pushed open the door to the suite they'd been given. "Pa?" Over her shoulder she said, "That's just in case, Laz. If he was here, he'd've stopped you going out."

Lyanz shrugged.

[2]

The small walled garden was a pleasant place with several shade trees, a graveled path that wound through flower beds now bright with harvest blooms and a fountain that shot water up twice the height of a man, water that came cascading back down a series of basins to merge with the pool again. It was quiet there in the deepening twilight. Overhead a few stars had emerged from the mother of the day, visible and not visible as the high, thin clouds blew across them.

Cymel sat on a stone bench beside the fountain, finding a welcome peace here away from the crowds of the Fair and the sense that everyone was watching her. Over the steady music of the fountain, she heard the crunch-crunch of Lyanz's feet as he ran round and round the garden, following the endless weaving of the path.

After what seemed like an hour, he flung himself down beside her, dark amber hair stringy with sweat falling into his eyes, those yellow cat eyes that seemed to look at everything and believe nothing. "Itch under skin," he said. "Gone now."

She shut her lips firmly and said nothing, though she wanted to remind him again that itch or no itch, if he didn't watch out he'd waste all their care by getting himself killed. She'd meant to tell him all the things she and Gryf had done at the Fair, but now he could just wait till tomorrow and find out from Gryf.

He lounged on the bench, his shoulders squeezed into the corner where the armrest came out, his heels resting on the rim of the fountain pool. He watched her from slitted eyes and she knew he knew what she was thinking and was ready to yell at her if she tried saying it.

She looked away. No little gods about. She never thought she'd miss the pests, but she did. Sort of like missing an itch when the rash went away. She missed the cows and the horses and the ullins and the colos and even the stupid chickens that nobody with sense would like. I don't want to be here, she thought. I hope Pa gets this poet business finished soon and we can go home. I don't want Lyanz there either. I want it to be just us two again. I could get some more kittens from one of the other farms and raise them and do my lessons.

She got to her feet. "Now you've run your itch off, we better get back to the suite."

"Don't want to."

"Then sit here and get yourself killed. See if I care." She stalked off, heading for the gate. A moment later she heard the crunch of his feet as he sauntered along beside her. She didn't have to look at him to know he was pretending he meant to come all along. Cat, she thought, just like Cyswe when he did something dumb.

Remembering poor ol' Cyswe who got himself killed for his daring, she shivered and tears burned her eyes. She ignored them and marched stolidly on.

[3]

Ellar was in the suite's parlor talking with two strangers when Lyanz followed Cymel into the room. He got to his feet. "This is the boy," he said.

Lyanz put his hands behind him, nodded to the men and started to edge toward the door. He knew who they had to be and he didn't want any part of them.

He didn't get far.

"Come here, Lyanz."

"I go lie down. Not feeling so good."

"You can lie down later. Come here. Cymel, you also."

Lyanz came reluctantly across the room and sat in the chair Ellar had ready for him. Cymel slid onto the chair beside him. When he glanced at her, she was scowling. He didn't know why and the way he was feeling now he didn't really care. All this business about Candidates and Heros and the rest of it—so maybe it was true, maybe he didn't have any choice. But who said he had to like that?

"Diawad Beirnaddson, Cadarn Meddygson, this is my daughter Cymel and the Candidate Lyanz Kurrin of the Merchant House of Kurrin in Nikawaid."

The one called Diawad was the older of the two. He was a lump of a man with a round and rather stupid face, broad in shoulder and hip with legs like tree trunks. He was the image of the bucolic fool, but Lyanz had a strong suspicion that the real fool would be whoever judged the man by his looks.

Cadarn was equally deceptive, slender and so blond he might have been dipped in bleach and all the color eaten out of him. His eyes were like ice, the pale tint changing with the shift of his moods, sometimes bluish, sometimes greenish, occasionally a pallid gray.

Ellar turned to his daughter. "Cymel, it was considerate of you to leave the note. I'm pleased you thought of it. I'd like a few more details, though, about this healing and the appearance of Dyf Tanew."

Cymel wriggled as if she were even more uncomfortable than Lyanz felt. "Well, you said to be back here by sundown, so Gryf and me, we went to see the jumps. We were going to go home as soon as that was over. Anyway, we watched for a while; Gryf liked it when one of the riders got dumped in the water and came up all over mud, but I didn't laugh. Then the sky started going crazier than it's ever done before. . . ." She scowled at nothing for a moment, calling back the awesome image of the god. Then she started talking again, telling them what she suspected when Dyf Tanew bent and dragged his hand through the Palace. "And when I got back here, it was so. Lyanz was coming down the stairs like he'd never been kicked."

Lyanz kept his eyes on the floor, though he sneaked looks at Ellar and the two men from University. He hadn't forgot the names Ellar mentioned back before they left the farm, and this confirmed what he'd suspected. They were his guards—no, not guards, wardens here to scoop him up and haul him off to some weird place up in the mountains where he might or might not be safe from the Mage, but would without doubt be ossified by boredom. They'd have to set him out in a garden for birds to perch on, because he sure wouldn't be good for anything else.

Ellar sat without speaking until Lyanz wanted to scream at him. Then he merely said, "I think you see what I was talking about in my letter."

Diawad inclined his heavy head and managed to look stupider than ever.

Cadarn brushed invisible crumbs from his knees. "Indeed," he said. "But it's not something to speak of here." His voice was musical but a trifle thin. "We could perhaps meet in the Temple in Tyst. Tomorrow. During the festivities there should be few folks bothering to worship."

"After today's manifestation?"

Diawad cleared his throat. "All of Foolsreign is worship." His voice was almost a squeak, absurd in a man his size and age.

Cadarn patted his arm. "You always were a dreamer, Dawy. It has been a long time since the games people play during these five days have had anything to do with devotion."

This had the flavor of an old argument between longtime friends, an impression strengthened by Diawad's response. "Does not matter the intent, Cad, the doing is sufficient."

"To return to the point . . ."

The dry bite to Ellar's voice was so much like Lyanz's tutor when Sah Muali was being acerbic that Lyanz felt a roughness in his throat and a great longing for his home. He swallowed a sigh because he didn't want these people knowing how he felt; that was a weakness they could pick at and use to make him do what they wanted.

"We'll meet to discuss details of how we mean to proceed in the Temple at third watch the first day of Choomis. I think meeting during Foolsreign would not be wise. Until then you will act as guards for young Lyanz here. You don't need to keep him in leading strings, just in sight. Cymel, Lyanz, I am asking you to join us at that time. Until then, I don't intend to keep you chained to your beds; enjoy Foolsreign, but be careful. You know the dangers well enough. Don't play tricks on Diawad and Cadarn. That would be stupid." He got to his feet. "I have to get back to the Common Room. The Tyrn has ordered the four of us to construct and oversee a play for Foolsreign's last night."

He walked round behind Lyanz, tapped him on the shoulder. "You were extraordinarily lucky, Laz. I hope you remember that." When he reached the door, he looked back, a sudden grin wrinkling his face. "I don't expect you will."

[4]

Talgryf waited while the gate guard checked his list for the third time, as if he couldn't believe a twig from the bothir could possibly have a high-level invitation into Carcalon. When he couldn't figure a way to question what was written there without handing his head to his Day Officer, he looked around, saw a gardener's boy shambling along, carrying a bucket filled with a stinking liquid. "Hoy, you! Yeh, you. Come over here." When the boy was standing in front of him, he pointed at Talgryf. "Take this'n"—he checked the list again—"to the Guest Quarters in the South Tower and make sure he goes straight there and keeps his hands to himself."

"Gimme script. They chase me if you don't."

"T' Tears!" The guard tore a scrap of paper from the list, scrawled a few words on it with a pencil stub he unearthed from a pocket and thrust it at the boy. "Lemme see y' backside going round the corner bau clau, y' hear?"

The boy took off at a quick trot, still carrying the bucket and careful that he didn't spill it. When Talgryf tried to talk to him, he scowled and muttered, "Bothir trash." And trotted even faster, as if he couldn't wait to wash his hands of this job.

Cymel was waiting for them, sitting on a bench beside the door into the South Tower. When she got up and came toward them, the gardener's boy turned and trotted away without bothering to say a word. She looked after him. "What was that about?"

Talgryf shrugged. "How's Laz?"

"Oh, he's fine. He said he was too jittery to hang around waiting so he's over at the stables fooling round the horses. He said to bring you round when you got here. I think he just didn't want to have to explain about Diawad and Cadarn. He figured I'd tell you and that'd save him the trouble."

"What's to explain?" He followed Cymel around the curve of the tower, trying not to feel irritated at Lyanz.

"Well, like I said yesterday, there's this Mage trying to kill him, so these two men from Cyfareth, the University, you know, they're hanging round watching him, bodyguards. So he doesn't have to be stuck with me all the time."

Talgryf grinned at the acid in her voice. He wasn't the only one Laz was rubbing wrong. He agreed with Laz, though. No fun to have a girl like your little sister dragging along because she's the only thing keeping you alive. Made his skin itch just thinking of his half sister Moaren at his back all the time because she was some kind of witch and could keep off the little gods so they wouldn't spoil the lifts. Mo wasn't a bad kid but T' Tears, her mouth was never shut and her tongue never still.

Lyanz was leaning on the fence watching Anrydd Barbranson taking his mount through slow circles, trot walk canter, over and over. Two men a short distance off were watching Laz. Those must be the bodyguards Cymel's father found for him. Odd-looking pair. They had to be magic players like Cymel, so Talgryf decided he didn't want any part of them. Probably wouldn't take them half a glance to peg him and his father. . . . He swallowed, remembering his father's gray face and the way he crept about the room that morning.

He wouldn't let Talgryf get a Healer in. Cost too much, he said.

With me not earning. And I don't want you pushing too hard. What happens to me and your sister if the Guards mark you and put a watch on you?

He stayed back as Cymel walked over and slapped Lyanz on the arm. Laz gets healed by the gods while my da . . . Talgryf shivered and tried to stop thinking about that.

Lyanz left the fence and came running to him. "Hey, Gryf." He punched Talgryf on the shoulder. "Good see you."

"Hey, Laz, they gonna be hanging round all the time?" Talgryf nodded at the two men standing back but obviously watching them.

"Yeh, but they not do anything, just watch." He turned, jerked a thumb at the rider on the other side of the corral fence. "Want see that?"

"He's the one Mel and me were watching when the god showed up. I don't think so. The parade's more fun. I know this, um, lady who has a window if them over there got some spare coin."

"No. Not let me go in house, I think. Is a place on street?"

"Late for that." He thought a moment. "Got some ideas. Let's go. Faster we get there, more chance there is of finding something."

[5]

Oerfel sat grim and alone in his tower office, watching in his new scrying mirror as the two boys and the girl ran hunched over along the wharf and swung onto a barge heading for Tyst, hunkering down behind some barrels with a tarp roped down over them. The two men following them, sour scowls on their faces, did the same, finding a place to conceal themselves as the bargemen finished the casting off and started downriver.

Watchers from University. Open about what they were. Or relatively so. Perhaps there were others screened from him. He could search and find out, but the search was more likely to uncover him than fetch any useful information.

He focused the mirror on the boy. If he'd had any doubts before, this would wipe them away. Healed by the hand of God. That was a hard thing to contemplate, but a god was little more than a skinful of concentrated Pneuma, his form and nature shaped by the minds of his worshipers. If one knew this, one could find ways to manipulate him or conceal things from him.

It was that "little more" that was the problem. Gods were chancy things, liable to acquire understanding and act from it in ways that were often rather final.

He touched the mirror, blanked it. You're safe, Hero. As long as you're in Tyst and Carcalon. Hm. Ellar sent for them. Why? Not just to guard the boy. If he doesn't know what his daughter is, he'll have a fair guess. The Vale of Caeffordian. They'll be taking him there as soon as Foolsreign is over. Barge? Probably. Saves trouble with the Broons, the charges on the toll roads and raids by the landless infesting the bosc. Hm. A series of traps. If one of them gets him, fine. If not, a long stretch of nothing then the last trap when they're in sight of the Vale, almost home. Yes. The cliffs at the mouth of the Vale. A deep spell encysted there, ready when triggered to drop half a mountain of stone on that brat. Let Dyf Tanew put that splatter together again. Hunh!

[6]

Cymel shivered at the noise, but for the first time the crowds of people shoving at her and shouting in her ears didn't upset her; they filled her with the same kind of lift she got on the first warm spring day when grass and leaves were new. She hung on to Lyanz's shirttail as he wriggled after Talgryf, using her elbows and the heels of her boots to keep up with him and clear the way for herself.

It seemed to take forever, but Talgryf knew what he was doing. He got them into a wide alley and in place against the windowless brick wall at the end of a row of shops, so close to the street that Cymel could lean her arms on one of the barriers the city guards had put up to keep the parade route clear.

BOOM BAA BOOM BAA BAA BOOM.

Capering round and round, kicking their feet up past their ribs, men in skeleton suits and skull masks banged on flat black drums a handwidth wide and half a man tall.

BOOM BAA BOOM BAA BAA BOOM.

Clowns in Fool masks went whirling by, turning somersaults, producing squawks from small split-mouthed horns and slapping at each other with painted bladders on sticks.

BOOM BAA BOOM BAA BAA BOOM.

Black dogs with circles of white painted about their eyes trotted beside fancy Raudaus, men made up and costumed as half male, half female, one side all black, the other all white, the female dress elaborate frothy creations, the male clothing with enormous codpieces, the arms, legs and shoulders padded to exaggerate musculature. They paced sedately along, nodding their heads with regal disdain to the shouting crowds that lined the street.

BAAAA BLAH BA BLAAA.

Five boys—younger sons in Broon families dressed in tights and ribbons and high black boots—marched along playing hunt horns with enthusiasm but little skill, making a glad noise and enjoying themselves mightily.

Cymel grunted as Talgryf dug his elbow into her ribs. "Be ready," he shouted in her ear. "It's gonna get wild in a minute because the Tafflers will be coming along. They throw boiled sweets in wax-paper twists. Folks think it's lucky to catch as many as they can, so watch out you don't get knocked off your feet. Once you down, it's you be having the luck if you get up again." He leaned away, shouted the same thing at Lyanz.

The next twenty minutes were like being in a pile of mud bugs with the itch, elbows everywhere, bodies thumping against them, slamming Cymel into the bricks of the wall, hands in her face, some idiot grabbing a hank of her hair and pulling till she screamed with rage, kicking backward and apparently connecting with the right person because whoever it was let go and went away. Because some of the Tafflers threw high and bounced the sweets off the walls, she also managed to catch more than a dozen of the throws and dump them down the front of her blouse to keep them away from the overeager hands of those around her.

When this squad of Tafflers had passed, taking the chaos along with them, Cymel pulled out one of the sweets, unwrapped it and popped it in her mouth. She didn't often get any kind of candy; her father thought it wasn't good for her. Tongue moving over and over the smooth lump, she wiped her hands down her sides and began watching the parade again. She was hot, sticky, bruised and tired and having a better time than she could remember.

After the Fooltyrn on his absurd boat-wagon rumbled round the bend and came toward them, Talgryf leaned against Cymel, his mouth close to her ear. "I gotta go," he said. "Gotta work the crowd when the Foolsride starts. Best time. Tell Laz bye after I'm gone, huh? He'd want to come, and with those wardens of his watching, can't be done."

"Luck, Gryf. Be careful, huh?"

"Always am. See you round." A light touch on her arm, then he was gone.

She made a face, then fished down her blouse for another sweet and went back to watching the parade.

After the Foolsride was over and the alley began emptying, Lyanz came over to Cymel, who was leaning against the wall feeling worn out and ready to go home. Well, not home, but back to the suite where, even if she couldn't have a bath like she could at the farm, she could change her clothes and wash the muck off her.

"Where Gryf?"

"He had to go work." She looked past him at the two men waiting at the far end of the alley, then wriggled her eyebrows to remind him of his guards. "You know. He said to say bye."

"Oh. What you want to do?"

"Huh." She rubbed her hands together, made a face as they stuck and came apart with a ripping sound. "This was fun but I'm kinda beat. And I'd like to wash my hands."

"And your face, Mel. Hoosh! you a mess."

"Look who's talking. Hey, I know. You swim?"

"No. What's swim?"

"You mean you were on a ship all that time and you couldn't even swim? Pa taught me soon's I could walk. There was the stream, you know, and he didn't want me falling in and not being able to get out."

"What is swim?"

Cymel looked down at her clothes. They couldn't get messier if she lay down and rolled in the muck of the alley, so getting them wet wouldn't hurt all that much, and she didn't give spit about what those snobs inside Carcalon thought about her, so why not? "Let's go walking down by the river, and if there's a good spot, I'll show you what is swim."

[7]

Lyanz watched Cymel pull her boots off, then was terrified to see her wade into the river. She bent down, brought a handful of water to her nose and sniffed. "Good," she called back. "The water wizard is doing his job, it's clean." She moved cautiously a few steps farther into the river. "Come on. Kick your boots off and wade over to me. Don't worry. I can hold you. Aunt Cory showed me how to anchor to worldheart."

The place Cymel had chosen was a deep bite out of the bank on the outside rim of the last curve as the river flowed into Tyst. In some storm a few years past a huge tree and several smaller ones had been blown over and they had carried with them part of the bank. The river had scooped out a hole, established an eddy and left one of the trees partially attached by its roots, something that helped to maintain the eddy and protect the water in the small cove from the tug of the main current. There were more trees growing between the bank and the Tyst road, making the demipond shady and cool.

Lyanz lowered himself onto the grass growing at the edge of the downslope and stared at the dark water swirling and circling below him. He remembered all too well the storm that had nearly drowned him. If he hadn't caught hold of the spar before he was washed overboard with it, his bones would be rolling about on the bottom of the sea, his flesh in the belly of fishes. Diawad and Cadarn were silent in the shadows behind him. They hadn't tried to stop Cymel so this business was probably safe enough. That thought didn't help at all.

He looked over his shoulder at the two men. They were squatting beside one of the trees, looking bored. Cadarn glanced at him, more than a touch of impatience in his pale gaze. He thought he saw contempt there, too, as if the man knew how afraid he was. He couldn't stand that, so he swung round and began pulling his boots off. He didn't say anything to Cymel because he didn't trust his voice.

He made his way cautiously down the slope. When he stepped into the river and felt mud and water swirling round his ankles, for a moment his body froze. He could not force himself to move until he took in how gentle was the teasing at his skin, and noticed the downed tree that lay half in the water. It was, in a way, like the spar that had saved his life, and somehow seeing it gave him the freedom to walk deeper into the pool and join Cymel by the root that thrust from the water, a root belonging to a tree completely submerged.

The footing was uncertain, stones and mud and wood, so he walked very carefully, but he reached her without anything but a minor slide before he recaught his balance. He lowered himself onto the trunk beside her and let the water coil about him, cool and pleasant. He was suddenly glad that she'd had this idea, because he could feel his terror melting away.

He hooked his hands around the half-rotten trunk and eased lower in the water, letting it slide over his shoulders. "Feel good."

"Yeh." Cymel swung round and got to her feet. "Time," she said, "we start teaching you to swim, Laz. What my father says, first comes floating. You're kinda doing that already, but you really got to do it on top of the water, not in it."

She came round behind him and he could feel her hands on his shoulders, then slipping between his arms and his sides. "Let your hands come up and straighten your legs out," she said. "I'll hold you. Trust me. I won't let you go."

It took a minute to make himself believe that, then he let go of the trunk and stretched out. Her hands were steady and strong. He relaxed more and felt himself floating up until he was stretched out on the water. It was holding him up, it really was; even with the weight of his clothes tugging at him, the water lifted and held him. He raised his head to look along his body and scared himself into a short panic as his feet came up and his bottom sank.

"Tchah! Relax, idiot. That's one thing you got to do with water, you fight it and it whaps you. Tease it gently and it loves you."

He could hear Ellar's voice behind those words. It wasn't the kind of thing Mela usually said. Thinking that took his mind off his body and the water lifted it again. So. Mela was right. Relax. Nothing to it. The water was cool. And it . . . yes . . . it teased at him. He could almost go to sleep.

Then Cymel pinched him. "Lazy boy, time to do some work. Don't worry, once you know how to float, you don't forget. So I'm going to shift you over to the root. Moving . . . moving . . . feel it? Good. Now reach over with your right hand and grab hold of it. That's good. Now flip over so you're belly down. Hold your face out of the water and just float again."

It wasn't as easy as she made it sound, but he managed.

"Now. Keep your legs straight and kick. Don't bend your knees, just move legs up and down, up and down. . . . There, that wasn't hard, was it? Can you feel yourself pushing up against that root?"

Lyanz kicked vigorously and felt himself moving in the water. It felt odd, as if he were some sort of weird mix of fish and duck. Grinning, he kicked and splashed and felt the root tremble from the pressure he was putting on it. His clothes dragged at him and he wondered what this swimming thing would be like without them, but not with Cymel hanging round.

"Right. You got that. Now hang on and watch me. Look at what I do with my arms. You must have seen dogs swimming. Same thing."

[8]

Oerfel pushed aside the plans for Opening of the new session of the Cyngrath; this was his first Opening and it had to go well. As well as the Closing had. Though his grip was firm on this Seat, he wanted to give no leverage to those who were looking for reasons to complain. Everything was planned to a hair. In a moment he'd descend to the kitchens to make sure that the serving staff were ready for the Grath Dinner, then the Hall to be sure they'd stocked the Cyngrathmen's offices and got the festboard set up, the chairs and linens ready to go. And he'd be up early in the morning to inspect the clerks' uniforms and their cubicles.

"Ready ready ready," he muttered to himself, then he lifted a sheet of paper from his scrying mirror, tapped it and found himself watching Cymel swimming industriously about in a kind of cove carved out of the south bank of the river. The Hero was clinging to a root jutting from the water, kicking water into a froth and watching the girl chug along with a laborious dogpaddle. For an instant he was tempted—it would only take a twitch to shift the main current, send it licking into that cove, snatch that miserable pair of pests and carry them off.

But only for an instant. Even all-knowing Dyf Tanew couldn't predict what that girl would do, but whatever it was, it would spoil everything. And the two Watchers standing guard were young and comparatively inexperienced, but even they could pull a couple of children from the water.

He watched a moment longer, teasing himself, enjoying his own frustration, then he went back to work.

[9]

Her father was waiting for Cymel as she came dripping through the door with Lyanz close behind. He rushed to her, caught her by the shoulders and shook her, then shook her again between each sentence of his scold. "What did you think you were doing?" Shake. "Why did you think no one would run and tell me about my wild daughter, looking sideways at me so I could see what they meant?" Shake. "Or did you think at all? Did you?" Shake. "Will you ever think before you do something stupid like that?" He flung his hands toward the ceiling. "If it isn't enough that you embarrass me before these people, you might have got Lyanz killed. The Mage has nearly drowned him twice, how many more opportunities do you mean to offer him?"

Lyanz knew he could slip away without being noticed, but he didn't feel right about that so he hovered in the doorway. He felt a sudden sharp bite of grief; his father used to shake him like that, whip him with his tongue like that. He was dripping over the floor, holding his boots because putting them on would have ruined them and he didn't know when he'd get more; his fingers were cramped and his eyes burned. From the river, he told himself.

Ellar thrust his fingers through his thinning brown hair, then began pacing about the room, talking more to himself than to them. "I've just been told," he said. "I've been appointed Court Poet. I'll have to rent the farm, maybe Dyrys will take it. Somebody has to care for the land and the animals. I thought for a while I could keep you here, Cymel. I thought I could find someone to teach you how to go on. You've just made it very clear how impossible that is. I have to think. I don't know what to do."

"Send me with Lyanz. To that Vale place. Then you won't have to worry about me or him either." Her voice was flat, tired.

"No!" The word exploded out of him. "No," he repeated more quietly. "That's out of the question."

"Why?"

"There are no women in the Vale. You're old enough that you're soon going to need a woman around to take care of you and teach you things. . . ." Blood reddened his cheeks. Lyanz thought it was horrible to see an old man blush like that. "Things I can't," Ellar finished in a rush, "that no man can."

"Aunt Cory."

"No!" Ellar dropped into a chair. "Cymel, think about Cyfareth. Little Noll's there; he can show you around, help you get settled." He drew in a breath, let it trickle out, the lines deeper in his face from weariness and frustration. "Go get yourself cleaned up, will you? We'll talk about this tomorrow. Every time I . . ." He looked past her at Lyanz. "That's all I need, the pair of you down sick with a flux."

As they went down the hall toward their rooms, Lyanz touched Cymel's arm. "Sorry," he said. "It is always me make trouble, yes?"

She jerked her arm away, glanced briefly at him, her face unhappy and full of anger, a mix he'd seen in her too often since she'd brought him to her home. She didn't say anything, just walked faster to leave him behind.

"Mela . . ."

"Just shut your mouth. You don't understand anything. Just shut up. Shut up. Shut up." She turned into her room, slammed the door in his face.

Shaking his head, he went into his own room, dropped the boots on the floor and stood flexing his fingers to get the feeling back into them. Nyd-Ifor was becoming easier to understand even though he still had some trouble speaking it, but his mind got so tired sometimes that it just stopped working and nothing made sense. "I want to go home," he said aloud in the Nikawarish that was like the cool river water against his ears. "I want words I can understand, I want people who act as they're supposed to and don't confuse you all the time, I want a place where things make sense without you having to puzzle at them. I don't want to be a stupid Hero."

18

Rebellion in Tilkos

By the secret calendar of the Watchers, events dating from the 29th day of Choomis, the sixth month in the 736th Glandairic year since the last Settling.

[1]

Whan sat on one of the lower limbs of a matete tree, his feet dangling, his face hidden in shadows, watching with distaste as the firelight turned the faces of the circle of swamp witches to masks of red and black. *We take our allies where we find them. Who would have believed I'd play devil for a Kale Mage and minion to a stinking Tilker pretty boy who thought he was being oppressed? Who didn't know what he was talking about. But we need him for now. Let him and his kind get rid of the Kale Born. Then we get rid of him.*

He twisted the hairs in his sparse beard as he waited with impatience for the witches to emerge from their separate trances and start doing something. Anything. These were powerful and holy folk, but he was almost nostalgic for Gurra. *The Tilker might be a hotheaded twit, but at least he got things done without talking them to death.*

A softwing, one of the white ones, fluttered into the circle of sitting men and women, flew a spiral about the fire, then plunged into it and burned to ash before it reached the red heart of the flames.

As if that were the signal they waited for, the witches stirred. Still they said nothing. The oldest of them rose to her feet finally and looked beyond the circle to Whan then to Taru and Rapa, who squatted at the base of the tree. "We are of the Dal Rawa and none of ours will go out from here. We do not understand the actions of the Kale Mage. We do not understand the sendings of Wai Kaha, all Blessèd be Her Name. We do not understand your doings, Stone Men. You say one thing to us and act another. We have seen this and we will not be part of it. These things we will not do."

An old man rose and stood beside her. "We are of the Dal Rawa, and though none of ours will go out from here, there are certain things we will do. Be assured that we will not turn from these tasks, for they will hold the Dal Rawa safe while the world changes. We will burn again the Snake Man fort that is a wound on the tip of the Finger of Wai. We will burn the Snake Man village that sits in its shadow. We will allow nothing to be built on their ashes. We will close the Finger of Wai to the Snake Men's ships and the trader's ships and all ships that come from outside. This we will do for as long as the Kale Mage turns his eyes from us. We cannot stand against him. We will flow before him and close behind him. He will do as he will."

A third witch stood. Unlike the others her face was covered and her form lost in a weaving of vines and leaves. When she spoke her voice was young and beautiful. It brought a flush of heat to Whan's face and loins and that angered him, but he stayed silent and listened.

"We are of the Dal Rawa and none of ours will go out from here. When this night is finished and the sun touches the leaves of the tallest hinapor, the Dal Rawa is closed to all outsiders. You will leave us now, Stone Men, and you will not come back. So say

the Maka of the Dal." She lifted a leafy arm and a boy came from
the shadows under the trees.

He waited for Whan to slide down from his branch, then he
turned and walked away. The hillmen followed him, having got
as much as they'd expected and nothing more.

[2]

Gurra Rasidal reached up and tugged the cowl farther forward
though the edge dropped in his eyes and made it difficult to see
anything but the toes of his boots. He pulled his cloak close
about him and knocked on the door.

He was in a noisome area on the landward side of Chierim, in
a lane that straggled into the barren hills above the port, the
weathered shacks on either side looking as if a heavy breath of
air would turn them into kindling and dust. Some of the houses
had meager gardens, a few rows of vegetables and a goat or two.
Others sat in barren plots and stank with the accumulated filth
of generations of poverty.

The door he knocked at belonged to one of the sturdier houses
one with a front thicket of naiyee reeds, each reed as big around
as a man's arm and twice his height. The door was made from
segments of those reeds and the roof was thatched with their
sword-shaped leaves.

The door opened and a wiry little man stood holding the handle of a small clay pot, wreathed in a cloud of stench so horrible that it brought tears to Gurra Rasidal's eyes and a rasp in his
throat so bad he couldn't speak. If he'd come to the right house
and it looked as if he had, this was the war wizard Shirgun
Jabb.

"I suppose you're the client Kirm was talking about," Jabb
said. His voice was surprisingly deep, so big that his body seemed
too slight to contain that much rumble. "Don't stand there like
a lump. Come inside. I haven't got all day."

Gurra Rasidal coughed, coughed again. His eyes were streaming and his head was starting to swim.

"Pah! Feeble, they're all feeble excuses for men these days." abb went away, his feet making an odd scratching sound as he walked.

Gurra reeled from the doorway, braced his back on the house wall and sucked in repeated lungfuls of the relatively clean air that hung about the small patch of barren earth between the house and the naiyee hedge.

When the wizard came back, Gurra followed him inside; at first he was reluctant to take anything but the shallowest of breaths, but when he settled himself in the chair the wizard abbed a thumb toward, he relaxed. The worst smell in this room was that of a solitary man who bathed less often than he should.

Now that he was here he didn't quite know how to ask what he wanted. It was impossible to visualize this little worm of a man running and hiding, riding in a scramble to hit a target, doing what damage he could, running back to his hole. Gurra had come here sure of himself; these doubts made him angry so when he spoke he was more abrupt than he'd planned. "War wizard, what do you do that makes you worth your fee?"

"I am a wizard of the air, so I do not do earth moving or waterflows. I do explosions to take out walls, accelerated dry rot in beams and rafters, unquenchable fire, attack stenches and wind-carried poisons—though because of the necessary dilution these do not kill, just make ill or uncomfortable all things that breathe. Given enough time I can produce whirlstorms sufficient to take down structures or disrupt any line of march, spook horses and other draft stock. Also, given time to arrange the proper conditions, I can generate lightning displays to produce fear and do damage. I won't bother listing the other, lesser items in my compendium. Do any of those meet your needs?"

Gurra grew calm and centered as he heard the eagerness tha
the Wizard couldn't hide. The hook was set. The man ached t
use his skills, and with no war for the past hundred years, thi
rebellion was his only chance. "No doubt all of them will prov
useful, if you are as proficient as you claim. We will want yo
working with us for the next year. Your go-between settled fo
thirty golds a month with a bonus at the end-of-the-year mont
of one thousand golds if you are still in our employ. There wi
be a trial period of six months. You will be expected to live roug
with the men, and on occasion you could be required to uphol
your end of defense either with weapons or with your magic. Yo
will be given two servants, one to deal with your bodily comfort
and one to take care of your riding string and your gear."

"Might I ask where this employment will take me?"

"You will be told that when you join us. Any notions tha
occur to you before then should be kept strictly to yourself."

"Of course. The fee?"

Gurra reached into his shirt, brought out the heavy purse tha
had been riding just above his belt. He set it on the table. "On
hundred eighty golds." He set a roll of parchment beside th
purse. "The agreement between us."

Jabb touched the parchment, drew his hand back. "That'
spell marked."

"It binds us both, or so I have been told. I have also been tol
that you will know this. The payment is for six months. The spe
binds for six months. Examine it if you have the skill."

"You are a cautious man."

"Very few would agree with you, but then there are very fev
wise men among my acquaintances."

Jabb got to his feet. "I need some . . . shall we say, tools."

Gurra rose. "Until I know yes or no, you and I will not par
company."

Jabb shrugged. "If I decided to betray you, Tilk, you could d
nothing to stop me. But have it as you wish."

* * *

An hour later Gurra Rasidal walked down the miserable lane, content with the world and with what such a small portion of his stolen coin had bought him.

[3]

In the foothills of the Ascarns, the mountain range that marked the boundary between Tilkos and Faiscar, two children played in the mud beside the well where their older sisters were walking the lift to keep the irrigation flume filled, as their mother guided the stream of water between rows of zamin plants about ready to give up their tubers to the grubbing hoe. The children were a boy and girl, twins about three years old. This was not free-hold land, but neither was it bound. It existed in the shadowland of the tied-acreage. It couldn't be sold without the consent of the Parashah and a third of the price would be paid to him, but it could be passed through inheritance to anyone who was designated heir by the current Tie.

The twins' father, who was the Tie of this farm, was in the lower meadows with his farmhands, marking the breeding stock for overwintering. All those not so marked would be slaughtered and the meat salted away in barrels. The winters were harsh in these uplands and there was no way to feed the full herd.

Two barrels of salt meat would be left on the oathstone, a bribe to keep the hillmen from raiding them once the snow was on the ground.

The boy dug in the leak-pool with a cracked wooden spoon, turning over the spoon to watch the mud splash down into the water, gurgling with pleasure at the sound. The girl ignored her brother and used her hands to shape mud into small round pies; like her brother she was soaked and happily dirt-covered, her small braids standing out from her head like the tails on a pair of very young kittens.

Something caught her attention. She lifted her head, over-

balanced out of her squat and plopped down in the puddl⟨
"Mar," she said. "Big mar." She pointed.

The head of an immense cowled serpent rose above the tree⟨
soaring higher into the sky than the peaks of the Ascarns behin⟨
it. It was a thing of colored light shimmering in the sunshine ⟨
if it had dreamed itself real—the Dark Wyrm that the hillme⟨
served come out from the great cavern where legend said it slep⟨

The boy let out a howl and began crying, his face red with th⟨
intensity of his need.

The sisters stopped their treading and gaped at the vision.

The mother called out when the water flow diminished, angr⟨
until she looked up and saw the looming Serpent. She ran fro⟨
the field to join her children and stand staring as the creatu⟨
swayed, its head turning and turning, terrible opaline eyes loo⟨
ing out across the land.

It began moving, undulating slowly southward, leaving behin⟨
it the scent of purpose and rage.

The mother slapped at the oldest girl's arm. "Well, it's gon⟨
Zam don't pay no mind to walking gods and hillman gods at tha⟨
so get you back to treading."

Late that night the Tieman woke to hoofbeats, several horse⟨
coming fast, then a pounding on the gate of the stockade ou⟨
side the small stone-walled farmhouse.

"With us or against us," a voice bawled from the darkness, the⟨
hoofbeats again as the riders left. The Tieman lay stiff with ange⟨
and fear. He knew that voice. Pakan the hillman.

There were creaks from the sleeping loft as the daughters wok⟨
"Pa, wha . . . ?"

The woman sat up in bed. "Chaya, it's nothing. Go back t⟨
sleep."

"Ma?"

"You too, Ruzasha. Don't let me hear a peep out of you." Sh⟨
lay back, took her husband's hand.

For a long time they lay awake wondering what they were going to do.

4]

The Buyegil Fort has fallen! The road has been cut between Murta Darset and the coast. Tilkos is in open revolt."

The Third Prince stalked into the Council Room, stood head up, feet apart, hands hooked into the belt of his ceremonial short sword. He repeated more quietly what he'd said after he sent the doors crashing open. "Three message tullins have arrived at the Karagh. One released from the Fort, two from Murta Darset. The Governor has called on the Yarashahs to provide men and supplies and has summoned the Subbashars from the smaller forts in the hill country. He requests support from the Olch Omir before winter closes the passes into Tilkos."

The Olch Omir was a man who had once been enormous but in recent years had lost flesh until his skin hung in great folds from his bones. Rumors about his health blew continually through the halls of the Palace. He sat unmoved, his head on the cushioned rest of his carved Seat of State, and stared coldly at his youngest surviving son. He lifted a finger on his left hand.

The Speaker to the Omir looked nervously at the finger, then in carefully round and resonant tones, he said, "The Olch Omir has heard you."

The Third Prince bowed, swung round and walked from the room, ignoring the hisses that followed him. His breach of custom had been deliberate, a challenge thrown down before his father and before the First Prince, who sat silent beside the Omir.

In his workroom, Mahara smiled. Events were marching in disciplined subservience to his plans. The First Prince would find his dreams interesting tonight, and perhaps tomorrow the Third Prince would find himself General of a punitive army sent to uphold the honor of his line. Got out of the city that way and ex-

pected to die in the process, perhaps given a slight shove ont
the Black Road.

Mahara looked in the mirror and chuckled aloud. The Aud
ence was ending with most of the agenda unheard, and the Firs
Prince was waving the Omir's Ichuged out of the corner wher
he stood in his dark robes and veil. "Already taken the point, hav
you? Hah! Rid of Zulam, rid of me at the same time. Two threat
converted to assets. It's almost a sin to wipe out such a suppl
mind."

He tapped the mirror and the scene in the Audience Chan
ber vanished. Then he leaned back in his chair and contemplate
the hands laced across his stomach, working out how he coul
maneuver so that the army was firmly in the Third Prince's gri
and the idea of conquest planted in the Third Prince's mind.

19

Marching North to the Grass Clans

By the secret calendar of the Watchers, events dating from the 1st day of Seimis, the seventh month in the 736th Glandairic year since the last Settling.

[1]

With Kamkajar the Merciful and Almighty, the Parter of Seasons, striding before them, his winged Alaeshin fluttering over his shoulders, the four clans rode into the farmlands of North Chusinkayan.

This was the way they came.

Nagar Burrik was to the left. Snop Kra was to the right. Dmar Spyonk and Ser Turuk took the center.

The men and the unchilded women rode their ponies in a wide fan before the supply wagons with mothers and children on board. Half a day's ride behind them, where they'd have the best chance of being safe from attack, were the herds of the clans, the boys not yet men moving them along and retrieving strays. The children the clans captured from the Apostates would be sent back to the boys and herded like the kakars.

The clans rode across stubble-filled fields, the grain and straw already carried away to the granaries. Shortly before noon they came to the first of the farmhouses.

It was the prerogative of the Dmar Spyonk as the first to whom
the Alaeshin had spoken to be the first to burn the taint of the
Unbelievers from the suffering land. Rinchay touched the torches
as the Spyonk rode in circles around her and each torch exploded
into flame with the lightest brush of her fingers.

Round and round the house they rode, and one by one they
threw their torches at it until the fire caught and the house
burned. Then they brought the wagons to the granary and trans-
ferred the grain into the leather sacks the women had sewn for
this moment. When the drive was complete and the god ap-
peased, the Lalumas of the clans would purify the grain, and it
could be used for winter feed.

They left ash behind and rode to join the clans once again, taking their place at the center.

Around mid-afternoon on the second day, the great fiery figure
of the god halted before the horde. He stood with his arms outstretched, rays of red light welling from his fingertips, reaching
from horizon to horizon.

The first village lay before them, sealed behind stone walls,
filled to bursting with the Apostates who fled from their farms
when they saw the god marching toward them.

The Lalumas of the clans let their chant drop into silence.
While the fighters of the clans stretched into a circle that held
the village at its center, they who dreamed moved into a knot and
stood assessing the spirit of the stone and wood that blocked their
purpose.

Rinchay Matan sat in her gur breathing the smoke of the jeglin
powder. When it was ready her soul sank into the earth and was
a serpent undulating through earth as a fish undulates through
water.

She knew when she was under the village wall; she could feel the weight of it. Around her, other soul serpents moved through the earth. She could feel their vibrations.

Roots dropped like fringe around her, moving slowly to the currents of the earth.

She sang to the roots, sang growth into them and fed them from the red heart of earth herself.

And she felt them grow.

She felt the walls groan above her.

She felt the stone cry out as roots writhed through it, breaking it to rubble.

Enough, she sang.

And the word came back to her threefold. Enough. Enough. Enough.

Rinchay Matan came from her gur and stood looking at the tumbled walls of the city.

Around her the Dmar Spyonk cried out in triumph and rode their ponies into the face of the arrows and spears of the Unbelievers and Apostates, knowing that should they fall, He Who Walks in Fire would reach out his golden hand to receive their souls.

[2]

Though the stream of landfolk fleeing the north Kays thickened daily, and rumors of death and destruction and the march of gods burned through the working and clerking classes around Banyakor, the Grand Council and the Kizoks domiciled in the guest wings of the Palace managed to ignore these events, and the Emperor was so caught in the entrancements Hudoleth provided for him that he wouldn't have noticed the earth opening beneath his feet. Life in the Palace encouraged this sense of separation from the hard realities the people who supported their ease had to face.

Hudoleth was content to have it so. The greater the need, the greater the army that would be raised to meet it.

The elegant drift of Court life was shattered irretrievably, though, when news came from the north that the Grass Clans had burned to ash and earth every structure in Kay Panok, including the Great House of the Kizok of Kay Panok, and were nearing the Finger Lakes area, Kay Yubihok and the Dedicated Lands of Kingakun University.

Instead of summoning her, the Chancellor of the University, in such humility as he could gather about himself, came to Hudoleth as she was in her office, dealing with problems her students brought to her. He waited until she was finished with one, then inserted himself in the place of the next.

Hudoleth sat behind a worktable making notes in a Daybook as she leafed through the papers in a folder bearing the name of the student who had the next appointment. She knew who had walked through the door, but concealed both her knowledge and her satisfaction for a few breaths, then looked up and established surprise on her face. She rose from her chair, pressed her palms together and bowed. "I am honored, Revered Sobakareth. How may I serve you?"

Chancellor Sobakareth cleared his throat. He was unhappy and uncomfortable as a suppliant; it was not a role he'd been in since the day he was weaned. "Scholar Hudoleth, the University lands near the Finger Lakes are threatened by the march of the Grass Clans."

"I see. What will Kingakun be doing? I will be sure to help in whatever way I can."

The Chancellor cleared his throat again. "It is necessary to reach the Emperor's ear. The Belovèd of Sugreta must arise from his august meditations and summon an army to drive those wretched animals back to their graze."

"The Belovèd of Sugreta will do what he will do," she murmured, savoring the frustration she could sense in him. She could afford to savor it since her plans were working out so well.

His mouth tightened. "The Kizok of Kay Panok and the Kizok of Kay Yubihok have endeavored to reach the Imperial Ear but their voices have been smothered by the layers of protection about him." He drew in a breath and let it out, then brought himself to state explicitly the request that she had refused to intuit. "You have pierced those smothering veils, Scholar Hudoleth. We ask, and by we I mean the Kizok of Kay Panok, the Kizok of Kay Yubihok, and I speaking for Kingakun, that you carry our plea to the Emperor."

Hudoleth inclined her head. "I am summoned to the Presence in two days. I will carry the message when I go."

She watched him leave and allowed herself to smile for just a moment, then she summoned the next student waiting for her.

On the seventeenth day of the seventh month, the month of Frost and First Snow, an Announcement was carried to the four corners of the land.

> *He who is Blood and Blessèd of Sugreta the Great and Merciful, the Emperor of all Chusinkayan, requires that the Kays of this Realm honor their Oaths of Fealty and Service and send a tenth part of men, armed, mounted and supplied, to the Army of the Realm, their term of service being Three Months of training and One Year beyond full induction.*

Kay Yubihok burned.

The University retreat cottages at the Finger Lakes burned.

The Grass Clans swarmed yet farther south.

From the walls and roofs of Banyakor people could see billows of smoke, some black, some white, some an indeterminate gray, and an occasional red flicker of fire.

* * *

The Army of the Realm finally assembled and marched north. The sun shone briefly on them, touching armor to bronze fire and turning helmet crests to jewel-colored spun glass. The clouds blew shut and a cold rain fell. The people on the roofs and walls went inside, reassured by what they'd seen and the evidence that of the Emperor's tender care for his folk.

Hudoleth watched the departure of the army in her mirrors, smiling grimly. They went with confidence that the barbarian invaders would be swept aside as easily as one brushed gnats from a sleeve. Those soft men would soon learn the folly of their belief. The biggest fools among the soldiers would die in that first clash. And she could judge which of the Generals were worth keeping and arrange for the worthless to die.

And this was only the first clash between Kay and Clan. Behind these four clans there were four more and another wave behind them. By the time the last wave rolled into Chusinkayan, her army would be hard and sharp, ready to move into Nikawaid.

She watched a while longer, then turned her attention to Mahara. She was pleased with what she saw. He was several months behind her, hadn't even got his army assembled yet.

She stretched and yawned, then went back to her delicate probes into Nikawaid, looking for hot spots where she could stir up trouble.

20

Scattered Efforts

By the secret calendar of the Watchers, events dating from the 7th day of Choomis, the sixth month in the 736th Glandairic year since the last Settling.

[1]

The stirring below tickled at Oerfel's mind as he gathered his sheaf of papers and prepared to attend the first meeting of the Cyngrath since the end of Foolsreign. He left the papers on the worktable beside his favorite ink bottle and the pen caddy and went to lean into the window of the Grathtower and look down toward the river. He could just see the landing where the barges tied up.

The Hero Candidate was having trouble leading a dun gelding onto the Northgoing barge. One of his escorts left his own mount and went to help. Guards. Oerfel drew his hand across his mouth. These men worried him not at all.

He turned away, settled his official gown about his thin body, moved the stone bottle and the pen caddy into the carrying case and slid the papers beside them. For the first time since he had taken up his new post, he wasn't pressed to do a dozen things at once. It would be three weeks before the boy and his guards reached the first of his traps. He could leave them to their travels and concentrate on the other aspects of his plans.

He went out, turned the key in the lock and dropped the chain about his neck. For the moment, all he had on his mind was the titular task for which he'd been appointed as Secretary to the Cyngrath, recording the acts of the Cyngrath, comparing his records to those of the clerks in his employ and finally overseeing the entry of those records into the great Daybook of Nyddys.

[2]

Silent, still so angry she didn't feel like talking to anyone, Cymel stood beside the pile that was her baggage and that of Hanner Corbswyf and glowered at Lyanz as he tried to get the horse up the planks and into its deck stall. He was having lots of trouble and she was glad of that. Aunt Cory wouldn't even talk to her last night when she tried to reach her. Cymel had seen her, but her aunt just shook her head and drew a hand between them, cutting off the Sight. Everybody was shoving at her, pushing her away.

The horse didn't like the footing and kept balking as Lyanz urged him onto the ramp. Finally the Watcher Diawad left his horse and went to help. Working together, they got the skittish gelding onto the deck and spring-tied into the stall.

Her father came through the Wallgate and stood beside her. At first she wouldn't look at him. She was hating him rather a lot and didn't care how much he hurt. Still, she didn't know when she'd see him again. She didn't want to bawl like a baby, she was almost a woman now. At the same time, she felt like howling. She looked at her feet.

"It's for the best, Mela. Even if all this hadn't happened. . . ."

She scuffed the soles of her boots against the landing planks and still wouldn't look at him.

He set his hand on her shoulder. "The five months will pass so fast you won't even know it. And it will be spring again, ice out of the river, time for visiting. I'll miss you, my Mela. But I have to do what's right."

The barge horn blew, a call for passengers to get on board.

Cymel gulped. She'd never been able to stay mad at him. It didn't seem fair, but there it was. She flung herself at her father, hugged him hard. Her face pressed against his neck, she said, "You have someone bring Ymfach and Oorta and the colos over here. I want letters, Pa. You write me, you promise?"

"I'll do what I can, Mela. Now you better get on board. It's time."

{ 3 }

Ellar came back to his too-quiet rooms and dropped into a chair, feeling at once wretched and relieved. He was already missing his daughter; he liked having her around and sending her off like this came close to hurting as much as the day he'd lost Doeta.

But he didn't like having her *here*. She was too accustomed to honest folk who didn't pretend to like and admire you then seek to destroy you behind your back. The capacity for hurt at this Court was beyond her experience, even her imagination.

Cyfareth wasn't ideal; there was a lot of ambition behind those walls and folk who'd do just about anything to get what they wanted, but Cymel's qualities of character and her potential for working the Pneuma Flow would win her a degree of respect. Something that wouldn't happen here.

"Sometimes you can tell the right thing to do by how much it hurts."

He looked up.

Corysiam stood with her hands clasped behind her, looking sympathetically down at him.

He shook his head. He hadn't felt her come across. That was dangerous. He'd let himself get too distracted. "Can't believe she's almost eleven." He rubbed his hand across his mouth. "Not to be unwelcoming, Scribe, but what are you doing here?"

"Cymel wanted me to intervene. I wouldn't speak to her, Ellar. I'm here to clean off a bit of that guilt. And to tell you that I'm sending a young Scribe, a Walker, to join your Watchers and help get the young Hero to Caeffordian."

"Hero? There are at least five other Candidates still alive."

"Barking at the moon, aren't you? Lyanz should be dead by now, would have been without extraordinary intervention. Why so reluctant to say what you must know is true? Ah! You needn't answer. I know why. Cymel." Corysiam touched his shoulder, then stepped back and changed the subject. "I'll need a letter with your seal on it for Amhar to give the Watchers so she can travel with them."

Once again Ellar drew his hands across his face, then he pushed onto his feet. "Come." He left the parlor and went into the small room he used as his office, sat at the worktable and wrote a brief note, then folded the paper over and melted a circle of wax across the ends. When the wax had set up enough, he used the seal he wore on a chain round his neck, then handed the packet to Corysiam. "I've included a code phrase in this so that Diawad and Cadarn will be certain I wrote it."

He leaned back. "Have you picked up anything more about the Siofray Mage?"

"He seems to be keeping his head down. I've heard rumors, that's all." She looked down at the small square in her hand. "The visions have begun. I . . ." She shrugged. "A ring of Messengers singing the glories of the Prophet. Very impressive. Disturbing to simple minds. I can see the seeds of things that frighten me very much." She took a step backward and her eyes focused on things unseen.

"Wait." He hesitated so long, she raised a sandy brow. "Look in on Cymel, will you? Make sure she's getting what she needs?" It was very hard for him to make that concession; the words came out like stones he was flinging at her. He couldn't help that. He still didn't fully trust her, but as he saw it, he had no choice.

Corysiam nodded. "I'll do that. Thanks, Ellar." Then she was gone.

Ellar sat for several minutes with his head in his hands, then he straightened, took his Daybook from the drawer in the work-table and began recording the events of the morning.

{ 4 }

With a wandering wind plucking at his thin hair, Oerfel poled the flatboat from eddy to eddy along the inner curve of the river. The moon had almost set, just a tip of the crescent still visible, curling over the hooked peak of Mount Tan. The day had been warmer than usual, and though there was a nip of frost in the air, the night wasn't cold enough to bother him. He could have taken a horse and gone by land, but even after a dozen days had passed he was enjoying the expansiveness that the departure of the Hero had brought him. No hurry. Take things easy. The plan was moving along nicely. There was a small problem with the Hero, but that, too, would be smoothed out. Later.

He brought the nose of the flatboat under the first of the river wharves, tied it in place. He took a moment to wind a cloak of Pneuma about himself to deflect the eyes of anyone who happened by, climbed onto the wharf and headed for the Grand Temple of Dyf Tanew.

The candles flickered around him, their flames reflected in the mirrors that hung about the hidden room deep below the Temple, mirrors that reflected Oerfel's meager naked body as he laid down the stencils and painstakingly brushed on his skin the complex knots of blue lines, the spirals, dots and jags that concentrated power for him.

When he was finished, he walked about awhile to let the paint dry. This wasn't like calling up the storm, but a much more subtle redirection of the Flow; he had to reach past the Tyrn's Sniffers and squeeze the man's heart just enough to frighten him, but not enough to kill him. It was time to lay down precedent for the day when the Tyrn had to die so the Heir could step into his place. Dengyn Feallson was a skilled manipulator and showman, given to personal excess but restraint in his rule. He was a popular Tyrn and as close to un-Seatable as any in history.

The Heir was different. He was much like his mother, handsome but rather stupid, an angry, frustrated man, suppressed for years by the ebullient, forceful personality of his father. Give him a year or two to let his personality run free and the Nyd-Ifor were going to loathe him. In Anrydd they'd see the rebirth of Tyrn Dengyn, and with the proper backing, the boy would take the Seat in a walk.

Oerfel drew in a long breath, savoring the smell of the hot wax and the ghosts of incense he'd burned here over the years, the faintly musty odor of rat droppings and old books, of mirror polish and furniture wax. This room was like an old robe, worn soft and comfortable.

He fetched thin white candles and set them into crystal bowls filled with distilled water. Moving very carefully so he wouldn't spill a drop of the precious liquid, he set each bowl at the point of the hexagram, then stepped inside, touching the silver line with his big toe in order to activate the pattern.

He stood in the center, very still for a long moment, then his arms lifted and his body began to sway like a sapling sways in a soft spring breeze.

He chanted:

> Cry cry
> Ululation
> Needle thrust into the lung
> Pain pain
> Excruciation
> Round the heart the thread is flung
> Leap leap
> Agitation
> Knot it tight, the thing is done.

He repeated the last word in a long exhalation, then dropped his arms to his sides and swayed where he stood, his senses linked to the Tyrn.

He felt the jolt as the heart juddered, stopped an instant, beat again, fast then slow then fast again. He could feel the bustle and fuss around the Tyrn, could feel the coolness of liquid sliding down the Tyrn's throat.

He sang:

> *Ease ease*
> *Alleviation.*
> *Unwind the thread, the pain is gone.*

He let the tie dissolve and opened his eyes. His work this night was done and done cleanly.

Oerfel stepped the flatboat's stubby mast, raised the triangular sail and puffed a bit of wind into the canvas, letting that directed wind push him against the current till he was moving slowly and easily back to Carcalon.

It was nearly time to shift Anrydd from the Court. That scene at the horse show began as rumor, but was turning rapidly to myth in the whispers that ran the halls of Carcalon and the streets of Tyst. The boy was riding high now and beginning to get careless with his reprisals for what he considered slights.

Barbrangan Lusor was growing increasingly impatient with him and only needed the slightest nudge to boot the boy out of his house. What kept him quiescent for the moment was his wife. Her family was a powerful one and to repudiate the boy was to brand her a whore.

The woman would have to die.

Use the death. Poison and rumors of poison. Hushed up, but running under the surface. Let Anrydd believe his name-father dropped the bane in his mother's food. Give the boy a strong boot toward revenge.

The little boat blew up to the barge landing. Oerfel tied it to a piling and went to his rooms in the Grathtower, quite satisfied with his night's work and his ponderings.

[5]

Cymel sat on the edge of the landing, kicking her feet and scowling at brown water curling about the pilings. Hanner was still on board the barge, dealing with the luggage. Take your pout out of here, she'd said. I'm tired of looking at it. If I didn't respect your father so much, I'd hire a nanny and a guard and wash my hands of you.

Cymel swished spit around her mouth and expelled it at the water, watched morosely as the current carried it under the landing. Breith hadn't talked to her in ages, not since the last time she'd been on a barge. And Lyanz was so busy with Diawad, practicing that hand-fighting stuff, he didn't want her round. Everyone was going away, like she had a plague or something.

She felt a burst of activity in the Flow and twisted around so she could look behind her.

Corysiam stepped round the corner of the Inn's Wardwall; she stopped, still in the shadow of the weedy bushes that had grown up beside the wall. A tall, lean girl stood in the deeper shadows behind her.

Cymel jumped to her feet, pleased laughter bubbling up through her body and a grin stretching her mouth till it almost hurt. "Aunt Cory, you came."

"Cym, bring Lyanz and the Watchers here, will you please?"

The brief flare of hope died. She turned away so her aunt wouldn't see the tears that burned her eyes, and she walked briskly up the ramp, avoiding the lines of local ladesmen carrying bundles, bales and other cargo on and off the barge.

【 6 】

Diawad broke the seal and opened the letter. He glanced at the words written there, then handed the letter to Cadarn. To Corysiam he said, "Why?"

"Why do I involve myself? Isn't that obvious? The Hero is as important to Iomard as he is to Glandair. I won't say more. You know why."

His eyes dull as gooideberries picked too long ago, he rubbed his hand over his plump chin and managed to look stupider than ever. On the first two days of this trip, Lyanz had learned to be wary of that look; it was entirely convincing and entirely misleading. "I see. But that's you, isn't it? What about the girl? She looks to be only a year or two older than the boy."

"Amhar is trained to hand, bow and sword to a degree that Watchers however talented never achieve. And she has experience teaching beginners."

"And you, young Scribe. Why?"

The girl stepped forward, set her hand on the older woman's shoulder. "Why not?" Her arms looked too thin and her hands were long and narrow; they seemed more bone than flesh. She had a hawkish nose and light green eyes with a fierce light in them that made Lyanz feel wary about trusting his body to her training.

He rubbed absently at the bruise on his shoulder and scowled at the girl. At least Diawad was a grown man. No shame to be thrown about by him. But a girl! He glanced at Cymel, saw her watching him. He moved his shoulders, feeling irritated. He hadn't done anything to her, but she acted as though he'd killed her cat or something.

Before any of them said anything else, Hanner came off the boat, followed by a wizened little man loaded down with gear. She frowned at Cymel, called to her. "We need to get started if we're to reach the hostel by nightfall. Come on."

Lyanz watched Cymel walk away, looking over her shoulder at the Iomardi woman as if she expected her to object. When the Scribe said nothing, Cymel sighed and walked after the poet, her feet dragging.

Cadarn refolded the letter, tapped it on the side of his hand. "Are you coming also, Scribe?"

"No. I have calls on me that I can't neglect any longer. Amhar can Walk between the worlds. She doesn't need me to Bridge her across, And she has an unusual sensitivity to the Flow. Listen carefully when she warns you of traps. I have felt the forces around this boy and they are powerful indeed." She turned. "Amhar, you know how to reach me."

The girl laughed. "Yes, yes. You don't have to play mama to me, Cory."

The first departure bell rang on the barge. Amhar made a quick dismissive gesture, gathered up the leather satchel lying at her feet and started up the ramp. Lyanz hung behind, wanting to see the Scribe take the first step of the Walk, but she just smiled at him as if she'd read his mind, shook her head and walked back around the corner of the wall.

[7]

Ellar shut the Daybook, leaned back and stretched his arms high above his head. He was getting flabby of body and brain. He used to complain about all the work the farm took. He'd never realized just how much he enjoyed getting out, using his hands, working with the animals, how valuable a break it was from the writing and the scanning that he'd considered the important part of his life. And how good solitude was.

As each day passed here, he loathed this place more. If he didn't get cut loose soon, he'd have to make himself sick enough to justify crawling off home to recover. Now that Cymel was safely away, there was no point in waiting longer. He patted a yawn, pushed his chair back. One more state dinner and that was it.

A knock on the door brought a frown to his face. There was no reason anyone would be coming to see him. The other poets were gone and he was of less than zero importance to most people at the Court. Besides, this was the time when the courtiers would be getting themselves prepared for the dinner.

When he opened the door, he saw a slender bald man in black tunic and trousers with only an elaborate gold chain to mark his office. The Master of the Inner Chamber. Not the Tyrn's body servant, but the director of all his servants. It was not usual for him to run his own errands.

"Ryn?"

The Master bowed. "If you will come with me, Ryn Poet. The Tyrn desires your presence in his chambers. You bring the cycle of poems you have titled 'Songs for a Dead Wife.' "

The Master took Ellar into a small anteroom where he clapped his hands. Two valets appeared. One brushed assiduously at his wrinkled clothing, pulling and tugging at it till it looked as good as it was going to. The second washed his face for him, then washed and creamed his hands.

A wave of the Master's hand sent them away. When they were alone again, he indicated a chair. "If you will sit there, Ryn Poet." He spoke gravely and with a careful formality that did not wholly conceal his feelings, but let him deal with them without embarrassing himself. "There are things that must be said. I will ask you to swear that you will not speak of anything you see and hear as long as you are in these rooms."

"You have my word of course, Ryn Master."

The Master stood with his hands clasped behind him, rocking back and forth on his heels. "Last night there was a very serious episode. The Tyrn's heart was involved and the Healers are worried about damage. The Heir will be Regent for the next several months while the Tyrn rests and repairs himself. He is not an easy patient and too likely to overreach his strength. As is natural in such circumstances, the Tyrn is contemplating death, seeking to reassure himself that he can face his end with the courage and intelligence with which he has confronted life."

"I see."

"The Healers have suggested that we allow him to control this search rather than agitate him further with unwelcome suggestions or attempts to comfort him. He was pleased with your tributes to your wife and wishes to hear more. You will read your poems and answer any questions that he asks, but you will not intrude yourself on his meditations."

"I see."

"You will wait here while I see if the Tyrn is ready for you."

[8]

Oerfel waited in his niche in the Dining Hall, a short distance from the raised table and chair of the Tyrn; his hands were flattened on the chest of his neat black robe, his chain of office the only color about him, flat gold links and the oval carnelian set in the pendant tag glowing red in the lamplight. The two guest tables below him stretched down the long hall, the Cyngrathmen and their wives, then the visiting Broons and their families, then merchants from Tyst and visitors from other lands. There was a low murmur of conversation as they waited for the Tyrn to enter.

Oerfel read the eddies of expectation and curiosity. Rumors had blown on the morning winds through Carcalon and even out to Tyst. Something had happened. Something. No one knew what. The Tyrn was dead. No. Not dead, but he'd had a stroke and couldn't talk or move. No. That was wrong. Poison. The Healers had saved his life but he was babbling like a child. And on and on, growing more bizarre as the sun rose higher in the sky.

The Controller of Ceremony stepped into the doorway, stood there a moment, then was gone.

Oerfel moved from his niche, beckoned to the Stentor. He spoke in short phrases, pausing between them to allow the Stentor to bellow them to the dinner guests.

"Tyrn Dengyn Feallson asks your pardon. . . .

He has suffered a minor flux and . . .

Requires rest for a short while. . . .

During this healing time . . .

He will be represented by his Heir . . .

Isel Dengynson . . .

Whom he commends to you . . .

As Regent to all Nyddys . . .

Until such time . . .

As he, Tyrn to all Nyddys . . .

Resumes his place."

Oerfel bowed, stepped back into his niche.

Blown in by a blare of tweekhorns, his consort silent beside him, the Heir came sedately into the Dining Hall, an unaccustomed flush on his face and a liveliness in his eyes that betrayed his excitement. Oerfel would have laughed if courtesy permitted. Isel had heard the rumors. He was too wary to trust them since he'd grown up with Court rumors seething about him and the Healers were too discreet to pass on more than the vaguest sketch of what was wrong, even to the Heir. It was obvious, though, that he was hoping there was some truth in what he'd heard. Hoping his time had come before he was to old to enjoy himself.

As the Heir walked along the aisle between the two tables, the guests applauded, the steady if muted sound like rain on a shingle roof. Though he tried to keep a modest demeanor, Isel's back straightened, his shoulders came down and his stride was freer. He took the Tyrn's Chair with a glitter in his eye and the deep satisfaction of a man who was where he belonged.

[9]

"How long has your wife been gone?"

"More than eight years, Sry."

"And you still grieve?"

"I don't know if you could call it grief, Sry. But I miss her, and there are times when I still turn to say something to her and then remember she isn't there. And there are times when I look at my daughter and see the face of my wife written into her face and I ache with wanting her back with me."

"You're a young man still so she was very young when she died. How did it happen?"

"Her father was gravely ill and she went to be with him, Sry. She was ambushed on the road and killed by outlaws. Not in Nyddys."

"You let her go alone?"

"There was no question of my letting her do anything, Sry. She was a woman of high courage who would not submit to the lightest rein."

"And your daughter is another such?"

"I'm afraid so, Sry. She is not a disobedient child and will be ruled by love where force would only rouse her stubbornness, but she will be a woman soon and I shudder to think where her impulses will lead her."

"Is she pretty?"

"Sry, right now she's coltish and more like a boy, but though I am her father and my judgment is suspect, I think she is going to be beautiful when she is grown."

"You should bring her to see me when next you come."

"Alas, Sry, I cannot. She is also a gifted child and I have sent her to Cyfareth for her further education."

"You are wiser than I, Poet. Carcalon is not the best place for a bright and not yet pretty girl. Read me another of your poems."

"Sry, this one is called 'Not Coming Home.' "

A scent
A hint of laughter
A shadow flowing
Past the corner of my eye
Kindling
Ache and anguish
And after
A melancholy memory of joy.
She is not coming home again.
I count on time to gentle pain.
I number
The days and watch
The slow march
Of the years.

[10]

The road to Cyfareth was a busy one with a village every few miles and lots of small farms. The land was held by the University rather than a Broon and the Regents ruled with a light hand. A large number of the families had been on their parcels for so many generations that they thought of the land as their own and counted the rent payments as merely a sort of tax. It was a peaceful, pleasant region of hills and narrow valleys, and after a day of riding along that road Cymel felt at home there.

She stopped pouting and feeling sorry for herself. These warm fall days and crisp nights were just too nice for nursing hurts. And she was starting to be curious about what Cyfareth was like.

Hanner was a silent woman and content to keep her conversation to the choir of seraphs in her head—at least that's what she called them when Cymel interrupted her one time to ask a pressing question. She was riding up ahead, her large body easy in the saddle. Her dark red hair was plaited into a single thick braid that she pinned on top her head. Over that knot she tied a kerchief to keep flies off her neck, and on top of which she wore a wide-brimmed hat woven of straw and secured in place with a long hatpin like the infant child of a ceremonial sword. She led the pack mule and let Cymel bring up the rear.

It was early afternoon and the road was full of traffic, travelers heading to the University, peddlers moving from village to village, farmers and farm wives on visiting rounds now that the harvest was done. Wains were piled high with apples and tubers, barrels of salt meat, rolls of leather, sacks of cotton and hemp for winter weaving and a thousand other items, all the surplus harvest going in both directions, some to Cyfareth for sale in the University shops, some for the river and the supply barges heading for Carcalon and Tyst. Buyers and agents for buyers were stationed at all the landings along this part of the river. The days after the end of Foolsreign and before the first snow were some of the busiest in the year.

Cymel waited till the road cleared for a stretch, then touched her mount into a faster walk until she was riding alongside Hanner. "Rynnat Hanner, what's Cyfareth like?"

"Bigger than Carcalon but quieter. There's the town called Cyfareth. Think of Tyst but smaller and without a harbor. You'll visit there from time to time, but you won't be living there. Your father has friends who teach and study at the University. You'll be staying with one of them until you're sixteen, then you'll move to a house with other girls your age and a house mother to set rules and keep order. Except for the children of the Scholars, there aren't many at University as young as you. Or as gifted— if your father hasn't exaggerated your abilities, Cym." She chuckled, a deep, friendly sound that made Cymel feel warm all over. "Parents do that, you know. Our children are wonders except when they're small demons."

"You have children?"

"Two sons and a daughter and not one of them interested in words and song. Ah well, that is the way it goes sometimes. They're grown and in their own homes and in a few months I'll be a grandmother as well as mother." She sighed. "It was an honor to be called to recite before the Tyrn, but it's an honor I could have lived without."

"Oh."

"What a sad little sound. No, Cym, I'm happy to do this favor for your father. He's a good friend and a colleague twice over. Cyfareth. It's a pretty place. I think you'll like it. Very quiet and peaceful once the snow sets in. There's music and talk. You'll have lessons like those your father set for you and others where a tutor comes and just talks with you about whatever it is you're studying with him. Or her. Your father says you like tending the tullins and colos. If you want, you can help in the birdhouses. And there'll be skiing and sledding and skating."

"What about time to . . . well, just fool around?"

"I'm afraid there won't be much of that your first few years. You'll be very busy, Cym. And this is a time of much trouble and uncertainty. You have to be ready to meet what comes."

"Oh."

There was a loud rumble ahead and a line of heavy wains came round the bend. To give them room, Cymel slowed the horse and let Hanner draw ahead again.

Hanner was wrong about one thing. Once she learned the rules and how the place was set up, she'd make time for just fooling around. And if they yelled at her, let them yell. Even her father couldn't make her do things she really didn't want to do. No dumb Scholar person was going to turn her into a quivering jelly like Tipri Dyrysdottar.

Breith's voice broke into her fierce musings. "Hey, Cym, where are you? What's happening?" His Talking Window was flickering in and out as he worked to keep pace with her. His face was longer and bonier than she remembered and there was a bright red pimple on the end of his nose that made her want to giggle. She didn't because she didn't want to make him mad.

"Well, you've been gone a long time."

"For one thing, there's been this bantar off the Domains who keeps showing up, and Da made me promise not to fiddle with the Window until he got her chased off, because she could use it to get at me and him. And in the meantime he and Amhar have been working me till I'm skin and bone and a river of sweat. But the Seer was gone this morning and Amhar took off somewhere a couple days ago, so I've finally got some time to myself. What is going on, Cym?"

"If you really want to know, Laz got kicked in the head by a horse and nearly was killed, and Dyf Tanew, that's a Big God, he came along and healed him, Laz I mean, and two Watchers came from the University and they're taking Laz someplace safe, and your Amhar came over here to help look after Laz."

"Huh? I thought you were doing that."

"Pa said I couldn't go, so here I am. He's sending me to Cyfareth where I'm supposed to have lessons and it all sounds like a huge bore."

"At least you're getting out from behind walls." Breith made a face. "I'm so tired of looking at the inside of ours that sometimes I feel like butting my head into them till they fall over or I do. How come the trees are that funny color? They sick or something?"

"Huh? Trees don't turn and drop their leaves on Iomard? Winter's coming, Bré. First snow's due before the month's out."

"Don't think I ever saw snow. Never even saw a mountain till I looked over where you were. Winter here in Valla Murloch is lots of rain and lots of wind, some of it hard enough to blow roofs off houses. Maybe a few days of frost, but that's it. And our trees do drop a leaf every so often. It dies and turns brown and blows off. Mostly trees stay green all year."

"Weird."

"Cym, talking about weird, are things getting funny over there? I mean not to laugh, just strange." He made a face. "Thing is, I saw a ring of Messengers in the sky. Their wings were huge and

beautiful and they were singing . . . something . . . I don't remember what except it made my bones ache."

"Uh-huh. What I told you, Dyf Tanew came strolling along the
day Laz got hurt. Like he was a farmer out checking his crops."
She was silent a minute. "I think it has something to do with what
Pa calls the Settling and why Laz is so important that a Mage is
trying to kill him. Aunt Cory says you call it the Corruption. I
think that's one of the things I'm supposed to learn about at the
University."

"My father is really steaming about the records we don't keep
here, the stuff the Domains don't want anyone to know about.
He'd give just about anything to be where you're going, I think."

"Tell you what. You teach me how to make the Window and
I'll hunt all the history I can get hold of, especially stuff about
Iomard, and I'll fix it so he can read it."

"You think they'll let you do that?"

Cymel grinned. "I think I'm not going to be asking anyone, I'll
just do it."

"You got a deal."

21

Dur Joins the Army of the Third Prince

By the calendar of the Domains of Iomard, the 3rd day of Ekhtos, the eighth month of the Iomardi year 6533, the 720th year since the last Corruption.

{ 1 }

Hook Bay was a talon shaped inlet at the south end of Isle Tuays. A narrow river laced with whitewater cascaded down the steep escarpment rising behind the cluster of stone houses at the point of the talon. Many of the houses were little better than huts, four walls with a thatched roof. There were a few larger houses with shingled roofs, the wood a sign of the prosperity of those who lived there. Three fishing boats rocked at the stone jetty, nets hung from the masts, spread out to dry in the winds that blew almost every day of the year. There were a number of smaller boats, sail dories used by the households to bring in fish for the daily meals and to salt down or smoke for the winter months when there was too much ice in the sea for all but the most desperate sailors. There were hot springs scattered about the slopes and on the floor of the bay, so the town stayed reasonably warm and the bay never froze over. The springs also brought thick fogs and the smell of sulfur blowing through the town.

The town was called Gavachtag, a word taken from the gutural language of the Hisay, a small, yellow-faced people who claimed to have lived here since the world began. The Hisay stayed away from Gavachtag except for a few days a year when they came from the hills to get drunk on muscar—a raw liquor that the villagers distilled from a mash made from grass seeds and chunks of a tuber called piltagh that grew everywhere but was mostly useless even as pony feed.

Though no one in Gavachtag was quite sure how he had managed it, Dur and the woman he'd brought with him had acquired one of the larger houses, and the former occupants had vanished, gone with the ship that had brought him, he said. Though they gossiped among themselves with great heat and little light over these events, Gavachers never asked questions about the former lives of their neighbors, nor did they allow newcomers into the gossip circles. Dur showed no sign he wanted to join them and the woman was a drunk who seldom left the house.

He had plenty of silver and kept the house supplied with food and clothing from the traders who brought their ships north when the ice cleared out.

There was more here to bring those traders than the bleak surroundings would suggest. The liver of a fish that existed only in Hook Bay was greatly prized as a heart medicine. A predator that the Hisay called t'how had a golden brown pelt speckled with black and white, and the pavhey, which the t'how hunted, had thick silky fur, pure white in the winter snows and a glossy black in summer. The Hisay traded their pelts for muscar and the Gavachers sold them to the buyers on the ships. There were seams of opal in the black mountains, and deposits of jade; those who knew the secret places could bring back enough of these stones to make a small fortune.

Life on Isle Tuays was harsh and often boring, but the Siofray who came here for sanctuary were not accustomed to soft days and silken nights, nor were they gentle souls fleeing oppression.

Men and women both, they were predators like the t'how and a lot more efficient about it.

Dur left the house and walked across the filthy, trampled snow into the tangle of low, crooked scrobarch trees that grew in a prickly profusion up a ravine cut into the scarp by a stream whose source was one of the hot springs. Mist eddied above the scummy water and the wind blew the stink of sulfur into his face as he followed a path that only those with the Sight could discern.

To ordinary eyes there was no break in the thicket that choked the ravine, but in some forgotten year a witch or outcast Seer or Mage had burned out a path and set spells to prevent the scrobarch from growing back and other spells to keep the path a secret. When Dur came here, the spells had gone ragged and weak, but he'd felt them out and repaired them.

The path led to a black basalt cliff and the spelled mouth of the Great Cavern that lived in folk tales passed around among daroc children, the one place where Siofray magic couldn't reach. The place of grand schemes of conquest and mystery. The first time Dur stepped into the Chamber of the Stone Candles, he gave a great shout. "They were true, the stories were true," he cried to the stalactites, and the echoes came back to him *true true true*.

He moved along the path, fending off the thorny tendrils of the scrobarch, scowling as he realized the sedentary life he'd been living the past three years had thickened his body enough to make walking the path more difficult. All that reading.

Books. More books stowed in side galleries off the main chambers than he'd seen even in his stolen glimpses of the Scribes' storehouses. Some so old that even with the spells protecting them, they'd crumbled when he touched them. Others in writing that neither he nor Fanach recognized—and her knowledge of the world's languages was the one thing she prided herself on. Many of the books that she could read frightened her so much she wouldn't touch them again no matter how he pressed her. He was learning what she could teach him, but that slowed him down so much that sometimes he wanted to strangle her. He could compel her to do anything he commanded, but he needed that extra spark, that step beyond the possible that she produced with frustrating irregularity.

Discovering the pleasures such as they were of the corrosive muscar had not been a good thing for her. She was rapidly pickling her brain and probably wouldn't survive this winter. He'd nursed her through the winters before, spending time he couldn't afford away from his reading and his probes into Glandair, but he knew he needed her and he gave her the attention and care that helped her weakened body make it to spring and the return of sunlight. He wasn't sure that he was willing to do that for another year. The Seers might have forgot him by now, turned their spite on more recent targets. A quick trip to the mainland to acquire another, healthier Scribe shouldn't be all that difficult.

He passed through the spell-curtain and entered the cave, his presence triggering the flames of the stone candles. He smiled as he always did. It was such an elegant small spell. It made him wonder about the witch who'd crafted it. He liked to think that they would have been friends, though he knew well enough that it wasn't likely.

The black water in the mirror pool at the heart of the Grand Chamber was blood-warm, yet the stone itself was dry. Another unobtrusive spell kept it so, probably crafted by the same person. He stripped, folded his clothing, glad to get rid of furs and wool that were now far too hot.

He took the wax stopper from the jar of paint, a crimson paste he'd matched as closely as he could to the color of the stone candles that lit the chamber. Using his forefinger, he stroked power signs onto his scarred body, signs he'd discovered in the books. He'd let his inner sight choose which he'd incorporate in his own web of power, for some signs leaped to his eyes and resonated with his soul. He'd started with one, the sign painted over his heart. Month by month he'd added others, painting them on his thighs and his forearms, on the backs of his hands. The web was not yet complete; he had not found the signs for his face, but there were piles of books left that he hadn't even opened.

The more complex and comprehensive the signweb grew, the surer his manipulation of the Flow became. When he painted the signs on his skin, his Eye sharpened and his range extended enormously, though he still could not see through the disturbance in the Flow that protected these islands from the Seers. If he wanted to scan mainland Saffroa, he'd have to take a ship beyond the Tangle.

He finished the signs, restoppered the jar and went to wash his hands in a small hot stream that ambled along the edge of the chamber, separated from the pool by a thick forest of stalagmites. Hands patted dry, he climbed to the stone chair that loomed high above the wide pool and settled himself there to scan the other world, looking with a very specific eye for what could help him to the goal he'd been working toward since he was a frightened twelve-year-old running from the gelding iron. Destroying the Domains, tearing down that damnable system of darocage and dependency.

He sang the words that brought images to the pool and scowled down at what he'd called into being. The Army of Chusinkayan was marching north, thousands of men moving across the land without picking it clean, supply wagons and missile throwers, spare horse herds, herds of bullocks for butchering, the support force greater in numbers than the armed fighters. He found the sight confusing, though it was obvious the men on the ground did not. He simply didn't understand what made it work.

Three years of hard labor, reading and watching and studying, had mostly taught him the enormity of his ignorance. No wonder the moment he became more than a pinprick in the toe of the Domains, it only took a single Seer to shut him down and drive him out. It was knowledge that beat him. He'd felt her touch and known her powerflow was a thread where his was a rope, but she knew how to use it with the precision of a swordmaster and if he had stayed to face her she would have cut him to ribbons.

He studied the army more closely, tried to see how the men in charge of groups controlled them. He caught what looked like hand signals, heard words he could understand—but their ordinary meanings didn't seem to match the actions evoked. Fanach might know what was happening, but she wasn't here.

He watched the marchers' faces, trying to read what they were thinking from their expressions. If his judgment was anywhere near accurate, most of them seemed to be thinking *My feet hurt. This armor itches. Cursed flies.*

He could not relate that to the difficulty he'd had controlling half a dozen men, getting them to follow him against the same targets and keeping them from doing wholly stupid things like getting drunk in river towns and boasting to bar girls about the raids they'd made and what they were going to do next summer.

He sang the scene dark, brought up the other army. No march yet, just a call-in of men from all over Kale, press-gangs hitting the streets of Yosun and Lim Ashir and the smaller smugglers' towns in coves along the coasts. It seemed far more chaotic than the gather in Chusinkayan. Also the faces in this army showed a greater variety, not only the purebred Rhudyar from the interior, but the mongrels from the seaports whose ancestry was so mixed it would take years just to sort out the strands that went into them.

Yet in the camp on the broad plateau outside the High City of Aile Kuvvet, there was a growing sense of order and purpose. And watching from the outside told him nothing about how it was being achieved.

He let the scene play on and sat back in the stone chair, thinking.

Something is going to happen. Something of vast importance

On Glandair the Mages of Chusinkayan and Kale were manipulating forces to produce war-hardened armies. Even the Nyddys Mage was busy in his secret way. Boys were being tracked down and killed along with the men escorting them. Local gods were putting on forms of light and marching across the land.

Here on Iomard circles of Messengers kept appearing, filling the sky, singing the Prophet's Praises. Turning the mush-headed and simpleminded frantic.

Iomard and Glandair were moving closer to each other. It got easier every day to look from one to the other. I don't know what this means. Except . . .

Something is going to happen.

The Mages know, but they don't talk about it and I have to be careful that they don't notice me hanging about. They're too dangerous. A few of the Scribes know. I don't dare go near them. Not yet. And I can't go near the Watchers.

He cursed his stupidity with that girl on Glandair. The Watcher's daughter. Little mongrel, half Glandairic, half Iomardi, with a Scribe for an aunt. Not only a Scribe but a Bridge. No wonder the child was such a tempting bundle of raw power. He'd felt the pull of it and pulled back as powerfully as he could, trying the impossible, trying to bring her across. And he might have done it, if her father hadn't slammed shut the door in his face. He still watched her occasionally, looking for a way he could use her.

Time. How much time do I have?

What is it that is going to happen?

Maybe it's in the books.

He slapped his hand on the stone arm of the chair. Piles and piles of books. I need Fanach here now.

He glanced at the scene in the pool, clicked his tongue and sang it dark, then turned it to his house.

In the dark water the image bloomed. Fanach was lying tan-

;led in damp quilts, one arm dangling over the edge of the
tovebed, skin turned pink by the lingering heat in the unglazed
iles. A stoneware jug lay on its side, a small pool of liquid dry-
ng under it.

As he watched, she shuddered awake, rolled onto her back, one
land on her belly. Her eyes opened, she stared at nothing for a
moment, then moved feebly, her legs scrabbling for some kind
f purchase. Eventually she half fell off the bed, half stood, back
ent, hands clutching the tiled edge where the mattress had
hifted enough to leave it clear.

She straightened and walked heavily out of the room, not
othering to find a wrap to cover herself.

At least she was awake and probably as close to sober as she
ver got. That wouldn't last long.

He waited till she got back to the bedroom, then he called to
er. "Fanach."

She stumbled to a stop, lifted her head. "Leave me alone. I told
ou I didn't want to do any more of that."

"Come here," he said. "Come to the cavern."

"No." There was no strength in her voice, no hope. She knew
he couldn't fight him but she wouldn't yield without that token
efusal.

"Get dressed and come here."

She bent to pick up the jug.

"No. No muscar. You can bring a jug with you, but bring it
ealed. Bring bread, cheese and cold meat also. It's going to be a
ong day."

"I . . ." She broke off, shrugged and turned toward the winter
lothing in a heap on the floor at the end of the bed.

2 }

'anach pushed her hair off her face, wiped her hand on her thigh
nd turned the page. "I think this is the one you want." She
ouched a finger to the line of characters. "*Marseoth, gan se blyan*

of se Truaill cen gaim mann and womann of aisteh warald galan dar cumm to Iomard. Thus it was that the year of the Corruptio began when men and women of the strange world Glandair cam to Iomard. *Marseoth ainso, gan mann and womann of Iomar wayen to galandar.* Thus it was also that men and women o Iomard began crossing to Glandair. The writer goes on to ask th blessing of the Prophet and to pray that this return of the Cor ruption not bring such blood and death to Saffroa as happene the last time."

She stopped reading, rested her hand across her eyes. "I nee a drink."

He scowled at her, then worked the rolled leather stopper from the jug of muscar and poured a thumbwidth in her glass. "Go on.

She gulped down the harsh distillate, shuddered, then sat moment with her eyes closed, her fingers twitching, making smal scraping sounds on the thick soft paper.

She shuddered again, opened her eyes but looked past him, a if she could only endure this if she pretended he wasn't there "We were taught about the Corruptions in Religion class. Th Brother said the Prophet sends them to try our faith and purif the people. Ghosts walk and strange things happen, the weathe changes, the earth opens beneath our feet. About every seve hundred years it happens. That last we weren't taught. I forge where I learned it."

"How many years left before the next one?"

"I don't know."

"Does the writer there give the date?"

"Somewhere. Probably."

"Well, find it."

She rubbed at her eyes, hunched over the book and began turn ing the pages, scanning them for any sign of numbers. By the tim she reached the end, her eyes were red from the book dust an her nose was running. She wiped the back of her hand across he nose repeatedly and kept turning.

"Ah. I think . . . Yes. She writes *Scriobben by Cosanto ait é
Piorra of Rivertown Teagartha in* . . . Um . . . she uses the old
numbers and it's hard to . . . *Twenty-one Seyos of se blayn* . . .
That's in the year of—it's hard to translate these letter numer-
als—I think it works out to Year of the Prophet 5813."

"Teagartha?"

"As far as I know there is no Teagartha these days."

"This is 6533. Seven hundred twenty years since that book was
written."

"You have what you want. Let me go."

"No. The timing is only the beginning. I need to know everything you can dig out of that record. Go back to the beginning
and tell me what the Scribe wrote."

"My throat is dry."

"I'll give you a drink of muscar for every twenty pages you finish. The rest of the time, you'll drink water."

[3]

Weary to the bone, eyes burning from too much poring over
crabbed script he could barely read, Dur slumped in the stone
chair and labored to relate what he'd discovered to the Iomard
he knew. The language wasn't the only thing that had changed
since Cosanto ait é Piorra of Rivertown Teagartha had written
her Daybook. He'd been astonished to find that the Riverine
Confluence hadn't existed in those days and almost equally surprised to see that life in the Domains had also changed in several ways, a life which he'd seen as so set in stone that one day
was the same as the next and each was the same as it always had
been. He'd learned to read and cipher. In Cosanto's time, anyone caught teaching these things to a daroc would be banished,
sometimes even executed.

He rubbed his hand across his eyes. If the last Corruption
brought that much change to darocs, there was hope for his

plans. He just had to find out how to make the proper lever and where to apply it.

Lever. Call it what it was. Army. Organized in a way the Domains never organized their patrols. His next step had become clear to him. He had to cross to Glandair and work his way into one of those armies. Kale would be best. When he gathered men to his banner, they'd be a patchwork of peoples like that one.

He looked down at Fanach with distaste. She slept on her side at his feet, the muscar jug in the curl of her arms, hugged against her breasts. She was nearly useless now. Except . . .

In one of the books he'd found a way to funnel his own power into her, to push her beyond her gift of Walking until she could Bridge him from world to world. This would likely burn out her brain, killing her or leaving her a babbling idiot, but she was doing that to herself already. Might as well squeeze one last service from her. His return to Iomard was simple enough. That Watcher's child—her aunt would come running if he threatened the girl. He laughed aloud at the thought. One way of getting his own back for the slap he'd taken.

He sang the pool awake again and began searching for a suitable place for his entry into Glandair.

[4]

Dur dropped the convulsing body on the beach and stepped away from it as Fanach gave a hoarse cry, shuddered and died.

He left her sprawled on the sand and ran for the tangle of vines and scrub trees that grew where the dunes and saltgrass ended.

He felt lighter as he ran and had to be careful he didn't overreach himself and fall flat on his face. The colors and the smells were different too, but the thing that bothered him most was the sun. He'd seen it, of course, when he looked across, but actually being here, feeling that light on his face, was more disturbing than he'd expected. It was the wrong color and brighter than

Iomard's sun; the shadows it cast were too sharp, as if the edges would cut him should he step on them.

He emerged on the other side of the thicket and stood looking around.

Beyond the choppy waste that ran in a narrow band along the shore, the land stretching to the eastern horizon was an undulation of pale green mixed with sun-yellowed grass; there were a few scattered clumps and lines of trees whose leaves were a much darker green. In the distance a large herd of black horses grazed without attendants. He smiled. No herdgirls to hunt him down, not this time.

Their tops visible above the weeds, he could see the stone cairns that marked the road he'd explored through visions in the pool. He picked his way through the thorny weeds, most of them dead and dry, and stepped onto a road of hard-packed alkali dirt. If he'd calculated properly, a small town lay beyond those stony undulations rising in the north and in a few moments a press-gang should be leaving it, heading for Lim Ashir with their catch of young men. He meant to allow himself to be added to that number.

Though his clothing and he were obviously foreign, he wasn't worried about intrusive questions. To the press-gang he was money on the hoof and they wouldn't waste time establishing his origins.

Overhead a soaring raptor was an angular black form against clouds like horsetails whipping across a sky that was a paler blue than the one he was used to seeing.

His boots thudded dully on the hard earth and his skin grew tight and hot. Despite the dampness and the nip in the wind, he felt as if he'd thrust his head into an oven. And he was getting dizzy. He began to wonder if this was such a good idea.

He'd been walking for several minutes when the press-gang came round a bend in the road, a handful of men on horseback and another driving a wicker-sided cart with a half-dozen men in the back. He ignored them and continued trudging along, shoulders rounded, eyes on the road. Presenting, he hoped, a tempting image.

[5]

After half a watch in the jolting, swaying cart, Dur's head was throbbing and he was feeling queasy. The chains on his arms rattled as he pressed his hands against his stomach.

"It's the sun what got him. Fool ain't got no hat."

He lifted his head, tried to pick out which of the men had spoken, but all he saw were watery wavers, hot white spikes and black spots with wriggling silver tails.

"Ahyah, sun. Must be from one a them north places. They say it rains every day in Hartaav. Don't see sun but twice a year."

"Look at 'im. He's turning green. I don't wanna spend the next couple hours breathing stink off his spew."

"Hey!" Sounds of iron manacles knocked hard against the bench. "Korkut, you better do something about the new herf or he's gonna snuff."

The jolting stopped, then the manacles on his wrists were unlocked and thrown aside, the chains clanking greasily as they hit the bench and slid off onto the floor. Hands caught hold of him, hauled him from the cart and dropped him without pretense of care onto the hardpan of the road. A moment later water splashed over him, soaking his hair and his clothing. Someone ripped the lacing of the leather tunic, pulled it off him. Hands lifted his head, forced his mouth open and poured a sour liquid into his mouth, not liquor, some sort of tonic, nearly strangling him until his body was tilted and hands were slapping his back.

More tonic.

They made him sit up and wrapped a sloppily wet strip of cloth about his head, turning and twisting it to make a kind of hat with the ends left to hang down and protect the back of his neck.

He was thrown back into the cart, his tunic wadded up for a pillow and a filthy piece of canvas pulled over him. When the driver snapped his whip and the horse started plodding, he was so drained that even the jolting couldn't keep him awake and he slipped into sleep as if he were drowning.

6]

Dur woke shuddering with cold. The pressmen had moved him from the cart and carried him inside. Enough light filtered through the greased paper in the window to show him his bunk was in the lowest row and nearest the door in a room filled with narrow bunk beds, the stacks three high, with just enough space left for a narrow walkway between them and the other wall. This dormitory smelled of stale sweat, dirt and urine.

The chain on one ankle had been locked into a heavy staple, but the manacles had been removed from his wrists and he had some freedom of movement, enough to slide out of bed and use the lidded can shoved under his bunk.

The straw-stuffed pad rustling under his knees, he crawled onto the bunk and pulled the thin blanket over him. So cold . . .

There was the sound of metal scraping against metal. A key turning in a lock.

The door creaked open and a woman walked in. The lamplight coming through the door behind her showed a worn, lined face, eyes like dark holes, straggly hair. A slattern, probably doubling as a convenience for men desperate enough to use her. She carried a tray covered by a ragged cloth.

"So you 'wake, eah?" Balancing the tray with the ease of long practice, she bent over him, placed the back of her hand against the side of his face. Her skin was dry and rough. "Ahyah, you sunsick right enough." She eased herself onto her knees, set the tray on the floor. "Got some broth and a toddy. Warm you up jes' fine."

She spooned the broth into him, wiping his face when his mouth leaked, giving him sips of water when she thought he needed it, talking to him as she fed him. "Too bad you down like this. Korkut, he always takes his catch to Memi Rospu's place to get 'em nice and set up for the turnover at Lim Ashir. Gets a higher fee if they looking bushy tail and ready to bite. But you don't wanna go hoping that being sick will make him dump you. What I hear, you're near pure profit, luck piece dropping in his hands like that. It's army for you, northman, sooner you settle to it, better off you gonna be. Not so bad either. They feed and find and if you show talent there's bonuses. There. That's a good boy. Ate it all." She touched his face again. "And the chill's took a walk. Get some more sleep and you be just fine. Next time, though, dress local and wear something on your head."

He listened to her loading up the tray, getting to her feet shuffling out with a tiredness in her step that reminded him suddenly of Fanach. His eyes filled with weak tears and for a breath or two he felt something like grief for her, then he was angry at such stupidity. The woman was killing herself; left alone to do it, that death would have been meaningless. At least she died in a grand cause. When the Domains were pulled down and the Lyns were disbanded and the land was free, he'd have a monument carved for her and her sacrifice would be celebrated in song and history.

Contemplating his own magnanimity, he drifted off to sleep

[7]

The high plateau outside of Aile Kuvvet was windswept and chill. In Kale, this time of the year was not only winter but the dry season; there was no rain, just thick fog nearly every morning, a fog that burned off no later than an hour after sunup. The only water in the camp came from the big tank wagons, and the foot soldiers in this army got a keg a day for drinking and keeping themselves clean. One of the war wizards kept the tanks full, lifting water from the river that ran along the base of the cliff on the far side of the city. There was plenty of food and tea to wash it down, but no alcohol. The horse soldiers provided their own uniforms but the foot wore issue.

Issue was two pairs of trousers sewn from heavy cotton twill, loose to the knee, then bound close to the leg to fit inside boots laced up the front. There were two shirts of cotton twill that laced up the front. The sleeves had long, heavy cuffs to act as arm protectors for the bowmen and a kind of simple armor for the pikemen. Over the shirt was a leather vest with the sigil of the Third Prince painted in bright colors on the back so that in a melee the men would know each other. And there was a leather helmet, the fit approximate at best.

They got two blankets which they rolled up and carried on their backs when marching. There was also a square of canvas, four tent pegs, two wooden rods and a hank of strong cord from which they were supposed to fashion small individual tents.

Dur stood near the wall of the enclosure feeling like a tribuf on the butcher's block. He and the others here had been rousted from their blankets at dawn, run past the quartermaster's wagon for their supplies, shoved into a series of round pits and left there long enough for the sun to reach into the pits and start cooking them. There were about thirty men in his pit, none of whom he'd seen before. Four Yuskova herdsmen had claimed a section of wall and were sleeping, their issue stacked inside the circle while a fifth stood watch. A Myndyar smuggler had produced dice from a recess deep inside the loose clothing he wore and was running a game in another section of the pit. Others were standing around listlessly, recovering from hangovers. Two men were arguing, but their dialect was so thick Dur had no idea what the quarrel was about. The rest were like him, hunkered down or standing, just waiting for something to happen.

After a while he began to hear a kind of singsong chant above them; he couldn't make out the words, just the rise and fall of a voice declaiming short phrases.

The herdsman on watch shook his cousins awake. The dice vanished again. Someone separated the quarrelers.

A short time later a dozen or more Kalemen were standing on the rim of the pit looking down at them. They wore issue much like the pressed had been given. A moment later another two individuals joined them. One wore a light twill robe that covered him from neck to ankles. The other was a dark-skinned boy with an iron chain about his neck and a neat white loincloth, a leather bag in his hands.

The robe man chanted, "Lots thirty-seven to forty-nine. Chits in hand, tegmals, the draw begins." He held out his hand, the boy reached into the sack and pulled out a small square piece of wood. The man chanted, "Lot thirty-seven. Three seven." He looked at the bit of wood. "Three go to thirty-seven."

One of the tegmals stepped forward, handed over a chit and stood looking over the men in the pit below him. "You," he said and pointed at Dur. "You." This time he chose the diceman. "You." The third choice was a quiet lanky man leaning against the wall, his arms folded.

When they were out of the pit, the tegmal marched them out of the pit area, called a halt and looked them over. "Got your issue? Last chance. Anything missing, your pay chits stay with me till the debt's wiped." He waited but Dur and the others didn't move or say anything. "You sorry lot of losers, first lesson. Me, I'm Tegmal Mical nin Menzil. Askerit five oh two. You call me Tegmal and you call five oh two home. It's mam and pap and little brother Guz to you. And me, I'm god. You keep that clear in your heads, we gonna have no trouble. Pish the sturd and you gonna be sorry you still breathing."

* * *

By his tenth day in the askerit, Dur began to understand how this mass of men was directed and kept in order.

A base-level askerit was twelve men and a full askerit was twenty-four. Askerit 502 had reached twenty-one with Dur, Bakuch the Myndyar and Caladeron the Faiscari. The rest of the new men were scattered through the other askerits. One thing he found interesting, cousins and friends were deliberately separated to break down old loyalties and build new ones.

Tegmal Mical did his best to made good his pronouncement— 502 was family, clan, home. He worked them to exhaustion every day, all day. They marched, they maneuvered, were never told the reason for any of the things they did but were expected to do them flawlessly. They learned the horn calls and the abbreviated bellows of their tegmal's commands, they policed their camp area, were punished with more work for the slightest irregularity in their possessions. Dur watched the effect on the men and his own reactions with considerable interest.

Small units, he told himself. Hundreds of small units. Manageable size. That can't be all there is to it, though. Not with this many men. How do you put the units together?

His skin went from bright red burn to dead flakes peeling off him to a darker color that made him more like the men around him, helped him to fit in a bit better.

He continued making notes and sought out new areas to watch. How the laundry was handled, how to dig latrines, how to set up drills, how to keep men so busy they didn't have time to think. Unit cohesion and how it worked. How to get supplies and water to large bodies of men without waste and confusion. The effects of corruption by the suppliers and quartermasters. How to work around that. The class differences between the tegmals and the higher officers and how that affected communication and discipline. How to handle incorrigibles among the men. How to deal with lazy and incompetent officers, especially those who could not be weeded out because they belonged to influential families.

He was very quiet, brooding a lot, trying to work out the patterns, especially at night, lying there in his too-short tent with his head out the end, staring up at unfamiliar stars. This seemed much harder than tying knots in the Pneuma, something he was born able to do. Patterns. How to start up, what history on Iomard could he twist to his purpose?

The secret seemed to lie in the same tactic that organized a mass of men into small units, then tied those units together into larger groups. Start with small and manageable tasks, do them over and over until they were graved in the bone, add more small tasks and keep adding them until very complex actions were possible. The individual fighter didn't have to understand anything, just do his particular job and stay alive as long as possible.

It was an interesting two months.

Then the horns blew assembly and the army was drawn up for inspection.

At first he thought it was the usual thing they held every ten days or so, but he began to suspect something unusual was going to happen when they stayed drawn up in their units, standing at ease but in silence. And the reviewing stand had a new profile with a half-pavilion of brightly painted canvas raised on a dais in the center. The usual officers and the army-aesthetes among the Born were nowhere in sight.

With a flourish of horns, a sound of hooves, a man rode a great black horse up onto the stand, onto the dais. He swung from the saddle and stood with the horse's elegant black head beside his own.

A whisper from the tegmal. "Sst, on your knees, you gormless herfs, that there's the Third Prince. Smooth and easy. Make mama proud."

As the askerit sank down, another man walked onto the stand and knelt beside the dais.

Dur went still. The waves of Pneuma swirling around the new-comer made him dizzy and told him who this had to be. Mahara. The Tower Mage.

"I hear that Tilkos girls are sweet and easy." The Third Prince's voice boomed out, amplified by the horn of Pneuma the Mage had shaped. Dur heard a breathy snicker from Bakuch, who knelt to his left, and a grunt from Durm on his right and felt a wave of surprised and barely suppressed laughter flashing across the asker-its around him.

"And restless. No men over there, just a lot of insects noisy with ambition, all talk, no follow-through. We're going to squash those bugs and tickle those girls. . . ."

Dur stopped listening to the words and considered the effect of the speech on the men around him. At first they'd paid a tepid attention, though the Third Prince had caught their ears with his first sentence, but as the speech went on, he could feel an arousal in the army. Arousal. It was an apt choice of word. He was courting the soldiers, seducing them.

By the time he reached the end of what he had to say and raised his fist in the air, he drew a roar out of the army, the men on their feet again, cheering him. Dur felt an echo of that enthusiasm in himself. The frenzy of the men around him seemed to wake a sympathetic response and by responding he gave himself over to the excitement of the mob of men.

"Yessss," the Third Prince cried. "Yesss." Then he held his hands out for silence and he got that too. "We march tomorrow at dawn." His voice was quiet now, serious. "I've given orders that a ration of harab be issued to all men and wood for fires. Tonight, over those fires, raise your cups to Kale and the Olch Omir."

He swung into the saddle and rode from the stand, his red-lined cloak blowing in wind of his passage, the hoofbeats of the royal Agirsade stallion loud in the quiet he left behind.

* * *

That night, Dur lay staring up at stars that still looked odd to him. Moving out in the morning. He had more than enough to keep his mind churning for the month it was going to take them to march across Kale and reach the mountains. Didn't need to do any thinking now. He pulled the blanket up and sank into a deep sleep.

22

Anrydd's Sorrows

By the secret calendar of the Watchers, events dating from the 1st day of Seimis, the eighth month in the 736th Glandairic year since the last Settling.

[1]

Their horses painted with whitewash to represent crude skeletons, five black-clad, black-masked riders met and milled in a tight group in a waste field at the edge of Tyst. The moon was down and the night was nearly finished, less than one night watch till dawn.

A whisper. "You all got torches? Your firepots?"

"Yeh, An—"

"No names!"

"Yeah, stupid."

"Who you calling stupid?"

"Wrap it! Let's go."

The last speaker turned his horse and rode into the lane that wound between the hovels of Beggar's Row. Still muttering insults, the other four followed him.

Deep in the bothrin, the leader lifted a hand to stop the others, then gestured to bring them around him. "All right," he said, his voice a hoarse whisper, "Number two, you're the one said the bitch cheated you and you wanted to teach her a lesson, so which house is it?"

"Gimme a minute. I know I said I could find the place, but I was drunk." The one called number two kneed his horse into a quick walk past the dark silent buildings, turned and rode back, his body tense as he tried to pierce the gloom and identify the house the whore had led him to. Finally he straightened and rode back to the others. "The third one."

"You sure?"

"Sure enough. They're all the same anyway, cheats and thieves and not worth the spit to drown them."

"All right. Let's do it."

The soaked torches flaring, the five rode at a gallop down the narrow street, whooping and howling. When they reached the building that was their target, they whirled the torches around their heads and flung them at the facade, two catching on balconies and the other three breaking through windows and burning even brighter as the force of the throws broke the bottles of oil tied to the poles.

The riders didn't stop to look back at their work, but went racing out of the bothrin, heading for the sea marshes south of Tyst where they planned to lose their traces and scrub the paint from their horses before they separated and crept one by one into Carcalon, returning the same way they'd left.

"Hoo, baby! Did you see that sucker go up!" Helcod, the erstwhile number three, tore up a new bundle of gromreeds. "Stand still, you dancing fool." He scrubbed at the shoulder of his grullar roan. "Gotta get this off you, gonna be one huge fuss when the Cyngrath gets going. Bunch of whey-faced hypocrites."

"Worth it." Cynfor, who'd been number five, yawned, twitched his nose as he rubbed the handful of reeds over the hindquarters of his mount. His black had a more docile nature and was standing patiently as he scrubbed. "Make that lot think twice before they fool with their betters."

"Yeeahhh, Tanew's Tears, I got my chiz back." Lyngyr, number two and the instigator of this expedition, kicked water into an exuberant spray. He grabbed the straps of the bridle as his horse squealed and tried to rear.

Anrydd laughed, but he said nothing and continued to clean the paint from Sernry's smooth coat. He was suffering from second thoughts. Though he hadn't mentioned it to his companions, he had more serious reasons than Lyngyr for torching that place. Last time he was there, he'd got carried away with one of the older women who looked rather like the Tyrn's wife if the light was low and you squinted hard. He'd said and done things that made him squirm when he remembered. Things that might be considered treasonous if the Heir ever heard of them.

I should have fixed that some other way. This was stupid.

The four had something they could tell about him and he suspected most of them were not going to keep their mouths shut. Especially Clebar, who was not saying anything and not looking at any of them. Anrydd bent to tear up a new twist of reeds and glanced at him.

Clebar's shoulders were hunched round. His gelding was acting very shifty, eyes rolling, head coming up, as if it had picked up on its rider's chancy mood.

Tanew's Teeth, I am a fool. Anrydd clicked his tongue at Sernry, scratched his poll to soothe him. He swished the reeds in the stinking water and scrubbed at the last lines of white on the smooth red-brown hair. *When Ol' Barbran hears about this, he'll kick me out for sure, never mind what Mama says.* He finished his scrubbing, walked round the horse, using the faint starlight to check for traces of white. *I've just given him the excuse he was looking for. Fool!*

He bundled the hood and cloak into a ball, used the cords of the cloak to tie it in that shape, then flung the ball deeper into the swamp. When he heard the splash, he turned and said, "Anybody not ready to go and wants a hand?"

Anrydd pushed Sernry hard and reached Carcalon considerably before the others. Cautiously he led the gelding into the paddock, then stopped to listen.

A horse snorted and shifted his footing, a nightadyr hooted softly—interrupted by a raucous snore. Anrydd grinned and wiped the sweat from his face. Last night he'd left a flask of drugged penty where the stableman would find it; the fool had slogged it down and was still snoring.

He stripped Sernry, led the horse into his stall. Working at top speed, he wiped down the saddle and settled it into place on the wood horse, wiped the bridle and hung it on its peg. He took a grooming brush to Sernry's sides just to make sure all the whitewash was off him, then tugged some grass hay from the hanging bale and tossed it in the manger.

He took off running, vaulted the paddock fence and scrambled up the side of a rocky knoll with a single olwyd tree growing gnarled and slump-shouldered on the top. He'd tried to make the others understand that it was important to ride back alone on separate routes so they'd leave less trace for trackers. Each was to make his own way back into his bed and come forth in the morning to publicly exclaim and secretly gloat over what had happened in the night.

He had to wait nearly fifteen minutes before another rider appeared. Lyngyr, riding slouched in the saddle, more than half asleep. *I must have had rats in my head when I listened to you whine. Ah, it was a lovely sight, that nest of bloodsuckers going up like that, but to let that clothead get his claws in me . . . If I do anything like this again, I swear I'm going to make sure whoever's with me has the sense Tanew give him.*

Cynfor came into sight. He spurred his tired horse into a brief run, caught up with Lyngyr, laughed and punched his shoulder. Then the two of them ambled toward the paddock gate. They left it ajar when they reached it, rode to the stables and vanished inside.

They came out just as Helcod reached the gate. They slapped hands then went on toward Southgate and the guard they'd bribed to let them in.

The sky was graying for dawn, a faint pink line along the horizon, when Clebar finally showed up. He was looking nervously about, jumpy as a mouse in a circle of cats. Anybody said boo to him, he'd fall on his face and babble the whole thing without waiting to be asked.

Anrydd launched himself from the knoll. The force of his leap drove Clebar from the saddle and they landed hard on the beaten earth of the road. Wind half knocked from him, half blind with fear and rage, Anrydd got his hands round Clebar's neck and started choking him. Clebar struggled, but he was smaller and weaker than Anrydd, whose arms and hands had been toughened by months of sword drill.

When he felt the body shudder and go still beneath him, Anrydd loosed one hand, groped for his belt dagger and cut his friend's throat, just to make sure. He wiped the dagger on Clebar's shirt, got to his feet and looked warily around. Still nobody in sight, but that wouldn't last. He dragged the body around behind the knoll, gave the horse a slap on the butt and sent it galloping off.

The yawning guard let him in. "You late, young rip. Good thing you got here now. My relief will be coming along any minute now. Whoosh! You look like you had yourself one damn fine night."

Anrydd forced a grin. "C'n say th-that again." He lurched by the guard and, as the man was hauling the gate shut, caught him by the hair and cut his throat. One more potential blackmailer gone. He hurried off to get himself washed and into his bed before the alarm was given.

[2]

Oerfel sat with his back against the bedstead and scowled at the mirror braced against his knees. He clicked his tongue with disgust as he watched Anrydd run for the knoll and fling himself down, then he began scanning the country around that side of Carcalon for early-rising dirtdiggers. The fool boy was acting as if he were the only one awake in the world. This business was incredibly stupid and he was going to have to work like twenty demons to keep Anrydd clear of it. Oerfel took a moment to check on the Watcher, but Ellar was deeply asleep; he hadn't got to bed until late because the Tyrn wouldn't let him leave. Until Ellar woke it should be safe enough to do some minor magics from this room.

" 'S Teeth, I thought so."

Watched by his grubbing crew, a farmhand over by the work paddock was backing a team of workhorses up to a tuber digger. If any of those men happened to look round, the knoll and its drooping olwyd tree would be plainly visible. Oerfel muttered a spell and set a compulsion on them to keep them from looking that way, then went on with his scrutiny of the walls and the area around them, blocking a guard's view, putting a servant back to sleep for a few minutes.

When he was finished, he watched the arrival of the other torchers and wondered if he was mistaken in Anrydd's intentions as three of them went undisturbed back to their beds.

"Ah!" He watched the murder of the fourth boy with considerable satisfaction, followed Anrydd through the gate and nodded approval as he dealt with the guard. "At least you're returning to your senses. Too late, but better late than never. Your friends are not going to like that guard's death, you know. They might keep their mouths shut for a while, but they'll start hinting and in the end they'll shove all the guilt on your shoulders. I'll deal with them, but that can wait till I've dealt with you."

He watched Anrydd washing the blood from his hands and clothing, then turning suddenly pale, staring at his hands, then vomiting into his chamberpot.

"Up till now you've kept your distance from your kills, my murderous little Hero. You don't like the personal touch, do you? Remember that and delegate. And choose your confidants a bit more wisely."

He tapped the mirror blank, passed his hand across his face. That young idiot had rushed his timetable and without a lot of scrambling on Oerfel's part might have ruined himself. There was going to be a loud outcry about this. Relations between Tyst and Carcalon were difficult at the best of times, and with the Heir on the seat of Power, times were nowhere near the best. Tyst was a port and as such part of the Tyrn's Portion, owing nothing to the Broons and their factions. And Tyst had the privilege of direct petition to the Tyrn for redress of grievances. They'd demand the torchers and it would take less than a day to find Anrydd and his idiot friends.

And they'd hang, the four left alive—the Heir would see to that. It would give him pleasure to bring low Broon families that had slighted him.

Oerfel changed the mirror and called up the face of a thin girl; she was not more than eight, a scrubbing maid in the House of Barbran gan Lusor. The sun was only just poking above the horizon, but she'd been up an hour already, doing the rough work that more skilled maids would finish off later in the day. He'd called her to him a week ago and laid a compulsion in her and handed her the packet of poison. Now all he had to do was whisper her name and her feet would walk the path laid down for her.

He smiled. "This is what you need to learn, my Hero. Find the

proper tools. And use them properly. Let people think you are
what you're not and please their fancies while you do what keeps
you where you want to be. Masks, my Hero. Learn to wear them.
You have a beautiful face and a splendid form and never a sign
of a heart inside it. There's your mask. And I'll teach you how to
make it brighter until women will look at you and sigh to think
they'll never have you and men will follow you to Tanew's cold
hell and back again."

He looked at the girl's intent face. "Let the training begin.
Time, Hinseal. Poison time."

[3]

The shriek cut through Anrydd's troubled sleep and brought him
sitting up before he was fully awake.

At first he thought it was about last night, then he heard the
sound change to a formal keening, the *ay ay ay ahhhh* for a
woman dead. He lay back, rubbed at his throbbing head. Too bad
it wasn't his reluctant father-by-name. Probably Great-aunt
Plawig; she'd been rotting away as long as he'd known her.

He yawned, then grimaced as he drew in the stink from the
chamber pot. His mouth felt almost as scummy. From the look
of the light creeping through the shutters, he'd only slept a watch,
or maybe a little more, but he didn't feel like hanging around this
room much longer.

He'd just finished dressing when there was a hesitant tapping at
his door. "Come," he said.

When the door opened, his father's secretary stood outside, a
little worm of a man, some kind of cousin. He palmed his hands,
bowed. "Ryn Anrydd, Ryn Barbran gan Lusor asks that you join
him in his cabinet. Immediately."

"Why?

"Gan Lusor wishes to inform you himself. It is a private matter." He bowed again, then dropped into that curious hovering mode he affected at such times.

Anrydd shrugged and crossed the room. "Lead on."

Barbran gan Lusor was standing by the window of his cabinet. He turned when he heard the door shut. Keeping his back to the light so that his features were obscured by shadow, he inspected Anrydd, then made a small sound of disgust. "It was you and your little band of layabouts. Don't waste your breath denying it. I wouldn't believe you if Soror Ubain herself swore witness for you. That's not why you're here. Or at least, only part of it. Your mother's dead. She died shortly after she woke, or so her women told me. I want you out of my house and out of Carcalon before sundown. You will not attend the funeral rites. If you try to defy me on this, I will have you removed by force and flogged. And you will not stay in Tyst. If I hear that you are in Tyst, I will have you put in chains and taken aboard the first ship leaving the harbor. Do you understand me?"

His world snatched away from him with a suddenness that left him dizzy, Anrydd couldn't bring himself to answer. Vomit rose in his throat and his eyes burned. If he spoke he knew his voice would crack and he could not endure the thought of Barbran gan Lusor watching him fall apart.

He turned and forced himself to stroll from the room as if he hadn't a care. The secretary waited outside. Anrydd nodded to him and kept walking.

In his room again, a room cleaned and straightened in the short time he'd been gone, he flung himself on the bed and lay staring up at the painted ceiling.

What am I going to do?

Mother's dead.

I don't believe it. She wasn't even sick.

What am I going to do?

As soon as they hear, Lyngyr and the others will run like rats. I should have killed them too. I must have been crazy, getting involved in the first place.

Dead. Tanew's Teeth, I was counting on her.

What am I going to do?

A light tapping at the door brought him upright. He sat staring at the panels wondering what more could go wrong. Whoever it was tapped again. He drew in a breath, pasted a smile on his face. "Come."

One of the maids came in with a tray and on it a letter folded and sealed with green wax. Eyes down, she dipped a bow and presented the tray, then went out. He saw her sneak a look at him just before she vanished down the hall. As usual the servants knew everything almost before it happened—as if they breathed it from the air. He listened to the faint patter of her feet and hated her for knowing about his humiliation.

He looked down at the letter. He didn't recognize the seal, though that color wax meant it was somebody official. The cold hollow in his middle grew colder and his eyes blurred. It couldn't be a summons for questioning. They'd have sent one of the Palace guards to bring him along, they wouldn't have bothered with a letter.

With shaking fingers he broke the seal and unfolded the letter.

The writing was small and cramped but easy enough to read and the message was short.

If you wish to learn something to your advantage, see me in my office today. When the bell sounds first watch after the noon meal.

Oerfel Hawlson
Secretary to the Cyngrath

He stared at the words, read them over and over. What they said was simple enough. What they meant was beyond him.

Hope, he thought. At least there's that.

He rolled off the bed and stood looking around the room. He had the morning to kill and better he pass that time away from here. He went to collect Sernry and go for a jaunt into the countryside.

[4]

Oerfel lifted his head and examined the young man standing on the far side of the worktable. The light from the tall window touched him lovingly, turning his hair to gold and his skin to ivory. He stood with a superb young arrogance, the only flaw the shallow emptiness of his dark blue eyes. A whiff of horse clung to him despite the rough grooming he'd given himself.

The arrogance was hollow, of course. The boy was shaking in the bone, hoping desperately that something would come of this interview, trying to avoid facing the probability that his life after this was going to be one long misery. He was learning about Masks.

Oerfel smiled, touched fingertip to fingertip. "My condolences," he said, "on the tragic loss to your family."

Anrydd bowed his head, long gold-brown lashes hiding the annoyance in his eyes. "That is graciously said," he murmured. "I thank you, Ryn Oerfel."

"When this news became known in certain circles, it was realized that your position in Barbran gan Lusor's Suite would become . . . um . . . shall we say, difficult? Yes, difficult. I was instructed to tell you that a haven has been prepared for you, a small Broony on the Western Shore. The Broony Brennin. If you are willing to accept this arrangement, there is a courier boat in port at Tyst—the *Cennad Clau*—which will carry you there. You will have no responsibility for the day-to-day life of the Broony. There are others who will do that. There is a reason for this. It is desired that you concentrate your efforts on training in arms and your studies of arts of war and governance. When the proper time comes, you will be brought back, given a high position in the Palace Guard and groomed for other things of which I may not speak at this moment."

Oerfel lowered his hands to the table and watched the boy contemplate the implications of those carefully chosen words. He knew the Tyrn was his father, that the Tyrn was disappointed in his Heir—and disliked Isel heartily. He wasn't naïve enough to convince himself that Dengyn would pass over his only surviving legitimate son, but that seed had been sown and would fruit later when Oerfel was ready to harvest it.

"So, Ryn Anrydd, your answer?"

"I am honored. Would it be possible to take my gelding Sernry with me?"

"That you would wish to do so has been recognized and arrangements have been made."

"And how soon will the *Cennad Clau* be leaving?"

"That waits on your decision, Ryn Anrydd."

"If it is to be, let it be now. My grief is a private matter and needs no public show for validation."

"An admirable sentiment, if I may be so bold." Oerfel stood. "May your journey be a pleasant one and your new home all you could wish."

As the door closed behind his Hero-to-be, Oerfel dropped into his chair and chuckled softly. "Everything I could have wished." He clasped his hands behind his head, tilted his chair back and lifted his feet onto the worktable. "Empty of conscience as a stone statue and clever as a snowsnake, though not so clever as he thinks he is. He's had a scare and perhaps has learned to control that vindictive streak."

He moved his shoulders, stretched again. "Back to business. The next step is distracting attention from him and his doings."

[5]

That night the Tyrn Dengyn suffered a massive heart attack and died before his doctors reached him. When the sun rose, the Death Knell was rung out from the Temple in Tyst and all of Nyddys went into mourning.

23

The Way to Caeffordian

By the secret calendar of the Watchers, events dating from the 7th day of Seimis, the seventh month in the 736th Glandairic year since the last Settling.

[1]

Amhar yelled, " 'Ware stone!"

Before Lyanz could ask her what she meant, she grabbed him round the waist and jumped over the side of the barge a breath before the side of the lock crumbled down on them. Half a ton of dressed stone blocks burst outward as if shoved from behind, slammed into the barge and crushed the gates. Though the lock was only half filled, the surge of water flung them at the hind gate and into a rough slide to the lower river, barrels, bales and fragments of the barge's superstructure swirling around them, along with bodies of sailors and a few other passengers, some struggling, others like sacks of meat being pummeled over and over by the debris. The noise from the water and the groaning shift of the stonework swallowed even the screams of the drowning.

A section of mast slammed into Amhar. She grunted and her grip on Lyanz was broken as she fought to free herself from the

ail it was dragging with it. Lyanz paddled furiously, keeping his
head mostly above the water until a barrel rolled over him.

He grabbed the net that was tangled round it, pulled himself
onto the barrel and finally straddled it as if it were a horse. His
weight took it down till the top curve barely broke the water, but
t held him afloat.

When he looked around he saw that Amhar was swimming
strongly, angling toward him. When she got close enough, he
reached down to pull her onto the barrel with him, but she waved
his hand away, maneuvered around behind him, caught hold of
the barrel's rim and began trying to shove it across the current,
moving very gradually closer to the shore.

A yell. Lyanz twisted around, saw Diawad fending off debris
and struggling to reach them. In a few moments he was adding
his strength to the push, and together, he and Amhar managed
to cut into the outer flow as the river swung round a wide bend.
Once they were into the outsway, the current no longer sucked
at them but nudged them toward the riverbank.

[2]

Panting and coughing up river water, Amhar crouched beside a
small crooked tree still clinging with a few roots to the stony
slope.

When she'd caught her breath, she shoved wearily at the tendrils of hair plastered to her face. "A spell," she said. "Tied to the
height of the water and you, Laz. I felt the Pneuma stir and saw
the wall bulge. If I hadn't been looking at just the right place . . ."
She brought her thick braid forward over her shoulder and began
squeezing the water out of it. "We need supplies and shelter. I
don't know this land. Diawad?"

He had a bad gash over one eye and bruises darkening along
his left side. He'd draped himself over a boulder and lay with
his head on his crossed arms, sucking in huge gulps of the chill
air. "Dimai Lock," he said. His teeth were starting to chatter.

"Dimffald village closest. Take a watch to walk there, were we in better shape. As it is, be lucky we get there by sundown."

While they talked, Lyanz climbed onto the tree, then pulled himself higher on the bank.

Amhar sneezed, saw him and said sharply, "Be careful. You don't know what mine is laid to catch you."

"Cadarn," he said. "I want see if I can see him."

"Cadarn's dead." Diawad's voice was flat, hard. "Chunk of rock took his head off."

[3]

"That won't be the last trap," Amhar said. She wore a shirt and trousers Diawad had bought for her from the Host of the WayInn. They were his son's second best, and though she was lean and small-breasted, she had to leave the shirt laces loose and the trousers fit like paint. She'd pulled her hair from the braid and it crinkled wildly about her cleanly sculpted face, a dark reddish-brown mane. Lyanz thought it made her exotic and beautiful, though definitely not cuddlesome. Be like cuddling a tigress.

He was sitting cross-legged on the narrow cot the Host had brought in for him. Diawad sat backward in the room's single chair, his arms crossed over the top rail, his face flushed with a touch of fever, the wound on his head bandaged finally, a small patch of red on the white cloth where blood had seeped through. He shivered, drew the back of his hand across his nose. "I know," he said. "I don't think Cadarn and I, we really believed Ellar before, but I do now."

"How long before we have to face more than frost in the morning?"

"He won't mess with snow."

"Why? Laz said the Mage sent a whirlstorm after him."

"Dyf Tanew holds Mastery of Snow on Nyddys. The Mage would not be such a fool as to bring Tanew's anger on his head."

"Oh. Well, I wasn't really asking about Mage snow, but the seasonal kind. Our lethal opponent seems to have a habit of working through natural forces. Spook the horses, leave us on foot in the middle of a blizzard with no gear and no food. That kind of thing. Would triggering an avalanche count as messing with snow?"

He wiped his nose again, grimaced. "Cursed rheum. First snow usually comes sometime round the middle of Seimis. Case you don't know, today's eighth Seimis. Which means a light fall could come any time in the next ten days. I don't smell it yet, if that's any comfort." He sneezed. "And I would, you know. I was born not far from here."

"Snow?" Lyanz leaned forward, excited. "I have not see snow."

"Prophet's Blood!" Amhar crossed the room in two long strides and stood in front of him, hands on her hips. "On your feet."

"Huh?" Lyanz slid off the cot and stood, embarrassed to be so close to her and to have his body showing that loud as a shout.

"I forgot you were a flatlander and a southron. You're going to need leather and fur before we go a step further. Turn around. I need to measure you."

Diawad coughed into a towel, wiped it across his mouth. "Where are you going to get that sort of outfit? Not here, if you're thinking that."

"Iomard. I have to replace my staff and bow anyway, might as well get us all stocked for winter travel." She walked her hands across Lyanz's shoulders; even through his shirt her fingertips tickled horribly. He bit his lip to keep from giggling.

"You can carry that much gear with you?"

"No. But Scribe Corysiam can. She's a Bridge, she could carry a horse if she had to." She circled Lyanz's neck briefly with her hands, then measured his waist. Her fingers were cool; she smelled like sunshine and green leaves. He stopped breathing.

"Useful."

"Done. You can sit down again, Laz." She crossed to Diawad,

laid her hand on his brow. "Thought so. It's more than just a rheum, you've got fever. Laz, go downstairs and ask the Host if his wife could heat up a good, thick meat broth and toast some bread. Tell her we've got a poor sick man up here who really needs it." She grinned over her shoulder at him. "Lay on the charm. You're good at that."

When Lyanz followed the Innwife into the room, Amhar was gone and Diawad in bed, the flush on his face darker, his skin hot and dry. Innwife Ellio pursed her lips and whistled softly. "Tanew Bless. The poor man. That was a bad, bad thing that happened at the lock. You run back downstairs, lad, and have my man give you a basin of cold water, some clean rags and a bottle of pinebleed."

Ellio was holding Diawad's head up and spooning broth into him when Lyanz came back with the tray. "Put those over here," she said, nodding at the small table by the window. "While I'm finishing this, you get the stopple out of the bottle and pour two good dollops of pinebleed into the water, then you get one of those rags good and wet."

The pinebleed had a sharp, acrid smell that reminded him of the trees on Cymel's mountain. As he sloshed the rag in the basin and used it to mix the stuff from the bottle with the water, he wondered what she was up to now, if she was lonesome or enjoying herself.

He missed her more than he expected. His father was drowned, he couldn't go back to his family, now Cadarn was dead and Cymel was way away somewhere. And Diawad was sick and maybe he'd die too. It was like everyone he'd ever been fond of was being taken away from him.

He heard the door open and looked over his shoulder. Amhar was back, dressed as she'd been the first time he saw her. Cymel's Aunt Cory was just behind her.

A weight rolled off his shoulders. He picked up the basin and

arried it to the bed, then stood beside Innwife Ellio, waiting for
ne of them to tell him what to do.

4]

They like Grass Clan ponies. I see them last year when the Shi-
oshan call a Convocation." Lyanz went cautiously toward the
ne pointed out as his pony, gave him a bit of carrot he'd begged
om Ellio. Even though he'd almost been killed by a horse, he
ked horses a lot better than boats and barges; at least they
tayed on solid ground, which didn't try to crawl inside you as
ater did.

Amhar nodded absently then walked off to check the saddle
n her mount, looking dubiously at the broad back and stubby
gs.

Diawad pulled himself into the saddle. He was still pale after
week in bed and his skin was hanging off his bones like an old
rinkled shirt. "Time to move." He flicked a thumb at the sky.
Rain, freezing rain round sundown. I want to get under cover
efore then."

Thick gray-black clouds were churning overhead and a chill
ind that blew dead leaves and other debris along the ground
urned Lyanz's face and turned his ears purple. Otherwise he was
arm. He stroked his hand down the front of the hooded leather
vertunic Amhar had brought over for him along with fur-lined
rousers; he'd thought it was peculiar that the fur was on the in-
ide, but the wind was telling him why. He swung into the sad-
le and settled himself. The pony was wider across the back than
ost of the full-sized horses he used to ride and the saddle was
oo big for him, but there wasn't much choice. At least the stir-
ups were adjusted properly.

He swung the pony into the wind and rode after Diawad.
mhar came after them. He looked back, saw her riding with her
ow strung and carried across the pommel. The hood of her over-
unic was tucked close to her ears but she hadn't pulled it up and

he shivered because he knew why. She wanted a clear field o
view.

The pony whuffed at him and he turned back round so h
could sit the saddle properly balanced. He pulled up the hood an
tied the face mask in place. The ruff of fur about his face pro
tected his eyes and he felt warm, almost cozy. This wasn't goin
to be so bad.

Five hours later his whole body ached and the pony's every ste
jarred him painfully. He wanted to stop, to rest. His mouth wa
dry and his eyes burned from looking into the wind. But Diawa
just kept pushing on and on as if something had whispered a com
mand in his ear that he could not disobey. At least the rain he'
talked about hadn't started yet.

Lyanz shifted in the saddle. Just ahead he could see a struc
ture of logs and the edge of a corral. Looked like some kind o
Way Stop. Maybe . . .

Diawad kept on going.

The place was empty, drifts of dead leaves piled up against th
wall, the roof shingles heavy with moss. He had a feeling the in
side would smell like wet dog or worse. But at least it *had* wall
and roof. There'd be a hearth of some kind and they could ligh
a fire.

He shifted in the saddle, trying to find a more comfortable seat
and thought of asking Diawad to stop. With a long sigh, he de
cided not.

The road winding through the dead-looking forest was un
paved dirt, with enough travel by wagon wheels and shod hoove
to wear it a handspan below the level of the ground on either side
though from the silence and emptiness of the countryside, Lyan
couldn't see where all that traffic had come from. Not even an
birds in the bare trees that swayed and groaned around them.

About a watch later, Diawad turned from the road and starte
off into the trees. Lyanz blinked but when he reached the turnof

e saw a faint path leading deeper into the trees. He nudged the weary pony onto the path and gritted his teeth as the bobbing jiggle of its gait worsened on the rough going and the steep incline of the path brought a whole new series of his own muscles into play. Much longer and my joints are going to freeze in this position, pony. Have to sleep with my knees bent and my arms up.

After a short while the path flattened out, curved round the side of the mountain and started down into a narrow mountain valley. At the end of the valley, near a narrow waterfall where a creek tumbled over the edge of a granite cliff, he saw a palisade made from tree trunks with sharpened points. He couldn't see any gate, but a faint twist of smoke rose from behind the walls.

Diawad lifted his hand to stop them. Over his shoulder he said, "Wait here. Don't move till I tell you."

He rode a short distance into the valley, stopped again at the beginning of a lane that ran between two high fences. He thrust two fingers into his mouth and produced a piercing whistle. He did that twice more, then sat patiently waiting.

A bell sounded.

He kneed the pony into a walk and went along the fenced lane, only his head visible over the top rails.

Lyanz glanced at Amhar. "What you think?"

"I think if it snows tonight, it'll be at least a week before we get away again."

"Huh?"

"Looks to me like Diawad has found a safe hole to dive down. If he's right, we get food and a quiet night. What happens tomorrow dawn?" She shrugged.

"That place, um, where we going. Like this you think?"

"Larger and higher in the mountains. You're going to have a close acquaintance with snow, young friend. It can be fun. I'll teach you how to ski." Her face flushed and her eyes sparkled. "It's as close to flying as folk without wings can get."

"Magic?"

"Not really, though it feels like—"

Diawad's shrill whistle interrupted her. He stood in his stirrup and waved to them.

"Well, shall we go down and meet our hosts?"

[5]

The snow started falling shortly after noon on the fourth day after they left the Inn at Dimffald. At first Lyanz didn't realize what was happening. They'd been riding through spatters of rain since morning, rain that had turned to hail for a few scary moments. Fortunately they'd climbed higher into the mountains and were in among the needle trees when the hail started, so it was easy to find shelter until the pelting stopped.

When he first saw tiny bits of white fluttering toward the ground he thought they were more hail, but they were soft and tentative and after a while he realized he was seeing snow. It was warmer than during the hailstorm and the wind had dropped until there was hardly a breath blowing past his face. The drifting, spiraling bits of white began to collect on branches and any other surface available to them, including his own sleeves.

He stared at the white powder, brushed at it. His gloves seemed to melt it before he could brush it off his sleeve. It was so quiet. Even the sounds of the ponies' hooves were muted. "Narn," he said aloud, then blinked at how strange his own language sounded in this place. "Snow," he said, after a minute. The Nyd-Ifor was more fitting. He took down the mask and tried to catch one of the bits on his tongue.

When his face started to prickle, he hooked the mask back into place and watched whiteness fall in eerie silence, thicker and thicker until Diawad was hardly more than a blob of darkness in front of him.

His fascination faded as the fall went on and on, endless white bits falling so gently and so inexorably, finding their way inside

is boots and every crease and crevice of his clothing and melt-
ng there until he was shivering and miserable.

And Diawad just kept riding.

Lyanz was shaken from his trance of misery when Amhar came
charging past him, forcing her tired pony into a trot so she could
catch up with Diawad. He caught a glimpse of her face as she
passed him. What little he could see was grim.

He tried to kick his pony into moving faster, but the beast ignored him and continued its slow plod.

Ahead of him the snow closed round Amhar and Diawad, leaving them shadows seen through a veil. He saw a shadow arm reach
out to touch a shadow shoulder. The second shadow's head
turned. Broken fragments of words blew back to him and he
ground his teeth because he couldn't make sense of them.

The shadows stopped moving and the words they exchanged
became clearer as Lyanz reached them. His pony halted and
stood head down, tail swishing.

"How many?" Diawad's growl.

"Thanks for not asking if I'm sure. Four under a tarp, one on
watch."

"Where?"

"Where the road bends between two rocky tors, with the lower
on the inside of the curve. They're on top of the lower. They've
got crossbows and short spears, no swords but several skinning
knives."

He went silent, tension visible in his shoulders.

Lyanz was confused for a moment, then he realized that
Diawad was trying to *see* as Amhar had. Magic. Tchah!

Finally Diawad grunted and let his shoulders drop. "I should
be able to pick up something."

"You're Glandairic. I'd say the Mage is blocking your Sight, but
he doesn't have a feel for Iomard and he can't block me."

"So you think this isn't just the usual sort of ambush? A clutch of hill lice thinking a man traveling alone with a woman and a boy would be easy meat."

"Didn't need to think anything. Disturbance in the Flow. I smelled it and looked and, behold, there they were. A shield thrown round them to block your Sight."

"They picked a good place. Can't ride off the road here. The going's too treacherous even in a soft snow like this."

"Speaking of sight, they won't be able to see us till we're right on top of them. Not with the snow coming down thicker every watch."

"Hear us."

"True, but sound's tricky. Hm. That gives me an idea." She hesitated. "Might be dangerous for you, though."

"Bait?"

"Uh-huh. I take Lyanz and make my way on foot round behind them. I don't need eyes to move on foot through this muck or to shoot when I'm in place. I figure I can take out at least three of them before they even notice something's happening. That leaves two on the loose, though."

"I can cast a shadow ahead of me. Let them try hitting what isn't there. You've . . . um . . . had to fight before?"

"I'm a Scribe. Maybe I still count as an apprentice, but I've ridden Rounds and fought scurds. I was blooded a good three years ago."

"Which is more than I've done. A Scholar's life does not prepare one for battle." He looked over his shoulder. "Laz, you heard all this. You understand what's going to happen?"

"Ah, some. I go with Amhar."

"And you do exactly what she tells you. Otherwise you could get all of us killed."

"I hear."

"Right. Let's get started."

6 }

Eyes on the ground, one hand holding on to a fold in the back of Amhar's overtunic, Lyanz concentrated on putting his feet down exactly where she did. Though it was mid-afternoon, they moved in a world of dark whiteness, where trees, brush and the occasional rock pile loomed at them as developing shadows and faded as quickly as they went past them. He couldn't understand how Amhar did it, but she never set a foot wrong, nor did she hesitate.

He followed her through that whiteness for what seemed like forever, moving in eerie silence broken only by the crunch of their boots and the occasional crack from a branch breaking because it was overweighted by the snow. Even the wind had died to almost nothing.

Though it too was quiet, almost a whisper, the man's voice came like a slap in the face. "I see somethin'. I think they're comin'."

Amhar grabbed Lyanz's shoulder, pointed to a tree a step away, then pushed down.

He nodded, moved to the tree and crouched behind the trunk.

She strode away until she was ghostly in the falling snow, stopped and positioned herself. Taking a cord from inside her overtunic, she strung the bow. She reached under again and brought out three arrows—one she nocked, the second she held between the third and fourth fingers of her drawing hand and the third she dropped point down into the snow beside her right leg.

Man's voice: "Big 'un first. Then the boy. Wait. Wait. Wait. Now!"

Amhar settled herself, drew the bow with a steady smooth flow to her arms, loosed the arrow, flipped the second arrow round, nocked it, drew and loosed it, swept up the third arrow and loosed that—and cried out with anger and frustration as a fireball bloomed where the hill lice had their ambush.

For a moment it was a blinding yellow-white glare, then it was gone, and all Lyanz could see was the after-illusion, tailed blue discs swooping about in front of his eyes.

He got shakily to his feet and ran behind Amhar as she trotted back the way they'd come, cursing in a language he'd never heard before. He could tell it was cursing from the tone of her voice and the way she spat the words out. She was mad at something, he didn't know what.

Diawad and the ponies were gone, all that was left of them a smear of black ash on the snow. Amhar contemplated that smear for a long moment, then she unstrung her bow, coiled the bow string and put it into its pocket. "I think I've just been very stupid and very lucky, Laz."

"Huh?" He turned and stared at her, not able to see anything lucky about this business. The ponies were ash. All their gear was ash. And the snow acted as if it were never going to stop.

"That ambush was only a distraction; the real trap was what got Diawad. If we hadn't taken that walk . . ." She slapped a hand against her side, the anger back. "If I'd just thought it through! It's my fault he's dead."

Lyanz shivered, but not from the cold. One more time he'd escaped getting killed by the width of a hair.

Amhar took hold of his shoulder, squeezed briefly. "You're sure hard on guardians, Laz. Come on. This is no place to hang about."

[7]

The snowfall diminished but the flakes kept drifting down, drifting down, drifting . . .

Lyanz was beyond fatigue, moving in a place where the only tie he had was the faint dark figure moving before him, sometimes just beyond reach, sometimes pulling ahead until he almost lost sight of her. The snow drifting down so soft and feathery turned to glue that sucked on his feet and multiplied the effort it took to lift them. Sometimes he forgot where he was and why he was doing this, got disoriented and started to lie down.

Then Amhar would come back, catch him by the arm and pull him along for a few steps. As soon as he was moving steadily, she went forging ahead, breaking a path through the drifts.

The faint gray light began fading and the cold was a jacket that squeezed tighter and tighter about him. He started to shiver. The air he was sucking through the mask felt lifeless, no good; his lungs were laboring.

A hand closed round his arm.

"Just a few more steps, Laz. Waystop, fire going, I can feel it. Come on. That's good. Hang on just a minute longer." He heard a drumming of fist on wood, then Amhar calling, "Open the negidda' door, will you? I've got a boy out here heading for cold-shock."

More sounds, then reddish light hit him in the face along with a gout of warm, moist air. His eyes blurred and burned and his legs turned to mush.

Hands caught him. Big hands. The smell of horse and sweat closed round him. "Get some blankets, Tylla. Elmas, dig out one of your shirts, gotta get this wet stuff off him."

[8]

Lyanz lay drowsing in his cocoon of blankets, listening to the exchange going on above his head.

Accompanied by the quick, light steps of the woman as she moved back and forth between the hearth and a worktable, making dinner for them all, the man's voice rumbled at Amhar. "What were you thinking of, the two of you out in weather like this and on foot too?"

"We had ponies and we weren't alone." Amhar's voice was hoarse and she coughed before she went on. "We were attacked, the rest killed. We got away in the snow and just kept walking."

In his cocoon, Lyanz smiled drowsily. Nothing like almost telling the truth to give the wrong impression. He didn't understand why she was doing that, but he was too limp to care.

"Where was that? You think they might still be hanging round there?"

"Don't know, back a ways. The road goes between two tors, though I suppose there are lots of places like that."

"You best come along with us. We'll be moving south soon as the snow lets up." The bench creaked as he rocked back and forth. "Weren't for Tylla's mum deciding to die right now, we wouldna be traveling either. No one with a grain of sense between their ears goes anywhere through these mountains once Seimis is well begun. I can tell by the way you talk and the look of the boy there that you're foreigners, so maybe you didn't know."

"We have reasons," Amhar said. Then she went silent.

Lyanz yawned and closed his mouth into a sleepy smile. Good luck in trying to think why we've got to keep going north when it's obvious we haven't got a hope of getting anywhere. But when he remembered what it would mean if they went back with these good people, a cold emptiness began growing in his middle. We can't do that, he thought. At least Diawad and Cadarn knew what might happen. He shivered.

Tylla saw that, knelt beside him, touching the back of her hand to his face. "T'k," she said. "Must have been a goose walking on your grave. You just stay quiet there and don't think about things. Little while and there's some nice soup to finish warming you up."

He watched her swing the pot off the fire. Hand wrapped in a fold of her skirt, she lifted the lid and hung it on the hook, then stirred the heating broth, scraping the wooden spoon across the bottom of the pot to be sure the goodness there was returned to the mix. Or that was what Cook used to say when he was back home and fussing round the kitchens.

Weak tears dribbled out of his eyes. He turned his head away so she wouldn't see him cry.

[9]

"Up." A whisper in his ear, a hand on his mouth. Amhar. "Quietly as you can. I've put sleep on them, but a sharp noise could break the trance."

The room was much colder and noisier than it was when he went to sleep. The fire was banked, giving out no light, and the shutters rattled loudly in a wind that howled round the corners of the cabin and crept through cracks to send icy drafts circling the walls. The darkness inside was so thick he could hardly see his hands as he sat up and pushed the blankets back.

"What . . ." he whispered.

"Scribe Corysiam is waiting outside. Get dressed. Here, let me . . ."

A moment later a faint blue light spread around him. Amhar was holding a thin bit of branch she'd taken from the woodbox. It shone as if it were the wick of a lamp. Magic. He was beginning to hate that stuff. All the more because he needed it to keep himself alive.

His underwear and his furs were hanging from a hook on the wall. They were mostly dry, but stiff and cold; he started shivering hard as he pulled them on. His teeth chattered and his jaws ached. And the thought of going out into that wind made his head hurt.

But he had to do it. He couldn't live with himself if he were responsible for getting these kind folks killed. He thought suddenly of the sailors on the *Kisa Sambai* and passengers on the barge, gulped and forced himself to concentrate on lacing up the front of the overtunic. "Amhar, when they see we're gone—"

"I left a note," she breathed. "On the table. Hurry. It's near dawn. I want to be well away before then."

He looked, saw a curl of paper pinned down by three small coins, gold far as he could tell. "What'd you say?"

"Not now, Laz. Get over here. I'm going to open the door just enough to let you slip through."

He started to ask what she was going to do, but she grabbed him before he could get the words out and stuffed him through the opening, then pushed the door shut behind him. Over the sound of the wind he heard the soft *chunk!* of the bar dropping home. He took a step and the wind hit him, almost shoving him off his feet.

Scribe Corysiam grabbed hold of him and pulled him around the corner into what shelter a lee wall could provide.

"Snow stop," he said. "Why get colder?"

"Wind. Night. Of course it's cold. Amhar, you all right? A quick doublestep like that can take it out of you."

Lyanz looked over his shoulder. Amhar was leaning against the wall near the corner. The hood of her overtunic wasn't pulled up and her face looked pinched and weary.

"I'm fine," she said. "Was just a little dizzy for a moment. They're coming?"

"Yes. One man with horses. Taymlo from the Vale. We'll meet on the road about an hour from here. You left a note for the folks inside?"

"Yes. Said not to worry or look for us, that I was a firewitch and the boy my charge and we had to get where we were going for reasons I couldn't explain and didn't want to argue about. You brought the sled?"

"Hmp. Said I would. Come on, Laz. Time to get you set up."

The sled was a fragile-looking arrangement of bent wood and wickerwork resting on slides made from long thin bones. There was a lump of fur tucked into the curve of the backframe and more furs in a heap toward the front. "Best Hisay make," Corysiam said. "Like your winter gear, Laz." She picked up the soft slippery lap robe. "Sit yourself in there, your back up against the supply pack, arms on the rests. Ah! That's good. Now . . ." She bent and tucked the robe about him, making sure his feet were well covered. "Best thing you can do to help is stay quite still, maybe lean a little into the curves once I get going."

She pulled her hood up, hooked the windmask into place and tightened the drawstrings. Voice muffled, she said, "Head out, Amhar. I'm going to pull Flow, so you'll need to stay at least a dozen strides ahead to read the ground."

Amhar nodded, checked her bowstave and was gone.

Corysiam stepped into the sled harness, settled it about her shoulders and waist. "Hang on to the sides, Laz. These first few steps will be rough. Once we make the road and I get into my stride, it'll be smoother and you can go right back to sleep."

He lay warm, comfortable, almost hypnotized by the steady dull beat of the Scribe's boots, the rhythmic and rather pleasant creak of the wickerwork, the hiss of the runners on the snow—not hiss exactly, but he didn't have the right word to name it nor was there anything in Nikawaid to compare it to.

Corysiam ran tirelessly, her form at the heart of a trembling blue flame. She seemed to glide above the snow, her feet not really touching it.

After a while, though he truly hadn't expect to, he did sleep.

[10]

" 'Ware stone!" Amhar called. "Don't come closer." She brought her Vale mount around and sent it trotting back to them. Lyanz shivered at those words, remembering the last time she'd used them.

She stopped at Corysiam's side. "There's a force knot buried in the left-side cliff. Can you drain the Pneuma out of it, Cory?"

Watcher Taymlo held up his hand. "What are you talking about?"

"Ryn Taymlo, bear with me a moment. Cory?"

The scribe frowned. "Your deep reach is more sensitive than mine. Hm. I think I see it. About a dozen spans in and shoulder high?"

"Yes, that's it." Corysiam turned to the simmering Watcher. "No shame to you for not sensing this, Taym. The Nyddys Mage is good at shielding his work, though not from Iomardi Sight."

"I see. What do you mean to do?"

"Untie the knot. You wait here." She turned to Lyanz. "You too, Laz. And don't worry. You're the trigger so I suspect nothing will happen until you go into that defile."

As Corysiam slid from the saddle and strode into the narrow crack between twin scarps, Lyanz rubbed at his eyes, shifted his seat and pulled the robe from the sled tighter about him. "Is what?"

Amhar turned her head. "Mage's work, Laz. A trap set to bring the cliff down on us when you get near enough to be caught in the fall. This time, Cory will stop it before it gets started, so don't you worry."

The Vale was white and green, gray and brown. High cliffs of granite with intricate drippings of icicles where the small river and the several smaller streams fell down them. Clouds of pale mist hovering over hot springs. Dark green conifers like feathery spearheads. Leafless trees in orchards planted in rows, their branches intertwining to make a kind of brown lace. Log houses and stone houses, red-brown shingles on the steeply pitched roofs.

Lyanz was cold and tired. Even with the fur robe wrapped around him he was frozen to the bone and wondering if he would ever be warm again. His soul was frozen, too. To these people, even Amhar, he was a Hero Candidate. Not Lyanz. Someone to be protected at the cost of their lives, but not a friend. At least Cymel had liked him for himself. When she argued with him, it was *him* she was yelling at.

He looked around as they rode along the lane between snow-covered fields and he wondered just what terror his being here would bring to this peaceful place. Corysiam had drained one sore, but she wouldn't stay and the Mage wouldn't stop. He pulled the hood closer about his face, slumped in the saddle, his eyes on the bobbing head of his mount as he followed Amhar and waited to find out what the Watchers meant to do with him.

24

The Mages of Nordomon and Nyddys Contemplate Conquest While Dur Continues His Education

By the secret calendar of the Watchers, events dating from the 21st day of Degamis, the final month in the 736th Glandairic year since the last Settling.

K A L E

The Mage Mahara stood on an outthrust of rock above the mountain pass, his black robes blowing in the icy wind, great gouts of steam swirling behind him, the only remnant of the snow his fires had blasted from the road.

A single mote in the river of men marching past below the Mage, Dur watched Mahara as long as he could see him. He'd carefully noted the pattern of Flowlines as the Mage cleared the passes and itched to see if he could play fire like that. He didn't try to light as much as a match. If Mahara felt another Mage active in the vicinity, he'd dig him out fast. And Dur knew only too well how vulnerable and ignorant he still was. Vulnerable and ignorant. Same thing to his mind.

As his askerit turned the last corner before the descent into Tilkos, he nearly walked onto the heels of the man in front of him, who had stopped dead in the middle of the road.

On the vast field of snow below them the rebel army was drawn up to meet them, but that wasn't where everyone was looking.

Two great forms of painted light rose from the valley floor, confronting each other.

Rueth, the Serpent of Kale. Winged dragon, mouth open, hissing, great teeth whiter than the snow on the peaks, scales glittering like plates of emerald, ruby and topaz. Body arched. Forearms lifted, ebon claws ready to strike.

The Dread Wyrm of Tilkos. Rising from coil upon coil of body, hood extended, poison teeth dripping ocher fire, eyes hotter than the sun at midsummer.

The gods of this world walk, Dur thought. And join battle like their worshipers.

Then their tegmal was on them, cursing them back into marching order, and they moved on. As they crossed from Kale to Tilkos, they changed from soldiers in training to the warriors that training was meant to create.

CHUSINKAYAN

A firedemon succubus curled herself about the Emperor and whispered in his ear, "Behold how even the gods turn away from your might, O Glorious One. Why stop when you've chastised these barbarian nothings? Nikawaid belongs to Chusinkayan. From the beginning of time it has belonged to you, O Belovèd of Sugreta. Reach out your hand and reclaim what is yours."

Sitting disregarded on her mat, maintaining the great mirror that allowed the Emperor to view the Harrowing of the Clans, Hudoleth knew what the demon whispered though she could not hear the words. They were her words, put in a mouth more apt to convince.

The Emperor's Niosul knelt in their corners and drowsed, grown complacent because the Mage had shown herself aware of her proper place and presented no threat to the Imperial Person.

In the mirror the God Kamkajar stood a moment longer, the light rays snuffed from his fingertips, his great face lifted to the heavens with tears gathering like rain in his ice-colored eyes. Then he vanished and his Alaeshin vanished with him.

This did not seem to dismay the Grass Clans but merely drove them into more frenzied attacks. The battle to drive them off was far from over and far from won. Hudoleth was pleased. Though many of the conscript soldiers died, the ones that were left were being honed into the weapons she needed. And she had sorted out the false from the true among the generals. My Generals, she thought. And she smiled.

NYDDYS

Oerfel watched Anrydd bloom as he stepped from the boat into the atmosphere of careful deference at Broony Brennin. It wasn't such a jog from his plan after all; the boy had needed a kick to force him to look at the dreadful future he could face if he didn't watch himself. Yes. A good lesson and a necessary one. But now it was needful to build back his arrogance and self-confidence.

He tapped the mirror and scowled as he saw Lyanz sliding from the saddle and being greeted by the other three boys at Caeffordian Vale. Interfering Iomardi bitches! At least I'm warned about you now. I'll be watching you, never doubt that.

He checked briefly on the two armies, then tapped the mirror off and leaned back in his chair, quietly satisfied with the way things were going. By the time the Empty Place formed, Mahara and Hudoleth would have battered each other into exhaustion and all he'd have to do was reach out a finger and flick them to ash. That slippery little Hero was only a minor irritation.

A tap at his door.

"Come."

His protocol secretary shouldered the door open and came shuffling into the office, arms filled with ledgers and stacks of paper. "Coronation records," he said and slid them carefully onto the worktable. He plucked off the top page and set it before Oerfel. "The names of the undersecretaries I'd like working with me on this. I've talked with High Priest Gwan. He's sending his Aide Bonyn to represent the needs of the Temple. If you'll approve my choices we should have an overview plan for you tonight."

Oerfel took the list of names and began running his finger along it, his other concerns set aside.

25

An End and a Beginning

By the secret calendar of the Watchers, events on the last day of Degamis, the final month in the 736th Glandairic year since the last Settling.

[1]

In the predawn darkness windrift snow swirled around Cymel and sizzled on the glass of the lantern she carried as she crossed the courtyard to the birdhouse. She opened the door carefully and slipped inside without letting in too much cold air or snow. "It's Mela," she called softly. "Come to do the feeding." Old Derdo had been spending the last few nights here, tending a sick bird, and he got nervous at unexpected sounds.

She set the food sack on the floor and hung the lantern on a hook, took off her coat and hung it on a wall peg, then sat on the bench by the door and pulled off her fur-lined overshoes. While she was slapping the snow off them, the inner door opened and Derdo looked in.

"You said you'd bring some bran mash."

"Did. There's a jar in the sack, wrapped to stay warm."

"Oh. Good. Jacy is perking up some and I want to get food down her before she does her daysleep."

"Great." Cymel dropped the boots and knelt beside the sack. She felt around inside until she came across the round shape, took it out. "I made it watery like you said and . . ." She felt about some more. "And I brought along a small scoop. When our Heddig was sick a couple of years ago and really picky, I found she'd eat better if I tilted little bits of mash against her beak. Anything special I should know before I feed the others?"

"No. Just do what you always do." He shuffled out, then stuck his head back through the door and winked at her. "You're a good kid, Mela." Then he was gone.

She flushed with pleasure at the praise, hefted the sack and went to do the feeding.

She was cleaning the last of the colo cups when the home-bell rang and she heard the flutter of wings in the catchbox. "I'll get it, Der," she called. It was easier for her; he'd have to scrub and change clothes and still worry about carrying sickness to the other tullins.

She climbed the ladder to the loft, lifted the wicker trap and crawled onto the planks, whistling the soft, breathy warble that calmed the message birds whether they were colos or tullins. The only light came through the wicker mesh of the two trapdoors, one into the colo cote, one into the tullin perch.

She listened to see which catchbox was filled, heard the imperious call of a tullin and giggled. "Peace, love, peace and patience. I'm coming. I'm coming."

When she reached the catchbox, she pulled on the leather glove and changed the soothing whistle to the quick *tsee tsee tsee* that meant she was going to reach into the box. The tullin stepped onto her wrist without a fuss and she brought it out into the loft. "There's the love. You did good. What hard flying it must have taken. Are you one of those who like to be stroked? We'll see in just a minute."

She unclipped the tube from the tullin's leg, tucked it in a pocket. The tullin shifted uneasily as her hand drew near, but as she ran the tops of her fingers very gently along its matte black feathers, it pushed against her hand and made a drawn-out grating sound like Heddig used to when she was stroked. "Oh yes, yes, what a love."

She lifted the trap and carried the bird down the ladder into the tullin house, settled it onto an empty perch and went to the food sack she'd left in here before heading into the colo house. There were some scraps of meat left and she took them to the tullin and smiled as it tore into them. "There. Home and fed. Wonder where you came from."

As she left the tullin house, she took the tube from her pocket and scowled at the tiny seal. The light was too dim, so she carried it to the antechamber and her lantern.

"Ah! The Vale. I bet this is another report about Laz." She smiled at the tube, bounced it in her hand. "Have to go see Scholar Barladd and find out how he's doing."

"Mela! What you dawdling for? That could be important."

"Getting it done, Der. Had to take care of the tullin first thing, didn't I?"

She dropped the tube in the collection box, rang the bell vigorously to let the Runners know a message was in, then went back to the colo house.

Hanner was right, she thought as she filled the feed cups. I like it here.

TOR
BOOKS The Best in Fantasy

ELVENBANE • Andre Norton and Mercedes Lackey
"A richly detailed, complex fantasy collaboration."—Marion Zimmer Bradley

SUMMER KING, WINTER FOOL • Lisa Goldstein
"Possesses all of Goldstein's virtues to the highest degree."—*Chicago Sun-Times*

JACK OF KINROWAN • Charles de Lint
Jack the Giant Killer and *Drink Down the Moon* reprinted in one volume.

THE MAGIC ENGINEER • L.E. Modesitt, Jr.
The tale of Dorrin the blacksmith in the enormously popular continuing saga of Recluce.

SISTER LIGHT, SISTER DARK • Jane Yolen
"The Hans Christian Andersen of America."—*Newsweek*

THE GIRL WHO HEARD DRAGONS • Anne McCaffrey
"A treat for McCaffrey fans."—*Locus*

GEIS OF THE GARGOYLE • Piers Anthony
Join Gary Gar, a guileless young gargoyle disguised as a human, on a perilous pilgrimage in pursuit of a philter to rescue the magical land of Xanth from an ancient evil.

TOR
BOOKS The Best in Fantasy

LORD OF CHAOS • Robert Jordan
Book Six of *The Wheel of Time*. "For those who like to keep themselves in a fantasy world, it's hard to beat the complex, detailed world created here....A great read."—*Locus*

STONE OF TEARS • Terry Goodkind
The sequel to the epic fantasy bestseller *Wizard's First Rule*.

SPEAR OF HEAVEN • Judith Tarr
"The kind of accomplished fantasy—featuring sound characterization, superior world-building, and more than competent prose—that has won Tarr a large audience."—*Booklist*

MEMORY AND DREAM • Charles de Lint
A major novel of art, magic, and transformation, by the modern master of urban fantasy.

NEVERNEVER • Will Shetterly
The sequel to *Elsewhere*. "With a single book, Will Shetterly has redrawn the boundaries of young adult fantasy. This is a remarkable work."—Bruce Coville

TALES FROM THE GREAT TURTLE • Edited by Piers Anthony and Richard Gilliam
"A tribute to the wealth of pre-Columbian history and lore."—*Library Journal*